FROM THE PAGES OF
THUS SPOKE ZARATHUSTRA

But when Zarathustra was alone, he spoke thus to his heart: "Could it then be possible! This old saint in his forest has not yet heard of it, that *God is dead!*" (page 9)

What is the ape to man? A laughing-stock or a painful embarrassment. And just the same shall man be to the Übermensch: a laughing-stock or a painful embarrassment. (page 9)

"What good is my virtue! As yet it has not made me passionate. How weary I am of my good and my evil! It is all poverty and pollution and wretched contentment!" (page 10)

I would believe only in a god who could dance. (page 38)

You may have only enemies whom you can hate, not enemies you despise. You must be proud of your enemy: then the successes of your enemy are your successes too. (page 43)

Through valuation only is there value; and without valuation the nut of existence would be hollow. Hear this, you creators! (page 53)

The true man wants two things: danger and play. Therefore he wants woman, as the most dangerous plaything. (page 58)

Life is a well of delight; but where the rabble drinks, too, all wells are poisoned. (page 85)

Mistrust all in whom the impulse to punish is powerful! (page 88)

Truly, I have often laughed at the weaklings, who think themselves good because their claws are blunt! (page 104)

Is not wounded vanity the mother of all tragedies? But where pride is wounded, there grows up something better than pride.
(page 124)

"Everything straight lies," murmured the dwarf, contemptuously. "All truth is crooked, time itself is a circle." (page 136)

"In everything one thing is impossible—rationality!" (page 143)

But down there—all speech is in vain! There, forgetting and passing-by are the best wisdom: *that* I have learned now! (page 158)

Willing liberates: for willing is creating: thus I teach. (page 177)

I, Zarathustra, the advocate of life, the advocate of suffering, the advocate of the circle—I call you, my most abysmal thought!
(page 185)

"Why do you conceal yourself? It is *the higher man* that cries for you!" (page 207)

"Because *you* once said, O Zarathustra: 'Spirit is life that itself cuts into life,' that led and seduced me to your teaching. And truly, with my own blood I have increased my own knowledge!" (page 214)

"Unless we are converted and become as cows, we shall not enter into the kingdom of heaven. For we ought to learn one thing from them: ruminating." (page 230)

Lift up your hearts, my brothers, high, higher! And do not forget your legs! Lift up your legs too, you good dancers, and better still, stand on your heads! (page 252)

Thus spoke Zarathustra and left his cave, glowing and strong, like a morning sun that comes out of dark mountains. (page 281)

THUS SPOKE ZARATHUSTRA

FRIEDRICH NIETZSCHE

A New Translation by Clancy Martin

With an Introduction by
Kathleen M. Higgins and Robert C. Solomon

and Notes by
Kathleen M. Higgins, Robert C. Solomon,
and Clancy Martin

GEORGE STADE
CONSULTING EDITORIAL DIRECTOR

BARNES & NOBLE CLASSICS
NEW YORK

BARNES & NOBLE CLASSICS

NEW YORK

Published by Barnes & Noble Books
122 Fifth Avenue
New York, NY 10011

www.barnesandnoble.com/classics

Also sprach Zarathustra was first published between 1883 and 1885.
The work appears here in a new translation by Clancy Martin.

Published in 2005 by Barnes & Noble Classics in a new translation with new
Introduction, Translator's Note, Notes, Biography, Chronology, Inspired By,
Comments & Questions, and For Further Reading.

Thus Spoke Zarathustra
ISBN-13: 978-1-59308-278-9
ISBN-10: 1-59308-278-9
LC Control Number 2005929144

Produced and published in conjunction with:
Fine Creative Media, Inc.
322 Eighth Avenue
New York, NY 10001

Michael J. Fine, President and Publisher

PRINTED IN THE UNITED STATES OF AMERICA

QM

3 5 7 9 10 8 6 4 2

FRIEDRICH NIETZSCHE

Friedrich Nietzsche, his thinking in confusion, collapsed on the streets of Turin, Italy, in 1889. The event marked the end of a decade during which the philosopher wrote and expanded his theories while migrating seasonally among favorite locales in Switzerland, Germany, France, and Italy, often in search of relief from chronic ailments and pain. Nietzsche's mental breakdown signaled the end of a period of creative brilliance that produced some of the most remarkable and influential contributions to modern philosophy.

Friedrich Wilhelm Nietzsche was born on October 15, 1844, in the Prussian town of Röcken. His father, the town's Lutheran pastor, died at an early age, and Friedrich, the household's sole male, was brought up by his mother, paternal grandmother, and two aunts. Early signs of his genius did not go unrecognized; he was awarded a full scholarship to Prussia's leading Protestant boarding school, where he wrote sophisticated essays and plays and composed music. An excellent student of German, Latin, and Greek, he attracted the attention of his teachers, who admired his obvious intelligence and deemed him an extraordinary talent.

In 1864 Nietzsche was admitted to the University of Bonn, where he studied theology and classical philology. Under the mentorship of his philology professor, he moved to the University of Leipzig, where he wrote essays on the ancient Greeks. On the basis of his published articles and the enthusiastic recommendations of his professors, he was offered a chair in philology at the University of Basel, Switzerland, in 1869. Nietzsche's philosophical inclinations emerged as his writings moved beyond the interpretation of ancient texts to observations on and dissections of Western culture. In 1872 Nietzsche published his first book, *The Birth of Tragedy*, which provoked the critical ire of his fellow academics. In the early 1870s his budding friendship with the composer Richard Wagner began to deepen.

Nietzsche's next major work, written over four years, was *Untimely Meditations*, a set of critiques of contemporary culture. In 1878 Nietzsche's friendship with Wagner dissolved over profound intellectual and philosophical differences. That same year Nietzsche published *Human, All Too Human*, which was roundly criticized by Wagner and his wife. His health failing, Nietzsche resigned his position at Basel in 1879 and began a lonely period characterized by frequent travel. During an extraordinary decade he published a book a year, including *The Gay Science* (1882), in which he proclaimed that "God is dead," *Thus Spoke Zarathustra* (1883–1885), *Beyond Good and Evil* (1886), and *On the Genealogy of Morals* (1887).

In the year before his breakdown Nietzsche completed *Twilight of the Idols* (1889), *The Antichrist* (1895), *Ecce Homo* (1908), *The Case of Wagner* (1888), and *Nietzsche Contra Wagner* (1895). He finished the last book on Christmas day 1888. Then, on January 3, 1889, Nietzsche intervened in the beating of a horse, throwing his arms around the animal's neck before collapsing in mental disarray on a street in Turin. He was returned to his mother's house in Naumburg, Germany, in a state of near-total dementia. After the death of his mother in 1897, he came under the care of his sister, Elisabeth, who promptly positioned herself as the sole editor and executor of his works. Friedrich Nietzsche died on August 25, 1900.

Married to a radical anti-Semite, Elisabeth edited her brother's writings through a prism of anti-Semitism. She ushered in a long and dark association of her brother's philosophy with Aryanism, which culminated in the Nazis' adoption of Nietzsche as a governing spirit. In the 1950s scholar and translator Walter Kaufmann revealed Elisabeth's motivations and began the process of uncovering Nietzsche's true philosophy.

TABLE OF CONTENTS

THE WORLD OF
FRIEDRICH NIETZSCHE AND
THUS SPOKE ZARATHUSTRA

1844 Friedrich Wilhelm Nietzsche is born on October 15 in the Prussian town of Röcken, near Leipzig. His father, Karl Ludwig, is the town's Lutheran pastor, an appointee of King Friedrich Wilhelm IV, for whom young Friedrich is named.

1846 Nietzsche's sister, Elisabeth is born; ultimately she will be the controversial executor of his estate. Søren Kierkegaard publishes *Afsluttende uvidenskabelig Efterskrift* (*The Concluding Unscientific Postscript*).

1848 Revolutions in France, Italy, Germany, and the Austrian Empire rock Europe. Karl Nietzsche injures his head and damages his brain. Nietzsche's brother Josef is born.

1849 Nietzsche's father dies at the age of thirty-five, leaving Friedrich and his siblings in the care of their mother, Franziska.

1850 Nietzsche's brother, Josef, dies just months after his father's death. The family has to vacate the pastor's house and moves to Naumburg. Friedrich will live for much of his childhood in a household of females: his mother, sister, two paternal aunts, and paternal grandmother.

1851 Friedrich starts studying the piano and soon after composes a short piece.

1853 After an unsuccessful stint at the local public school, he is enrolled at a private school to prepare him for the Domgymnasium, a preparatory school.

1854 Friedrich enters the Domgymnasium.

1855 Herbert Spencer publishes *Principles of Psychology*.

1858 Friedrich receives a scholarship to Schulpforta, Germany's leading Protestant boarding school.

1859 Charles Darwin's *On the Origin of Species* is published.

1862 Otto von Bismarck becomes prime minister of Prussia.

1864 An excellent student, Nietzsche graduates from Schulpforta with a solid classical education and enters the University of Bonn to study theology and classical philology (literature and language). His academic performance suffers due to enmity between two of his classics professors. He continues to write musical compositions.

1865 Following his philology professor, Friedrich Wilhelm Ritschl, Nietzsche transfers to the University of Leipzig, where he cements his academic reputation in articles published in Ritschl's journal. For the first time he reads philosopher Arthur Schopenhauer's *Die Welt als Wille und Vorstellung* (1819; *The World as Will and Idea*). Gregor Mendel presents findings to a scientific society that are to lay the groundwork for the study of genetics.

1866 Nietzsche discovers philosopher Friedrich A. Lange's *Geschichte des Materialismus* (1866; *History of Materialism*), which will have an influence on his thinking.

1867 In October Nietzsche begins a year of mandatory military service in the cavalry of an artillery regiment. Bismarck defeats the Austrian army in the Austro-Prussian war and opens the path to the establishment of the German Empire. Karl Marx publishes the first volume of *Das Kapital.*

1868 While serving in the military, Nietzsche is seriously injured as he mounts his horse. His wounds are slow to heal, but he returns to his studies in Leipzig in the fall. Already drawn to Richard Wagner's operas, Nietzsche meets the composer, with whom he begins a profoundly affecting friendship that involves considerable intellectual debate. Fyodor Dostoevsky publishes *The Idiot.*

1869 With the strong recommendation of Ritschl, Nietzsche is offered a professorship in classical philology at the University of Basel, in Switzerland, which he accepts.

1870 At the outbreak of the Franco-Prussian War Nietzsche leaves Basel and volunteers as a medical orderly. He contracts dysentery and diphtheria, which will lead to lifelong health problems.

1871   France surrenders to Prussia, ending the war. The German Empire is established, with Bismarck as chancellor. Nietzsche's interest in philosophy grows, but he is denied a chair in the university's philosophy department. He rekindles his friendship with Wagner, now living in Triebschen, Switzerland, with his wife, Cosima, daughter of composer Franz Liszt. The serialization of *Middlemarch*, by English novelist George Eliot, begins.

1872   Nietzsche spends many weekends and holidays with Wagner and his wife and the artists and intellectuals of their circle. *Die Geburt der Tragödie* (*The Birth of Tragedy*), Nietzsche's first book, is published; an original work, it stirs controversy among academics.

1873   Nietzsche publishes an attack on a popular theologian and culture critic with "David Strauss der Bekenner und der Schriftsteller" ("David Strauss, the Confessor and the Writer"), the first of the four parts of *Unzeitgemässe Betrachtungen* (*Untimely Meditations*), a critique of European culture. Suffering from eye pain and headaches, he dictates his manuscripts at times.

1874   Two more meditations are published: "Vom Nutzen und Nachteil der Historie für das Leben" ("On the Uses and Disadvantages of History for Life") and "Schopenhauer als Erzieher" ("Schopenhauer as Educator").

1875   Frequently ill, Nietzsche travels to Germany to "take a cure." Though a doctor helps alleviate his stomach discomfort, he continues to suffer from stomach pain and headaches, and his health deteriorates.

1876   The final meditation, "Richard Wagner in Bayreuth," is published. Because of ill health, Nietzsche takes a year's leave from the university. A schism in his friendship with Wagner opens over intellectual and artistic disagreements.

1878   *Menschliches Allzumenschliches* (*Human, All Too Human*), a book of philosophical aphorisms, is published; it is criticized by many, including the anti-Semitic Wagner, who sees it as too favorable to the Jews.

1879   Worsening health forces Nietzsche to resign his professorship at Basel. "Vermischte Meinungen und Sprüche" ("Mixed

Opinions and Maxims")—an appendix to *Human, All Too Human*—is published.

1880 Plagued by health problems, Nietzsche begins a lonely, peripatetic life, traveling almost every year during the coming decade between various French, Swiss, Italian, and German cities, always focusing on his writing. The second and final sequel to *Human, All Too Human*—"Der Wanderer und sein Schatten" ("The Wanderer and His Shadow") is published.

1881 *Die Morgenröte: Gedanken über die moralischen Vorurteile (Daybreak: Thoughts on the Prejudices of Morality)* is published; it contains themes that Nietzsche will develop more fully in later writings. Russian tsar Alexander II is assassinated.

1882 *Die fröhliche Wissenschaft (The Gay Science)* is published; in it Nietzsche introduces his concepts of "eternal recurrence" and the death of God. In Rome Nietzsche meets and falls in love with Lou Andreas-Salomé, a young student who is also admired by Nietzsche's close friend Paul Rée. Nietzsche's attempts to woo Andreas-Salomé fail.

1883 Nietzsche publishes the first part of his masterpiece *Thus Spoke Zarathustra*. Richard Wagner dies. Elisabeth, whose relationship with her brother is often strained, announces her engagement to Bernhard Förster, a noted anti-Semite.

1884 The second part of *Zarathustra* is published; as in the case of the first part, few copies are sold. Soon after, the third part, also a poor seller, appears in print.

1885 Nietzsche privately prints the fourth part of *Zarathustra*. Elisabeth Nietzsche marries Förster, inciting the anger of her brother, who unequivocally opposes her husband's anti-Semitism.

1886 Nietzsche publishes *Jenseits von Gut und Böse (Beyond Good and Evil)*. Elisabeth travels to Paraguay to help her husband found an Aryan society. Nietzsche begins to revisit and rework some of his earlier writings. The first three parts of *Zarathustra* are published together for the first time.

1887 *Zur Genealogie der Moral (On the Genealogy of Morals)* is published.

1888 In a year of intense productivity, Nietzsche writes a polemic against Christianity, *Der Antichrist* (1895; *The Antichrist*); *Die Götzen-Dämmerung* (1889; *Twilight of the Idols*), a critique of esteemed philosophers and cultural figures; *Ecce Homo* (1908), in which he examines his own work; and *Nietzsche contra Wagner* (1895). He writes and publishes an attack on Wagner, *Der Fall Wagner* (*The Case of Wagner*).

1889 In January Nietzsche collapses in the streets of Turin, Italy, suffering a complete breakdown of his mental abilities from which he will never recover. Franz Overbeck, Nietzsche's close friend, takes him to a psychiatric clinic in Basel, but soon afterward he is transferred to an asylum in Jena, Germany. Bernhard Förster, deep in debt, commits suicide.

1890 Nietzsche is released from the clinic into the care of his mother in Naumburg. William James publishes *The Principles of Psychology*.

1891 The first English edition of *Thus Spoke Zarathustra*, translated by Thomas Common, is published.

1893 Elisabeth returns from Paraguay for the last time and establishes the Nietzsche Archive, a library of Nietzsche's letters, manuscripts, and published writings.

1894 In a French case fueled by anti-Semitism, Capt. Alfred Dreyfus is convicted of giving military secrets to the Germans.

1895 Pressured by Elisabeth, Nietzsche's mother signs away all rights to his works, allowing Elisabeth to assume complete control over her brother's writings.

1896 Richard Strauss's tone poem *Thus Spoke Zarathustra* premieres.

1897 Nietzsche's mother dies, and Elisabeth moves her brother to Weimar, where she will take care of him until his death.

1900 Friedrich Nietzsche dies on August 25. Some say his condition is symptomatic of syphilis; however, recent research points to a brain tumor as the cause of his physical and mental disease. Sigmund Freud publishes *Die Traumdeutung* (*The Interpretation of Dreams*).

1901 Cobbling together notes by Nietzsche, including many he had used in his works, but with important changes, Elisabeth publishes *Der Wille zur Macht* (*The Will to Power*), which she claims represents her brother's true philosophy.

1903 George Bernard Shaw publishes his play *Man and Superman*.

1914 World War I begins following the assassination of Archduke Franz Ferdinand, heir to the throne of the Austro-Hungarian Empire, by a Slav nationalist.

1918 World War I ends with the defeat of the Central Powers (Austria-Hungary, Germany, and Italy).

1930 Elisabeth becomes associated with the Nazis; through her influence so, too, does the work of Nietzsche.

1933 The Nietzsche Archive receives financial support from Hitler's government.

1935 Elisabeth Nietzsche dies; her funeral is attended by Adolf Hitler.

1939 World War II begins as Germany invades Poland.

1945 The Nazis's unconditional surrender on May 7 brings an end to World War II in Europe.

1950 Walter Kaufmann, who will become one of the primary modern translators of Nietzsche's work, publishes *Nietzsche: Philosopher, Psychologist, Antichrist*. The book exposes Elisabeth's manipulations of her brother's writings and ushers in a new era of Nietzsche scholarship that distances the philosopher's work from the taint of Nazism.

INTRODUCTION

In 1880, as the science and industry of Western Europe were redefining the modern world and a newly unified Germany flexed its muscles, a lone philosopher, hiking by a breathtaking lake in the Alps, began resurrecting an ancient Persian prophet to send him into the contemporary world. Friedrich Nietzsche published the first part of his *Also sprach Zarathustra* (*Thus Spoke Zarathustra*) in 1883, and the completed volume became his best-known book. He considered it his most important work, and toward the end of his life he immodestly described it in *Ecce Homo* (1908) as "the greatest present" that had been made to humanity so far. In the same book, he no less outrageously proclaims that it is "not only the highest book there is . . . but it is also the *deepest*, born out of the innermost wealth of truth." So we should not be surprised to find that *Zarathustra* is an extremely enigmatic and often pretentious work and by no means easy to understand or to classify. It is not clearly philosophy, or poetry, or prophecy, or satire. Sometimes it seems to be all of the above. It is also difficult because it is filled with learned allegories and allusions—to the Bible, Plato, Shakespeare, Goethe's *Faust*, Ludwig Feuerbach, Arthur Schopenhauer, Nietzsche's former friend Richard Wagner, and others—references that might not be readily recognizable by most contemporary readers. *Zarathustra*'s subtitle, "A Book for All and None," also sounds like a challenge, if not a direct affront, suggesting that while anyone might pick it up and read it, no one can really understand it. In the then anxious world of modern Europe, already preparing for the calamities and traumas of the twentieth century, *Zarathustra* would find itself curiously at home.

The basic format of *Zarathustra* is familiar. It tells a story in biblical style. *Zarathustra* is an epic that resembles no other book so

much as the New Testament, a work that Nietzsche, who had originally intended to enter the ministry (and whose father and grandfathers had all been ministers), knew very well. Like Jesus in the
New Testament, the titular character of Nietzsche's book goes into
solitude at the age of thirty and returns to humanity with a mission—
to share his wisdom with others, to challenge them to reform their
lives. But like Jesus, Zarathustra is seriously misunderstood. The
book thus chronicles the protagonist's efforts and wanderings, his
coming to understand who he is and what he stands for, by way of
his interactions with the various and often odd characters he meets
along the way.

Nevertheless, there are obvious and dramatic differences between
Zarathustra and the Gospels. To begin with, unlike Jesus, who returns from solitude after forty days, Zarathustra enjoys solitude for
ten years before beginning his mission. And while the story of Jesus
is completed with his death and resurrection, Zarathustra's story is
never finished. Indeed, the book starts exactly as it begins, with
Zarathustra's leaving his mountain cave and descending once again
to humanity. While Jesus is presented as enlightened throughout his
teaching mission, Zarathustra matures only gradually. His whole
story can be understood as an instance of the popular German genre
of *Bildungsroman*—that is, a novel chronicling the education of its
protagonist. Most important, the "gospel" that Zarathustra brings
contrasts sharply with the teachings of Jesus. In Nietzsche's version,
Zarathustra utterly rejects the distinction between good and evil,
and with it the basic premise of Judeo-Christian morality. He also
denounces the "otherworldly" outlook of Christianity, its emphasis
on a "better" life beyond this one. Zarathustra's philosophy, summa-
rized in a single phrase, is a celebration of what is "this-worldly." It
is a "yes-saying" to life, *this* life; for Zarathustra (like Nietzsche)
thinks that there is no other. The combined allusions to and dis-
crepancies from the New Testament in *Zarathustra* make it appropriate to think of it as a parody, although it should not be thought
of just as satire, which ridicules its target. On the blasphemous side,
however, Zarathustra is treated as a figure whose seriousness and
importance are comparable to those of Jesus.

Many readers may not know that Nietzsche's titular character is
a very important historical religious figure. Zarathustra, also known
as Zoroaster, probably lived in the seventh century B.C.E. (possibly

from 628 to 551). He was a Persian who founded his own religion. Zoroastrianism, in turn, had a profound influence on both Judaism and Christianity. Zarathustra remained a fantasy figure in the West for many centuries, long before his writings were translated in the eighteenth century. Central to the teachings of the historical Zarathustra was the idea that the world is a stage on which cosmic moral forces, the power of good and the powers of evil, fight it out for dominance over humanity. This conflict between good and evil is central to both Judaism and Christianity, and given Nietzsche's rejection of this dichotomy, it is highly significant as well as ironic that Nietzsche chose the supposed originator of that distinction as his central character and ostensibly as his spokesman. Nietzsche tells us in *Ecce Homo* that as the first to invent the opposition of good and evil, Zarathustra should be the first to recognize that it is a "calamitous error," for he has more experience and is more truthful than any other thinker. Nietzsche's Zarathustra is the historical religious leader updated, offering insight into the modern world, just as the original Zarathustra addressed the circumstances of his era.

One could argue that Nietzsche used his fictional Zarathustra much as Plato used his teacher, Socrates (who never wrote down his teachings), to express his own views. And given that Nietzsche had a doctorate in classical philology and taught the classics for many years, we should not be surprised to find that Nietzsche's book makes extensive references to Plato's dialogues and their hero. Socrates, along with Jesus, remained one of the focal points of Nietzsche's philosophy from his first book to his last. Socrates is a figure of profound importance to the Western tradition. In Nietzsche's first book, *Die Geburt der Tragödie* (1872; *The Birth of Tragedy*), he called Socrates "the one vortex and turning-point" of Western culture. In one of his last books, *Die Götzen-Dämmerung* (1889; *Twilight of the Idols*), he devotes an entire chapter to "The Problem of Socrates," which is nothing less than the problem of Western civilization as such. In his life, Socrates was a self-styled gadfly to his contemporaries, provoking them to question their basic beliefs, which for the most part they held just because others held them too. His unrelenting challenge to common morals and public authority ultimately led to his being convicted on trumped-up charges and executed. Nietzsche's Zarathustra is similarly devoted to challenging both "common sense" and the authority of tradition, and he similarly arouses hatred in those committed to them.

Yet again there are sharp differences between Socrates and Zarathustra. Socrates was devoted to what Nietzsche came to see an "absurd rationality" that undervalued the emotions and other irrational aspects of our nature. Moreover, Plato's Socrates contends that the philosophical life is a long practice in learning how to die, and he offers an ethereal vision of truth in a separate, heavenly plane. According to Plato's hero, the body drags the soul down and distracts it from this true reality, which can be grasped only by reason. Consequently, Nietzsche sees Platonism as otherworldly and life-denying, a prefiguring of the Judeo-Christian worldview in its negativism; in *Jenseits von Gut und Böse* (1886; *Beyond Good and Evil*) he calls Christianity "Platonism for the masses." Nietzsche's Zarathustra is a parodic counterpart to Plato's Socrates, for Zarathustra urges appreciation of this world, the body, and our passions, directly contradicting Plato's account of the purely rational, otherworldly philosophical life.

Thus the opening of *Zarathustra* recalls the Myth of the Cave from Plato's *Republic* 7. In that work, Socrates describes a cave in which people bound to a wall see shadows cast onto the cave's wall; the shadows are the entirety of their experience. One individual, who represents the philosopher, manages to get loose and emerge from the cave, where he discovers the whole world that the sun illuminates. He returns to his companions in the cave to tell them what he has found. But his companions want none of his reports. They are convinced that he has ruined his eyesight, since it took him some time to readjust to the darkness, and they want to kill him. Zarathustra similarly emerges from the cave, but the wisdom he has to share comes from his experiences inside it. The sun, which represents the all-illuminating form of the Good for Plato, is also the image of Apollo, the god of reason and order. Nietzsche describes Greek tragedy in *The Birth of Tragedy* as combining the wisdom of Apollo with that of Dionysus, the god of drunkenness, passion, and the irrational powers of the psyche. Nietzsche insists that Apollo alone or Dionysus alone represents only part of the human experience, and that the psychological reality of the human being as a whole requires a combination of what these gods represent. Zarathustra appreciates both the insights of his cave and the illumination of the sun, in that his wisdom appreciates both parts of our nature, while Plato addresses only one.

Thus Spoke Zarathustra opens with a prologue that is a minidrama unto itself. Its plot, in brief, is this: Zarathustra emerges in the morning from his mountain cave and sings a hymn to the sun, vowing like the sun to bestow his riches on humanity, which in Zarathustra's case amounts to the wisdom he has discovered in his solitude. He descends and meets an ascetic saint in the forest, who urges him not to go to humanity. Continuing his descent, Zarathustra comes upon a group of people who have gathered for a circus performance. It is here that Zarathustra addresses them and attempts to inspire them with a speech about the *Übermensch* ("superman"), but he is grotesquely misunderstood. The people think that Zarathustra is a circus barker and that the *Übermensch* is the tightrope walker about to perform above their heads. As the tightrope walker begins his performance, he is taunted by a jester and falls to his death. Zarathustra comforts the performer as he dies and promises to bury him. Taking the corpse with him, Zarathustra is threatened by the jester and some gravediggers. He wanders in the forest and takes refuge in the home of a hermit, who offers him and his dead companion bread and wine to eat. After burying the corpse in a hollow tree, Zarathustra, feeling misunderstood, takes stock and concludes that he should seek companions, or at least like-minded individuals, instead of addressing crowds en masse. At the end of the Prologue, an eagle and a snake join Zarathustra, who calls them "my animals" and compares them to his pride and his wisdom. (Such comparisons with animals occur throughout *Zarathustra*.)

The Prologue reads a bit like a dream report, yet it serves as a kind of overture to *Zarathustra* as a whole, raising many of the book's main themes and suggesting the basic problems that Zarathustra will confront. The opening section of the Prologue, Zarathustra's hymn to the sun, is virtually identical to the last section of Nietzsche's previous book, *Die fröhliche Wissenschaft* (*The Gay Science*, 1882; also translated as *The Joyous Wisdom*). In that work, the section is titled "Incipit tragoedia," Latin words meaning "the tragedy begins." Nietzsche had suggested at the beginning of *The Gay Science* that tragic ages are those that seek some purpose to human existence and accept the doctrines of some moral teacher about the nature of values, good, and evil. Thus there is the hint that Zarathustra's hymn initiates a tragedy. But according to Nietzsche, also in *The Gay Science*, tragic ages give way to comic ages, in which the meaning or purpose of life is no longer raised as a question, for life is assumed to be valuable just as it is. The recovery of that sense that life is valuable for its own sake is also the goal of *Zarathustra*.

The second section of the Prologue announces one of Nietzsche's most famous lines and one of the central themes of *Zarathustra*, the idea that "God is dead." Zarathustra takes this idea for granted, for after his encounter with the old saint he remarks to himself, " 'Could it then be possible? This old saint in his forest has not yet heard of it, that *God is dead*!' " (p. 9). Nietzsche does not have in mind any metaphysical claim about a Supreme Being here; he is referring instead to people's *belief* in the Judeo-Christian God. His claim is that many people who think that they believe in God really do not believe. That is, their "belief" makes no difference in their lives, a fact that they betray through their actions and feelings. By comparison with medieval Europe, in which people based their sense of place in the world directly on their ideas about God and his relation to humanity, the modern world understands a person's role in completely secular terms, whether or not an individual considers himself or herself a Christian, Muslim, or Jew.

At the same time, many of the corollaries to the West's previous belief in a supernatural Almighty, which in *The Gay Science* Nietzsche calls "the shadows of God," remain alive and well. For example, the views that our significance is compromised by the discovery that our planet is in an undistinguished part of the universe, and that nature is somehow deficient, and that our lives are without mooring unless they are lived under the watchful eye of Providence remain implicit in the modern person's worldview, even if these are not conscious beliefs. Since they no longer have a real sense of the presence of God in human life, these background beliefs promote a sense that our lives are meaningless and that our values are without grounding. This is the condition that Nietzsche calls "nihilism." Zarathustra's role is to address modern humanity in this situation and to suggest possibilities that might lead us beyond the crisis of nihilism.

In Zarathustra's speech to the circus audience, he gives us the single most famous image from *Zarathustra*, the idea of the *Übermensch* ("superman"). The *Übermensch* is often envisioned as a cartoonish character not unlike Conan the Barbarian, brute strength combined with an utter lack of sophistication or civilization. Combined with the fact that Nietzsche celebrates what he calls "the will to power" (a topic we consider below), the *Übermensch* would seem to suggest that Nietzsche has an unhealthy enthusiasm for unbridled, unrefined, naked power. But Nietzsche was among the most refined men of his generation. He had exquisite taste, and he had little but contempt for those who did not appreciate the finer things in life, such as music, art, and poetry. In fact, the *Übermensch* idea appears only briefly in *Zarathustra* (and nowhere else), with few mentions beyond the first part of the book. (The popularity of the image was greatly enhanced by the playwright George Bernard Shaw, who gave the "Superman" a role in one of his funniest plays, *Man and Superman*.) There is very little in *Zarathustra* or in any other of Nietzsche's texts to support the importance given to the *Übermensch* in popular conceptions of Nietzsche and his philosophy. Once again, it is important to take a careful look at what Nietzsche actually wrote as opposed to snatching a quotation or an image from its context.

The idea of the *Übermensch* is not prophecy but a provocative image, characterized in a number of brief but powerful statements. Zarathustra announces in his first speech, "*I teach you the Übermensch.* Man is something that shall be overcome. . . . What is the ape to man? A laughing-stock or a painful embarrassment. And just the same shall man be to the Übermensch: a laughing-stock or a painful embarrassment" (p. 9) and "Man is a rope stretched between the animal and the Übermensch" (p. 11). But as we mentioned in our summary of the Prologue, the scene of Zarathustra's speech is ironic, his speech is thoroughly misunderstood, and the whole scene is quite embarrassing to him. The crowd hears him not as a prophet or a sage but mistakes him for a circus barker and takes the *Übermensch* not as an inspiring vision but as another circus performer.

What did Nietzsche have in mind? He had read and appropriated Darwin, whose *On the Origin of Species* had been published in 1859. Thus Zarathustra's image of the *Übermensch* might well be taken to suggest a further stage of evolution, beyond humanity. But Nietzsche makes very clear that such progress is anything but assured. We could live our lives in such a way that humanity progresses toward this higher stage, but Nietzsche seems to think that for most people this is highly implausible. More likely, we will collectively hasten human devolution. Thus Zarathustra juxtaposes his talk of the *Übermensch* with a much less flattering image of what humanity might become: "the last man." The last man is the ultimate couch potato. He proclaims, "We have invented happiness" and blinks, wilfully ignoring anything that would interrupt his dull contentment. But whereas the *Übermensch* is a fantasy, Nietzsche rightly fears that the last man is all too real—humanity devoid of striving and creativity, reduced to a life of mere comfort and contentment. Zarathustra presents this image to the townspeople to horrify them. Instead, they welcome the world of the last man as utopia.

In Zarathustra's portrait of the last man, Nietzsche is taking on a formidable foe: the English philosophy of utilitarianism, which calls for the greatest good for the greatest number of people and defines "good" in terms of pleasure and the absence of pain. In *Beyond Good and Evil*, Nietzsche cracks, "Man does not live for pleasure. Only the Englishman does." The centrality of pleasure and happiness (the utilitarians did not carefully distinguish these) seems to Nietzsche both banal and psychologically false. Pleasure and pain go hand in hand, in his view, and to minimize one is to minimize the other. He also rejects utilitarianism's doctrine that every person's interests should be counted equally. Nietzsche's conception of "the greater good" is anything but egalitarian. For him, the greater good is determined by and for the exceptional individual, "the higher man." Thus the political appeal of Nietzsche's fantasy of the *Übermensch* in the new militaristic Germany of the twentieth century.

After the tightrope walker's accident, the jester who caused it threatens Zarathustra; he says, " 'Leave this town, O Zarathustra. . . . The good and just hate you, and call you their enemy and despiser; the believers in the true faith hate you, and call you a danger to the multitude' " (p. 16). This anticipates Zarathustra's opposition to conventional morality and his assault on both the Judeo-Christian and the Platonic traditions. The morality that Nietzsche attacks is the Judeo-Christian and Platonic morality of absolute codes of right and wrong—a morality that treats good and evil as metaphysical abstractions. In opposition, Nietzsche contends that "good" and "evil" are always reflections of the interests and aspirations of historically situated groups of people, and that these notions have varied over time and even among groups within a single society. Moral values are, accordingly, "relative," and they are also political tools employed by the powerful to maintain or establish control. Nietzsche described himself as an "immoralist" (and in one of his last books, even as "the Antichrist"), and he called for a radical "revaluation of values," a deep questioning of the values of Christianity in particular. This was particularly shocking as the nineteenth century was drawing to a close, with the usual panic and apocalyptic thinking that have typically marked the turn of centuries in Europe. The stage was set for such a "revaluation of values," and Nietzsche's philosophy was well-suited to the role.

Zarathustra can be read as a seminal text in this revaluation of basic values. Essential to this project is Nietzsche's diagnosis of human motives, the hidden purposes behind our actions. These often differ from what the moral tradition has commended and what we ourselves are willing to acknowledge. Much of what we consider to be altruistic (and hence "good") behavior is actually subtly selfish. Many acts judged harshly, on the other hand, have the same motives as those judged to be good. Underlying all of our actions, Nietzsche hypothesizes, is the "will to power," the drive to express and enhance one's vitality and to control one's circumstances.

The expression "will to power" is exciting and seductive, and it caught on in the increasingly war-mongering years after Nietzsche's death. Certainly Nietzsche means for this expression to draw attention to the role of sheer strength in the world, but he by no means restricts the idea to military power and political domination. *Zarathustra* describes the will to power as "the unexhausted procreating will of life" (p. 100), indicating that it is creative, not merely controlling, and that it represents self-mastery, not just power over others.

The will to power is also posed in opposition to the metaphysical Will or "will to existence" of Arthur Schopenhauer (1788–1860), a philosopher whom Nietzsche very much admired but whose views he came to reject. Schopenhauer contended that the nature of reality, expressed in human beings and every other creature or entity, was Will, and that the Will in various creatures struggled with the Will in others; the result was suffering all around. Schopenhauer's emphasis, however, was on the creature's drive to maintain itself in existence, and he contended that ultimately we should overcome our tendency to struggle and suffer by recognizing that all of reality is driven by the same will. Thus Schopenhauer called for renunciation of the Will within us as the only route to release from suffering, an idea he inherited from Buddhism and its Four Noble Truths. Despite the seeming similarity of their language, Nietzsche's will to power is an explicit rejection of Schopenhauer's philosophy of renunciation. With the will to power, Nietzsche advocates an appreciation of life with all of its "overcomings" as it exists within us and outside us, in its exuberance and excess. Nietzsche acknowledges that life involves suffering, much of which stems from conflict; but, against Schopenhauer, he insists that we can make the most of suffering by our willing participation in the world. Far from pointless, as Schopenhauer argued, life is joyful and well worth the price of suffering.

In the popular imagination, however, the coinage "will to power" continued to have overtones of imperialistic ambition. After World War I, Nietzsche was reviled throughout Europe because he had become associated with German nationalism, and a few years later he was interpreted as a precocious spokesman for the Nazis. It did not help that his sister Elisabeth became part of a proto-Nazi group and then promoted her brother's philosophy to the new Nazi party. (There is a famous photograph of Hitler nose to nose with a bust of Nietzsche, staged by Elisabeth.) But Nietzsche despised anti-Semitism, and he was no lover of German nationalism. It was not until the middle of the twentieth century that his reputation started to be disentangled from the Nazi horror, and even then, Nietzsche's antimoral and antireligious stance kept him marginalized even in academic and intellectual circles. Nevertheless, some of Nietzsche's concerns (for example, his critique of modernity, his insistence on willing participation in the world, and "the death of God") made him attractive to the existentialists of the mid-twentieth century (in particular, Karl Jaspers and Martin Heidegger).

In the latter part of the twentieth century, history caught up with Nietzsche. By that time, the legacy of two world wars, the Great Depression, the Holocaust, fascism, Stalinism, and a new appreciation for relativity, in science as well as in culture, made

Nietzsche, who stressed the modern crisis in values, the darling of the avant garde and a figure of importance for intellectuals and academics everywhere. Nietzsche's reception in intellectual history parallels the course of Zarathustra's mission in the *Prologue*. What is initially offered to the world at large is misunderstood, and Zarathustra must content himself with the search for like-minded individuals. This gives us a more sympathetic sense of the book's subtitle; Nietzsche offers his book to whoever cares to read it, but he doubts that he will find any contemporary readers receptive to it. Thus Zarathustra's speeches include Nietzsche's "untimely" complaints about the folly of his time and the directions he saw his contemporaries taking. But in Nietzsche's philosophy, critiques of human foolishness and warnings about the horrors of the future are always tempered by an abstract hope and a concrete love of life. This is the tone that is set in *Zarathustra*. Like the New Testament, which it both imitates and mocks, it is ultimately a book of hope, enthusiasm, and good cheer.

This good cheer is evident, in part, in Nietzsche's brilliant, buoyant, and enthusiastic writing style. He is often said to be among the very best writers of German prose, comparable to the great poet Goethe (who is in turn often compared with Shakespeare). But his style also raises philosophical concerns. Philosophers tend to be tediously literal, but Nietzsche was a flamboyant rhetorician who rarely shied away from even the most outrageous overstatements and accusations. As a consequence, he seems to invite all sorts of wild interpretations that go far beyond what he could have literally intended. Nevertheless, it is evident that he was willing to be misunderstood if that was the price of attracting our attention. The pseudobiblical style of Zarathustra is but one example of this. Another is his sometimes vehement attack on the Judeo-Christian worldview, despite the fact that he himself was very much a product of it. This attack is a provocation to "self-overcoming," making a revolutionary change in our lives and the way we see the world.

Reading *Zarathustra*, it is clear that Nietzsche intends to shock and provoke us because it is only by being shocked and provoked that we will feel compelled to undertake a serious and critical self-examination. What is not so clear is exactly how we should take the many outrageous things Zarathustra seems to say. But part of the problem is that quotations are so often snatched out of context from Nietzsche's texts. For instance, he often wrote in a hypothetical way ("What if . . ."), suggesting a thought-experiment or an ironic expression. He sometimes puts words in the mouth of one or another fictional character, not clearly expressing his own opinion at all. The overall fictional context of *Zarathustra* makes the question "What is Nietzsche saying to us?" particularly complicated. One notorious example is the oft-quoted line " 'You go to women? Do not forget the whip!' " (p. 59). This line is often attributed to Nietzsche, as if he offered this as advice, demonstrating his extreme misogyny. However, the line is quoted by Zarathustra as the comment of a little old woman with whom he has been speaking. The meaning and seriousness of the comment is thus deeply in question. It certainly does not follow that Nietzsche is an unenlightened woman-hater. In fact, just before he wrote *Zarathustra*, his most intimate soul mate was the young Lou Andreas-Salomé, one of the most liberated women in Europe at the time.

So, too, there are serious questions about how we should take Zarathustra's (and Nietzsche's) denunciations of the sentiment of pity (*Mitleid*—literally, "suffering with," also translated as "compassion" and "empathy"). Historically, these are part of his attack on Christianity, on Schopenhauer (who insisted that compassion was the basis of all morality), and, by implication, on Buddhism. Nevertheless, Nietzsche's comments are prone to misunderstanding. Nietzsche and his Zarathustra frequently claim that pity is useless and hypocritical, a claim that leads readers to believe that Nietzsche was misanthropic, devoid of concern for other people. And Nietzsche does seem at times even to make fun of weakness and poverty. But we know both from his letters and from the reports of those who knew him that Nietzsche was an extremely compassionate and sensitive man. So how should we understand the extreme things he says?

Nietzsche's condemnation of pity is a discomforting example of his diagnosis of the underlying motives behind human morals. A person who pities, Nietzsche suggests, is relishing his or her own superior position with respect to the person pitied. Far from being altruistic, the pitying person is hypocritically gaining a psychological advantage through another person's misfortune. Being pitied, on the other hand, is psychologically debilitating; it makes the person pitied feel his or her weakness and inferiority by comparison to the supposed benefactor; and it encourages the person to doubt his or her ability to cope with the difficulties at hand. Regarding the "compassion" that the moral tradition promotes, Nietzsche contends that tough love and a stance of not allowing oneself to become debilitated by "suffering with" another person is really the more compassionate approach.

Perhaps the most interesting idea to make its appearance in *Zarathustra* (and in several of Nietzsche's other books) is "eternal recurrence," which he immodestly claims to be his greatest idea and the fundamental conception of the book. Eternal recurrence is the idea that the sequence of events, including the events that make up one's life, has already happened and will recur again and again and again. This metaphor (although there is some evidence that he took it literally) underscores Nietzsche's endorsement of the affirmation of *this* life, exactly as it is. True, life always involves suffering. The proper response to suffering, however, is not resentment or disengagement but wholehearted "Dionysian" acceptance. Embracing the idea of eternal recurrence, being willing to endure one's life, with all of its pains as well as its pleasures, indicates a real love of life. Resentment, regret, and remorse, by contrast, suggest an unwillingness to accept one's life as it is and thus an unwillingness to live one's life again. There is a difference implied here between loving one's life because of its achievements and enjoyments and loving one's life for the sake of life itself. It is one thing to relish one's victories and successes. It is something else to love one's life despite or even *because of* one's failures and suffering.

Near the end of *The Gay Science*, Nietzsche gives us a provocative description of eternal recurrence:

> What, if some day or night a demon were to steal after you into your loneliest loneliness and say to you: "This life as you now live it and have lived it, you will have to live once more and innumerable times more; and there will be nothing new in it, but every pain and every joy and every thought and sigh and everything unutterably small or great in your life will have to return to you, all in the same succession and sequence—even this spider and this moonlight between the trees, and even this moment and I myself. The eternal hourglass of

existence is turned upside down again and again, and you with it, speck of dust!"

Would you not throw yourself down and gnash your teeth and curse the demon who spoke thus? Or have you once experienced a tremendous moment when you would have answered him, "You are a god and never have I heard anything more divine." If this thought gained possession of you, it would change you as you are or perhaps crush you. The question in each and every thing, "Do you desire this once more and innumerable times more?" would lie upon your actions as the greatest weight. Or how well disposed would you have to become to yourself and to life *to crave nothing more fervently* than this ultimate confirmation and seal? (pp. 273–274).

The same proposition is repeated in *Zarathustra*: "*not* . . . a new life or a better life or a similar life" but "this identical and selfsame life" (p. 190). This phrase, "this identical and selfsame life," can be interpreted in a variety of ways. It certainly seems to mean "the same *in every minute detail*." Indeed, we have all observed, perhaps to our dismay, that changing even one small event in the past might have resulted in any number of dramatic alterations of the present. Indeed, if one had been born only five minutes earlier, so the argument goes, one would have been, in some significant sense, *a different person*. If one regrets having gone to business school instead of pursuing one's true love of literature, or having never gotten married and had children so young, the question of who one might otherwise be is truly bewildering.

So considered, the eternal recurrence is not an archaic theory of time but a psychological test: "How would you feel if . . . ?" To be sure, it is a model of time that has ancient and illustrious roots, back to the Indian Vedas and the pre-Hellenic Greeks, but there is little evidence that Nietzsche seriously intended to embrace such metaphysical systems of which this view of time is a part. The eternal recurrence, certainly as it is presented in *Zarathustra*, is a thought-experiment. Its significance lies not in the details but rather in the general affirmation of one's life. Commentator Maudemarie Clark offers this nice explanation of eternal recurrence: At the end of a long marriage, would one be willing to do it again? In other words, was it worth it, all things considered? A few minor changes here or there, or perhaps even some major changes, would not affect your view. It is rather the whole of the marriage— the whole of your life for that considerable amount of time—that is in question. If you would gnash your teeth and curse the very suggestion, you would have to say that you do not really value your married life. If, on the other hand, you claim to have no regrets, all things considered, then that is what we would call a happy marriage. It is also what makes for a happy life.

Although eternal recurrence is a dominant idea in *Zarathustra*, it emerges only gradually over the course of the book, which presents Zarathustra's discovery and articulation of this idea, as well as his various reactions to it. When the idea of eternal recurrence itself first appears in Zarathustra's mind, he does not want to admit it. It appears in various formulations in the third part of the book, and not all of these seem life-affirming. Zarathustra worries that eternal recurrence might be seen as condemning us to repeat the same traumas over and over, and that all of life's pettiness might be made eternal if this vision were true. He has real ambivalence over this idea, suggesting that it is more easily accepted intellectually than existentially. Eventually, however, he learns to embrace the entirety of his life. But first he has to recognize that what is needed to redeem humanity is the elimination of "the spirit of revenge" against the past, the kind of chip on one's shoulder that, because of past events, one can no longer change. Zarathustra concludes that to overcome this vindictive attitude, one needs to have a sense that the past does not coerce one to do anything. The past does not determine our will, but our will shapes our lives in the future. The third part of *Zarathustra* ends with a rapturous wedding song to eternity, indicating his willingness to spend his life bound to time's cyclical recurrence.

Only in the fourth part of the book, however, does Zarathustra tie his affirmation of life to his actual work in the world. We should note that Nietzsche wrote the parts of the book separately, each of them in a fit of inspiration, with months elapsing between one outburst and another. But the fourth part is in a distinctively different style than the first three parts, with a more prominent narrator, several ironic characters ("the higher men"), and a humorous, sometimes slapstick, tone. (Some commentators think that *Zarathustra* should have ended with the third part and view the fourth part as something of an afterthought, an add-on, a view with which we

disagree.) In the fourth part, the parodic aspects of *Zarathustra* take
on their most comical qualities, with satires of the Last Supper and
Moses' return from Mount Sinai, for example. These were not to
everyone's taste, and Nietzsche himself published it only privately
for fear of public censure. We believe, however, that the fourth part
performs a vital role in the work as a whole. In it Zarathustra objects to the higher men's "betrayal" of his doctrines and realizes that
he has been distracted from his mission by his pity for them, his
"final sin," an admission that he has lost touch with his original
message. He laughs at himself and shares with the higher men a
song (a "round") celebrating eternal recurrence. The fourth book
ends with Zarathustra emerging from his cave in the morning and
seeing what he takes to be signs that he is approaching his spiritual
goal. He concludes, "Should I strive for my *happiness*? I strive for my
work!" (p. 281). The comparison and contrast with Jesus is again evident. Zarathustra, too, is devoted to his mission, but that mission
is opposed, not furthered, by pity.

So the book ends as it begins, with Zarathustra again descending
from his mountain home to resume spreading his wisdom to others.
Zarathustra has yet to find companions who are really prepared for
his message. In this sense, he has not accomplished anything of his
purpose over the course of the book. But the book has demonstrated
his achievement of a transformation, an endogenous attitudinal
transformation. He has reached the stage of embracing his life in all
of its fullness. Although his beginning and end may look the same
from an external point of view, his work and the entirety of his
life have become transfigured. So, too, we find after reading Nietzsche and struggling with his ideas and images that we are transformed. Not that we now fancy ourselves *Übermenschen*, but we do
find ourselves thinking with just a bit more imagination, aspiration, and inspiration than when we began this curious and sometimes infuriating book.

Kathleen M. Higgins and **Robert C. Solomon** are professors of
philosophy at the University of Texas at Austin. Together they have
written *What Nietzsche Really Said* and *A Short History of Philosophy*
and co-edited *Reading Nietzsche*. They have also made an audio-video
"Superstar Teacher" tape on Nietzsche for the Teaching Company,

The Will to Power: The Philosophy of Friedrich Nietzsche. Higgins is also the author of *Nietzsche's Zarathustra* and *Comic Relief: Nietzsche's Gay Science.* Solomon is also the author of *Living with Nietzsche, The Joy of Philosophy,* and *Spirituality for the Skeptic.* They are married and live in Austin, Texas.

TRANSLATOR'S NOTE

Why a new translation of Nietzsche's masterpiece *Also sprach Zarathustra*? There are three other English translations of the book: the first by Thomas Common, made at the end of the nineteenth century, and then two others, undertaken almost simultaneously in the 1950s by Walter Kaufmann and R. J. Hollingdale.

Over the decades, Walter Kaufmann's has proved to be the most popular translation. The first time I read *Thus Spoke Zarathustra*, when I was a high school student in Calgary, Alberta, I read Kaufmann's translation. But for all its strengths, Kaufmann's edition takes large and often unjustified liberties with Nietzsche's text. While translating this book, I occasionally felt that Nietzsche needed an editor: Fifty years after Nietzsche died (and thus could no longer control any editorial decisions) Kaufmann took it upon himself to become this editor. Thus Kaufmann made paragraphs where there were none before, changed punctuation, sometimes changed words, and in places altered both the literal and the philosophical meaning of Nietzsche's text. In many cases he had good reasons: Nietzsche is always inflammatory, and Kaufmann was damping the flame of a thinker who was at Kaufmann's time strongly associated with Hitler's rhetoric and with Nazism in general. But in this translation, with Nietzsche's alleged anti-Semitism and war mongering thoroughly debunked, I have been able to be true to the metaphors Nietzsche actually used and the language he actually wrote.

Some mistakes in Kaufmann's translation are a consequence of the unreliable German edition of *Thus Spoke Zarathustra* available to him. Hollingdale worked with the same flawed edition. Happily for my purposes, a thoroughly revised and corrected edition of *Also sprach Zarathustra* has since become available, and the present translation has benefited from it.

Like Kaufmann's, this translation began as a revision of the Thomas Common edition. But, also like Kaufmann, I quickly became so frustrated with Common that I started again from scratch. (Common's translation suffers from large and systematic problems made worse by the fact that he worked with a particularly poor German edition of the work.) That said, all three of us—Kaufmann, Hollingdale, and now Martin—have a real debt to Common. He hits a lot of bad notes, but now and then he finds a line that rings true, and we all steal it from him. The same holds, in my own case, for the best words, phrases, and even sentences of Kaufmann and Hollingdale. Accordingly this translation is a kind of collaboration among the four of us that retains, I hope, the voice of Nietzsche, although it is inevitably tuned to and by my own ear. Here I would like to thank Common, Hollingdale, and Kaufmann: Without their work this translation would have many more weaknesses than it presently has, and many fewer handsome lines.

My coeditors and I decided that we would not translate the notorious word *Übermensch*, which was translated accurately by Hollingdale as "superman" and inaccurately by Kaufmann as "overman." (Kaufmann avoided "superman" because he was worried that the concept would be trivialized in the minds of Nietzsche's American readers by the popular comic book hero.) How the *Übermensch* fits into Nietzsche's larger philosophical project has been a matter of scholarly debate for years, and the debate shows no signs of ending. Probably the best way to sort out what Nietzsche means by *Übermensch* is to read the book. The concept is introduced early in *Zarathustra* but is developed throughout the book, and the good reader will resist coming to hasty conclusions about its meaning.

Nietzsche loves puns: I have captured only a few of them. When I have missed a pun entirely, I have tried to indicate that fact in the footnotes. English cannot easily accommodate Nietzsche's gender-neutral formulations, which he usually prefers, reserving the male- or female-gendered words for emphasis or for a particular point about the sexes. For example, in English we can use the gender-neutral construction of "one" (as in "one says"), but it is clumsy and often sounds forced. Therefore I have followed the practice of previous translators and generally used "man" in place of "one." As a result, this translation makes Nietzsche appear much more gender-focused than he is in the original German. Contrary to popular myth, Nietzsche was not a sexist. Even *Übermensch* should be "super*human*," not "super*man*."

This translation has benefited greatly from the many improvements suggested by Kathleen M. Higgins and Robert C. Solomon. My deepest thanks to both of them.

I dedicate this translation to my daughters, Zelly and Margaret.

—*Clancy Martin*

THUS SPOKE ZARATHUSTRA

A BOOK FOR ALL AND NONE

CONTENTS

Contents

ZARATHUSTRA'S PROLOGUE

1

When Zarathustra was thirty years old, he left his home and the lake of his home and went into the mountains.[1] There he enjoyed his spirit and solitude and for ten years did not weary of it. But at last his heart changed—and rising one morning with the dawn, he stood before the sun and spoke to it thus:

"You great star! What would your happiness be if you had not those for whom you shine!

"For ten years you have climbed here to my cave: you would have wearied of your light and of this journey, without me, my eagle and my serpent.

"But we awaited you every morning, took from you your overflow and blessed you for it.

"Behold, I am weary of my wisdom, like the bee that has gathered too much honey. I need hands outstretched to take it.

"I want to give away and distribute, until the wise have once more become happy in their folly, and the poor happy in their riches.

"Therefore I must descend into the depths: as you do in the evening, when you go behind the sea and bring light also to the underworld, you exuberant star!

"Like you must I *go under*[2]—as men say, to whom I shall descend.

"Bless me then, you tranquil eye, that can behold even an all-too-great happiness without envy!

"Bless the cup that wants to overflow, that the waters may flow golden from him and carry everywhere the reflection of your joy!

"Behold, this cup wants to be empty again, and Zarathustra wants to be man again."

Thus Zarathustra began to go under.

2

Zarathustra went down the mountain alone and met no one. But when he entered the forest, there suddenly stood before him an old man, who had left his holy hut to look for roots. And the old man spoke thus to Zarathustra:

"This wanderer is no stranger to me: he passed by here many years ago. He was called Zarathustra; but he has changed.

"Then you carried your ashes into the mountains: would you now carry your fire into the valleys?[3] Do you not fear the punishment for arsonists?

"Yes, I recognize Zarathustra. His eye is pure, and no loathing lurks about his mouth. Does he not walk like a dancer?

"Zarathustra is changed, Zarathustra has become a child, Zarathustra is an awakened one: what do you want now in the land of the sleepers?

"You lived in your solitude as in the sea, and it has borne you up. Alas, would you now climb ashore? Alas, would you again drag your own body?"

Zarathustra answered: "I love mankind."

"Why," said the saint, "did I go into the forest and the desert? Was it not because I loved men far too well? Now I love God: men, I do not love. Man is for me too imperfect a thing. Love of man would kill me."

Zarathustra answered: "Did I speak of love! I bring men a gift."

"Give them nothing," said the saint. "Take rather part of their load, and carry it along with them—that will be most agreeable to them: if only it agrees with you!

"And if you want to give to them, give them no more than alms, and let them beg for that!"

"No," replied Zarathustra, "I give no alms. I am not poor enough for that."

The saint laughed at Zarathustra and spoke thus: "Then see to it that they accept your treasures! They are distrustful of hermits, and do not believe that we come with gifts.

"Our footsteps ring too lonely through their streets. And just as at night, when they are in bed and hear a man abroad long before sunrise, so they ask themselves concerning us: where is the thief going?

"Do not go to men, but stay in the forest! Go rather even to the animals! Why not be like me—a bear among bears, a bird among birds?"[4]

"And what is the saint doing in the forest?" asked Zarathustra.

The saint answered: "I make songs and sing them; and in making hymns I laugh and weep and hum: thus I praise God.

"With singing, weeping, laughing, and humming I praise the god who is my god. But what do you bring us as a gift?"

When Zarathustra had heard these words, he bowed to the saint and said: "What could I have to give you! Let me rather hurry away lest I take something from you!"—And thus they parted from one another, the old one and the man, laughing, just like two schoolboys laugh.

But when Zarathustra was alone, he spoke thus to his heart: "Could it then be possible! This old saint in his forest has not yet heard of it, that *God is dead!*"[5]

3

When Zarathustra arrived at the nearest town at the edge of the forest, he found many people assembled in the marketplace: for it had been announced that a tightrope walker would give a performance. And Zarathustra spoke thus to the people:

I teach you the Übermensch.[6] Man is something that shall be overcome.[7] What have you done to overcome him?

All beings so far have created something beyond themselves: and you want to be the ebb of that great tide, and would rather go back to the beast than overcome man?

What is the ape to man? A laughing-stock or a painful embarrassment. And just the same shall man be to the Übermensch: a laughing-stock or a painful embarrassment.

You have made your way from worm to man, and much within you is still worm. Once you were apes, and even yet man is more of an ape than any ape.[8]

Even the wisest among you is only a conflict and hybrid of plant and ghost. But do I bid you become ghosts or plants?

Behold, I teach you the Übermensch!

The Übermensch is the meaning of the earth. Let your will say: The Übermensch *shall be* the meaning of the earth!

I beseech you, my brothers, *remain true to the earth*, and do not believe those who speak to you of otherworldly hopes! They are poison-mixers, whether they know it or not.

They are despisers of life, themselves the decaying and poisoned, of whom the earth is weary: so away with them!

Once the sin against God was the greatest sin; but God died, and those sinners died with him. To sin against the earth is now the most dreadful sin, and to esteem the entrails of the unknowable higher than the meaning of the earth!

Once the soul looked contemptuously on the body, and then that contempt was the supreme thing:—the soul wished the body meager, ghastly, and famished. Thus it thought to escape from the body and the earth.

Oh, that soul was herself meager, ghastly, and famished; and cruelty was the delight of that soul! But you, also, my brothers, tell me: what does your body say about your soul? Is your soul not poverty and pollution and wretched contentment?

Truly, man is a polluted stream. One must be a sea to receive a polluted stream without becoming impure.

Behold, I teach you the Übermensch: he is that sea; in him your great contempt can be submerged.

What is the greatest thing you can experience? It is the hour of great contempt. The hour in which even your happiness becomes loathsome to you, and so also your reason and virtue.

The hour when you say: "What good is my happiness! It is poverty and pollution and wretched contentment. But my happiness should justify existence itself!"

The hour when you say: "What good is my reason! Does it long for knowledge as the lion for his food? It is poverty and pollution and wretched contentment!"

The hour when you say: "What good is my virtue! As yet it has not made me passionate. How weary I am of my good and my evil! It is all poverty and pollution and wretched contentment!"

The hour when you say: "What good is my justice! I do not see that I am flame and fuel. The just, however, are flame and fuel!"

The hour when you say: "What good is my pity! Is not pity the cross on which he is nailed who loves man? But my pity is not a crucifixion."

Have you ever spoken thus? Have you ever cried thus? Ah, would that I had heard you crying thus!

It is not your sin—it is your stinginess that cries to heaven; your very thrift in sin cries to heaven!

Where is the lightning to lick you with its tongue? Where is the frenzy with which you should be inoculated?

Behold, I teach you the Übermensch: he is that lightning, he is that frenzy!—

When Zarathustra had thus spoken, one of the people called out: "Now we have heard enough of the tightrope walker; it is time now for us to see him!" And all the people laughed at Zarathustra. But the tightrope walker, who thought the words were directed to him, began his performance.

4

Zarathustra, however, looked at the people and wondered. Then he spoke thus:

Man is a rope stretched between the animal and the Übermensch—a rope over an abyss.

A dangerous crossing, a dangerous on-the-way, a dangerous looking-back, a dangerous trembling and halting.

What is great in man is that he is a bridge and not a goal: what is lovable in man is that he is an *over-going* and a *going under*.

I love those that do not know how to live except by going under, for they are those who go over.

I love the great despisers, because they are the great adorers and arrows of longing for the other shore.

I love those who do not first seek a reason beyond the stars for going under and being sacrifices, but sacrifice themselves to the earth, that the earth may some day become that of the Übermensch.

I love him who lives in order to know, and seeks to know in order that the Übermensch may live some day. And thus he wants to go under.

I love him who labors and invents to build the house for the Übermensch, and to prepare for him earth, animal, and plant: for thus he wants to go under.

I love him who loves his virtue: for virtue is the will to going under, and an arrow of longing.

I love him who reserves not one drop of spirit for himself, but wants to be wholly the spirit of his virtue: thus he strides as spirit over the bridge.

I love him who makes his virtue his addiction and his catastrophe: thus, for the sake of his virtue, he wants to live on and to live no more.

I love him who does not want too many virtues. One virtue is more of a virtue than two, because it is more of a noose on which his catastrophe can hang.

I love him whose soul is extravagant, who wants no thanks and returns none: for he always gives away and does not want to preserve himself.

I love him who is ashamed when the dice fall in his favor and then asks: "Am I a gambler who cheats?" For he wants to perish.

I love him who scatters golden words ahead of his deeds, and always does even more than he promises: for he wants to go under.

I love him who justifies the future ones, and redeems the past ones: for he wants to perish of the present.

I love him who chastens his god because he loves his god: for he must perish of the wrath of his God.

I love him whose soul is deep, even in being wounded, and who may perish through a minor matter: thus he goes willingly over the bridge.

I love him whose soul is so overfull that he forgets himself, and all things are in him: thus all things become his going under.

I love him who has a free spirit and a free heart: thus his head is only the guts of his heart; his heart, however, causes his going under.

I love all who are like heavy drops falling one by one out of the dark cloud that lowers over man: they herald the coming of the lightning, and as heralds they perish.

Behold, I am a herald of the lightning, and a heavy drop out of the cloud: the lightning, however, is the *Übermensch*."

5

When Zarathustra had spoken these words, he again looked at the people and was silent. "There they stand," he said to his heart; "there they laugh: they do not understand me; I am not the mouth for these ears.

"Must one first batter their ears, that they may learn to hear with their eyes? Must one clatter like kettledrums and preachers of repentance? Or do they only believe the stammerer?

"They have something they are proud of. What do they call it, that which makes them proud? Education, they call it; it distinguishes them from the goatherds.

"Therefore they dislike to hear of 'contempt' of themselves. So I will appeal to their pride.

"I will speak to them of the most contemptible thing: but that is *the last man!*"

And thus spoke Zarathustra to the people:

It is time for man to set himself a goal. It is time for man to plant the germ of his highest hope.

His soil is still rich enough for it. But that soil will one day be poor and domesticated, and no tall tree will any longer be able to grow in it.

Alas! There comes the time when man will no longer shoot the arrow of his longing beyond man—and the string of his bow will have forgotten how to whir!

I tell you: one must still have chaos in oneself to give birth to a dancing star. I tell you: you still have chaos in yourselves.

Alas! There comes the time when man will no longer give birth to a star. Alas! There comes the time of the most despicable man, who can no longer despise himself.

Behold! I show you *the last man.*

"What is love? What is creation? What is longing? What is a star?"—so asks the last man and he blinks.

The earth has become small, and on it hops the last man who makes everything small. His species is ineradicable like that of the flea; the last man lives longest.

"We have invented happiness"—say the last men, and blink.[9]

They have left the regions where it was hard to live: for one needs warmth. One still loves one's neighbor and rubs against him: for one needs warmth.

Becoming sick and being suspicious are sinful to them: one proceeds carefully.

He is a fool who still stumbles over stones or human beings!

A little poison now and then: that makes pleasant dreams. And much poison at last for a pleasant death.

One still works, for work is a pastime. But one is careful lest the pastime should hurt one.

One no longer becomes poor or rich; both are too burdensome. Who still wants to rule? Who still wants to obey? Both are too burdensome.

No shepherd, and one herd! Everyone wants the same; everyone is the same: whoever feels different goes willingly into the madhouse.

" 'Formerly all the world was insane,' "—say the subtlest of them and blink.

One is clever and knows all that has happened: so there is no end of derision. One still argues, but one is soon reconciled—otherwise it spoils the digestion.

One has one's little pleasures for the day and one's little pleasures for the night, but one has a regard for health.

"We have invented happiness,"—say the last men, and blink.

And here ended the first speech of Zarathustra, which is also called "The Prologue,"[10] for at this point the shouting and mirth of the multitude interrupted him. "Give us this last man, O Zarathustra,"—they called out—"make us into these last men! Then we will make you a present of the Übermensch!" And all the people exulted and smacked their lips. But Zarathustra turned sad and said to his heart:

"They do not understand me: I am not the mouth for these ears.

"Too long, perhaps, have I lived in the mountains; too long have I listened to the brooks and trees: now I speak to them as to the goatherds.

"My soul is calm and bright as the mountains in the morning. But they think I am cold and I jeer and make terrible jests.

"And now they look at me and laugh: and while they laugh they hate me too. There is ice in their laughter."

6

Then, however, something happened which made every mouth mute and every eye stare. For meanwhile the tightrope walker had commenced his performance: he had come out at a little door, and was going along the rope which was stretched between two towers, so that it hung above the marketplace and the people. When he was just midway across, the little door opened once more, and a gaudily-dressed fellow like a jester sprang out, and went rapidly after the first one. "Go on, lame foot," cried his frightful voice, "go on, lazy-bones, interloper, sallow-face!—or I will tickle you with my heel! What are you doing here between the towers? In the tower is the place for you, you should be locked up; you block the way of your better!"—And with every word he came nearer and nearer. When, however, he was but a step behind, there happened the frightful thing which made every mouth mute and every eye stare—he uttered a yell like a devil, and jumped over the other who was in his way. But the latter, when he thus saw his rival triumph, lost both his head and his footing on the rope; he threw his pole away, and shot downwards faster than it, like an eddy of arms and legs, into the depth. The marketplace and the people were like the sea when a storm comes on: they all flew apart and over one another, especially where the body was about to fall.

But Zarathustra did not move, and the body fell just beside him, badly broken and disfigured, but not yet dead. After a while consciousness returned to the shattered man, and he saw Zarathustra kneeling beside him. "What are you doing there?" he said at last, "I knew long ago that the devil would trip me up. Now he will drag me down to hell: will you prevent him?"

"On my honor, my friend," answered Zarathustra, "there is nothing of all that you speak of: there is no devil and no hell. Your soul will be dead even sooner than your body: fear nothing further."

The man looked up distrustfully. "If you speak the truth," he said, "I lose nothing when I lose my life. I am not much more than an animal that has been taught to dance by blows and a few scraps."

"Not at all," said Zarathustra, "You have made danger your calling; there is nothing contemptible in that. Now you perish by your calling: for that I will bury you with my own hands."

When Zarathustra had said this the dying one did not reply further; but he moved his hand as if he sought Zarathustra's hand in gratitude.

7

Meanwhile the evening came on, and the marketplace veiled itself in gloom. Then the people dispersed, for even curiosity and terror grow weary. Zarathustra, however, still sat beside the dead man on the ground, absorbed in thought: so he forgot the time. But at last it became night, and a cold wind blew upon the lonely one. Then Zarathustra rose and said to his heart:

"Truly, Zarathustra has made a fine catch of fish today![11] It is not a man he has caught, but a corpse.

"Human life is uncanny and as yet without meaning: a jester may be fatal to it.

"I want to teach men the sense of their existence: the Übermensch, the lightning out of the dark cloud of man.

"But I am still far from them, and my sense does not speak to their senses. To men I am still the mean between a fool and a corpse.

"Dark is the night, dark are the ways of Zarathustra. Come, you cold and stiff companion! I carry you to the place where I shall bury you with my own hands."

8

When Zarathustra had said this to his heart, he put the corpse upon his shoulders and set out on his way. Yet he had not gone a hundred steps when a man crept up to him and whispered in his ear—and behold, it was the jester from the tower. "Leave this town, O Zarathustra," he said, "there are too many here who hate you. The good and just hate you, and call you their enemy and despiser; the believers in the true faith hate you, and call you a danger to the multitude. It was your good fortune to be laughed at: and truly you spoke like a jester. It was your good fortune to associate with the dead dog; by so humiliating yourself you have saved your life today. Depart, however, from this town,—or tomorrow I shall jump over you, a living man over a dead one." And when he had said this, the jester vanished; but Zarathustra went on through the dark streets.

At the gate of the town the gravediggers met him: they shone their torch on his face, and, recognizing Zarathustra, they mocked him. "Zarathustra is carrying away the dead dog: a fine thing that Zarathustra has turned a gravedigger! Our hands are too clean for that roast. Will Zarathustra steal the bite from the devil? Well then, we wish you a hearty meal. If only the devil is not a better thief than Zarathustra!—he will steal them both, he will eat them both!" And they laughed and put their heads together.

Zarathustra did not say a word and went on his way. When he had walked for two hours, past forests and swamps, he had heard too much of the greedy howling of the wolves, and he himself became hungry. So he halted at a lonely house where a light was burning.

"Hunger attacks me," said Zarathustra, "like a robber. Among forests and swamps my hunger attacks me, and late in the night.

"My hunger is certainly capricious. Often it comes to me only after a meal, and all day it has failed to come: where has it been?"

And at that Zarathustra knocked on the door of the house. An old man appeared; he carried a light and asked: "Who comes to me and my bad sleep?"

"A living man and a dead one," said Zarathustra. "Give me something to eat and drink, I forgot about it during the day. Whoever feeds the hungry refreshes his own soul: thus speaks wisdom."

The old man withdrew, but came back immediately and offered Zarathustra bread and wine. "A bad country for the hungry," he said; "that is why I live here. Animal and man come to me, the hermit. But bid your companion eat and drink also, he is wearier than you." Zarathustra answered: "My companion is dead; I shall hardly be able to persuade him to eat." "That does not concern me," said the old man sullenly; "whoever knocks at my door must take what I offer him. Eat, and be off!"[12]—

After that, Zarathustra walked another two hours, trusting the road and the light of the stars: for he was used to walking at night and liked to look into the face of all that slept. When the morning dawned, however, Zarathustra found himself in a thick forest, and no path was any longer visible. So he put the dead man into a hollow tree—for he wanted to protect him from the wolves—and laid himself down on the ground and moss. And immediately he fell asleep, his body fatigued but his soul untroubled.

9

For a long time Zarathustra slept; and not only dawn passed over his face but also the morning. At last, however, his eyes opened, and amazed he gazed into the forest and the stillness, amazed he gazed into himself. Then he rose quickly, like a seafarer who suddenly sees the land; and he shouted for joy: for he saw a new truth. And thus he spoke to his heart:

"An insight has come to me: I need companions—living ones; not dead companions and corpses, which I carry with me where I please.

"But I need living companions, who will follow me because they want to follow themselves—wherever I please.

"An insight has come to me. Not to the people is Zarathustra to speak, but to companions! Zarathustra shall not be the shepherd and dog of a herd![13]

"To lure many from the herd—for that I have come. The people and the herd shall be angry with me: Zarathustra wants to be called a robber by the shepherds.

"Shepherds, I say, but they call themselves the good and just. Shepherds, I say, but they call themselves believers in the true faith.

"Behold the good and just! Whom do they hate most? The man who breaks their tablets of values, the breaker, the lawbreaker:—he, however, is the creator.

"Behold the believers of all faiths! Whom do they hate most? The man who breaks their tablets of values, the breaker, the lawbreaker—he, however, is the creator.

"Companions, the creator seeks, not corpses—and not herds or believers either. Fellow creators the creator seeks—those who write new values on new tablets.

"Companions, the creator seeks, and fellow reapers: for everything about him is ripe for the harvest. But he lacks a hundred sickles: so he plucks ears of corn and is annoyed.

"Companions, the creator seeks, and such as know how to whet their sickles. Destroyers, they will be called, and despisers of good and evil. But they are the reapers and rejoicers.

"Fellow creators, Zarathustra seeks; fellow reapers and fellow rejoicers, Zarathustra seeks: what has he to do with herds and shepherds and corpses!

"And you, my first companion, farewell! I have buried you well in your hollow tree; I have hidden you well from the wolves.

"But I part from you; the time has arrived. Between dawn and dawn a new truth has come to me.

"I am not to be a shepherd, I am not to be a gravedigger. Never again shall I speak to the people; for the last time have I spoken to the dead.

"I shall join the creators, the reapers, and the rejoicers: I shall show them the rainbow and all the steps to the Übermensch.

"To the hermits I will sing my song, to the lonesome and the twosome; and to him who still has ears for the unheard—I will make his heart heavy with my happiness.

"To my goal will I go—on my own way; over those who hesitate and loiter I shall leap. Thus let my going be their going under."

10

This is what Zarathustra had said to his heart when the sun stood high at noon. Then he looked inquiringly aloft,—for he heard above him the sharp call of a bird. And behold! An eagle swept through the air in wide circles, and on him there hung a serpent, not as prey but as a friend: for she kept herself coiled round the eagle's neck.

"They are my animals," said Zarathustra, and rejoiced in his heart.

"The proudest animal under the sun, and the wisest animal under the sun,—they have come out to search.

"They want to know whether Zarathustra still lives. Truly, do I still live?

"I have found life to be more dangerous among men than among animals; on dangerous paths walks Zarathustra. Let my animals lead me!"

When Zarathustra had said this he remembered the words of the saint in the forest. Then he sighed and spoke thus to his heart:

"Would that I were wiser! Would that I were wise from the very ground, like my serpent!

"But I am asking the impossible. Therefore I ask my pride to go always with my wisdom!

"And if my wisdom should some day forsake me:—ah! it loves to fly away!—may my pride then fly with my folly!"

Thus Zarathustra began to go under.

—*1883*

ZARATHUSTRA'S SPEECHES

FIRST PART

[1883]

ON THE THREE METAMORPHOSES

I TELL YOU OF three metamorphoses of the spirit: how the spirit becomes a camel, the camel a lion, and the lion at last a child.

There is much that is difficult for the spirit, the strong reverent spirit that would bear much: but its strength demands the difficult and the most difficult.

What is difficult? so asks the spirit that would bear much; then it kneels down like a camel wanting to be well laden.

What is the most difficult, you heroes? so asks the spirit that would bear much, that I may take it upon me and rejoice in my strength.

Is it not this: to humiliate oneself in order to mortify one's pride? To exhibit one's folly in order to mock at one's wisdom?

Or is it this: to abandon our cause when it celebrates its triumph? To climb high mountains to tempt the tempter?

Or is it this: to feed on the acorns and grass of knowledge, and for the sake of truth to suffer hunger of soul?

Or is it this: to be sick and dismiss comforters, and make friends of the deaf, who never hear your requests?

Or is it this: to go into foul water when it is the water of truth, and not repulse cold frogs and hot toads?

Or is it this: to love those who despise us, and give one's hand to the ghost when it is going to frighten us?

All these most difficult things the spirit that would bear much takes upon itself: and like the camel, which, when laden, hastens into the desert, so hastens the spirit into its desert.

But in the loneliest wilderness the second metamorphosis occurs: here the spirit becomes a lion who would conquer his freedom and be master in his own desert.

Here he seeks his last master: he wants to fight him and his last god; for final victory he wants to fight with the great dragon.

Who is the great dragon whom the spirit will no longer call lord and god? "Thou shalt," is the name of the great dragon. But the spirit of the lion says, "I will."

"Thou shalt," lies in his path, sparkling with gold—a beast covered with scales; and on every scale glitters a golden, "Thou shalt!"

The values of a thousand years glitter on those scales, and thus speaks the mightiest of all dragons: "All the value of all things glitters on me.

"All value has long been created, and I am all created value. Truly, there shall be no more 'I will'." Thus speaks the dragon.

My brothers, why is there a need of the lion in the spirit? Why is not the beast of burden, which renounces and is reverent, enough?

To create new values—that, even the lion cannot accomplish: but to create freedom for oneself for new creating—that the might of the lion can do.

To create freedom for oneself, and give a sacred "No" even to duty: for that, my brothers, the lion is needed.

To assume the right to new values—that is the most terrifying assumption for a reverent spirit that would bear much. Truly, to him it is preying, and the work of a beast of prey.

He once loved "thou shalt" as most sacred: now he must find illusion and arbitrariness even in the most sacred things, that he may steal his freedom from his love: the lion is needed for such prey.

But say, my brothers, what can the child do that even the lion could not do? Why must the preying lion still become a child?

The child is innocence and forgetting, a new beginning, a game, a self-propelled wheel, a first movement, a sacred Yes-saying.

Yes, for the game of creating, my brothers, a sacred Yes-saying is needed: the spirit now wills his own will, and he who had been the world's outcast now conquers his own world.

I have told you of three metamorphoses of the spirit: how the spirit became a camel, the camel a lion, and the lion at last a child.—

Thus spoke Zarathustra. And at that time he lived in the town that is called: The Motley Cow.[1]

On the Teachers of Virtue[2]

A WISE MAN WAS praised to Zarathustra, as one who could speak well about sleep and virtue: he was said to be honored and rewarded highly for it, and all the youths were said to be sitting at his feet. Zarathustra went to him, and sat among the youths at his feet. And thus spoke the wise man:

Respect sleep and be modest in its presence! That is the first thing! And avoid all who sleep badly and keep awake at night!

Even the thief is modest in the presence of sleep: he always steals softly through the night. Shameless, however, is the night watchman; shamelessly he carries his horn.

It is no small art to sleep: for that purpose you must keep awake all day.

Ten times a day you must overcome yourself: that makes you good and tired and is opium for the soul.

Ten times you must reconcile again with yourself; for overcoming is bitterness, and the unreconciled sleep badly.

Ten truths you must find during the day; otherwise you will seek truth during the night, and your soul will remain hungry.

Ten times you must laugh during the day, and be cheerful; otherwise your stomach, the father of gloom, will disturb you in the night.

Few people know it, but one must have all the virtues in order to sleep well. Shall I bear false witness? Shall I commit adultery?

Shall I covet my neighbor's maid? All that would go ill with good sleep.

And even if one has all the virtues, there is still one thing one must know: to send the virtues themselves to sleep at the right time.

That they may not quarrel with one another, the fair little women, about you, child of misfortune!

Peace with God and your neighbor: so good sleep demands. And peace also with your neighbor's devil! Otherwise it will haunt you in the night.

Honor the magistrates and obey them, and also the crooked magistrates! Good sleep demands it. Is it my fault that power likes to walk on crooked legs?

He who leads his sheep to the greenest pasture, shall always be for me the best shepherd: that goes well with good sleep.

I do not want many honors, nor great treasures: they inflame the spleen. But one sleeps badly without a good name and a little treasure.

A little company is more welcome to me than evil company: but they must come and go at the right time. That goes well with good sleep.

Well, also, do the poor in spirit please me: they promote sleep. Blessed are they, especially if one always tells them they are right.

Thus the virtuous pass the day. And when night comes, then I take good care not to summon sleep. It dislikes to be summoned—sleep, the master of the virtues!

But I think of what I have done and thought during the day. Chewing the cud, I ask myself, patient as a cow: Well, what were your ten overcomings?

And what were the ten reconciliations, and the ten truths, and the ten laughters with which my heart edified itself?

Weighing such matters and rocked by forty thoughts, it overtakes me suddenly, sleep, the unsummoned, the lord of the virtues.

Sleep taps on my eyes: they turn heavy. Sleep touches my mouth: it stays open.

Truly, on soft soles he comes to me, the dearest of thieves, and steals from me my thoughts: I stand stupid like this chair here.

But not for long do I stand like this: I already lie—

When Zarathustra heard the wise man thus speak he laughed in his heart: for an insight had come to him. And he spoke thus to his heart:

This wise man with his forty thoughts is a fool: but I believe he knows well how to sleep.

Happy is he that even lives near this wise man! Such sleep is contagious—contagious even through a thick wall.

There is magic even in his teaching chair. And it is not in vain that the youths sit before this preacher of virtue.

His wisdom is: to keep awake in order to sleep well. And truly, if life had no sense and had I to choose nonsense, then I too would consider this the most sensible nonsense.

Now I understand clearly what was once sought above all else when teachers of virtue were sought. Good sleep was sought, and opiate virtues to promote it!

For all these much praised sages who were teachers of virtue, wisdom was the sleep without dreams: they knew no better meaning of life.

Even today, to be sure, there may still be a few like this preacher of virtue, and not all so honest: but their time is up. And not much longer do they stand: there they already lie.

Blessed are the sleepy ones: for they shall soon fall off.—

Thus spoke Zarathustra.

ON THE AFTERWORLDLY[3]

AT ONE TIME ZARATHUSTRA also cast his fancy beyond man, like all the afterworldly. The work of a suffering and tortured god, the world then seemed to me.

A dream and a fiction of a god the world then seemed to me; colored smoke before the eyes of a dissatisfied deity.

Good and evil and joy and pain and I and you—colored smoke they seemed to me before creative eyes. The creator wanted to look away from himself, so he created the world.

It is drunken joy for the sufferer to look away from his suffering and lose himself. Drunken joy and loss of self, did the world once seem to me.

This world, eternally imperfect, the image of an eternal contradiction, an imperfect image—a drunken joy to its imperfect creator: thus did the world once seem to me.

Thus, at one time, I also cast my fancy beyond man, like all afterworldly. Beyond man indeed?

Ah, you brothers, that god whom I created was humanly made madness, like all gods!

Man he was, and only a poor fragment of a man and his "I":[4] out of my own ashes and glow it came to me, that ghost, and truly! It did not come to me from beyond!

What happened, my brothers? I overcame myself, the sufferer; I carried my own ashes to the mountains; I invented a brighter flame for myself. And behold! At that the ghost *fled* from me!

Now it would be suffering for me and agony for the convalescent to believe in such ghosts: now it would be suffering for me, and humiliation. Thus I speak to the afterworldly.

It was suffering and impotence—that created all afterworlds; and that brief madness of bliss which is experienced only by those who suffer most deeply.

Weariness, which seeks to get to the ultimate with one leap, with one death-leap; a poor ignorant weariness, unwilling even to will any longer: that created all gods and afterworlds.

Believe me, my brothers! It was the body that despaired of the body—it groped with the fingers of a deluded spirit at the ultimate walls.

Believe me, my brothers! It was the body that despaired of the earth—it heard the belly of being speaking to it.

And then it sought to get through these ultimate walls with its head—and not only with its head—over there to "that world."

But "that world" is well concealed from humans, that dehumanizing inhuman world, which is a heavenly nothing; and the belly of being does not speak to man except as man.

Truly, it is hard to prove all being, and hard to make it speak. Tell me, you brothers, is not the strangest of all things best proved?

Yes, this "I", with its contradiction and perplexity, speaks most honestly of its being—this creating, willing, valuing "I", which is the measure and value of all things.

And this most honest being, the "I"—it speaks of the body, and still implies the body, even when it muses and raves and flutters with broken wings.

Ever more honestly it learns to speak, the "I"; and the more it learns, the more words and honors it finds for the body and the earth.

A new pride my "I" taught to me, and I teach that to men: no longer to thrust one's head into the sand of heavenly things, but to carry it freely, a terrestrial head, which creates a meaning to the earth!

A new will I teach men: to will this way which man has walked blindly, and to affirm it—and no longer to slink aside from it, like the sick and decaying!

The sick and decaying—it was they who despised the body and the earth, and invented the heavenly world, and the redeeming drops of blood; but even those sweet and dark poisons they borrowed from the body and the earth!

From their misery they sought escape, and the stars were too remote for them. Then they sighed: "O that there were heavenly paths by which to steal into another existence and into happiness!" Then they contrived for themselves their sneaky ruses and bloody potions!

Beyond the sphere of their body and this earth they now fancied themselves transported, these ungrateful ones. But to what did they owe the convulsion and rapture of their transport? To their body and this earth.

Zarathustra is gentle with the sick. Truly, he is not indignant at their kind of consolation and ingratitude. May they become convalescents and overcomers, and create higher bodies for themselves!

Neither is Zarathustra indignant at a convalescent who looks tenderly on his delusions, and at midnight steals round the grave of his god; but even so his tears still betray a sickness and a sick body to me.

Many sick ones have there always been among those who muse, and languish for God; violently they hate the lover of knowledge and that youngest among the virtues, which is called "honesty."

They always gaze backwards toward dark ages: then, indeed, delusion and faith were something different. The rage of reason was godlikeness, and doubt was sin.

All too well do I know those godlike ones: they insist on being believed in, and that doubt is sin. All too well, also, do I know what they themselves most believe in.

Truly, not in afterworlds and redeeming drops of blood: but in the body they also believe most; and their own body is for them their thing-in-itself.

But it is a sickly thing to them, and gladly would they get out of their skin. Therefore they listen to the preachers of death, and themselves preach afterworlds.

Listen rather, my brothers, to the voice of the healthy body; it is a more honest and purer voice.

More honestly and purely speaks the healthy body that is perfect and perpendicular; and it speaks of the meaning of the earth.

Thus spoke Zarathustra.

ON THE DESPISERS OF THE BODY

I WANT TO SPEAK to the despisers of the body. I would not have them learn and teach differently, but merely say farewell to their own bodies—and thus become silent.

"Body am I, and soul"—so says the child. And why should one not speak like children?

But the awakened one, the knowing one, says: "Body am I entirely, and nothing more; and soul is only the name of something about the body."[5]

The body is a great reason, a plurality with one sense, a war and a peace, a herd and also a shepherd.

An instrument of your body is also your little reason, my brother, which you call "spirit"—a little instrument and toy of your great reason.

"I," you say, and are proud of that word. But the greater thing—in which you are unwilling to believe—is your body with its great reason; it says not "I," but does it.

What the sense feels, what the spirit discerns, never has its end in itself. But sense and spirit would like to persuade you that they are the end of all things: that is how vain they are.

Instruments and toys are sense and spirit: behind them still lies the self. The self also seeks with the eyes of the senses, it also listens with the ears of the spirit.

Always the self listens and seeks; it compares, masters, conquers, and destroys. It rules, and is in control of the "I" too.

Behind your thoughts and feelings, my brother, there is a mighty lord, an unknown sage—his name is self; he dwells in your body, he is your body.

There is more reason in your body than in your best wisdom. And who knows why your body requires precisely your best wisdom?

Your self laughs at your "I" and its bold leaps. "What are these leaps and flights of thought to me?" it says to itself. "A detour to my end. I am the leading strings of the 'I', and the prompter of its concepts."

The self says to the "I": "Feel pain!" And at that it suffers, and thinks how it may put an end to it—and for that very purpose it is *made* to think.

The self says to the "I": "Feel pleasure!" At that it is pleased, and thinks how it might often be pleased again—and for that very purpose it is *made* to think.

I want to speak to the despisers of the body. It is their respect that produces their contempt. What is it that created respect and contempt and worth and will?

The creating self created respect and contempt, it created pleasure and pain. The creative body created spirit as a hand for its will.

Even in your folly and contempt you each serve your self, you despisers of the body. I tell you, your self itself wants to die and turns away from life.

No longer can your self do that which it desires most:—to create beyond itself. That is what it would do above all else; that is its fervent desire.

But it is now too late to do so:—so your self wants to go under, you despisers of the body.

To go under—so wishes your self; and therefore you have become despisers of the body. For you can no longer create beyond yourselves.

And therefore now you are angry with life and with the earth. An unconscious envy is in the squint-eyed glance of your contempt.

I shall not go your way, you despisers of the body! You are no bridge to the Übermensch!—

Thus spoke Zarathustra.

On Enjoying and Suffering the Passions

My brother, when you have a virtue, and she is your own virtue, you have her in common with no one.

To be sure, you want to call her by name and caress her; you want to pull her ear and have fun with her.

And behold, now you have her name in common with the people, and have become one of the people and the herd with your virtue!

You would do better to say: "Ineffable and nameless is that which is agony and sweetness to my soul and is even the hunger of my entrails."

Let your virtue be too exalted for the familiarity of names, and if you must speak of her, then do not be ashamed to stammer about her.

Then speak and stammer: "This is *my* good, this do I love, thus does it please me entirely, thus only do *I* desire the good.

"I do not want it as a divine law; I do not want it as a human law or a human need; it shall not to be signpost for me to over-earths and paradises.

"It is an earthly virtue that I love: there is little prudence in it, and least of all the reason of every man.

"But this bird built its nest with me: therefore, I love and caress it—now it dwells with me, sitting on its golden eggs."

Thus you shall stammer and praise your virtue.

Once you suffered passions and called them evil. But now you have only your virtues left: they grew out of your passions.

You commended your highest aim to the heart of these passions: then they became the virtues and passions you enjoy.

And whether you came from the race of the choleric or the voluptuous or the fanatic or the vindictive:

All your passions in the end became virtues, and all your devils angels.

Once you had wild dogs in your cellar: but they changed at last into birds and charming singers.

Out of your poisons you brewed your balsam; you milked your cow, misery—now you drink the sweet milk of her udder.

And nothing evil grows in you any longer, unless it is the evil that grows out of the conflict of your virtues.

My brother, if you are fortunate, then you will have only one virtue and no more: thus you will go more easily over the bridge.

It is illustrious to have many virtues, but a hard lot; and many have gone into the desert and killed themselves, because they were weary of being the battle and battlefield of virtues.

My brother, are war and battle evil? But this evil is necessary; necessary are the envy and mistrust and calumny among the virtues.

Behold, how each of your virtues covets the highest place; each wants your whole spirit that it might become *her* herald, each wants your whole strength, in wrath, hatred, and love.

Each virtue is jealous of the others, and jealousy is a dreadful thing. Virtues too can perish of jealousy.

Surrounded by the flames of jealousy, the jealous one winds up, like the scorpion, turning the poisoned sting against himself.

Ah, my brother, have you never seen a virtue backbite and stab itself?

Man is something that has to be overcome: and therefore you will love your virtues,—for you will perish of them.

Thus spoke Zarathustra.

ON THE PALE CRIMINAL

YOU DO NOT WANT to kill, you judges and sacrificers, until the animal has nodded? Behold, the pale criminal has nodded: out of his eyes speaks the great contempt.

"My 'I' is something that shall be overcome: to me my 'I' is the great contempt of man": so it speaks out of that eye.

When he judged himself—that was his supreme moment; do not the sublime relapse again into his baseness!

There is no salvation for him who thus suffers from himself, unless it is speedy death.

Your slaying, you judges, shall be pity, and not revenge; and as you kill, see to it that you yourselves justify life!

It is not enough that you should reconcile with him whom you kill. Let your sorrow be love of the Übermensch: thus you will justify your own survival!

"Enemy" you shall say but not "villain," "sick" you shall say but not "wretch," "fool" you shall say but not "sinner."

And you, red judge, if you would say aloud all you have done in thought, then everyone would cry: "Away with this filth and this poisonous worm!"

But the thought is one thing, the deed another, and the image of the deed still another. The wheel of causality does not roll between them.

An image made this pale man pale. He was equal to his deed when he did it, but he could not endure its image after it was done.

Now he always saw himself as the doer of one deed. Madness, I call this: the exception became the essence for him.

A streak of chalk stops a hen; the stroke he himself struck stopped his weak reason—madness *after* the deed I call this.

Listen, you judges! There is yet another madness, and it comes *before* the deed. Ah, you have not yet crept deep enough into this soul!

Thus speaks the red judge: "Why did this criminal commit murder? He meant to rob." I tell you, however, that his soul wanted blood, not robbery: he thirsted for the bliss of the knife!

But his poor reason did not understand this madness, and it persuaded him. "What matters blood!" it said; "don't you want, at least, to commit a robbery with it? Or take revenge?"

And he listened to his poor reason: its words lay upon him like lead—so he robbed when he murdered. He did not want to be ashamed of his madness.

And now once more the lead of his guilt lies upon him, and once more his poor reason is so stiff, so paralyzed, so heavy.

If only he could shake his head, then his burden would roll off; but who shakes that head?

What is this man? A pile of diseases that reach out into the world through the spirit; there they want to catch their prey.

What is this man? A coil of wild serpents that are seldom at peace among themselves—so they go forth singly and seek prey in the world.

Look at that poor body! What it suffered and craved, the poor soul interpreted to itself—it interpreted it as murderous lust and greed for the bliss of the knife.

Those who fall sick today are overcome by that evil which is evil today: he seeks to hurt with that which hurts him. But there have been other ages and another evil and good.

Once doubt was evil, and the will to self. Then the sick became heretics or witches; as heretics or witches they suffered and sought to inflict suffering.

But this will not go in your ears; it hurts your good people, you tell me. But what do your good people matter to me!

Much in your good people nauseates me, and truly, it is not their evil. Indeed, I wish they had a madness by which they might perish like this pale criminal!

Truly, I wish their madness were called truth or fidelity or justice: but they have their virtue in order to live long and in wretched contentment.

I am a railing by the torrent; grasp me, those who can grasp me! Your crutch, however, I am not.—

Thus spoke Zarathustra.

ON READING AND WRITING

OF ALL THAT IS written I love only what a man has written with his blood. Write with blood, and you will find that blood is spirit.

It is no easy task to understand strange blood; I hate those readers who idle.

Whoever knows the reader, does nothing more for the reader. Another century of readers—and spirit itself will stink.

That every one may learn to read in the long run corrupts not only writing but also thinking.

Once the spirit was God, then it became man, and now it even becomes herd.

Whoever writes in blood and aphorisms does not want to be read but to be learned by heart.

In the mountains the shortest way is from peak to peak, but for that one must have long legs. Aphorisms should be peaks, and those who are addressed, tall and lofty.

The atmosphere rare and pure, danger near and the spirit full of a gay malice: these go well together.

I want to have goblins about me, for I am courageous. The courage that scares away ghosts creates goblins for itself—courage wants to laugh.

I no longer feel as you do; the cloud which I see beneath me, this blackness and gravity at which I laugh—that is your thunder-cloud.

You look up when you long for elevation. And I look down because I am elevated.

Who among you can laugh and be elevated at the same time?

Whoever climbs on the highest mountains laughs at all tragic plays and tragic seriousness.

Brave, unconcerned, mocking, violent—thus wisdom wants us: she is a woman and always loves only a warrior.

You tell me, "Life is hard to bear." But why would you have your pride in the morning and your resignation in the evening?

Life is hard to bear: but do not pretend to be so delicate! We are all of us fine beasts of burden, male and female asses.

What do we have in common with the rosebud, which trembles because a drop of dew lies on it?

It is true: we love life, not because we are used to living, but because we are used to loving.

There is always some madness in love. But there is always also some reason in madness.

And to me also, as I am well disposed toward life, butterflies and soap bubbles and whatever among men is of their kind seem to know most about happiness.

To see these light, foolish, pretty, lively little souls flutter—that seduces Zarathustra to tears and songs.

I would believe only in a god who could dance.

And when I saw my devil I found him serious, thorough, profound, and solemn: he was the spirit of gravity—through him all things fall.

Not by wrath does one kill but by laughter. Come, let us kill the spirit of gravity!

I learned to walk: ever since, I let myself run. I learned to fly: ever since, I do not want a push before moving along.

Now I am light, now I fly, now I see myself beneath myself, now a god dances through me.

Thus spoke Zarathustra.

On the Tree on the Mountain

ZARATHUSTRA'S EYE HAD OBSERVED that a youth avoided him. And as he walked alone one evening over the hills surrounding the town called "The Motley Cow": behold, there he found the youth sitting leaning against a tree and gazing wearily into the valley. Zarathustra laid hold of the tree under which the youth was sitting and spoke thus:

"If I wished to shake this tree with my hands I should not be able to do so.

"But the wind, which does not see, tortures and bends it in whatever direction it pleases. We are bent and tortured worst by invisible hands."

At that the youth arose in consternation and said: "I hear Zarathustra, and just now was I thinking of him." Zarathustra answered:

"Why should that frighten you?—But it is the same with man as with the tree.

"The more he seeks to rise into the height and light, the more vigorously do his roots struggle earthward, downward, into the dark, the deep—into evil."

"Yes, into evil!" cried the youth. "How is it possible that you discovered my soul?"

Zarathustra smiled and said: "Some souls one will never discover, unless one invents them first."

"Yes, into evil!" the youth cried once more.

"You have spoken the truth, Zarathustra. I no longer trust myself since I sought to rise into the height, and nobody trusts me any longer; how did this happen?

"I change too quickly: my today refutes my yesterday. I often skip steps when I climb: no step forgives me that.

"When I am at the top I always find myself alone. No one speaks to me, the frost of solitude makes me tremble. What do I seek on the height?

"My contempt and my longing increase together; the higher I climb, the more I despise the climber. What does he seek on the height?

"How ashamed I am of my climbing and stumbling! How I mock at my violent panting! How I hate the flier! How tired I am on the height!"

Here the youth was silent. And Zarathustra contemplated the tree beside which they stood and spoke thus:

"This tree stands lonely here in the mountains; it grew high above man and beast.

"And if it wanted to speak it would have none who could understand it: so high has it grown.

"Now it waits and waits—for what is it waiting? It dwells too close to the seat of the clouds: surely it waits for the first lightning?"

When Zarathustra had said this the youth called out with violent gestures: "Yes, Zarathustra, you speak the truth. I longed to go under when I desired to be on the height, and you are the lightning for which I waited! Behold, what am I since you have appeared among us? It is the *envy* of you that has destroyed me!"—Thus spoke the youth and wept bitterly. But Zarathustra put his arm about him and led the youth away with him.

And when they had walked a while together, Zarathustra began to speak thus:

It tears my heart. Better than your words express it, your eyes tell me of all your dangers.

As yet you are not free; you still *search* for freedom. Your search has made you overtired and over awake.

You want the free heights, your soul thirsts for the stars. But your wicked drives also thirst for freedom.

Your wild dogs want freedom; they bark for joy in their cellar when your spirit plans to open all prisons.

To me you are still a prisoner who is plotting his freedom: ah, in such prisoners the soul becomes clever, but also deceitful and bad.

And even the liberated spirit must still purify himself. Much prison and mustiness still remain in him: his eyes must still become pure.

Yes, I know your danger. But by my love and hope I beseech you: do not throw away your love and hope!

You still feel noble, and others too sense your nobility, though they bear you a grudge and send you evil glances. Know that the noble one stands in everybody's way.

The noble one stands in the way of the good too: and even when they call him one of the good, they thus want to do away with him.

The noble man wants to create something new and a new virtue. The good want the old, and that the old should be preserved.

But this is not the danger of the noble man, that he might become one of the good, but a know-it-all, a mocker, a destroyer.

Ah, I have known noble ones who lost their highest hope. And then they disparaged all high hopes.

Then they lived shamelessly in brief pleasures and barely cast their aims beyond the day.

"Spirit too is lust"—so they said. Then the wings of their spirit broke: and now their spirit creeps about and soils what it gnaws.

Once they thought of becoming heroes: now they are voluptuaries. The hero is for them an offense and a terror.

But by my love and hope I beseech you: do not throw away the hero in your soul! Hold holy your highest hope!—

Thus spoke Zarathustra.

On the Preachers of Death

There are preachers of death: and the earth is full of those to whom one must preach renunciation of life.

The earth is full of the superfluous; life is marred by the all-too-many. May they be lured out of this life by the "eternal life"!

The preachers of death wear yellow or black. But I want to show them to you in other colors as well.

There are the terrible ones who carry about in themselves the beast of prey and have no choice except lust or self-laceration. And even their lust is still self-laceration.

They have not yet become men, those terrible ones: let them preach renunciation from life and pass away themselves!

There are those with consumption of the soul: hardly are they born when they begin to die and to long for teachings of weariness and renunciation.

They would like to be dead and we should welcome their wish! Let us beware of waking those dead ones and of disturbing those living coffins!

They meet a sick man or an old man or a corpse—and immediately they say: "Life is refuted!"

But only they themselves are refuted, and their eyes, which see only one aspect of existence.

Shrouded in thick melancholy and eager for the little accidents that bring death: thus they wait and grind their teeth.

Or else they reach for sweets while laughing at their own childishness: they clutch at the straws of their lives and make fun of their still clutching straws.

Their wisdom speaks thus: "Only a fool remains alive, but such fools are we! And that is surely the most foolish thing about life!"

"Life is only suffering"—so say others, and do not lie: see to it then that *you* cease! See to it then that the life which is only suffering ceases!

And let this be the teaching of your virtue: "Thou shalt kill yourself! Thou shalt steal away from thyself!"—

"Lust is sin"—so say some who preach death—"let us go apart and beget no children!"

"Giving birth is troublesome"—say others—"why still give birth? One bears only unfortunates!" And they too are preachers of death.

"Pity is necessary,"—so says a third group. "Take what I have! Take what I am! So much less does life bind me!"

Were they consistently pitiful then they would make their neighbors sick of life. To be evil—that would be their genuine goodness.

But they want to be rid of life: what do they care if they bind others still more tightly with their chains and gifts!—

And you too, for whom life is furious work and unrest: are you not very weary of life? Are you not very ripe for the preaching of death?

All of you to whom furious work is dear, and the rapid, new, and strange—you tolerate yourselves badly; your diligence is flight and the will to forget yourselves.

If you believed more in life, then you would devote yourselves less to the momentary. But you do not have contents enough in yourselves for waiting—nor even for idleness!

Everywhere the voice of those who preach death resounds; and the earth is full of those to whom death must be preached.

Or "eternal life": it is all the same to me—if only they pass away quickly!—

Thus spoke Zarathustra.

On War and Warriors

WE DO NOT WANT to be spared by our best enemies, nor by those either whom we love thoroughly. So let me tell you the truth!

My brothers in war![6] I love you thoroughly,[7] I am and I was of your kind. And I am also your best enemy. So let me tell you the truth!

I know of the hatred and envy of your hearts. You are not great enough not to know hatred and envy. Then be great enough not to be ashamed of them!

And if you cannot be saints of knowledge, at least be its warriors. They are the companions and forerunners of such sainthood.

I see many soldiers: would that I saw many warriors! One calls what they wear a "uniform": would that what it conceals were not uniform!

You should have eyes ever seeking for an enemy—for *your* enemy. And some of you hate at first sight.

You shall seek your enemy, you shall wage your war, and for the sake of your thoughts! And if your thoughts are vanquished, then your honesty should still find triumph in that!

You shall love peace as a means to new wars—and the short peace more than the long one.

To you I advise not work but battle. To you I advise not peace but victory. Let your work be a battle, let your peace be a victory!

One can be silent and sit still only when one has arrow and bow: otherwise one chatters and quarrels. Let your peace be a victory!

You say it is the good cause that hallows even war? I say to you: it is the good war that hallows any cause.

War and courage have done more great things than love of the neighbor. Not your pity but your courage has so far saved the unfortunate.

"What is good?" you ask. To be brave is good. Let the little girls say: "To be good is what is both pretty and touching."

They call you heartless: but you have a heart, and I love you for being ashamed to show it. You are ashamed of your flow, while others are ashamed of their ebb.

You are ugly? Well then, my brothers, wrap the sublime about you, the mantle of the ugly!

And when your soul becomes great, then it becomes playful, and in your sublimity there is malice. I know you.

In malice the prankster and the weakling meet. But they misunderstand one another. I know you.

You may have only enemies whom you can hate, not enemies you despise. You must be proud of your enemy: then the successes of your enemy are your successes too.

Recalcitrance—that is the nobility of slaves. Let your nobility be obedience. Let your commanding itself be obeying!

To the good warrior "thou shalt" sounds more pleasant than "I will." And all that is dear to you, you shall first have it commanded to you.

Let your love of life be love of your highest hope: and let your highest hope be the highest thought of life!

Your highest thought, however, you should receive as a commandment from me—and it is: man is something that shall be overcome.

So live your life of obedience and of war! What matters long life! What warrior wants to be spared!

I do not spare you, I love you thoroughly, my brothers in war!—

Thus spoke Zarathustra.

On the New Idol

SOMEWHERE THERE ARE STILL peoples and herds, but not where we live, my brothers: here there are states.

State? What is that? Well! Now open your ears to me, for now I shall speak to you about the death of peoples.

State is the name of the coldest of all cold monsters. Coldly it tells lies too; and this lie crawls from its mouth: "I, the state, am the people."

It's a lie! It was creators who created peoples and hung a faith and a love over them: thus they served life.

It is destroyers who lay traps for the many and call them "state": they hang a sword and a hundred cravings over them.

Where there is still a people, there the state is not understood but hated as the evil eye and as the sin against laws and customs.

This sign I give to you: every people speaks its tongue of good and evil: and the neighbor does not understand it. It has invented its own language of customs and rights.

But the state lies in all the tongues of good and evil; and whatever it says it lies—and whatever it has it has stolen.

Everything about it is false; it bites with stolen teeth, this biter. Even its entrails are false.

Confusion of tongues of good and evil: this sign I give to you as the sign of the state. Truly, this sign signifies the will to death! Truly, it beckons to the preachers of death!

All-too-many are born: for the superfluous the state was invented!

See just how it entices them to it, the all-too-many! How it swallows and chews and rechews them!

"On earth there is nothing greater than I: it is I who am the ordering finger of God"—thus roars the monster. And not only the long-eared and the shortsighted fall upon their knees!

Ah, even in your ears, you great souls, it whispers its dark lies! Ah, it detects the rich hearts which like to squander themselves!

Yes, it detects you too, you vanquishers of the old god! You have grown weary of fighting, and now your weariness serves the new idol!

It would surround itself with heroes and honorable ones, the new idol! It basks happily in the sunshine of good consciences—the cold monster!

It will give *you* everything if *you* worship it, the new idol: thus it purchases the luster of your virtue and the look of your proud eyes.

It would use you as a bait for the all-too-many! Yes, a hellish artifice has here been devised, a death-horse jingling with the trappings of divine honors!

Yes, a dying for many has here been devised, which glorifies itself as life: truly, a great service to all preachers of death!

State, I call it, where all drink poison, the good and the bad: state, where all lose themselves, the good and the bad: state, where the slow suicide of all—is called "life."

Just see the superfluous! They steal the works of the inventors and the treasures of the sages for themselves: "education," they call their theft—and everything becomes sickness and trouble to them!

Just see the superfluous! They are always sick; they vomit their bile and call it a newspaper. They devour one another and cannot even digest themselves.

Just see the superfluous! They gather riches and become poorer with them. They want power and first the lever of power, much money—the impotent paupers!

See them clamber, these nimble monkeys! They clamber over one another and thus tumble one another into the mud and the deep.

They all want to get to the throne: it is their madness—as if happiness sat on the throne! Often mud sits on the throne—and often also the throne on mud.

Madmen they all seem to me, clambering monkeys and overeager. To me their idol smells foul, the cold monster: to me they all smell foul, these idolaters.

My brothers, do you want to suffocate in the fumes of their snouts and appetites? Rather break the windows and spring to freedom!

Escape from the bad smell! Escape from the idolatry of the superfluous!

Escape from the bad smell! Escape from the steam of these human sacrifices!

The earth is free even now for great souls. There are yet many empty seats for the lonesome and the twosome, wafted by the aroma of still seas.

A free life is even now free for great souls. Truly, whoever possesses little is that much less possessed: praised be a little poverty!

Only where the state ends, there begins the human being who is not superfluous: there begins the song of necessity, the unique and inimitable tune.

Where the state *ends*—look there, my brothers! Do you not see it, the rainbow and the bridges of the Übermensch?—

Thus spoke Zarathustra.

On the Flies in the Marketplace

FLEE, MY FRIEND, INTO your solitude! I see you deafened with the noise of the great men and pricked by the stings of the little men.

Forest and rock know well how to be silent with you. Be like the tree again, the wide branching tree which you love: silently and attentively it hangs over the sea.

Where solitude ends, there the marketplace begins; and where the marketplace begins, there begins also the noise of the great actors and the buzzing of the poisonous flies.[8]

In the world even the best things are worthless without those who first present them: people call these presenters great men.

The people have little comprehension of greatness, that is to say: creativeness. But they have a taste for all presenters and actors of great things.

The world revolves around the inventors of new values: invisibly it revolves. But around the actors revolve the people and fame: so the world goes.

The actor has spirit, but little conscience of the spirit. He always believes in that with which he most powerfully produces belief—produces belief in *himself*!

Tomorrow he will have a new faith and the day after tomorrow a newer one. He has sharp perceptions, like the people, and capricious moods.

To overthrow—to him that means: to prove. To drive mad—to him that means: to convince. And blood is to him as the best of all arguments.

A truth that penetrates only sensitive ears he calls a lie and nothing. Truly, he believes only in gods who make a great noise in the world!

The marketplace is full of solemn jesters—and the people boast of their great men! These are their masters of the hour.

But the hour presses them: so they press you. And from you they also want a Yes or a No. Ah, would you put your chair between For and Against?

Do not be jealous, lover of truth, of those unconditional and impatient ones! Never yet has truth clung to the arm of the unconditional.

Return to your security because of these abrupt men: only in the marketplace is one assailed by Yes? or No?

The experience of all deep fountains is slow: they must wait long until they know *what* has fallen into their depths.

All that is great takes place away from the marketplace and from fame: the inventors of new values have always lived away from the marketplace and from fame.

Flee, my friend, into your solitude: I see you stung all over by the poisonous flies. Flee to where a rough, strong breeze blows!

Flee into your solitude! You have lived too closely to the small and the pitiable. Flee from their invisible vengeance! Towards you they have nothing but vengeance.

Do not raise an arm against them! They are innumerable and it is not your fate to be a fly swatter.

The small and pitiable ones are innumerable; and raindrops and weeds have already been the ruin of many a proud building.

You are not stone, but already these many drops have made you hollow. You will yet break and burst through these many drops.

I see you exhausted by poisonous flies, I see you bloodily torn at a hundred spots; and your pride refuses even to be angry.

They want blood from you in all innocence, their bloodless souls crave blood—and therefore they sting in all innocence.

But you, profound one, you suffer too profoundly even from small wounds; and before you have recovered, the same poisonous worm is again crawling over your hand.

You are too proud to kill these sweettooths. But take care that it does not become your fate to suffer all their poisonous injustice!

They buzz around you even with their praise: and their praise is importunity. They want to be close to your skin and your blood.

They flatter you, as one flatters a god or devil; they whimper before you, as before a god or devil. What does it come to! They are flatterers and whimperers and nothing more.

And they are often kind to you. But that has always been the prudence of the cowardly. Yes! The cowardly are prudent!

They think a great deal about you with their narrow souls—you are always suspicious to them! Whatever is thought about a great deal is at last thought suspicious.[9]

They punish you for all your virtues. They forgive you entirely—your mistakes.

Because you are gentle and just-minded, you say: "They are blameless in their small existence." But their narrow souls think: "All great existence is blameworthy."

Even when you are gentle towards them, they still feel you despise them; and they repay your kindness with secret unkindness.

Your silent pride always offends their taste; they rejoice if ever you are modest enough to be vain.

What we recognize in a man we also inflame in him. Therefore be on your guard against the small ones!

In your presence they feel themselves small, and their baseness gleams and glows against you in invisible vengeance.

Did you not see how often they became dumb when you approached them, and how their strength left them like smoke from a dying fire?

Yes, my friend, you are a bad conscience to your neighbors: for they are unworthy of you. Therefore they hate you and would dearly like to suck your blood.

Your neighbors will always be poisonous flies: what is great in you, that itself must make them more poisonous and ever more fly-like.

Flee, my friend, into your solitude and to where a rough strong breeze blows. It is not your fate to be a fly-swatter.—

Thus spoke Zarathustra.

ON CHASTITY

I LOVE THE FOREST. It is bad to live in cities: too many of the lustful live there.

Is it not better to fall into the hands of a murderer than into the dreams of a lustful woman?

And just look at these men: their eyes say it—they know of nothing better on earth than to lie with a woman.

Filth is at the bottom of their souls; and it is worse if this filth still has spirit in it!

Would that you were perfect—at least as animals! But to animals belongs innocence.

Do I exhort you to kill your instincts? I exhort you to innocence in your instincts.

Do I exhort you to chastity? Chastity is a virtue with some, but with many almost a vice.

These people abstain, to be sure: but the bitch Sensuality leers enviously out of all that they do.

This restless beast follows them even into the heights of their virtue and into the depths of their cold spirit.

And how nicely the bitch Sensuality knows how to beg for a piece of spirit, when a piece of flesh is denied her!

You love tragedies and all that breaks the heart? But I am distrustful of your bitch Sensuality.

Your eyes are too cruel for me, and you search lustfully for sufferers. Has your lust not merely disguised itself and called itself pity?

And I also give this parable to you: not a few who meant to drive out their devil have themselves entered into swine.

Those for whom chastity is difficult should be dissuaded from it, lest it become the road to hell—that is, to filth and lust of soul.

Do I speak of dirty things? That does not seem to me the worst I could do.

It is not when the truth is dirty, but when it is shallow, that the enlightened man is reluctant to step in its waters.

Truly, there are those who are chaste through and through: they are gentler of heart and laugh better and oftener than you.

They laugh at chastity too, and ask: "What is chastity?

"Is chastity not folly? But the folly came to us and not we to it.

"We offered that guest shelter and love: now it dwells with us— let it stay as long as it will!"—

Thus spoke Zarathustra.

ON THE FRIEND

"ONE IS ALWAYS ONE too many around me"—thus thinks the hermit. "Always once one—in the long run that makes two!"

I and Me are always too earnestly in conversation: how could it be endured, if there were not a friend?

For the hermit the friend is always the third person: the third person is the cork that prevents the conversation of the other two from sinking into the depths.

Ah, there are too many depths for all hermits. That is why they long so much for a friend and for his heights.

Our faith in others betrays wherein we would like to have faith in ourselves. Our longing for a friend is our betrayer.

And often with our love we only want to leap over envy. And often we attack and make an enemy in order to conceal that we are vulnerable to attack.

"At least be my enemy!"—thus speaks the true reverence, which does not venture to solicit friendship.

If one would have a friend, then one must also be willing to wage war for him: and in order to wage war, one must be *capable* of being an enemy.

One ought still to honor the enemy in one's friend. Can you go near to your friend without going over to him?

In one's friend one shall have one's best enemy. You should be closest to him with your heart when you oppose him.

Do you wish to go naked before your friend? It is in honor of your friend that you show yourself to him as you are? But he sends you to the devil for that!

He who makes no secret of himself enrages: so much reason have you to fear nakedness! If you were gods you could then be ashamed of your clothes!

You cannot adorn yourself too well for your friend: for you should be to him an arrow and a longing for the Übermensch.

Have you ever watched your friend asleep—and discovered how he looks? What is the face of your friend anyway? It is your own face, in a rough and imperfect mirror.

Have you ever watched your friend asleep? Were you not startled that your friend looked like that? O my friend, man is something that must be overcome.

A friend should be a master at guessing and in keeping silence: you must not want to see everything. Your dream should tell you what your friend does when awake.

Let your pity be a guessing: to know first if your friend wants pity. Perhaps what he loves in you is the unmoved eye and the glance of eternity.

Your pity for your friend should conceal itself under a hard shell, and you should break a tooth on it. Thus it will have delicacy and sweetness.

Are you pure air and solitude and bread and medicine to your friend? Some cannot loosen their own chains and can nevertheless redeem their friend.

Are you a slave? Then you cannot be a friend. Are you a tyrant? Then you cannot have friends.

All-too-long have a slave and a tyrant been concealed in woman. Therefore woman is not yet capable of friendship: she knows only love.

In woman's love there is injustice and blindness towards all she does not love. And even in the knowing love of a woman there is still always surprise attack and lightning and night along with the light.

Woman is not yet capable of friendship: women are still cats and birds. Or at best, cows.

Woman is not yet capable of friendship. But tell me, you men, who among you is capable of friendship?

Oh your poverty, you men, and the meanness of your souls! As much as you give to your friend I will give even to my enemy, and will not have grown poorer in doing so.

There is comradeship: may there be friendship!

Thus spoke Zarathustra.

On the Thousand and One Goals

ZARATHUSTRA HAS SEEN MANY lands and many peoples: thus he has discovered the good and evil of many peoples. Zarathustra has found no greater power on earth than good and evil.

No people could live without first valuing; if a people will maintain itself, however, it must not value as its neighbor values.

Much that seemed good to one people was regarded with scorn and contempt by another: thus I found. I found much that was called evil in one place was in another decked with purple honors.

One neighbor never understood another: his soul always marveled at his neighbor's madness and wickedness.

A tablet of the good hangs over every people. Behold, it is the tablet of their overcomings; behold, it is the voice of their will to power.

Whatever seems difficult to a people is praiseworthy; what is indispensable and difficult is called good; and whatever relieves the greatest need, the rarest, the most difficult of all—that they call holy.

Whatever makes them rule and conquer and shine, to the dread and envy of their neighbors, that is to them the high, the first, the measure, the meaning of all things.

Truly, my brother, if you only knew a people's need and land and sky and neighbor, you could surely divine the law of its overcomings, and why it climbs up that ladder to its hope.

"You should always be the first and outrival all others: your jealous soul should love no one, unless it be the friend"—that made the soul of a Greek quiver: thus he walked the path of his greatness.

"To speak the truth and to handle bow and arrow well"—this seemed both dear and difficult to the people from whom I got my name—the name which is both dear and difficult to me.

"To honor father and mother, and from the root of the soul to do their will"—another people hung this tablet of overcoming over itself and became powerful and eternal thereby.

"To practice loyalty, and for the sake of loyalty to risk honor and blood even in evil and dangerous things"—another people mastered itself with this teaching, and thus mastering itself it became pregnant and heavy with great hopes.

Truly, men have given to themselves all their good and evil. Truly, they did not take it, they did not find it, it did not come to them as a voice from heaven.

Only man assigned values to things in order to maintain himself— he created the meaning of things, a human meaning! Therefore, calls he himself: "Man," that is: the evaluator.

Evaluation is creation: hear this, you creators! Valuation itself is of all valued things the most valuable treasure.

Through valuation only is there value; and without valuation the nut of existence would be hollow. Hear this, you creators!

Change of values—that is a change of creators. Whoever must be a creator always destroys.

First, peoples were creators; and only in later times, individuals. Truly, the individual himself is still the latest creation.

Once peoples hung a tablet of the good over themselves. Love which would rule and love which would obey have together created such tablets.

Joy in the herd is older than joy in the "I": and as long as the good conscience is identified with the herd, only the bad conscience says: "I".

Truly, the cunning "I", the loveless one, that seeks its advantage in the advantage of many—that is not the origin of the herd, but its going under.

Good and evil have always been created by lovers and creators. The fire of love glows in the names of all the virtues and the fire of wrath.

Zarathustra has seen many lands and many peoples: Zarathustra has found no greater power on earth than the works of the lovers— "good" and "evil" are their names.

Truly, this power of praising and blaming is a monster. Tell me, O brothers, who will subdue it for me? Tell me, who will throw a yoke upon the thousand necks of this beast?

A thousand goals have there been so far, for a thousand peoples have there been. Only the yoke for the thousand necks is still lacking: the *one* goal is lacking. As yet humanity has no goal.

But tell me, my brothers, if the goal of humanity is still lacking, is there not also still lacking—humanity itself?—

Thus spoke Zarathustra.

On Love of the Neighbor

You crowd around your neighbor and have beautiful words for it. But I tell you: your love of the neighbor is your bad love of yourselves.[10]

You flee from yourselves to your neighbor and would like to make a virtue out of that: but I see through your "selflessness."

The You is older than the I; the You has been consecrated, but not yet the I: so man crowds toward his neighbor.

Do I recommend love of the neighbor to you? Sooner should I recommend even flight from the neighbor and love of the farthest!

Higher than love of the neighbor stands love of the farthest and the future; higher still than the love of man I account the love of things and ghosts.

The ghost that runs on before you, my brother, is fairer than you; why do you not give him your flesh and your bones? But you are afraid and you run to your neighbor.

You cannot endure to be alone with yourselves and do not love yourselves enough: so you want to mislead your neighbor into love and gild yourselves with his error.

I wish rather that you could not endure to be with any kind of neighbor or your neighbor's neighbor; then you would have to create your friend and his overflowing heart out of yourselves.

You call in a witness when you want to speak well of yourselves; and when you have misled him into thinking well of you, you then think well of yourselves.

It is not only he who speaks contrary to what he knows who lies, but even more he who speaks contrary to his ignorance. And thus you speak of yourselves in your dealings with others and deceive your neighbor with yourselves.

Thus speaks the fool: "Association with other people spoils the character, especially when one has none."

One man goes to his neighbor because he seeks himself, and another because he wants to lose himself. Your bad love of yourselves makes solitude a prison to you.

It is those farther away who must pay for your love of your neighbor; and when there are five of you together, a sixth must always die.

I do not love your festivals either: I found too many actors there, and even the spectators often behaved like actors.

I do not teach you the neighbor but the friend. Let the friend be the festival of the earth to you, and a foretaste of the Übermensch.

I teach you the friend and his overflowing heart. But you must know how to be a sponge if you want to be loved by overflowing hearts.

I teach you the friend in whom the world stands complete, a vessel of the good,—the creating friend who has always a completed world to give away.

And as the world unrolled itself for him, so it rolls together again for him in rings, as the becoming of the good through evil, as the becoming of purpose out of chance.

Let the future and the farthest be the motive of your today: in your friend you shall love the Übermensch as your motive.

My brothers, I do not recommend to you love of the neighbor: I recommend to you love of the farthest.

Thus spoke Zarathustra.

On the Way of the Creator

Do you want, my brother, to go into solitude? Would you seek the way to yourself? Pause just a moment and listen to me.

"He who seeks may easily get lost himself. All solitude is guilt": thus speaks the herd. And you have long belonged to the herd.

The voice of the herd will still echo in you. And when you say, "I no longer have a common conscience with you," then it will be a lament and an agony.

For see, that agony itself was born of *one and the same* conscience: and the last glimmer of that conscience still glows on your affliction.

But you want to go the way of your affliction, which is the way to yourself? Then show me your right and your strength to do so!

Are you a new strength and a new right? A first motion? A self-propelling wheel? Can you also compel stars to revolve around you?

Ah, there is so much lusting for the heights! There is so much convulsion of the ambitious! Show me that you are not one of the lustful and the ambitious!

Ah, there are so many great thoughts that do no more than a bellows: they puff up and make emptier.

You call yourself free? I want to hear your ruling thought, and not that you have escaped from a yoke.

Are you one of those *entitled* to escape from a yoke? There are many who cast away their final worth when they cast away their servitude.

Free from what? What does that matter to Zarathustra! But your eye should clearly show me: free *for what*?

Can you give to yourself your evil and your good and hang up your will above yourself as a law? Can you be judge for yourself and avenger of your law?

It is terrible to be alone with the judge and avenger of one's own law. Thus is a star thrown forth into the void and into the icy breath of solitude.

Today you still suffer from the multitude, you individual: today you still have all your courage and your hopes.

But one day the solitude will weary you, one day your pride will yield and your courage quail. You will one day cry: "I am alone!"

One day you will no longer see your loftiness and will see your lowliness all-too-near; your sublimity itself will frighten you as a ghost. You will one day cry: "All is false!"

There are feelings that want to kill the lonesome one; if they do not succeed, well, they themselves must die! But are you capable of being a murderer?

Have you ever known, my brother, the word "contempt"? And the anguish of your justice in being just to those who despise you?

You force many to think differently about you; they charge that heavily to your account. You came near them and yet went past: that they will never forgive you.

You go above and beyond them: but the higher you rise, the smaller you appear to the eye of envy. But the one who flies is hated most of all.

"How could you be just to me!"—you must say—"I choose your injustice as my due portion."

They throw injustice and filth at the lonely one: but my brother, if you would be a star, you must shine no less for them on that account!

And beware the good and just! They would like to crucify those who devise their own virtue—they hate the lonely one.

Beware also of holy simplicity! All that is not simple is unholy to it; it likes to play with fire too—and the stake.

And beware also the assaults of your love! The lonely one offers his hand too quickly to any one he meets.

To many men you may not give your hand, but only the paw; and I want your paw to have claws too.

But the worst enemy you can meet will always be you yourself; you lie in wait for yourself in caverns and forests.

Lonely one, you are going the way to yourself! And your way goes past yourself, and past your seven devils!

You will be a heretic to yourself and witch and soothsayer and fool and doubter and unholy one and villain.

You must be ready to burn yourself in your own flame: how could you become new, if you had not first become ashes!

Lonely one, you are going the way of the creator: you would create a god for yourself out of your seven devils!

Lonely one, you are going the way of the lover: you love yourself, and therefore you despise yourself as only lovers despise.

The lover wants to create, because he despises! What does he knows of love who has not had to despise precisely what he loved!

With your love go into your loneliness and with your creation, my brother; and only much later will justice limp after you.

With my tears go into your loneliness, my brother. I love him who seeks to create over and beyond himself and thus perishes.—

Thus spoke Zarathustra.

On Little Old and Young Women[11]

"Why do you steal along so furtively in the twilight, Zarathustra? And what do you hide so carefully under your cloak?

"Is it a treasure you have been given? Or a child born to you? Or do you yourself now follow the ways of thieves, you friend of the evil?"—

"Truly, my brother," said Zarathustra, "it is a treasure that has been given me: it is a little truth that I carry.

"But it is naughty like a young child: and if I do not hold its mouth, it screams too loudly.

"As I went on my way alone today, at the hour when the sun goes down, there I met a little old woman who spoke thus to my soul:[12]

"Much has Zarathustra spoken also to us women, but he never spoke to us concerning woman."

And I answered her: "About woman one should speak only to men."

"Speak to me also of woman," she said: "I am old enough to forget it immediately."

And I obliged the old woman and spoke thus to her:

Everything about woman is a riddle, and everything about woman has one solution: it is called pregnancy.

For woman man is a means: the end is always the child. But what is woman for man?

The true man wants two things: danger and play. Therefore he wants woman, as the most dangerous plaything.

Man should be trained for war and woman for the recreation of the warrior: all else is folly.

All-too-sweet fruit—the warrior does not like it. Therefore he likes woman; even the sweetest woman is also bitter.

Woman understands children better than man does, but man is more childlike than woman.

In the true man a child is hidden: it wants to play. Come, you women, and discover the child in man!

Let woman be a plaything, pure and fine, like a precious stone, illumined with the virtues of a world not yet come.

Let the beam of a star shine through your love! Let your hope say: "May I bear the Übermensch!"

In your love let there be courage! With your love you should go forth to him who inspires you with fear!

Let there be honor in your love! Little does woman understand of honor otherwise. But let this be your honor: always to love more than you are loved, and never to be second.

Let man fear woman when she loves: then she makes every sacrifice, and everything else she considers worthless.

Let man fear woman when she hates: for man in his innermost soul is merely evil, but woman is bad.

Whom does woman hate most?—Thus spoke the iron to the magnet: "I hate you most because you attract, but are not strong enough to pull me to you."

The happiness of man is: I will. The happiness of woman is: he wills.

"Behold, just now the world has become perfect!"—thus thinks every woman when she obeys with all her love.

And woman must obey, and find a depth for her surface. Woman's nature is surface, a mobile stormy film over shallow water.

But a man's nature is deep, his current roars in subterranean caverns: woman senses its strength, but does not comprehend it.—

Then the little old woman answered me: "Zarathustra has said many fine things, especially for those who are young enough for them.

"It's strange, Zarathustra knows little about woman, and yet he is right about them! Is this because with women nothing is impossible?

"And now accept as thanks a little truth! I am surely old enough for it!

"Swaddle it up and hold its mouth: otherwise it will scream too loudly, this little truth."

"Give me, woman, your little truth!" I said. And thus spoke the little old woman:

"You go to women? Do not forget the whip!"—

Thus spoke Zarathustra.

On the Adder's Bite

ONE DAY ZARATHUSTRA HAD fallen asleep under a fig tree, for it was hot, with his arms over his face. And an adder came and bit him on the neck, so that Zarathustra cried out in pain. When he had taken his arm from his face he looked at the snake: and it recognized the eyes of Zarathustra, wriggled awkwardly and wanted to get away. "Oh no," said Zarathustra, "you have not yet received my thanks! You awoke me in time, my way is still long." "Your way is short," the adder said sadly; "my poison is fatal." Zarathustra smiled. "When did a dragon ever die from a snake's poison?"—he said. "But take back your poison! You are not rich enough to give it to me." Then the adder fell upon his neck again and licked his wound.

When Zarathustra once told this to his disciples, they asked: "And what, O Zarathustra, is the moral of your story?" Then Zarathustra answered thus:

The destroyer of morals, the good and just call me: my story is immoral.

But if you have an enemy, do not requite him good for evil: for that would shame him. But prove that he has done something good to you.

And rather be angry than make ashamed! And when you are cursed, I do not like it that you want to bless. Rather join a little in the cursing!

And should a great injustice be done to you, then quickly add five little ones. He who bears injustice alone is hideous to behold.

Did you already know this? A wrong shared is half right. And he who can bear it should take the wrong upon himself!

A little revenge is more human than no revenge at all. And if the punishment is not also a right and an honor for the transgressor, I do not like your punishing.

It is nobler to declare oneself wrong than to maintain one is right, especially if one is right. Only one must be rich enough for that.

I do not like your cold justice; and out of the eye of your judges there always gazes the executioner and his cold steel.

Tell me, where can one find that justice which is love with open eyes?

Then invent for me the love that bears not only all punishment but also all guilt!

Then invent for me the justice that acquits every one except the judge!

Do you still want to hear this too? To him who wants to be just through and through, even a lie becomes philanthropy.

But how could I be just through and through! How can I give each his own! Let this be enough for me: I give each my own.

Finally, my brothers, beware of doing wrong to any hermit. How could a hermit forget! How could he requite!

A hermit is like a deep well. It is easy to throw in a stone; but if it should sink to the bottom, tell me, who will bring it out again?

Beware of insulting the hermit! But if you have done so, well then, kill him too!

Thus spoke Zarathustra.

On Child and Marriage

I HAVE A QUESTION for you alone, my brother: like a sounding lead I cast this question into your soul, to discover how deep it is.

You are young and wish for children and marriage. But I ask you: are you a man *entitled* to wish for a child?

Are you the victor, the self-conqueror, the ruler of your senses, the master of your virtues? Thus I ask you.

Or is it the animal and need that speak in your wish? Or loneliness? Or discord in you?

I would have your victory and your freedom long for a child. You shall build living monuments to your victory and your liberation.

You shall build over and beyond yourself. But first you must be built yourself, perpendicular in body and soul.

Not only forward shall you propagate yourself, but upward! May the garden of marriage help you to do it!

You shall create a higher body, a first movement, a self-propelled wheel—you will create a creator.

Marriage: thus I name the will of two to create the one that is more than those who created it. Reverence for one another, as those willing with such a will, is what I name marriage.

Let this be the meaning and the truth of your marriage. But that which the all-too-many call marriage, those superfluous ones—ah, what shall I call it?

Ah, the poverty of soul in partnership! Ah, the filth of soul in partnership! Ah, the pitiable contentment in partnership!

Marriage they call this; and they say their marriages are made in heaven.

Well, I do not like it, that heaven of the superfluous! No, I do not like them, those animals tangled in the heavenly net!

And let the god who limps near to bless what he has not joined stay far from me!

Do not laugh at such marriages! What child has not had reason to weep over its parents?

This man seemed worthy to me and ripe for the meaning of the earth: but when I saw his wife, the earth seemed to me a house for the senseless.

Yes, I wished that the earth would shake with convulsions when a saint and a goose mate with one another.

This one went forth in quest of truth like a hero, and at last he captured for himself a little dressed-up lie. He calls it his marriage.

That one was reserved in his dealings and chose choicely. But all at once he spoiled his company forever: he calls it his marriage.

That one sought a maid with the virtues of an angel. But suddenly he became the maid of a woman, and now he needs to become an angel too.

I have found all buyers to be cautious now, and all of them have cunning eyes. But even the most cunning among them buys his wife while she is still wrapped.

Many brief follies—that is what you call love. And your marriage puts an end to many brief follies, with *a single* long stupidity.

Your love of woman and woman's love of man: ah, if only it were sympathy for suffering and veiled gods! But generally two animals sense one another.

But even your best love is only a passionate impersonation and a painful ardor. It is a torch that should light you to loftier paths.

One day you shall love beyond yourselves! So *learn* first to love. And for that you had to drain the bitter cup of your love.

Bitterness lies in the cup of even the best love: thus it arouses longing for the Übermensch, thus it arouses thirst in you, the creator!

A creator's thirst, arrow and longing for the Übermensch: tell me, my brother, is this your will to marriage?

Holy I call such a will and such a marriage.

Thus spoke Zarathustra.

On Voluntary Death

MANY DIE TOO LATE, and a few die too early. Still the teaching sounds strange: "Die at the right time!"

Die at the right time: thus teaches Zarathustra.

To be sure, how could those who never live at the right time die at the right time? Better if they had never been born!—Thus I advise the superfluous.

But even the superfluous still make a great thing of their dying, and even the hollowest nut still wants to be cracked.

Every one regards death as an important matter: but as yet death is not a festival. As yet men have not learned how to consecrate the most beautiful festivals.

I show you the consummating death, which shall be a spur and a promise to the survivors.

He that consummates his life dies his death triumphantly, surrounded by those with hope and promise.

Thus one should learn to die; and there should be no festivals where such a dying one does not consecrate the oaths of the living!

To die thus is best; but the next best is: to die in battle and to squander a great soul.

But equally hateful to the fighter as to the victor is your grinning death, which steals near like a thief—and yet comes as master.

My death, praise I to you, the voluntary death, which comes to me because *I* want it.

And when shall I want it?—Whoever has a goal and an heir, wants death at the right time for the goal and the heir.

And out of reverence for the goal and the heir, he will hang up no more withered wreaths in the sanctuary of life.

Truly, I do not want to resemble the rope makers: they spin out their yarn and always walk backwards.

Many a one grows too old even for his truths and triumphs; a toothless mouth no longer has the right to every truth.

And everyone who wants to have fame must take leave of honor in good time and practice the difficult art of—going at the right time.

One must stop letting oneself be eaten when one tastes best: that is known by those who want to be long loved.

To be sure, there are sour apples whose lot is to wait until the last day of autumn: and they become ripe, yellow, and shriveled all at once.

In some the heart ages first and in others the spirit. And some are old in their youth: but those who are young late stay young long.

To many men life is a failure: a poison-worm gnaws at their heart. Then let them see to it that their dying is all the more a success.

Many never become sweet; they rot even in the summer. It is cowardice that holds them fast to their branches.

All-too-many live and all-too-long they hang on their branches. Would that a storm came and shook all this rottenness and worm-eatenness from the tree!

Would that there came preachers of *speedy* death! Those would be the appropriate storms and shakers of the trees of life! But I hear only slow death preached, and patience with all that is "earthly."

Ah, you preach patience with what is earthly? It is the earthly that has too much patience with you, you blasphemers!

Truly, too early died that Hebrew whom the preachers of slow death honor: and to many it has proved a calamity that he died too early.

As yet he had known only tears and the melancholy of the Hebrews, together with the hatred of the good and just—the Hebrew Jesus: then he was seized with the longing for death.

Had he but remained in the wilderness and far from the good and just! Perhaps he would have learned to live and to love the earth—and laughter too!

Believe it, my brothers! He died too early; he himself would have recanted his teaching had he lived to my age! He was noble enough to recant!

But he was still immature. The youth loves immaturely and immaturely too he hates man and earth. His mind and the wings of his spirit are still bound and heavy.

But there is more child in the man than in the youth, and less melancholy: he has a better understanding of life and death.

Free for death and free in death, able to say a holy No when there is no longer time for Yes: thus he understands death and life.

That your dying may not be a blasphemy against man and earth, my friends: that is what I beg from the honey of your soul.

In your dying your spirit and your virtue should still glow like a sunset around the earth: otherwise your dying has turned out badly.

Thus I want to die myself, that you friends may love the earth more for my sake; and I want to become earth again, to have rest in her that bore me.

Truly, Zarathustra had a goal, he threw his ball: now you friends are the heirs of my goal, I throw the golden ball to you.

Best of all I like to see you too, my friends, throwing the golden ball! And so I still linger a little on the earth: forgive me for it!

Thus spoke Zarathustra.

On the Gift-Giving Virtue

1

When Zarathustra had taken leave of the town to which his heart was attached and which was called "The Motley Cow," many who called themselves his disciples followed him and escorted him. Thus they came to a crossroad: there Zarathustra told them that now he wanted to walk alone: for he liked to walk alone. But his disciples handed him in farewell a staff, with a golden handle on which a serpent twined round the sun. Zarathustra was delighted with the staff and leaned upon it; then he spoke thus to his disciples:

Tell me: how did gold come to have the highest value? Because it is uncommon and useless and shining and soft in luster; it always gives itself.

Only as an image of the highest virtue did gold come to have the highest value. Goldlike beams the eye of the giver. Golden luster makes peace between moon and sun.

The highest virtue is uncommon and useless, it is shining and soft in luster: a gift-giving virtue is the highest virtue.

Truly, I divine you well, my disciples, you strive like me for the gift-giving virtue. What could you have in common with cats and wolves?

You thirst to become sacrifices and gifts yourselves: and therefore you thirst to heap up all riches in your soul.

Your should strives insatiably for treasures and jewels, because your virtue is insatiable in wanting to give.

You compel all things to come to you and into you, that they may flow back again from your fountain as the gifts of your love.

Truly, such a gift-giving love must approach all values as a robber; but I call this selfishness healthy and holy.—

There is another selfishness, an all-too-poor and hungry kind that always wants to steal—the selfishness of the sick, the sick selfishness.

It looks with the eye of the thief upon all that is lustrous; with the greed of hunger it measures him who has plenty to eat; and it is always skulking around the tables of those who give.

Sickness speaks from such craving, and invisible degeneration; the thieving greed of this longing speaks of a sick body.

Tell me, my brothers: what do we consider bad and worst of all? Is it not *degeneration*?—And we always suspect degeneration where the gift-giving soul is lacking.

Our way goes upward from genus to super-genus. But the degenerate sense that says "Everything for me" is a horror to us.

Upward flies our sense: thus is it a parable of our body, a parable of elevation. Such parables of elevations are the names of the virtues.

Thus the body goes through history, becoming and fighting. And the spirit—what is it to the body? The herald, companion and echo of its battles and its victories.

All names of good and evil are parables;[13] they do not speak out, they only hint. He who seeks knowledge of them is a fool.

Watch for every hour, my brothers, in which your spirit[14] wants to speak in parables: there is the origin of your virtue.

Then your body is elevated and risen up; it enraptures the spirit with delight, so that it becomes creator and valuer and lover and benefactor of all things.

When your heart surges broad and full like a river, a blessing and a danger to those living near: there is the origin of your virtue.

When you are exalted above praise and blame, and your will wants to command all things as the will of a lover: there is the origin of your virtue.

When you despise the soft bed and what is pleasant and cannot bed yourself far enough from the soft: there is the origin of your virtue.

When you will with *one* will, and you call this cessation of all need necessity: there is the origin of your virtue.

Truly, she is a new good and evil! Truly, a new deep murmur and the voice of a new well!

She is power, this new virtue; she is a ruling thought, and around her a subtle soul: a golden sun, and around it the serpent of knowledge.

2

Here Zarathustra fell silent for a while and regarded his disciples lovingly. Then he continued to speak thus—and his voice had changed:

Stay true to the earth, my brothers, with the power of your virtue! Let your gift-giving love and your knowledge serve the meaning of the earth! Thus I beg and beseech you.

Do not let them fly away from earthly things and beat with their wings against eternal walls! Ah, there has always been so much virtue that has flown away!

Lead, like me, the flown virtue back to the earth—yes, back to body and life: that it may give the earth its meaning, a human meaning!

A hundred times so far has spirit as well as virtue flown away and blundered. Ah, all this delusion and blundering still dwells in our bodies: it has there become body and will.

A hundred times so far has spirit as well as virtue attempted and erred. Yes, man was an experiment. Ah, much ignorance and error has become body in us!

Not only the reason of millennia—also their madness breaks out in us. It is dangerous to be an heir.

We are still fighting step by step with the giant Chance, and over the whole of humanity there has ruled so far only nonsense, the senseless.

Let your spirit and your virtue serve the sense of the earth, my brothers: let the value of everything be determined again by you! For that shall you be fighters! For that shall you be creators!

The body purifies itself with knowledge; experimenting with knowledge it elevates itself; to the discerning all instincts become holy; in the elevated the soul becomes gay.

Physician, heal yourself: thus you will heal your patient too. Let his best cure be to see with his own eyes the man who heals himself.

There are a thousand paths that have never yet been trodden, a thousand healths and hidden islands of life. Man and man's earth are still unexhausted and undiscovered.

Awake and listen, you lonely ones! From the future come winds with stealthy wing-beats; and good tidings are proclaimed to delicate ears.

You lonely ones of today, you that are drawing away, you shall one day be a people: out of you who have chosen yourselves, shall a chosen people arise—and out of them the Übermensch.

Truly, the earth shall yet become a place of healing! And even now a new fragrance surrounds it, bringing salvation—and a new hope!

3

When Zarathustra had spoken these words he paused like one who had not said his last word; he weighed the staff doubtfully in his hand for a long while. At last he spoke thus:—and his voice had changed.

Now I go alone, my disciples! You too now go away and alone! So I will it.

Truly, I advise you: go away from me and guard yourselves against Zarathustra! And better still: be ashamed of him! Perhaps he has deceived you.

The man of knowledge must not only love his enemies, he must also be able to hate his friends.

One repays a teacher badly if one remains always only a student. And why do you not want to pluck at my wreath?

You revere me; but what if your reverence tumbles one day? Beware that a statue does not slay you!

You say you believe in Zarathustra? But what matters Zarathustra? You are my believers: but what matter all believers!

You had not yet sought yourselves: then you found me. Thus do all believers; therefore all belief comes to so little.[15]

Now I bid you lose me and find yourselves; and only when you have all denied me will I return to you.

Truly, with other eyes, my brothers, shall I then seek my lost ones; with another love shall I then love you.

And once again you shall have become friends to me and children of *one* hope: then I will be with you the third time, that I may celebrate the great noon with you.

And this is the great noon, when man stands in the middle of his road between animal and Übermensch and celebrates his way to the evening as his highest hope: for it is the way to a new morning.

Then he who goes under will bless himself, for being one who goes over and beyond; and the sun of his knowledge will stand at noon for him.

"Dead are all gods: now we want the Übermensch to live."—at the great noon let this be our last will !—

Thus spoke Zarathustra.

SECOND PART

—and only when you have all denied me will I return to you.
   Truly, with other eyes, my brothers, shall I then seek my lost ones;
with another love shall I then love you.

—*Zarathustra, "On the Gift-Giving Virtue"*

[1883]

The Child with the Mirror

After this Zarathustra returned again into the mountains to the solitude of his cave and withdrew himself from men: waiting like a sower who has scattered his seed. His soul, however, became impatient and full of longing for those whom he loved: because he still had much to give them. For this is hardest of all: to close the open hand out of love and to keep a sense of shame as a giver.

Thus months and years passed for the solitary; but his wisdom increased and caused him pain by its abundance.

One morning, however, he awoke before dawn, reflected long on his bed, and at last spoke to his heart:

"Why was I so startled in my dream that I awoke? Did not a child step up to me, carrying a mirror?

" 'O Zarathustra'—the child said to me—'look at yourself in the mirror!'

"But when I looked into the mirror, I shrieked, and my heart was shaken: for it was not myself I saw, but a devil's grimace and sneering laughter.

"Truly, I understand the dream's sign and admonition all-too-well: my *teaching* is in danger, weeds want to be called wheat!

"My enemies have grown powerful and have distorted the meaning of my teaching, so that my dearest ones are ashamed of the gifts I gave them.

"I have lost my friends; the hour has come to seek my lost ones!"—

With these words Zarathustra sprang up, but not like a frightened man seeking the air, rather like a seer and a singer whom the spirit has moved. His eagle and serpent regarded him with amazement: for a coming happiness lit up his face like the dawn.

What has happened to me, my animals?—said Zarathustra. Have I not changed? Has not bliss come to me like a storm wind?

My happiness is foolish and will say foolish things: it is still too young—so have patience with it!

I am wounded by my happiness: all sufferers shall be physicians to me!

I may go down again to my friends and also to my enemies! Zarathustra may again speak and give and show love to the beloved!

My impatient love overflows in torrents, downward, toward sunrise and sunset. Out of silent mountains and storms of pain my soul rushes into the valleys.

I have longed and looked into the distance too long. I have belonged to solitude too long: thus I have forgotten how to be silent.

I have become mouth through and through, and the brawling of a brook from high rocks: I want to hurl my speech down into the valleys.

And let the stream of my love plunge into impassable ways! How should a stream not finally find its way to the sea!

Indeed a lake is in me, secluded and self-sufficient; but the stream of my love draws it down with it—to the sea!

I go new ways, a new speech comes to me; I grow tired, like all creators, of the old tongues. My spirit no longer wants to walk on worn out soles.

All speech runs too slowly for me—I leap into your chariot, storm! And I will whip even you with my malice!

Like a cry and a yawp I want to traverse wide seas, till I find the happy islands where my friends are dwelling:—

And my enemies among them! How I now love any one to whom I may but speak! My enemies too are part of my bliss.

And when I want to mount my wildest horse, it is always my spear that helps me up best: it is the ever-ready servant of my foot:—

The spear that I hurl at my enemies! How grateful I am to my enemies that at last I can hurl it!

The tension of my cloud was too great: between laughters of lightning I want to cast hail showers into the depths.

Violently then my chest will heave, violently it will blow its storm over the mountains: thus comes its relief.

Truly, my happiness and my freedom come like a storm! But my enemies shall think that *the evil one* rages over their heads.

Yes, you too will be terrified, my friends, by my wild wisdom; and perhaps you will flee from it along with my enemies.

Ah, that I knew how to lure you back with shepherds' flutes! Ah, that my lioness wisdom would learn to roar tenderly! And we have already learned so much with one another!

My wild wisdom became pregnant on lonely mountains; on the rough stones she bore her young, the youngest.

Now she runs foolishly through the harsh desert and seeks and seeks the soft grass—my old wild wisdom!

On the soft grass of your hearts, my friends!—upon your love she would bed her most dearly beloved!—

Thus spoke Zarathustra.

On the Happy Islands[1]

THE FIGS ARE FALLING from the trees, they are good and sweet; and as they fall their red skins burst. I am a north wind to ripe figs.

Thus, like figs, do these teachings fall for you, my friends: now drink their juice and eat their sweet flesh! It is autumn all around and clear sky and afternoon.

Behold, what fullness is around us! And from such overflow it is delightful to look out upon distant seas.

Once one said God when one looked upon distant seas; but now I have taught you to say: Übermensch.

God is a conjecture: but I want your conjecturing not to reach beyond your creative will.

Could you *create* a god?—So be silent about all gods! But you could well create the Übermensch.

Perhaps not you yourselves, my brothers! But you could transform yourselves into fathers and forefathers of the Übermensch: and let that be your best creation!—

God is a conjecture: but I should like your conjecturing to be bounded by the thinkable.

Could you *conceive* a god?—But may the will to truth mean this to you: that everything be changed into what is conceivable for man, visible for man, touchable by man! You should think through your own senses to the end!

And what you have called the world shall be created only by you: your reason, your image, your will, your love shall thus become the world! And truly, for your bliss, you knowers!

And how would you endure life without that hope, you knowers? Neither in the inconceivable could you have been born, nor in the irrational.

But let me reveal my heart to you entirely, my friends: *if* there were gods, how could I bear not to be a god! *Therefore* there are no gods.

Indeed I have drawn the conclusion; however, now it draws me.—

God is a conjecture: but who could drink all the agony of this conjecture without dying? Shall his faith be taken from the creator and from the eagle his soaring to eagle heights?

God is a thought that makes crooked all that is straight, and makes all that stands reel. How? Should time be gone, and all that is impermanent be only a lie?

To think this is giddiness and vertigo for human bones, and even vomiting to the stomach: truly, I call it the reeling sickness to conjecture such.

I call it evil and misanthropic: all that teaching about the One and the Plenum and the Unmoved and the Sufficient and the Permanent!

All the Permanent—that is only a parable! And the poets lie too much.—

But the best parables should speak of time and of becoming: let them be a praise and a justification of all impermanence!

Creation—that is the great redemption from suffering, and life's becoming light. But that the creator may be, much suffering itself is needed and much change.

Yes, there must be much bitter dying in your life, you creators! Thus you are advocates and justifiers of all impermanence.

For the creator himself to be the newborn child, he must also be willing to bear the child and to endure the pains of childbirth.

Truly, through a hundred souls I went my way, and through a hundred cradles and birth pains. I have said many a farewell; I know the heartbreaking last hours.

But so wills my creative will, my fate. Or, to speak to you more honestly: just such a fate—wills my will.

All feeling suffers in me and is in prison: but my will always comes to me as my liberator and comforter.

Willing liberates: that is the true teaching of will and freedom— thus Zarathustra teaches it to you.

No longer willing and no longer valuing and no longer creating! ah, that this great weariness may always stay far from me!

In knowledge too I feel only my will's joy in procreating and becoming; and if there is innocence in my knowledge, it is because the will to procreation is in it.

Away from God and gods this will has lured me; what would there be to create, if gods—existed!

But it always drives me again toward man, my fervent creative will; just as the hammer is driven to the stone.

Ah, you men, in the stone there sleeps an image, the image of my images! Ah, that it must sleep in the hardest, ugliest stone!

Now my hammer rages cruelly against its prison. Fragments fall from the stone: what is that to me?

I want to perfect it: for a shadow came to me—the stillest and lightest of all things once came to me!

The beauty of the Übermensch came to me as a shadow. Ah, my brothers! What are the gods to me now!—

Thus spoke Zarathustra.

On the Pitying

My friends, a gibe was told to your friend: "Just look at Zarathustra! Doesn't he walk among us as if among animals?"

But it is better said so: "The knower walks among men *as* among animals."[2]

To the knower man himself is: the animal that has red cheeks.

How has that happened to him? Is it not because he has had to be ashamed too often?

O my friends! Thus speaks the knower: shame, shame, shame— that is the history of mankind!

And that is why the noble bids himself not to shame: he is ashamed himself before all sufferers.

Truly, I do not like them, the merciful who feel blessed in their pity: they are much too lacking in shame.[3]

If I must pity, at least I do not want it named so; and if I do, it is preferably from a distance.

I should also like to shroud my head and flee before I am recognized: and thus I enjoin you to do, my friends!

May my fate always lead those, like you, who do not suffer to cross my path, and those with whom I *may* share hope and meal and honey!

Truly, I may have done this and that for sufferers: but I always seem to have done better when I learned to feel better joys.

Since there have been men, man has enjoyed himself too little: that alone, my brothers, is our original sin!

And learning better to feel joy, we unlearn best how to hurt to others or to plan hurts for them.

Therefore I wash my hand when it has helped the sufferer, therefore I also wipe even my soul.

For in seeing the sufferer suffer, I was ashamed on account of his shame; and in helping him, I sorely wound his pride.

Great indebtedness does not make men grateful, but vengeful; and if a small kindness is not forgotten, it becomes a gnawing worm.

"Be reserved in accepting! Distinguish by accepting!"—thus I advise those who have nothing to give.

But I am a gift-giver: I like to give, as friend to friends. But strangers and the poor may pluck for themselves the fruit from my tree: that causes less shame.

But beggars should be entirely done away with! Truly, it annoys one to give to them and it annoys one not to give to them.

And likewise sinners and bad consciences! Believe me, my friends: the bite of conscience teaches one to bite.

The very worst, however, are petty thoughts. Truly, better to have done evilly than to have thought pettily!

To be sure, you say: "The delight in petty evils saves us from many a big evil deed." But here one should not wish to save.

An evil deed is like a boil: it itches and irritates and breaks open—it speaks honestly.

"Look, I am disease,"—so speaks the evil deed: that is its honesty.

But the petty thought is like an infection: it creeps and hides and wants to be nowhere—until the whole body is decayed and withered by petty infections.

But to him who is possessed by the devil I whisper this word in his ear: "Better for you to rear up your devil! Even for you there is still a path to greatness!"—

Ah, my brothers! One knows a little too much about every one! And some become transparent to us, but yet we can by no means pass through them.

It is difficult to live among men, because it is so difficult to be silent.

And we are most unfair not to him who is offensive to us, but to him who does not concern us at all.

But if you have a suffering friend, be a resting place for his suffering, but like a hard bed, a field cot: thus you will serve him best.

And if a friend does you wrong, then say: "I forgive you what you have done to me; that you have done it to *yourself*, however—how could I forgive that!"

Thus speaks all great love: it surpasses even forgiveness and pity.

One should hold fast one's heart; for when one lets it go, how soon one's head runs away!

Ah, where in the world has there been greater folly than among the pitying? And what in the world has caused more suffering than the folly of the pitying?

Woe to all lovers who do not have a height that is above their pity!

Thus spoke the devil to me once: "God too has his hell: it is his love of man."

And most recently I heard him speak this word: "God is dead: God died of his pity for man."—

So be warned against pity: *from there* a heavy cloud yet comes to man! Truly, I understand weather signs!

But also mark this word: all great love is even above all its pity: for it still seeks—to create the beloved!

"I sacrifice myself to my love, *and my neighbor as myself*"—so goes the language of all creators.

But all creators are hard.—

Thus spoke Zarathustra.

The Priests

And once Zarathustra gave a sign to his disciples and spoke these words to them:

"Here are priests: and though they are my enemies, pass by them quietly and with sleeping swords!

"Among them too there are heroes; many of them have suffered too much—: so they want to make others suffer.

"They are evil enemies: nothing is more vengeful than their meekness. And whoever attacks them readily soils himself.

"But my blood is related to theirs; and I want to know that my blood is honored even in theirs."—

And when they had passed, pain gripped Zarathustra; and he had not wrestled long with the pain when he began to speak thus:

My heart moves for those priests. They also go against my taste; but that is the smallest matter to me, since I am among men.

But I suffer and have suffered with them: They are prisoners to me and marked ones. He whom they call Savior put them in fetters:—

In fetters of false values and delusive words! Oh, that some one would yet save them from their Savior!

They believed once that they had landed on an island, when the sea tossed them about; but look, it was a sleeping monster!

False values and delusive words: these are the worst monsters for mortals—calamity sleeps and waits long in them.

But at last it comes and wakes and eats and devours and what built huts upon it.

Oh, just look at those huts which these priests have built! Churches they call their sweet-smelling caves!

Oh, that falsified light, this musty air! Here, where the soul is not permitted to soar to its height!

For thus their faith commands: "Up the stairs on your knees, you sinners!"

Truly, I would rather see even the shameless than the contorted eyes of their shame and devotion!

Who created for themselves such caves and stairways of repentance? Was it not those who wanted to conceal themselves and were ashamed under the pure sky?

And only when the pure sky looks again through broken ceilings, and down upon grass and red poppies near ruined walls—will I again turn my heart to the haunts of this God.

They called God that which opposed and afflicted them: and truly, much was heroic in their worship!

And they did not how to love their God other than by nailing man to the cross!

They meant to live as corpses; in black they draped their corpses; out of their speech too I still smell the foul odor of slaughterhouses.

And whoever lives near them lives near black pools, where the toad sings his song with sweet melancholy.

They would have to sing better songs for me to learn to believe in their Savior: and his disciples would have to look more saved!

I would like to see them naked: for only beauty should preach repentance. But who would be persuaded by that muffled misery!

Truly, their saviors themselves did not come from freedom and freedom's seventh heaven! Truly, they themselves have never walked on the carpets of knowledge!

The spirit of those saviors consisted of emptiness; but into every empty gap they put their delusion, their stopgap, which they called God.

Their spirit was drowned in their pity; and when they were swollen and overswollen with pity, it was always a great folly that swam on top.

They drove their herd over their path eagerly and with shouts: as if there were but a *single* path to the future! Truly, these shepherds also belonged among the sheep!

These shepherds had small spirits and spacious souls: but, my brothers, what small lands have even the most spacious souls been so far!

They left marks of blood along the way they went, and their folly taught that with blood the truth is proved.

But blood is the worst witness of truth; blood poisons even the purest teaching and turns it into delusion and hatred of the heart.

And if a man goes through fire for his teaching—what does that prove! It is truly more when one's teaching comes from one's own burning!

A sultry heart and a cold head: where these two meet there arises the roaring wind, the "Savior."

There have been those truly greater and higher born than those whom the people call saviors, those blowhards who carry away!

And by ones still greater than any of the saviors must you, my brothers, be saved, if you would find the way to freedom!

Never yet has there been an Übermensch. I saw both of them naked, the greatest and the smallest man:—

They are still all-too-similar to one another. Truly, even the greatest I found—all-too-human!—

Thus spoke Zarathustra.

On the Virtuous

One must speak to indolent and sleepy senses with thunder and heavenly fireworks.

But beauty's voice speaks gently: it creeps only into the most awakened souls.

My shield gently trembled and laughed today; it was beauty's holy laughter and tremor.

About you, you virtuous, my beauty laughed today. And thus its voice came to me: "They still want—to be paid!"

You still want to be paid, you virtuous! Do you want rewards for virtue and heaven for earth and eternity for your today?

And now are you angry with me for teaching that there is no reward-giver nor paymaster? And truly, I do not even teach that virtue is its own reward.

Ah, this is my sorrow: they have lied reward and punishment into the foundation of things—and now even into the basis of your souls, you virtuous!

But my words shall like the boar's snout tear up the foundation of your souls; you will call me a ploughshare.

All the secrets of your heart shall be brought to light; and when you lie uprooted and broken in the sun, then too your lies will be separated from your truth.

For this is your truth: you are *too pure* for the dirt of the words: revenge, punishment, reward, retribution.

You love your virtue as the mother her child; but when did one hear of a mother wanting to be paid for her love?

It is your dearest self, your virtue. The ring's thirst is in you: every ring strives and turns to reach itself again.

And like a dying star is every work of your virtue: its light is ever on its way and wandering—and when will it cease to be on its way?

Thus the light of your virtue is still on its way, even when its work is done. Though it be forgotten and dead: its ray of light still lives and wanders.

That your virtue is your self, and not something foreign, a skin, a cloak: that is the truth from the foundation of your souls, you virtuous ones!—

But indeed there are those to whom virtue means writhing under the lash: and you have listened too much to their shrieks!

And there are others who call it virtue when their vices grow lazy; and once their hatred and jealousy stretch themselves to rest, their "justice" becomes lively and rubs its sleepy eyes.

And there are others who are drawn downward: their devils draw them. But the more they sink, the more fervently their eye shines and the lust for their God.

Ah, their shrieks have also reached your ears, you virtuous: "What I am *not*, that, that to me are God and virtue!"

And there are others who come along, heavy and creaking like carts bearing stones downhill: they talk much of dignity and virtue—they call their brake virtue!

And there are others who are like everyday clocks wound up; they make their tick-tock and want one to call tick-tock—virtue.

Truly, I have fun with these: wherever I find such clocks I shall wind them up with my mockery; and therefore they shall even ring for me!

And others are proud of their handful of justice and commit wanton outrage upon all things for its sake: so that the world is drowned in their injustice.

Ah, how ill the word "virtue" sounds in their mouths! And when they say: "I am just," it always sounds like: "I am just—revenged!"[4]

They want to scratch out the eyes of their enemies with their virtue; and they ennoble themselves only to debase others.

And again there are those who sit in their swamp, and speak thus from the rushes: "Virtue—that is to sit quietly in the swamp.

"We bite no one, and stay out of the way of those who want to bite; and in all matters we hold the opinion that is given us."

And again, there are those who love posing and think: virtue is a sort of pose.

Their knees always adore, and their hands are eulogies of virtue, but their heart knows nothing about it.

And again there are those who regard it as virtue to say: "Virtue is necessary"; but fundamentally they believe only that the police are necessary.

And some who cannot see the sublime in man call it virtue to see his baseness all-too-closely: thus they calls their evil eye virtue.—

And some want to be edified and raised up and call it virtue: and others want to be cast down—and call it virtue, too.

And thus almost all believe that they participate in virtue; and at the very least every one wants to be an expert on "good" and "evil."

But Zarathustra has not come to say to all these liars and fools: "What do *you* know of virtue! What *could* you know of virtue!"—

Rather, that you, my friends, might grow weary of the old words you have learned from the fools and liars:

That you might grow weary of the words "reward," "retribution," "punishment," "just revenge."—

That you might grow weary of saying: "An action is good when it is unselfish."

Ah, my friends! That *your* self be in your action, as the mother is in the child: let that be *your* word on virtue!

Truly, I have taken a hundred words and your virtue's favorite toys away from you; and now you scold me, as children scold.

They played by the sea—then a wave came and swept their toys into the deep: and now they cry.

But the same wave shall bring them new toys and pour out new colored seashells before them!

Thus they will be comforted; and like them shall you also, my friends, have your comforting—and new colored seashells!—

Thus spoke Zarathustra.

On the Rabble

LIFE IS A WELL of delight;[5] but where the rabble drinks, too, all wells are poisoned.

I like all that is clean; but I dislike seeing the grinning maws and the thirst of the unclean.

They cast their eyes down into the well: now their revolting smile shines up at me out of the well.

They have poisoned the holy water with their lustfulness; and when they called their filthy dreams delight, they poisoned the language too.

The flame is frustrated when they put their damp hearts to the fire; the spirit itself bubbles and smokes when the rabble approaches the fire.

In their hands all fruit grows syrupy and over-ripe: their glance makes the fruit tree unsteady and withered at the crown.

And many a one who turned away from life, turned away only from the rabble: he did not want to share well and flame and fruit with the rabble.

And many a one who went into the wilderness and suffered thirst with the beasts of prey merely did not want to sit around the cistern with filthy camel drivers.

And many a one who came along as a destroyer and as a hailstorm to all orchards, merely wanted to put his foot into the jaws of the rabble and so to stop its throat.

And the bite on which I gagged the most was not knowing that life itself requires hostility and death and torture-crosses:—

But once I asked and almost suffocated on my question: What? Does life have *need* of the rabble too?

Are poisoned wells necessary, and stinking fires and soiled dreams and maggots in the bread of life?

Not my hatred but my nausea gnawed hungrily at my life! Ah, I often grew weary of spirit when I found even the rabble rich in spirit!

And I turned my back on the rulers when I saw what they now call ruling: bargaining and haggling for power—with the rabble!

I dwelt with closed ears among people with strange tongues: so that the language of their bargaining and their haggling for power might remain strange to me.

And holding my nose, I walked displeased through all of yesterday and today: truly all of yesterday and today smells foully of the writing rabble!

Like a cripple who has gone deaf and blind and dumb—thus have I long lived, that I might not live with the power- and writing- and pleasure-rabble.

Wearily my spirit climbed steps, and cautiously; alms of delight were its refreshment; and life crept along like the blind on a cane.

Yet what happened to me? How did I save myself from nausea? Who rejuvenated my eyes? How did I fly to the height where the rabble no more sits at the well?

Did my nausea itself create wings for me and water-divining powers? Truly, I had to fly to the loftiest height to find the well of delight again!

Oh, I have found it, my brothers! Here on the loftiest height the well of delight gushes up for me! And here there is a life at which no rabble drinks!

You stream almost too violently, fountain of delight! And often you empty the cup again, by wanting to fill it!

And I must yet learn to approach you more modestly: all-too-violently my heart still streams towards you:—

My heart on which my summer burns, short, hot, melancholy, overjoyful: how my summer heart longs for your coolness!

Gone is the lingering distress of my spring! Gone the malice of my snowflakes in June! Summer have I become entirely, and summer noon!

A summer on the loftiest height with cold wells and blissful stillness: oh come, my friends, that the stillness may become yet more blissful!

For this is *our* height and our home: we live here too high and steep for all the unclean and their thirst.

Only cast your pure eyes into the well of my delight, friends! How should that make it muddy! It shall laugh back at you with *its* purity.

We build our nest on the tree Future; in our solitude eagles shall bring us food in their beaks!

Truly, food which the unclean could not share! They would think they were eating fire and burn their mouths!

Truly, we keep no homes here for the unclean! Their bodies and their spirits would call our happiness an ice cave!

And we want to live above them as strong winds, neighbors to the eagles, neighbors to the snow, neighbors to the sun: thus live strong winds.

And like a wind I will one day blow among them and with my spirit take the breath from their spirit: thus my future wills it.

Truly, Zarathustra is a strong wind to all the low; and he offers this advice to his enemies and all that spits and spews: "Take care not to spit *against* the wind!"—

Thus spoke Zarathustra.

ON THE TARANTULAS

SEE, THIS IS THE tarantula's hole![6] Do you want to see the tarantula itself? Here hangs its web: touch it, so that it trembles.

There it comes willingly: welcome, tarantula! Your triangle and symbol sit black upon your back; and I also know what sits in your soul.

Revenge sits in your soul: wherever you bite, a black scab grows; your poison makes the soul giddy with revenge!

Thus I speak to you in a parable, you who make the soul giddy, you preachers of *equality*! To me you are tarantulas and the secretly vengeful!

But soon I will bring your hiding places to light: therefore I laugh in your faces my laughter of the heights.

Therefore I tear at your web, that your rage may lure you from your hole of lies, and your revenge may leap forth from behind your word "justice."

For *that man be redeemed from revenge*: for me that is the bridge to the highest hope, and a rainbow after long storms.

But of course the tarantulas would have it otherwise. "That the world may become full of the storms of our revenge, let precisely that be called justice by us"—thus they talk to one another.

"We shall wreak vengeance and insult on all who are not as we are"—thus the tarantula-hearts promise themselves.

"And 'will to equality'—that itself shall henceforth be the name of virtue; and against everything that has power we will raise our outcry!"

You preachers of equality, the tyrant-madness of impotence cries thus in you for "equality": thus your most secret tyrant appetite disguises itself in words of virtue!

Soured conceit, repressed envy, perhaps your fathers' conceit and envy: they erupt from you as flame and frenzy of revenge.

What was silent in the father speaks out in the son; and I often found the son to be the father's secret revealed.

They resemble the inspired: yet it is not the heart that inspires them—but revenge. And when they become refined and cold, it is not spirit, but envy, that makes them refined and cold.

Their jealousy leads them also upon thinkers' paths; and this is the sign of their jealousy—they always go too far: so that their weariness has at last to lie down and sleep even on the snow.

Revenge sounds out of all their complaints, a malevolence is in all their praise; and to be judge seems bliss to them.

But thus I counsel you, my friends: mistrust all in whom the impulse to punish is powerful!

They are people of a bad race and lineage; out of their faces peer the hangman and the bloodhound.

Mistrust all those who talk much of their justice! Truly, it is not only honey that their souls lack.

And when they call themselves "the good and just," do not forget, that nothing is lacking to make them Pharisees except—power!

My friends, I do not want to be mixed up and confused with others.

There are those who preach my doctrine of life: and are at the same time preachers of equality and tarantulas.

That they speak well of life, though they sit in their hole, these poisonous spiders, with their backs turned on life: this is because they want to do harm.

They want to harm those who now have power: for with those the preaching of death is still most at home.

Were it otherwise, then the tarantulas would teach otherwise: and they themselves were formerly the best slanderers of the world and burners of heretics.

I do not want to be mixed up and confused with these preachers of equality. For justice speaks thus *to me*: "Men are not equal."[7]

And neither should they become so! What would my love of the Übermensch be, if I spoke otherwise?

They should press on to the future on a thousand bridges and paths, and there should be more and more war and inequality among them: thus my great love makes me speak!

In their hostilities they shall become inventors of images and ghosts, and with those images and ghosts they shall yet fight the highest fight against one another!

Good and evil, and rich and poor, and high and low, and all names of the values: they shall be weapons and ringing signs that life must overcome itself again and again!

Life wants to build itself up into the heights with columns and stairs: it wants to look into the far distance and out towards joyful beauties—*therefore* it needs height!

And because it needs height, it needs steps and conflict among the steps and the climbers! Life wants to climb and in climbing overcome itself.

And just look, my friends! Here, where the tarantula's hole is, there rises up the ruins of an ancient temple—just look at it with enlightened eyes!

Truly, he who once piled up his thoughts here in stone, knew as well as the wisest about the secret of all life!

That there is battle and inequality even in beauty, and war for power and superpower: that is what he teaches us here in the plainest parable.

How divinely vault and arches break through each other here in the wrestling match: how they strive against each other with light and shade, the godlike strivers.—

Thus assured and beautiful let us also be enemies, my friends! Divinely will we strive *against* one another!—

Alas! Now the tarantula, my old enemy, has bitten me! Divinely assured and beautiful it bit me on the finger!

"There must be punishment and justice"—thus it thinks: "and here he shall not sing songs in honor of enmity in vain!"

Yes, it has revenged itself! And ah! now it will also make my soul dizzy with revenge!

That I may *not* veer round, my friends, bind me fast to this pillar! I would rather be a stylite than a whirl of revenge!

Truly, Zarathustra is no cyclone or whirlwind: and if he is a dancer, he will never dance the tarantella!—

Thus spoke Zarathustra.

On the Famous Wise Men[8]

YOU HAVE SERVED THE people and the people's superstition, you famous wise men!—and *not* the truth! And it is just for that reason they paid you respect.

And also for that reason they tolerated your unbelief, because it was a joke and a diversion for the people. Thus the master indulges his slaves and even enjoys their insolence.

But he who is hated by the people as a wolf is by the dogs: he is the free spirit, the enemy of fetters, the non-worshipper, the dweller in the woods.

To hunt him out of his lair—that was always called "sense of right" by the people: they have always set their sharpest-toothed dogs upon him.

"For the truth is there: where the people are! Woe, woe to the seekers!" Thus has it echoed through all time.

You would justify your people in their reverence: you called that "Will to Truth," you famous wise men!

And your heart has always said to itself: "I have come from the people: from there also came to me the voice of God."

You have always been stiff-necked and clever, like the ass, as the advocate of the people.

And many a powerful one who wanted to fare well with the people has harnessed in front of his horses—a little ass, a famous wise man.

And now I should wish, you famous wise men, that you would finally throw off entirely the lion's skin!

The speckled skin of the beast of prey, and the matted hair of the investigator, the searcher, and the conqueror!

Ah, for me to learn to believe in your "truthfulness," you would first have to break your will to revere.

Truthful—so would I call him who goes into godless deserts and has broken his revering heart.

In the yellow sands and burnt by the sun he may well peer thirstily at the islands filled with springs, where the living repose under shady trees.

But his thirst does not persuade him to become like those comfortable ones: for where there are oases, there are also idols.

Hungry, violent, lonely, godless: thus the lion-will wants itself.

Free from the happiness of slaves, redeemed from gods and worship, fearless and fearful, great and lonely: thus is the will of the truthful.

The truthful, the free spirits, have always dwelt in the desert, as lords of the desert; but in the cities dwell the well-fed famous wise men—the beasts of burden.

For they always pull the *people's* cart as asses!

Not that I am angry with them for that: but for me they are still servants and beasts in harness, even though they glitter in harnesses of gold.

And often they have been good servants and praiseworthy. For thus speaks virtue: "If you must be a servant, seek him whom you can serve best!

"The spirit and virtue of your master should flourish because you are his servant: thus you yourself will flourish with his spirit and virtue!"

And truly, you famous wise men, you servants of the people! You yourselves have flourished with the people's spirit and virtue—and the people by you! I say it to your honor!

But to me even in your virtue you are still of the people, the people with purblind eyes—the people who do not know what *spirit* is!

Spirit is the life that itself cuts into life: by its own agony it increases its own knowledge—did you already know that?

And the spirit's happiness is this: to be anointed and consecrated with tears as a sacrificial beast—did you already know that?

And the blindness of the blind and his seeking and groping shall yet testify to the power of the sun into which he has gazed—did you already know that?

And the enlightened shall learn to *build* with mountains! It is a small thing for the spirit to move mountains—did you already know that?

You know only the sparks of the spirit: but you do not see the anvil it is, and the cruelty of its hammer!

Truly, you do not know the spirit's pride! But still less could you endure the spirit's modesty, should it ever want to speak!

And never yet could you cast your spirit into a pit of snow: you are not hot enough for that! Thus you also do not know the delight of its chill.

In all respects, however, you are too familiar with the spirit; and you have often made of wisdom a poorhouse and a hospital for bad poets.

You are no eagles: thus you have never experienced the happiness of the spirit's terror. And he who is not a bird should not roost over abysses.

You are lukewarm to me: but all deep knowledge flows cold. The innermost wells of the spirit are ice-cold: a refreshment to hot hands and handlers.

You stand there respectable and stiff and with straight backs, you famous wise men!—no strong wind or will drives you.

Have you never seen a sail crossing the sea, rounded and swollen and trembling with the violence of the wind?

Like the sail trembling with the violence of the spirit, my wisdom crosses the sea—my wild wisdom!

But you servants of the people, you famous wise men—how *could* you go with me!—

Thus spoke Zarathustra.

The Night Song

IT IS NIGHT: NOW all gushing fountains speak louder. And my soul too is a gushing fountain.

It is night: now only do all songs of lovers awaken. And my soul too is the song of a lover.

Something unstilled, unstillable, is within me; it wants to speak out. A craving for love is within me, that itself speaks the language of love.

I am light: ah, that I were night! But it is my loneliness to be girded with light!

Ah, that I were dark and nocturnal! How I would suck at the breasts of light!

And I would bless you, you twinkling small stars and glowworms above!—and rejoice in your gifts of light.

But I live in my own light, I drink into myself again the flames that break forth from me.

I do not know the happiness of those who receive; and I have often dreamt that stealing must be more blessed than receiving.

It is my poverty that my hand never rests from giving; it is my envy that I see expectant eyes and the illumined nights of longing.

Oh the misery of all givers! Oh eclipse of my sun! Oh craving to crave! Oh ravenous hunger in satiety!

They take from me: but do I yet touch their souls? There is a gap between giving and receiving; and the smallest gap must finally be bridged.

A hunger grows out of my beauty: I should like to hurt those for whom I shine; I should like to rob those to whom I give—thus I hunger for malice.

Withdrawing my hand when another hand already stretches out to it; hesitating like the waterfall that hesitates even in its plunge—thus I hunger for malice!

Such revenge does my abundance plot: such spite wells up out of my loneliness.

My happiness in giving died in giving, my virtue became weary of itself by its abundance!

The danger of one who always gives is that he may lose his shame; the hand and heart of him who always distributes become callous by his very distributing.

My eye no longer overflows with the shame of suppliants; my hand has become too hard for the trembling of hands that have been filled.

Where have the tears of my eyes gone and the down of my heart? Oh the loneliness of all givers! Oh silence of all who bring light!

Many suns circle in empty space: to all that is dark they speak with their light—to me they are silent.

Oh this is the hostility of light to what brings light, it travels its course pitilessly.

Unfair in its heart to all that shines, cold toward suns—thus travels every sun.

Like a storm the suns fly along their courses: that is their traveling. They follow their inexorable will: that is their coldness.

Oh, it is only you, you dark, nocturnal ones, that extract warmth from the shining! Oh, only you drink milk and refreshment from the udders of light!

Ah, there is ice around me, my hand is burned with ice! Ah, there is thirst in me, that pants after your thirst!

It is night: ah, that I must be light! And thirst for the nocturnal! And loneliness!

It is night: now my longing breaks forth in me as a well—I long for speech.

It is night: now all gushing fountains speak louder. And my soul too is a gushing fountain.

It is night: now all songs of lovers awaken. And my soul too is the song of a lover.—

Thus sang Zarathustra.

THE DANCE SONG

ONE EVENING ZARATHUSTRA WAS walking through the forest with his disciples; and while looking for a well, behold, he came upon a green meadow peacefully surrounded with trees and bushes: on it girls were dancing together. As soon as the girls recognized Zarathustra, they stopped dancing; Zarathustra, however, approached them in a friendly way and spoke these words:

"Do not stop your dance, you lovely girls! No spoilsport, no enemy of girls, has come to you with an evil eye.

"I am God's advocate with the devil: he, however, is the spirit of gravity. How could I, you light-footed ones, be an enemy of godlike dances? or of girls' feet with fine ankles?

"To be sure, I am a forest and a night of dark trees: but he who is not afraid of my darkness will find banks full of roses beneath my cypresses.

"And he will even find the little god whom girls love best: he lies beside the well, still, with closed eyes.

"Truly, he fell asleep in broad daylight, the slacker! Did he chase after butterflies too much?

"Do not be angry with me, you beautiful dancers, if I reprimand the little god somewhat! He may cry and weep—but he is laughable even when weeping!

"And with tears in his eyes he should ask you for a dance; and I myself will sing a song to his dance:

"A dance- and mocking-song on the spirit of gravity, my supreme, most powerful devil, who is said to be 'the master of the world.' "—

And this is the song that Zarathustra sang while Cupid and the girls danced together:

Lately I gazed into your eye, O life! And I seemed to sink into the unfathomable.

But you pulled me out with a golden rod; you laughed mockingly when I called you unfathomable.

"All fish talk like that," you said; "what *they* do not fathom is unfathomable.

"But I am merely changeable and wild and in every way a woman, and no virtuous one:

"Though I be called by you men the 'profound,' or 'faithful,' 'eternal,' 'mysterious.'

But you men always endow us with your own virtues—ah, you virtuous men!"

Thus she laughed, the incredible woman; but I never believe her and her laughter when she speaks evil of herself.

And when I spoke secretly with my wild wisdom, she said to me angrily: "you will, you desire, you love, that is the only reason you *praise* life!"

Then I almost answered indignantly and told the truth to the angry one; and one cannot answer more indignantly than when one "tells the truth" to one's wisdom.

For things stand thus with us three. In my heart I love only life— and truly, most when I hate her!

But that I am fond of wisdom, and often too fond, is because she reminds me so strongly of life!

She has her eye, her laugh, and even her golden fishing rod: is it my fault that both are so alike?

And when life once asked me: "Who is she then, this wisdom?"— then I said eagerly: "Ah, yes! Wisdom!

"One thirsts for her and is not satisfied, one looks at her through veils, one grasps for her through nets.

"Is she beautiful? What do I know! But the canniest old fish are still lured by her.

"She is changeable and capricious; I have often seen her bite her lip and comb against the grain of her hair.

"Perhaps she is wicked and false and altogether a woman; but when she speaks ill of herself, just then she is most seductive."

When I had said this to life, she laughed maliciously and shut her eyes. "Of whom do you speak?" she said. "Perhaps of me?

"And if you were right—should one say *that* to my face! But now speak of your wisdom, too!"

Ah, and now again you have opened your eyes, O beloved life! And into the unfathomable I again seemed to sink.—

Thus sang Zarathustra. But when the dance was over and the girls had departed, he became sad.

"The sun has long since set," he said at last, "the meadow is damp, and from the forest comes coolness.

"An unknown presence is about me and gazes thoughtfully. What! You still live, Zarathustra?

"Why? Wherefore? By what? Whither? Where? How? Is it not folly still to live?—

"Ah, my friends, it is the evening that asks thus through me. Forgive me my sadness!

"Evening has come: forgive me that evening has come!"

Thus sang Zarathustra.

THE GRAVE SONG

"YONDER IS THE GRAVE island, the silent isle; yonder also are the graves of my youth. I will carry an evergreen wreath of life there."

Resolving thus in my heart I crossed the sea.—

Oh, you sights and scenes of my youth! Oh, all you gleams of love, you divine fleeting gleams! How could you perish so soon for me! I think of you today as my dead ones.

From you, my dearest dead ones, comes to me a sweet savor, heart-opening and melting. Truly, it convulses and opens the heart of the lone seafarer.

I am still the richest and most to be envied—I, the loneliest one! For I *had* you and you have me still. Tell me: to whom have there ever fallen such rosy apples from the tree as have fallen to me?

I am still your love's heir and heritage, blooming to your memory with many-hued, wild-growing virtues, O you dearest ones!

Ah, we were made for one another, you gentle, strange marvels; and you came to me and my longing not like timid birds—no, but as trusting ones to him who trusts!

Yes, made for faithfulness, like me, and for fond eternities: must I now name you by your faithlessness, you divine glances and moments: I have as yet learned no other name.

Truly, you died too soon, you fugitives. Yet you did not flee from me, nor did I flee from you: we are innocent to each other in our faithlessness,

To kill *me*, they strangled you, you songbirds of my hopes! Yes, at you, you dearest ones, malice always shot its arrows—to strike my heart!

And they struck! Because you were always my dearest, my possession and my being possessed: *therefore* you had to die young, and all-too-early!

The arrow was shot at my most vulnerable possession—at you, whose skin is like down and even more like a smile that dies at a glance!

But I will say this word to my enemies: What is all murder of men compared with what you have done to me!

You did a worse thing to me than any murder; you took from me the irretrievable—thus I speak to you, my enemies!

You murdered my youth's visions and dearest marvels! You took my playmates from me, those blessed spirits! I lay this wreath and this curse to their memory.

This curse upon you, my enemies! You cut short my eternity, like a tone breaks off in a cold night! It came to me for barely the blink of divine eyes—a mere moment!

Thus spoke my purity once in a happy hour: "All beings shall be divine to me."

Then you haunted me with foul phantoms; ah, where has that happy hour fled now!

"All days shall be holy to me"—so spoke once the wisdom of my youth: truly, the language of a gay wisdom!

But then you enemies stole my nights and sold them to sleepless torment: ah, where has that gay wisdom fled now?

Once I longed for happy omens from the birds: then you led a monstrous owl across my path, an adverse sign. Ah, where did my tender longings flee then?

I once vowed to renounce all disgust: then you transformed those near and nearest to me into abscesses. Ah, where did my noblest vow flee then?

I once walked as a blind man on blessed paths: then you cast filth on the blind man's path: and now the old footpath disgusts him.

And when I performed my hardest task and celebrated the victory of my overcomings, then you made those who loved me scream that I hurt them most.

Truly, it was always your doing: you embittered my best honey and the industry of my best bees.

To my charity you have ever sent the most impudent beggars; around my pity you have ever crowded the incurably shameless. Thus you have wounded my virtue's faith.

And when I offered what was holiest to me as a sacrifice, immediately your "piety" put its fatter gifts beside it: so that what was holiest to me suffocated in the fumes of your fat.

And once I wanted to dance as I had never yet danced: beyond all heavens I wanted to dance. Then you seduced my favorite singer.

And then he struck up a gruesome dismal tune; ah, he tooted in my ears like a mournful horn!

Murderous singer, instrument of malice, most innocent yourself! Already I stood prepared for the best dance: then you murdered my rapture with your tones!

I know how to speak the parable of the highest things only in the dance—and now my greatest parable has remained unspoken in my limbs!

Unspoken and unrealized my highest hope has remained! And all the visions and consolations of my youth are dead!

How did I ever bear it? How did I survive and overcome such wounds? How did my soul rise again from those graves?

Yes, something invulnerable, unburiable is within me, something that rends rocks: it is called *my will*. It goes silently and unchanged through the years.

It will go its course upon my feet, my old will; its nature is hard of heart and invulnerable.

Invulnerable am I only in the heel. You live there and are always the same, most patient one! You will always break out of every grave!

What was unrealized in my youth still lives on in you; and as life and youth you sit hopefully here on the yellow ruins of graves.

Yes, for me you are still the demolisher of all graves: Hail to you, my will! And only where there are graves are there resurrections.—

Thus sang Zarathustra.

On Self-Overcoming

You call it "will to truth," you wisest men, that which impels you and fills you with lust?

A will to the thinkability of all being: thus *I* call your will!

You would *make* all being thinkable: for you doubt with a healthy mistrust whether it is already thinkable.

But it shall yield and bend to you! So wills your will. It shall become smooth and serve the spirit as its mirror and reflection.

That is your entire will, you wisest men, as a Will to Power;[9] and that is even when you speak of good and evil and of valuations.

You want to create a world before which you can kneel: such is your ultimate hope and drunkenness.

The ignorant, to be sure, the people—they are like a river on which a boat floats along: and in the boat sit the valuations, solemn and disguised.

You put your will and your valuations on the river of becoming; what the people believe to be good and evil betrays to me an old will to power.

It was you, you wisest men, who put such guests in this boat, and gave them grandeur and proud names—you and your ruling will!

The river now carries your boat onward: it *must* carry it. Small matter if the rough wave foams and angrily resists its keel!

It is not the river that is your danger and the end of your good and evil, you wisest men, but that will itself, the will to power—the unexhausted procreating will of life.

But that you may understand my teaching on good and evil, I shall relate to you my teaching on life and the nature of all the living.

I have followed the living, I walked in the broadest and narrowest paths to learn its nature.

With a hundred-faced mirror I caught its glance when its mouth was shut, so that its eye might speak to me. And its eye spoke to me.

But wherever I found the living, there too I heard the language of obedience. All that lives, obeys.

And this is the second point: he who cannot obey himself is commanded. Such is the nature of the living.

But this is the third thing I heard: that commanding is more difficult than obeying. And not only because the commander bears the burden of all who obey, and because this burden may easily crush him:—

All commanding seemed to me to be an experiment and a risk: and whenever it commands, the living risks itself.

Yes, even when it commands itself, it must still pay for its commanding. It must become the judge and avenger and victim of its own law.

How does this happen! so I asked myself. What persuades the living thing to obey and to command and even to be obedient in commanding?

Listen now to my word, you wisest men! Test in all seriousness whether I have crept into the heart of life itself and into the very roots of its heart!

Wherever I found the living, there I found will to power; and even in the will of the servant I found the will to be master.

That the weaker shall serve the stronger, to that it is persuaded by its own will, which would be master over what is weaker still: that pleasure alone it is unwilling to forego.

And as the lesser surrenders to the greater that he may have delight and power over the least of all, so even the greatest surrenders himself, and for the sake of power stakes—life.

That is the surrender of the greatest—that they face risk and danger and roll dice for death.

And where there is sacrifice and service and loving glances, there is also the will to be master. By secret paths the weaker slinks into the castle and even into the heart of the more powerful—and there steals power.

And life itself spoke this secret to me. "Behold," it said, "I am that *which must ever overcome itself.*

"To be sure, you call it a will to procreate or a drive toward a goal, towards the higher, remoter, more manifold: but all that is one and the same secret.

"I would rather perish than renounce this one thing; and truly, where there is perishing and the falling of leaves, behold, there life sacrifices itself—for power!

"That I must be struggle and becoming and goal and conflict of goals: ah, he who divines my will surely divines on what *crooked* paths it must tread!

"Whatever I create and however much I love it—soon I have to oppose it and my love: so my will wills it.

"And even you, knowing one, are only a path and footstep of my will: truly, my will to power even steps on the feet of your will to truth!

"He certainly did not hit the truth who shot at it the doctrine, 'will to existence': this will—does not exist!

"For what is not cannot will; but that which is in existence—how could it still strive for existence!

"Only where there is life is there also will: but not will to life, rather—so I teach you—will to power!

"Much is valued more highly than life itself by the living; but out of the valuing itself speaks—the will to power!"—

Thus life taught me once: and thereby, you wisest men, I solve the riddle of your hearts.

Truly, I say to you: unchanging good and evil—do not exist! From out of themselves they must overcome themselves again and again.

With your values and doctrines of good and evil, you exercise power, you valuers: and that is your secret love, and the sparkling, trembling, and overflowing of your souls.

But a stronger power grows out of your values, and a new over-coming: egg and eggshell break against them.

And he who must be a creator of good and evil: truly, he must first be a destroyer and break values.

Thus the greatest evil belongs with the greatest good: that, however, is the creative good.—

Let us speak of this, you wisest men, even if it be bad. To be silent is worse; all suppressed truths become poisonous.

And let everything break that is able to be broken by our truths! Many a house is still to be built!—

Thus spoke Zarathustra.

THE SUBLIME ONES

STILL IS THE BOTTOM of my sea: who would guess that it hides sportive monsters!

Imperturbable is my depth: but it sparkles with swimming riddles and laughter.

I saw a sublime one today, a solemn one, a penitent of the spirit: oh, how my soul laughed at his ugliness!

With upraised breast, and like those who draw in their breath: thus he stood, the sublime one, and in silence:

Overhung with ugly truths, the spoil of his hunting, and rich in torn clothes; many thorns also hung on him—but I saw no rose.

He had not yet learned laughing and beauty. This hunter returned gloomily from the forest of knowledge.

He returned home from the fight with wild beasts: but even yet a wild beast gazes out of his seriousness—an unconquered wild beast!

He always stands like a tiger about to spring; but I do not like those strained souls, my taste does not favor all these withdrawn men.

And you tell me, friends, that there is to be no dispute about taste and tasting? But all life is a dispute about taste and tasting!

Taste: that is weight and at the same time scales and weigher; and ah for every living thing that would live without any dispute about weight and scales and weigher!

If he became weary of his sublimity, this sublime one, only then would his beauty begin—and then only will I taste him and find him savory.

And only when he turns away from himself will he overleap his own shadow—and truly! into *his* sun.

Far too long he sat in the shade; the cheeks of the penitent of the spirit became pale; he almost starved on his expectations.

Contempt is still in his eye, and loathing hides in his mouth. To be sure, he now rests, but he has not yet lain down in the sunshine.

He should behave like the ox; and his happiness should smell of the earth, and not of contempt for the earth.

I would like to see him as a white ox, snorting and bellowing as he walks before the plough: and his bellowing should also praise all that is earthly!

His face is still dark; the shadow of his hand dances upon it. The sense of his eye too is overshadowed.

His deed itself is still the shadow upon him: his doing obscures the doer. He has not yet overcome his deed.

To be sure, I love in him the shoulders of the ox: but now I want to see also the eye of the angel.

He must unlearn his heroic will too: he shall be an exalted one, and not only a sublime one:—the ether itself should raise him, the will-less one!

He has subdued monsters, he has solved enigmas. But he should also redeem his monsters and enigmas; into heavenly children he should transform them.

As yet his knowledge has not learned to smile and to be without jealousy; as yet his gushing passion has not become calm in beauty.

Truly, not in satiety shall his longing cease and disappear, but in beauty! The generosity of the magnanimous should include gracefulness.

His arm across his head: that is how the hero should rest, and thus too he should overcome his rest.

But it is precisely to the hero that *beauty* is the hardest thing of all. Beauty is unattainable by all violent wills.

A little more, a little less: precisely this is more here, here it is the most.

To stand with relaxed muscles and with unharnessed will: that is the hardest for all of you, you sublime ones!

When power becomes gracious and descends into the visible: I call such descent beauty.

And from no one do I want beauty so much as from you, you powerful one: let your goodness be your last self-conquest.

I believe you capable of all evil: therefore I desire the good from you.

Truly, I have often laughed at the weaklings, who think themselves good because their claws are blunt!

You will strive after the virtue of the pillar: the higher it rises, the more beautiful and graceful it becomes, but inwardly harder and able to bear more weight.

Yes, you sublime one, one day you will also be beautiful, and hold up the mirror to your own beauty.

Then your soul will shudder with divine desires; and there will be worship even in your vanity!

For this is the secret of the soul: only when the hero has abandoned it does the superhero approach it in dreams.—

Thus spoke Zarathustra.

THE LAND OF CULTURE[10]

I FLEW TOO FAR into the future: a horror seized me.

And when I looked around me, behold! there time was my only contemporary.

Then I flew backwards, homewards—and always faster. Thus I came to you, you men of the present, and into the land of culture.

For the first time I brought an eye to see you and healthy desires: truly, I came with longing in my heart.

But how did it turn out with me? Although so alarmed—I had yet to laugh! Never did my eye see anything so mottled!

I laughed and laughed, while my foot still trembled and my heart as well: "Here indeed, is the home of all the paint pots,"—I said.

With fifty patches painted on faces and limbs—so you sat there to my astonishment, you men of the present!

And with fifty mirrors around you, which flattered your play of colors and repeated it!

Truly, you could wear no better masks, you men of the present, than your own faces! Who could—*recognize* you!

Written all over with the characters of the past, and these characters also penciled over with new characters—thus you have concealed yourselves well from all interpreters of signs!

And even if one could try the reins, who still believes that you have reins! You seem to be baked out of colors and scraps of paper glued together.

All times and peoples gaze many-colored from your veils; all customs and beliefs speak many-colored in your gestures.

He who would strip you of veils and wrappers, and paints and gestures, would have just enough left to scare the crows.

Truly, I am myself the scared crow that once saw you naked and without paint; and I flew away when the skeleton flirted with me.

I would rather be a day laborer in the underworld among the shades of the bygone!—Indeed the underworldlings are fatter and fuller than you!

This, yes this, is bitterness to my entrails, that I can endure you neither naked nor clothed, you men of the present!

All that is unfamiliar in the future, and whatever makes strayed birds shiver, is truly more familiar and cozy than your "reality."

For thus you speak: "We are wholly real and without belief or superstition": thus you thump your chests—ah, even with hollow chests!

Indeed, how would you be *able* to believe, you many-colored ones!—you who are pictures of all that has ever been believed!

You are walking refutations of belief and a fracture of all thought. *Unbelievable*: thus *I* call you, you real men!

In your spirits all ages babble in confusion; and the dreaming and babbling of all ages were even more real than your waking lives!

You are unfruitful: *therefore* you lack belief. But he who had to create, has always had his prescient dreams and astrological signs—and believed in belief!—

You are half-open doors at which gravediggers wait. And this is *your* reality: "Everything deserves to perish."

Ah, how you stand there before me, you unfruitful ones; how lean your ribs! And indeed many of you have noticed that.

Many a one has said: "Surely a god stole something from me secretly while I slept? Truly, enough to make a little woman for himself!

"The poverty of my ribs is amazing!" thus many a man of the present has spoken.

Yes, you are laughable to me, you men of the present! And especially when you marvel at yourselves!

And woe to me if I could not laugh at your marveling, and had to swallow all that is repugnant in your bowels!

As it is, however, I will take you more lightly, since I have to carry what is *heavy*; and does it matter if beetles and dragonflies also alight on my load!

Truly, it shall not on that account become heavier to me! And not from you, you men of the present, shall my great weariness arise.—

Ah, where shall I now ascend with my longing! From all mountains I look out for fatherlands and motherlands.

But I have nowhere found a home: I am unsettled in every city and I depart from every gate.

The men of the present, to whom my heart once drove me, are alien to me and a mockery; and I have been driven from fatherlands and motherlands.

Thus I love only my *children's land*, undiscovered in the remotest sea: I bid my sails to search and search for it.

To my children I will make amends for being the child of my fathers: and to all the future—for *this* present!—

Thus spoke Zarathustra.

On Immaculate Perception

WHEN THE MOON ROSE yesterday I thought it was about to bear a sun: so broad and pregnant did it lie on the horizon.

But it was a liar with its pregnancy; and I will sooner believe in the man in the moon than in the woman.

To be sure, he is not much of a man either, that timid night-reveler. Truly, with a bad conscience he stalks over the roofs.

For he is covetous and jealous, the monk in the moon; covetous of the earth, and all the joys of lovers.

No, I do not like him, that tomcat on the roofs! I hate all that slink around half-closed windows !

Piously and silently he stalks along on carpets of stars—but I do not like light-stepping feet on which not even a spur jingles.

Every honest man's step speaks; the cat, however, steals along over the ground. Behold, the moon comes along cat-like and dishonestly.—

This parable I speak to you sentimental hypocrites, to you "pure knowers!" *I* call you—lustful!

You too love the earth and the earthly: I have seen through you!—but shame is in your love and a bad conscience—you are like the moon!

Your spirit has been persuaded to despise the earthly, but your entrails have not: these, however, are the strongest in you!

And now your spirit is ashamed to be at the service of your entrails, and goes by-ways and lying ways to escape its own shame.

"That would be the highest thing for me"—so your lying spirit says to itself—"to gaze upon life without desire, and not like the dog with its tongue hanging out,

"To be happy in gazing: with a dead will, free from the grip and greed of selfishness—cold and grey as ash in body but with intoxicated moon-eyes![11]

"That would be the dearest thing to me"—thus does the seduced one seduce himself—"to love the earth as the moon loves it, and with the eye only to feel its beauty.

"And this I call *immaculate* perception of all things: to want nothing else from them, but to be allowed to lie before them as a mirror with a hundred eyes."—

Oh, you sentimental hypocrites, you lustful ones! You lack innocence in your desire: and therefore now you slander desire!

Truly, you do not love the earth as creators, procreators, and those who have joy in becoming!

Where is innocence? Where there is will to procreation. And he who seeks to create beyond himself in my view has the purest will.

Where is beauty? Where I *must will* with my whole will; where I will love and perish, that an image may not remain merely an image.

Loving and perishing: these have rhymed from eternity. Will to love: that is to be willing also to die. Thus I speak to you cowards!

But now your emasculated leers wish to be "contemplation!" And that which can be examined with cowardly eyes is to be christened "beautiful!" Oh you befoulers of noble names!

But it shall be your curse, you immaculate ones, you pure knowers, that you shall never give birth, even though you lie broad and pregnant on the horizon!

Truly, you fill your mouth with noble words: and we are to believe that your heart overflows, you great liars?

But *my* words are poor, despised, crooked words: I gladly pick up what falls from the table at your meals.

I can still use them to speak—the truth to hypocrites! Yes, my fishbones, shells, and prickly leaves shall—tickle the noses of hypocrites!

Bad air always surrounds you and your meals: your lustful thoughts, your lies and secrets are indeed in the air!

Only dare to believe in yourselves—in yourselves and in your entrails! He who does not believe in himself always lies.

You have put on a god's mask, you "pure" ones: into a god's mask your dreadful coiling snake has crawled.

Truly, you deceive, you "contemplative ones!" Even Zarathustra was once the dupe of your godlike exterior; he did not guess at the serpent's coil with which it was stuffed.

I once thought I saw a god's soul at play in your games, you pure knowers! Once I thought there was no better art than your arts!

Distance concealed from me the serpent's filth and foul odor: and that a lizard's cunning crawled around lecherously.

But I came *near* to you: then the day dawned for me—and now it dawns for you—the moon's love affair is at an end!

See there! Caught and pale it stands there—before the dawn!

For already she comes, the glowing one—*her* love to the earth comes! All solar love is innocence and creative desire!

See there, how she comes impatiently over the sea! Do you not feel the thirst and the hot breath of her love?

She wants to suck at the sea and drink its depths to her height: now the desire of the sea rises with its thousand breasts.

It *wants* to be kissed and sucked by the thirst of the sun; it *wants* to become air and height and light's footpath and light itself!

Truly, I love life like the sun and all deep seas.

And *to me* this is knowledge: all that is deep shall ascend—to my height!—

Thus spoke Zarathustra.

Scholars

As I lay asleep, a sheep ate at the ivy-wreath on my head—ate and said: "Zarathustra is no longer a scholar."

It said this and went away stiffly and proudly. A child told me this.

I like to lie here where the children play, beside the ruined wall, among thistles and red poppies.

I am still a scholar to the children, and also to the thistles and red poppies. They are innocent even in their malice.

But to the sheep I am no longer a scholar: thus my fate will have it—bless it!

For this is the truth: I have left the house of the scholars and slammed the door behind me.

My soul sat hungry at their table for too long: I have not been schooled, as they have, to crack knowledge as one cracks nuts.

I love freedom and the air over fresh soil; I would rather sleep on ox skins than on their honors and dignities.

I am too hot and scorched with my own thought: often it is ready to take away my breath. Then I have to go into the open air and away from all dusty rooms.

But they sit coolly in the cool shade: they want to be mere spectators in everything and they take care not to sit where the sun burns on the steps.

Like those who stand in the street and gape at the passers-by: thus they too wait and gape at the thoughts that others have thought.

If one lays hold of them they involuntarily raise a dust like sacks of flour: but who could guess that their dust came from corn and from the yellow delight of summer fields?

When they pose as wise their petty sayings and truths make me shiver: their wisdom often smells as if it came from the swamp; and it's true, I have even heard the frog croak in it!

They are clever, they have nimble fingers: what is *my* simplicity next to their multiplicity! Their fingers understand all threading and knitting and weaving: thus they knit the socks of the spirit!

They are good clocks: only be careful to wind them up properly! Then they indicate the hour without mistake and making a modest noise.

They work like mills and like pestles: just throw seed corn to them!—they know how to grind corn small and make white dust out of it.

They keep a sharp eye on one another and do not properly trust each other. Ingenious in little artifices, they wait for those whose knowledge walks on lame feet—they wait like spiders.

I have seen how carefully they prepare their poisons; and they always put on glass gloves to do it.

They also know how to play with loaded dice; and I found them playing so eagerly that they sweated.

We are strangers to each other, and their virtues are even more repugnant to my taste than their falsehoods and false dice.

And when I lived with them I lived above them. Therefore they took a dislike to me.

They wanted to hear nothing of any one walking above their heads; and so they put wood and earth and rubbish between me and their heads.

Thus they muffled the sound of my steps: and so far I have been least heard by the most learned.

All mankind's faults and weaknesses they put between themselves and me—in their houses they call it a "false ceiling."

But nevertheless I walk with my thoughts *above* their heads; and even if I walk on my own errors, still I am above them and their heads.

For men are *not* equal: so speaks justice. And what I desire *they* may not desire!—

Thus spoke Zarathustra.

On Poets[12]

"Since I have known the body better"—said Zarathustra to one of his disciples—"the spirit has been spirit only figuratively; and all that is 'imperishable'—that too is only a simile."

"I heard you say so once before," answered the disciple, "and then you added: 'But the poets lie too much.' Why did you say that the poets lie too much?"[13]

"Why?" said Zarathustra. "You ask why? I am not one of those who may be questioned about their why.

"Is my experience only from yesterday? It was long ago that I experienced the reasons for my opinions.

"Should I not have to be a barrel of memory if I wanted to carry my reasons around with me?

"It is already too much for me even to retain my opinions; and many a bird flies away.

"And now and then I also find an unfamiliar stray in my dovecote, which trembles when I lay my hand upon it.

"But what did Zarathustra once say to you? That the poets lie too much?—But Zarathustra too is a poet.

"Now you believe that he spoke the truth here? Why do you believe it?"

The disciple answered: "I believe in Zarathustra." But Zarathustra shook his head and smiled.—

Belief does not make me blessed, he said, least of all belief in me.

But granting that some one did say in all seriousness that the poets lie too much: he was right—*we* do lie too much.

We also know too little and are bad learners: so we have to lie.

And which of us poets has not adulterated his wine? Many a poisonous mishmash has been produced in our cellars, many an indescribable thing has been done there.

And because we know little, therefore the poor in spirit please our hearts, especially when they are young women!

And we desire even those things which old women tell one another in the evening. This we call the eternal-feminine in us.

And we believe in the people and their "wisdom" as if there were a special secret entrance to knowledge which is *blocked* to those who have learned anything.

This, however, all poets believe: that whoever pricks up his ears when lying in the grass or on lonely slopes, learns something of the things that are between heaven and earth.

And if they experience tender emotions, then the poets always think that nature herself is in love with them:

And that she steals to their ear to whisper secrets into it, and amorous flatteries: of this they boast and pride themselves before all mortals!

Ah, there are so many things between heaven and earth of which only the poets have dreamed![14]

And especially *above* the heavens: for all gods are poet's parables, poet's prevarications!

Truly, it always lifts us upward—that is to the land of the clouds: on these we set our motley bastards and call them gods and Übermenschen:[15]—

Are they not light enough for those chairs!—all these gods and Übermenschen?—

Ah, how weary I am of all these inadequate beings that are insisted on as actual! Ah, how weary I am of the poets!

When Zarathustra spoke thus his disciple was angry with him but was silent. And Zarathustra was silent too; and his eye looked inward as if it gazed into the far distance. At last he sighed and drew breath.—

I am of today and before, he said then; but something is in me that is of tomorrow, and the day following, and time to come.

I became weary of the poets, of the old and of the new: to me they are all superficial and shallow seas.

They have not thought deeply enough: therefore their feeling did not touch bottom.

Some lust and some boredom: these have as yet been their best reflection.

All the jingling of their harps is to me the breathing and coughing of ghosts; what have they known so far of the fervor of tones!—

They are also not pure enough for me: they all muddy their waters to make them seem deep.

And they would like to prove themselves reconcilers: but to me they are mediators and meddlers, and half-and-half and impure!—

Ah, I cast my net into their sea and meant to catch good fish; but I always drew out the head of some old god.

Thus the sea gave the hungry a stone. And they themselves may well have come from the sea.

Certainly, one finds pearls in them: in that way they are the more like hard mollusks. And instead of a soul I often found salty slime in them.

They have learned vanity too from the sea: is not the sea the peacock of peacocks?

It unfurls its tail even before the ugliest of all buffaloes it spread out its tail, it never tires of its lace fan of silver and silk.

The buffalo looks on disdainfully, his soul like the sand, more yet like the thicket, but most like the swamp.

What is beauty and sea and peacock-splendor to him! This parable I speak to the poets.

Truly, their spirit itself is the peacock of peacocks, and a sea of vanity!

The spirit of the poet seeks spectators: even if they are also buffaloes!—

But I became weary of this spirit: and I see the time coming when it will become weary of itself.

Already I have seen the poets transformed and their glance turned towards themselves.

I saw ascetics of the spirit approach: they grew out of the poets.

Thus spoke Zarathustra.

ON GREAT EVENTS

THERE IS AN ISLAND in the sea—not far from the happy islands of Zarathustra—on which a volcano always smokes; the people, and especially the old women among them, say that this island is placed as a rock before the gate of the underworld: but that the narrow downward path which leads to this gate goes through the volcano itself.

Now about the time that Zarathustra was living on the happy islands, it happened that a ship anchored at the island of the smoking mountain; and the crew went ashore to shoot rabbits. About noon, however, when the captain and his men were together again, they suddenly saw a man coming towards them through the air, and a voice said distinctly: "It is time! It is high time!" But when the figure was nearest to them—it flew past quickly however, like a shadow, in the direction of the volcano—then they recognized with the greatest surprise that it was Zarathustra; for they had all seen him before except the captain himself, and they loved him as the people love: in such a way that love and awe were combined in equal degree.

"Look at that!" said the old helmsman, "there goes Zarathustra to hell!"

About the same time that these sailors landed on the fire island, there was a rumor that Zarathustra had disappeared; and when his friends were asked about it, they said that he had gone on board a ship by night, without saying where he was going.

Thus there arose some uneasiness; but after three days the story of the ship's crew came to add to this uneasiness—and now all the people said that the devil had taken Zarathustra. Of course his disciples laughed at this talk; and one of them even said: "I would sooner believe that Zarathustra has taken the devil." But at the bottom of their hearts they were all full of anxiety and longing: so their joy was great when on the fifth day Zarathustra appeared among them.

And this is the story of Zarathustra's conversation with the firedog:

The earth, he said, has a skin; and this skin has diseases. One of these diseases, for example, is called: "man."

And another of these diseases is called "fire dog": men have told many lies and been told many lies about *him*.

To fathom this secret I went over the sea: and I have seen truth naked, truly! barefoot to the neck.

Now I know how it is concerning the fire dog; and likewise concerning all the overthrow- and scum-devils which not only old women fear.

"Up with you, fire dog, out of your depth!" I cried, "and confess how deep that depth is! Whence comes that which you snort up?

"You drink deeply at the sea: your salty eloquence betrays that! Truly, for a dog of the depth you take your nourishment too much from the surface!

"At best I regard you as the ventriloquist of the earth: and every time I heard overthrow- and scum-devils speak, I found them like you: salty, lying, and superficial.

"You understand how to roar and to darken with ashes! You are the best braggarts, and have sufficiently learned the art of making mud boil.

"Where you are, there must always be mud at hand, and much that is spongy, hollow, and compressed: it wants to be freed.

" 'Freedom' you all roar most eagerly: but I have unlearned belief in 'great events,' when there is much roaring and smoke about them.

"And believe me, friend hellish-noise! The greatest events—are not our loudest but our stillest hours. The world revolves not around the inventors of new noise but around the inventors of new values; it revolves *inaudibly*.

"Admit it! Once your noise and smoke passed away not much had taken place. What did it matter if a city had become mummified and a statue lay in the mud!

"And this I say also to the overthrowers of statues. It is certainly the greatest folly to throw salt into the sea and statues into the mud.

"The statue lay in the mud of your contempt: but just this is its law, that out of contempt its life and living beauty grow again!

"With more divine features it now arises, seductive in its suffering; and truly! it will yet thank you for overthrowing it, you subverters!

"But I offer this advice to kings and churches, and to all that is weak with age or virtue—let yourselves be overthrown! That you may again come to life, and that virtue may come to you!—"

Thus I spoke before the fire dog: then he interrupted me sullenly and asked: "Church? What is that?"

"Church?" I answered, "that is a kind of state, and indeed the most mendacious. But be silent, you deceptive dog! You surely know your own kind best!

"Like yourself the state is a deceptive dog; like you it likes to speak with smoke and roaring—to make believe, like you, that it speaks out of the belly of things.

"For it seeks by all means to be the most important beast on earth, the state; and people believe it too."

When I had said this, the fire dog acted as if he were furious with envy. "What!" he cried, "the most important beast on earth? And people believe it too?" And so much steam and terrible shrieking came out of his throat that I thought he would choke with vexation and envy.

At last he became calmer and his panting subsided; but as soon as he was quiet I said laughingly:

"You are angry, fire dog: so I am right about you!

"And that I may continue to be right, hear about another fire dog: he really speaks from the heart of the earth.

"His breath exhales gold and golden rain: so his heart wants it. What are ashes and smoke and hot mud to him now!

"Laughter flutters from him like a mottled cloud; he does not like your gargling and spewing and griping of the bowels!

"But the gold and laughter—he takes these out of the heart of the earth: for, that you may know it—*the heart of the earth is gold.*"

When the firedog heard this he could no longer bear to listen to me. Abashed he drew in his tail, said "bow-wow!" in a cowed voice and crept down into his cave.—

Thus related Zarathustra. But his disciples hardly listened to him: so great was their eagerness to tell him about the sailors, the rabbits, and the flying man.

"What am I to think of it!" said Zarathustra. "Am I indeed a ghost?

"But it must have been my shadow. Surely you have heard something of the Wanderer and his Shadow?

"But this is certain: I must guard it more closely—otherwise it will ruin my reputation."

And once more Zarathustra shook his head and wondered. "What am I to think of it!" he said once more.

"Why did the ghost cry: 'It is time! It is high time!'

"*For what* then is it—high time?"

Thus spoke Zarathustra.

The Soothsayer

"—And I saw a great sadness come over mankind. The best grew weary of their works.

"A teaching appeared, a faith ran beside it: 'All is empty, all is alike, all has been!'[16]

"And from all hills there re-echoed: 'All is empty, all is alike, all has been!'

"To be sure we have harvested: but why have all our fruits become rotten and brown? What fell last night from the evil moon?

"All our labor was in vain, our wine has become poison, an evil eye has seared our fields and hearts.

"We have all become dry; and if fire should fall on us, then we should scatter like ashes—yes we have wearied fire itself.

"All our wells have dried up, even the sea has receded. The earth wants to break open, but the depths will not swallow us!

" 'Ah, where is there still a sea in which one could drown': thus our cry rings—across shallow swamps.

"Truly, we have grown too tired even to die; now we stay awake and live on—in sepulchers!"

Thus Zarathustra heard a soothsayer speak; and his prophecy touched his heart and transformed him. He went about sorrowfully and wearily; and he became like those of whom the soothsayer had spoken.—

"Truly," he said to his disciples, "the long twilight is not far off. Ah, how shall I preserve my light through it! That it may not smother in this sorrowfulness! It shall be a light to remoter worlds and also to remotest nights!"

Thus Zarathustra went about grieved in his heart, and for three days he took no meat or drink, had no rest and forgot speech. At last it came to pass that he fell into a deep sleep. But his disciples sat around him in long watches of the night and waited anxiously to see if he would awake and speak again and recover from his misery.

And this is the speech that Zarathustra spoke when he awoke; his voice, however, came to his disciples as if from afar:

"Hear the dream that I dreamed, my friends, and help me to read its meaning!

"It is still a riddle to me, this dream; the meaning is hidden in it and encaged and does not yet fly above it on free wings.

"I dreamed I had renounced all life. I had become a night- and grave-watchman on the lonely mountain castle of death.

"There I guarded his coffins: the musty vaults stood full of those trophies of his victory. Out of glass coffins vanquished life gazed upon me.

"I breathed the odor of dusty eternities: my soul lay sultry and dusty. And who could have aired his soul there!

"The brightness of midnight was all around me, loneliness crouched beside her; and as a third, the rasping stillness of death, the worst of my friends.

"I carried keys, the rustiest of all keys; and I understood how to open with them the most creaking of all doors.

"Like a bitterly angry croaking the sound rang through the long corridors when the wings of this door opened: this bird cried fiendishly, it was unhappy at being awakened.

"But it was more frightful and more heart stopping yet when it again became silent and still all around, and I sat alone in that malignant silence.

"Thus time passed with me and slipped by, if there still was time: how should I know! But at last that happened which awoke me.

"Three strikes struck at the door like thunder, three times again the vaults resounded and howled: then I went to the door.

"Alpa! I cried, who carries his ashes to the mountain? Alpa! Alpa! Who carries his ashes to the mountain?

"And I turned the key and pulled at the door and exerted myself. But it was not yet open a finger's-breadth:

"Then a raging wind tore its wings from one another: whistling, shrilling and piercing it threw a black coffin to me:

"And in the roaring and whistling and shrilling the coffin burst open and spewed out a thousand peals of laughter.

"And from a thousand grimaces of children, angels, owls, fools, and butterflies as big as children it laughed and mocked and roared at me.

"At this I was terribly frightened: it threw me to the ground. And I cried with horror as I never cried before.

"But my own crying awoke me:—and I came to my senses."—

Thus Zarathustra related his dream and then was silent: for as yet he did not know the interpretation of it. But the disciple whom he loved most arose quickly, seized Zarathustra's hand, and said:

"Your life itself interprets this dream for us, O Zarathustra!

"Are you not yourself the shrilly whistling wind which bursts open the doors of the fortress of death?

"Are you not yourself the coffin full of colorful sarcasms and the angelic grimaces of life?

"Truly, like a thousand peals of children's laughter Zarathustra comes into all sepulchers, laughing at those night- and gravewatchmen and whoever else rattles with gloomy keys.

"With your laughter you will frighten them and throw them to the ground: and your power over them will make them faint and wake them.

"And when the long twilight comes and the mortal weariness, even then you will not perish in our heaven, you advocate of life!

"You have shown us new stars and new nocturnal glories: truly, you have spread laughter itself out over us like a canopy of many colors.

"Now children's laughter will always flow from coffins; now a strong wind will always comes victoriously to all mortal weariness: of this you are yourself the pledge and the prophet!

"Truly, *just this is what you dreamed*, your enemies: that was your hardest dream.

"But as you awoke from them and came to yourself, so shall they awaken from themselves—and come to you!"

Thus spoke the disciple; and all the others then thronged around Zarathustra and grasped him by the hands and tried to persuade him to leave his bed and his sadness and return to them. But Zarathustra sat upright on his bed, and with an absent look. Like one returning from a long journey in a strange land he looked at his disciples and examined their faces; but still he did not know them. But when they raised him and set him on his feet, behold, suddenly his eye changed; he understood everything that had happened, stroked his beard, and said with a strong voice:

"Well! This too has its time; but see to it, my disciples, that we have a good meal, and soon! Thus I mean to atone for bad dreams!

"But the soothsayer shall eat and drink at my side: and truly, I will yet show him a sea in which he can drown!"

Thus spoke Zarathustra. But then he gazed long into the face of the disciple who had interpreted the dream, and shook his head.

ON REDEMPTION

WHEN ZARATHUSTRA WAS GOING over the great bridge one day, the cripples and the beggars surrounded him, and a hunchback spoke thus to him:

"Behold, Zarathustra! Even the people learn from you and come to believe in your teaching: but for them to believe fully in you, one thing is still necessary—you must first of all convince us cripples! Here now you have a fine selection, and truly, an opportunity with more than one forelock! You can heal the blind, and make the lame run; and from him who has too much behind him you could well take a little away—that, I think, would be the right method to make the cripples believe in Zarathustra!"

But Zarathustra replied thus to him who so spoke: "When one takes his hump from the hunchback, then one takes his spirit from him—so the people teach. And when one gives the blind man eyes, then he sees too many bad things on the earth: so that he curses him who healed him. He, however, who makes the lame man run, inflicts upon him the greatest injury; for hardly can he run, when his vices run away with him—so the people teach concerning cripples. And why should not Zarathustra also learn from the people, when the people learn from Zarathustra?

"But it is the smallest thing to me since I have been among men, to see: 'this one person lost an eye and this other an ear and a third a leg, and there are others, who have lost the tongue or the nose or the head.'

"I see and have seen worse things and many things so hideous that I should neither like to speak of all of them nor yet even once keep silent about some of them: namely, men who lack everything, except one thing that they have too much of—men who are nothing more than a big eye or a big mouth or a big belly or something else big—I call such people inverse cripples.

And when I came out of my solitude and crossed this bridge for the first time, I did not believe my eyes but looked again and again and said at last: "That is an ear! An ear as big as a man!" I looked still more attentively—and actually there did move under the ear something that was pitiably small and poor and slim. And in truth this immense ear was perched on a small thin stalk—but the stalk was a man! If one used a magnifying glass one could even further recognize a small envious face, and also a bloated little soul dangling at the stalk. The people told me, however, that the big ear was not only a man, but a great man, a genius. But I have never believed the people when they spoke of great men—and I maintain my belief that it was an inverse cripple, who had too little of everything and too much of one thing."

When Zarathustra had spoken thus to the hunchback and to those whose mouthpiece and advocate the hunchback was, he turned to his disciples in profound dismay and said:

"Truly, my friends, I walk among men as among the fragments and limbs of human beings!

"This is the terrible thing to my eye, that I find man broken up, and scattered about, as on a battle- and butcher-ground.

"And when my eye flees from the present to the past it always finds the same: fragments and limbs and fearful chances—but no men!

"The present and the past upon earth—ah! my friends—that is *my* most unbearable burden; and I would not know how to go on living if I were not a seer of what is to come.

"A seer, a willer, a creator, a future itself, and a bridge to the future—and ah, also as a cripple on this bridge: all that is Zarathustra.

"And you also asked yourselves often: 'Who is Zarathustra to us? What shall he be called by us?' And like me you gave yourselves questions for answers.

"Is he a promiser? Or a fulfiller? A conqueror? Or an inheritor? A harvest? Or a ploughshare? A physician? Or a convalescent?

"Is he a poet? Or a truthteller? A liberator? Or a subjugator? A good? Or an evil?

"I walk among men as among the fragments of the future: that future which I contemplate.

"And it is all my art and aim, to compose into one and gather together what is fragment and riddle and fearful chance.

"And how could I bear to be a man if man were not also poet and guesser of riddles and redeemer of chance!

"To redeem what is past, and to transform every 'It was' into 'Thus would I have it!'—that alone do I call redemption!

"Will—so the liberator and joy-bringer is called: thus I have taught you, my friends! But now learn this as well: the will itself is still a prisoner.

"Willing liberates: but what is it that puts even the liberator in chains?

" 'It was': thus the will's teeth-gnashing and loneliest tribulation is called. Powerless against that which has been done, it is an angry spectator of all that is past.

"The will cannot will backwards; that it cannot break time and time's desire—that is the will's loneliest tribulation.

"Willing liberates: what does willing itself devise in order to get free from its tribulation and mock at its prison?

"Ah, every prisoner becomes a fool! The imprisoned will too always foolishly releases itself.

"That time does not run backward, that is its wrath; 'That which was'—that is the name of the stone it cannot roll.

"And thus it rolls stones out of wrath and irritation, and takes revenge on whatever does not, like it, feel wrath and irritation.

"Thus the will, the liberator, becomes a torturer: and it takes revenge on all that is capable of suffering, because it cannot go backward.

"This, yes, this alone is *revenge* itself: the will's antipathy to time and its 'It was.'

"Truly, a great foolishness dwells in our will; and it became a curse to all humanity, that this foolishness acquired spirit!

"*The spirit of revenge*: my friends, that has so far been the subject of man's best reflection; and where there was suffering, there was always supposed to be punishment.

" 'Punishment,' is what revenge calls itself: it feigns a good conscience for itself with a hypocritical lie.

"And because in the willer himself there is suffering, because he cannot will backwards—thus was willing itself and all life supposed to be—punishment!

"And then cloud after cloud rolled over the spirit: until at last madness preached: 'Everything passes away, therefore everything deserves to pass away!'

" 'And this itself is justice, the law of time, that he must devour his children': thus madness preached.

" 'Things are morally ordered according to justice and punishment. Oh, where is there deliverance from the flux of things and from the punishment of 'existence'?' Thus madness preached.

" 'Can there be deliverance when there is eternal justice? Ah, the stone, 'It was' cannot be rolled away: all punishments too must be eternal!' Thus madness preached.

" 'No deed can be annihilated: how could it be undone by the punishment! That existence too must eternally become deed and guilt, this, this is what is eternal in the punishment 'existence'!'

" 'Unless the will should at last deliver itself and willing become not willing—': but you know, my brothers, this fable of madness!

"I led you away from those fables when I taught you: 'The will is a creator.'

All 'It was' is a fragment, a riddle, a fearful chance—until the creating will says to it: 'But I willed it thus!'"—

Until the creating will says to it: "But I will it thus! Thus shall I will it!"

But did it ever speak thus? And when does this happen? Has the will been unharnessed from its own folly?

Has the will become its own deliverer and joy-bringer? Has it unlearned the spirit of revenge and all teeth-gnashing?

And who has taught it reconciliation with time, and something higher than all reconciliation?

The will that is the will to power must will something higher than all reconciliation—but how does that happen? Who has taught it also to will backwards?"

—But at this point in his speech Zarathustra suddenly paused and looked exactly like one who has received a severe shock. With terror in his eyes he gazed on his disciples; his glances pierced their thoughts and afterthoughts[17] as with arrows. But in a short time he laughed again and said calmly:

"It is difficult to live among men because keeping silent is so difficult. Especially for a babbler."—

Thus spoke Zarathustra. The hunchback, however, had listened to the conversation and had covered his face during the time; but when he heard Zarathustra laugh, he looked up with curiosity, and said slowly:

"But why does Zarathustra speak to us differently than to his disciples?"

Zarathustra answered: "What is surprising in that! With hunchbacks one may well speak in a hunchbacked way!"

"Very good," said the hunchback; "and with pupils one may well tell tales out of school.

"But why does Zarathustra speak differently to his pupils—than to himself?"—

On Human Prudence

NOT THE HEIGHT: THE precipice is terrible!

The precipice, where the gaze plunges *downward* and the hand grasps *upward*. There the heart becomes giddy through its double will.

Ah, friends, have you divined also my heart's double will?

This, this is *my* precipice and my danger, that my gaze shoots towards the summit, and my hand would like to clutch and lean—on the depth!

My will clings to man, I bind myself to man with chains, because I am pulled upwards to the Übermensch: for there my other will tends.

And *therefore* I live blindly among men; as if I did not know them: that my hand may not entirely lose belief in firmness.

I do not know you men: this gloom and consolation is often spread around me.

I sit at the gateway for every rogue, and ask: Who wishes to deceive me?

This is my first human prudence, that I allow myself to be deceived, so as not to be on my guard against deceivers.

Ah, if I were on my guard against man, how could man be an anchor to my ball! I would be pulled upwards and away too easily!

This providence is over my fate, that I must be without foresight.

And he who does not want to die of thirst among men, must learn to drink out of all glasses; and he who wants to keep clean among men, must know how to wash himself even with dirty water.

And thus I often comforted myself: "Well then! Cheer up! Old heart! One misfortune missed you: enjoy that as your—fortune!"

But this is my second human prudence: I spare the *vain* more than the proud.

Is not wounded vanity the mother of all tragedies? But where pride is wounded, there grows up something better than pride.

For life to be pleasant to watch, its play must be well acted; for that, however, it needs good actors.

I found all the vain to be good actors: they act and will that others shall want to watch them—all their spirit is in this will.

They act themselves, they invent themselves; I like to look at life in their vicinity—it cures melancholy.

Therefore I spare the vain because they are the physicians of my melancholy and keep me tied to man as to a play.

And further: who can estimate the full depth of the modesty of the vain! I love and pity him for his modesty.

He would learn his belief in himself from you; he feeds upon your glances, he eats praise out of your hands.

He believes even your lies if you lie favorably about him: for his heart sighs in its depths: "What am *I*?"

And if true virtue is that virtue which is unconscious of itself: well, the vain man is unconscious of his modesty!—

But this is my third human prudence: I do not let the sight of the *evil* be spoiled for me by your timidity.

I am happy to see the marvels the hot sun hatches: tigers and palms and rattlesnakes.

Also among men a beautiful breed hatches in the hot sun and much that is marvelous in the evil.

Indeed, as your wisest did not seem to me so very wise, so I also found that human evil did not live up to its reputation.

And I often shook my head and asked: why go on rattling, you rattlesnakes?

Truly, there is still a future even for evil! And the hottest South is still undiscovered by man.

How many things are now called the worst evil, which are only twelve feet wide and three months long! But some day greater dragons will come into the world.

For that the Übermensch may not lack his dragon, the superdragon, that is worthy of him: for that much hot sun must yet burn on damp jungles!

Your wild cats must first become tigers and your poisonous toads crocodiles: for the good hunter shall have a good hunt!

And truly, you good and just! In you there is much to be laughed at, and especially your fear of what has so far been called "the devil!"

What is great is so foreign to your souls that to you the Übermensch would be *frightful* in his goodness!

And you wise and knowing ones, you would flee from the burning sun of wisdom in which the Übermensch joyfully baths his nakedness!

You highest men whom my eyes have seen! This is my doubt of you and my secret laughter: I suspect you would call my Übermensch—a devil!

Ah, I became tired of those highest and best: from their "height" I longed to go up, out, and away to the Übermensch!

A horror came over me when I saw those best ones naked: then there grew for me the wings to soar away into distant futures.

Into more distant futures, into more southerly Souths than ever artist dreamed of: there, where gods are ashamed of all clothes!

But I want to see *you* disguised, you neighbors and fellow men, and well dressed and vain and dignified as 'the good and just.'—

And disguised I will myself sit among you—that I may *mistake* you and myself: for that is my last human prudence.—

Thus spoke Zarathustra.

THE STILLEST HOUR

WHAT HAS HAPPENED TO me, my friends? You see me troubled, driven forth, unwillingly obedient, ready to go—ah, to go away from *you*!

Yes, once more Zarathustra must retire to his solitude: but this time the bear goes unhappily back to his cave!

What has happened to me? Who orders this?—Ah, my angry mistress wants it so, so she told me; have ever I told you her name?

Yesterday towards evening *my stillest hour* spoke to me: that is the name of my terrible mistress.

And thus it happened—for I must tell you everything, so that your heart may not harden against the suddenly departing!

Do you know the terror of him who falls asleep?—

He is terrified to the very toes, because the ground gives way under him, and the dream begins.

This I speak to you in a parable. Yesterday at the stillest hour the ground gave way under me: the dream began.

The hour hand moved on, the timepiece of my life drew breath—I had never heard such stillness around me, so that my heart was terrified.

Then voicelessly it spoke to me: *"You know it, Zarathustra?"*—

And I cried in terror at this whispering, and the blood left my face: but I was silent.

Then once more voiceless it spoke to me: "You know it, Zarathustra, but you do not say it!"—

And at last I answered defiantly: "Yes, I know it, but I will not say it!"

Then again voicelessly it spoke to me: "You *will* not, Zarathustra? Is this true? Do not hide behind your defiance!"—

And I wept and trembled like a child, and said: "Ah, I would indeed, but how can I do it! Spare me this! It is beyond my strength!"

Then again voicelessly it spoke to me: "What do you matter, Zarathustra! Speak your word and break!"

And I answered: "Ah, is it *my* word? Who am *I*? I await the worthier one; I am not worthy even of being broken by it."

Then again voicelessly it spoke to me: "What do you matter? You are not yet humble enough for me. Humility has the thickest skin."—

And I answered: "What has the skin of my humility not endured! I dwell at the foot of my height: how high my summits are no one has yet told me. But I know my valleys well."

Then again voicelessly it spoke to me: "O Zarathustra, he who must move mountains also moves valleys and plains."—

And I answered: "As yet my word has not moved mountains and what I have spoken has not reached man. I went, indeed, to men, but I have not yet found them."

Then again voicelessly it spoke to me: "What do you know *of that*! The dew falls on the grass when the night is most silent."—

And I answered: "They mocked me when I found and walked in my own path; and certainly my feet trembled then.

"And thus they spoke to me: You have forgotten the way, now you also forget how to walk!"

Then again voicelessly it spoke to me: "What does their mockery matter! You have unlearned to obey: now you will command!

"Do you not know who is most needed by all? He who commands great things.

"To do great things is difficult: but the more difficult task is to command great things.

"This is the most unforgivable thing in you: you have the power and you will not rule."

And I answered: "I lack the lion's voice for command."

Then again as a whispering it spoke to me: "It is the stillest words that bring the storm. Thoughts that come on doves' feet guide the world.

"O Zarathustra, you will go as a shadow of that which is to come: thus you will command and in commanding go first."—

And I answered: "I am ashamed."

Then again voicelessly it spoke to me: "You must yet become a child and without shame.

"The pride of youth is still in you, you are late in growing young: but he who would become a child must overcome even his youth."—

And I considered a long while, and trembled. At last, however, I said what I had said at first. "I will not."

Then laughter broke out all around me. Ah, how that laughter tore my entrails and cut open my heart!

And for the last time it spoke to me: "O Zarathustra, your fruits are ripe, but you are not ripe for your fruits!

"So you must go again into solitude: for you will yet become mellow."—

And again there was laughter, and it fled: then it became still around me as with a double stillness. But I lay on the ground, and the sweat flowed from my limbs.

—Now you have heard everything, and why I must return into my solitude. I have kept nothing from you, my friends.

But you have heard even this from me, *who* still is the most taciturn of all men—and will be so!

Ah, my friends! I should have something more to say to you, I should have something more to give to you! Why do I not give it? Am I so stingy?—

But when Zarathustra had spoken these words, the violence of his pain and a sense of the nearness of his departure from his friends overwhelmed him, so that he wept aloud; and no one knew how to console him. But that night he went away alone and left his friends.

THIRD PART

You look up when you long for elevation. And I look down because I am elevated.

Who among you can laugh and be elevated at the same time?

Whoever climbs on the highest mountains laughs at all tragic plays and tragic seriousness.

—Zarathustra, "On Reading and Writing"

[1884]

The Wanderer

It was about midnight when Zarathustra went his way over the ridge of the island, so that he might arrive early in the morning at the other coast: because he meant to embark there. For there was a good harbor in which foreign ships also liked to anchor: those ships took with them many people, who wished to cross over from the Happy Islands. So when Zarathustra thus ascended the mountain, he thought on the way of his many solitary wanderings from youth onwards, and how many mountains and ridges and summits he had already climbed.

I am a wanderer and mountain climber, he said to his heart, I do not love the plains, and it seems I cannot sit still for long.

And whatever may still overtake me as fate and experience—it will be a wandering and a mountain climbing: in the end one experiences only oneself.

The time is now past when accidents could befall me; and what *could* now fall to my lot which would not already be my own!

It only returns, it comes home to me at last—my own self, and such of it as has been long abroad, and scattered among things and accidents.

And I know one thing more: I stand now before my last summit, and before that which has been longest reserved for me. Ah, I must climb my hardest path! Ah, I have begun my loneliest wandering!

He, however, who is of my nature does not avoid such an hour: the hour that says to him: only now you go the way to your greatness! Summit and abyss—these are now united together!

You go the way to your greatness: now it has become your last refuge, what was so far your last danger!

You go the way to your greatness: it must now be your best courage that there is no longer any path behind you!

You go the way to your greatness: here no one shall steal after you! Your foot itself has erased the path behind you, and over it stands written: Impossibility.

And when all footholds disappear, then you must learn to climb upon your own head: how could you climb upward otherwise?

Upon your own head, and beyond your own heart! Now the gentlest in you must become the hardest.

He who has always overindulged himself is at last sickened by his overindulgence. Praises on what makes hardy! I do not praise the land where butter and honey—flow!

In order to see *much* one must learn to *look away from* oneself— this hardness is needed by every mountain climber.

But he who as a knower is over-eager with his eyes, how can he ever see more of anything than its foreground!

But you, O Zarathustra, would view the ground of everything, and its background: thus you must climb even above yourself—up, upwards, until you have even your stars *under* you!

Yes! To look down upon myself, and even upon my stars: only that would I call my *summit*, that has remained for me as my *last* summit!—

Thus spoke Zarathustra to himself while ascending, comforting his heart with harsh maxims: for he was sore at heart as he had never been before. And when he had reached the top of the mountain ridge, behold, there lay the other sea spread out before him: and he stood still and was long silent. The night, however, was cold at this height, and clear and starry.

I recognize my destiny, he said at last, sadly. Well! I am ready. Now has my last loneliness begun.

Ah, this black somber sea below me! Ah, this brooding nocturnal reluctance! Ah, fate and sea! To you must I now *go under*!

I stand before my highest mountain, and before my longest wandering: therefore I must first go deeper down than I ever ascended:

—Deeper down into pain than I ever ascended, even into its darkest flood! So wills my fate. Well! I am ready.

From where do the highest mountains come? so I once asked. Then I learned that they come out of the sea.

That testimony is inscribed on their stones, and on the walls of their summits. Out of the deepest the highest must come to its height.—

Thus spoke Zarathustra on the ridge of the mountain where it was cold: but when he came into the vicinity of the sea, and at last stood alone among the cliffs, he had become weary on his way and more yearning than he was before.

Everything sleeps as yet, he said; even the sea sleeps. Drowsily and strangely its eye gazed upon me.

But it breathes warmly—I feel it. And I feel also that it dreams. It tosses about dreamily on hard pillows.

Hark! Hark! How it groans with evil recollections! Or evil expectations?

Ah, I am sad along with you, you dusky monster, and angry with myself even for your sake.

Ah, that my hand has not strength enough! Gladly, indeed, would I free you from evil dreams!—

And while Zarathustra thus spoke, he laughed at himself with melancholy and bitterness. What! Zarathustra, he said, will you even sing consolation to the sea?

Ah, you amiable fool, Zarathustra, you all-too-blindly confiding one! But you have always been thus: you have always approached everything terrible confidently.

You want to caress every monster. A whiff of warm breath, a little soft tuft on its paw—: and immediately you were ready to love and lure it.

Love is the danger of the loneliest one, love to anything, *if only it lives*! Laughable, truly, is my folly and my modesty in love!—

Thus spoke Zarathustra and laughed again: but then he thought of his abandoned friends—, and he was angry with himself, as if he had wronged them with his thoughts. And like that it came to pass that the laugher wept—with anger and longing Zarathustra wept bitterly.[1]

On the Vision and the Riddle

1

When word spread among the sailors that Zarathustra was on board the ship—for a man who came from the Happy Islands had gone on board along with him—there was great curiosity and expectation. But Zarathustra kept silent for two days, and was cold and deaf with sadness, so that he answered neither looks nor questions. On the evening of the second day, however, he opened his ears again, though he still kept silent: for there were many curious and dangerous things to be heard on board the ship, which came from afar and was to go still further. Zarathustra, however, was a friend to all who make distant voyages and do not like to live without danger. And behold! when listening, his own tongue was at last loosened, and the ice of his heart broke: then he began to speak thus:

To you, the daring venturers and adventurers, and whoever has embarked with cunning sails upon frightful seas,—

—to you the riddle-drunk, the twilight-enjoyers, whose souls are allured by flutes to every treacherous gulf:

—for you dislike to grope at a thread with a cowardly hand; and where you can *guess*, you hate to *calculate*—

—to you alone I tell the riddle that I *saw*—the vision of the loneliest.—

Lately I walked gloomily in corpse-colored twilight—gloomily and sternly, with compressed lips. Not only one sun had set for me.

A path which ascended defiantly among boulders and rubble, an evil, lonesome path, no longer cheered by an herb or shrub: a mountain-path crunched under the defiance of my foot.

Striding mute over the mocking clatter of pebbles, trampling the stone that made it slip: thus my foot forced its way upward.

Upward:—in spite of the spirit that drew it downward, towards the abyss, the spirit of gravity, my devil and archenemy.

Upward:—although it sat upon me, half-dwarf, half-mole; paralyzed, paralyzing; dripping lead in my ear, and thoughts like drops of lead into my brain.

"O Zarathustra," it whispered scornfully, syllable by syllable, "you philosopher's stone"![2] You threw yourself high, but every thrown stone must—fall!

"O Zarathustra, you philosopher's stone, you sling stone, you destroyer of stars! You threw yourself so high—but every thrown stone—must fall!

"Condemned by yourself and to your own stoning: O Zarathustra, far indeed you threw your stone—but it will fall back upon *you*!"

Then the dwarf was silent; and it lasted long.[3] But the silence oppressed me; and to be thus as two is surely more lonesome than to be alone!

I ascended, I ascended, I dreamed, I thought—but everything oppressed me. I resembled an invalid, whom bad torment wearies, and who as he falls asleep is reawakened by a still worse dream.—

But there is something in me that I call courage: it has so far slain for me every discouragement. This courage at last bade me stand still and say: "Dwarf! You! Or I!"—

For courage is the best slayer—courage that *attacks*: for in every attack there is triumphant shout.

But man is the most courageous animal: hence he has overcome every animal. With a triumphant shout he has overcome every pain; human pain, however, is the sorest pain.

Courage also slays giddiness at abysses: and where does man not stand at an abyss! Is not seeing itself—seeing abysses?

Courage is the best slayer: courage also slays pity. But pity is the deepest abyss: as deeply as man looks into life, so deeply does he also look into suffering.

But courage is the best slayer, courage that attacks: it slays even death itself; for it says: "Was *that* life? Well then! Once more!"

But in such speech there is much shouting of triumph. He who has ears to hear, let him hear.—

2

"Halt, dwarf!" I said. "I! Or You! But I am the stronger of the two—you do not know my abysmal thought! *That*—you could not endure!"

Then something happened which lightened me: for the dwarf, the curious one, sprang from my shoulder! And he squatted on a stone in front of me. But a gateway stood just where we halted.

"Look at this gateway! Dwarf!" I continued: "it has two faces. Two roads come together here: no one has yet followed either to its end.

"This long lane backwards: it continues for an eternity. And that long lane forward—that is another eternity.

"They are opposed to one another, these roads; they offend each other face to face—and it is here, at this gateway, that they come together. The name of the gateway is inscribed above: 'Moment.'

"But should one follow them further—and ever further and further on, do you think, dwarf, that these roads would be eternally opposed?"—

"Everything straight lies," murmured the dwarf, contemptuously. "All truth is crooked, time itself is a circle."

"You spirit of gravity!" I said angrily, "do not take it too lightly! Or I shall leave you squatting where you are, lamefoot[4]—and I carried you *high*!

"Behold," I continued, "this moment! From this gateway Moment a long, eternal lane runs *backward*: behind us lies an eternity.

"Must not all things that *can* run already have run along that lane? Must not all things that *can* happen already have happened, been done, and passed by?

"And if everything has been here before: what do you think, dwarf, of this moment? Must not this gateway already also—have been?

"And are not all things closely bound together in such a way that this moment draws all coming things after it? *Therefore*—itself too?

"So, for all things that *can* run: also in this long lane *forward*—it *must* once more run!—

"And this slow spider which creeps in the moonlight, and this moonlight itself, and you and I in this gateway whispering together, whispering of eternal things—must we not all have been here before?

"—And must we not return and run in that other lane out before us, that long weird lane—must we not eternally return?"—

Thus I spoke, and always more softly: for I was afraid of my own thoughts and afterthoughts. Then suddenly I heard a nearby dog *howl*.

Had I ever heard a dog howl thus? My thoughts ran back. Yes! When I was a child, in my most distant childhood:

—Then I heard a dog howl thus. And saw it too, bristling, its head up, trembling in the stillest midnight, when even dogs believe in ghosts:

—so that it moved me to pity. For just then the full moon passed, silent as death, over the house, just then it stood still, a round glow—still upon the flat roof, as if on another's property:—

that was what had terrified the dog: for dogs believe in thieves and ghosts. And when I heard such howling again, it moved me to pity again.

Where was the dwarf gone now? And the gateway? And the spider? And all the whispering? Was I dreaming then? Had I awoken? Suddenly I stood between wild cliffs, alone, dreary, in the dreariest moonlight.

But there lay a man! And there! The dog, springing, bristling, whining—now it saw me coming—then it howled again, then it *shrieked*—had I ever heard a dog shriek so for help?

And truly, I had never seen the like of what I then saw. I saw a young shepherd, writhing, choking, convulsed, his face distorted, and a heavy black snake hung out of his mouth.[5]

Had I ever seen so much disgust and pale dread a *single* face? Had he perhaps been asleep? Then the snake had crawled into his throat—and there bit itself fast.

My hand tore at the snake and tore—in vain! It could not tear the snake out of his throat. Then it cried out of me: "Bite! Bite!

"The head off! Bite!"—so it cried out of me, my horror, my hatred, my disgust, my pity, all my good and my bad cried out with a *single* cry.—

You bold ones around me! You venturers, adventurers, and those of you who have embarked with cunning sails on unexplored seas! You enjoyers of riddles!

Solve for me the riddle that I saw, interpret for me the vision of the loneliest!

For it was a vision and a premonition—*what* did I see in a parable? And *who* is it that must come some day?

Who is the shepherd into whose throat the snake crawled thus? *Who* is the man into whose throat all that is heaviest and blackest will crawl thus?

—But the shepherd bit as my cry had admonished him; he bit with a good bite! Far away he spat the head of the snake—and sprang up.—

No longer shepherd, no longer man—a transfigured being, radiant, *laughing*! Never yet on earth had a man laughed as *he* laughed!

O my brothers, I heard a laughter which was no human laughter—and now a thirst gnaws at me, a longing that is never stilled.

My longing for that laughter gnaws at me: oh how can I yet bear to live! And how could I bear to die now!

Thus spoke Zarathustra.

On Involuntary Bliss

WITH SUCH RIDDLES AND bitternesses in his heart Zarathustra sailed over the sea. But when he was four days journey from the Happy Islands and from his friends, he had overcome all his pain— triumphantly and with firm feet he stood on his destiny again. And then Zarathustra spoke thus to his exulting conscience:

I am alone again, and I like to be so, alone with the pure heaven, and the open sea; and again the afternoon is around me.

On an afternoon I found my friends for the first time; on an afternoon, also, I found them a second time:—at the hour when all light becomes stiller.

For whatever happiness is still on its way between heaven and earth, now seeks a luminous soul for its lodging: *with happiness* all light has now become stiller.

O afternoon of my life! Once my happiness descended also to the valley that it might seek lodging: then it found those open hospitable souls.

O afternoon of my life! What did I not surrender that I might have one thing: this living plantation of my thoughts, and this dawn of my highest hope!

He who creates once sought companions, and children of *his* hope: and lo, it turned out that he could not find them unless he himself first created them.

Thus I am in the midst of my work, going to my children and turning from them: for the sake of his children Zarathustra must perfect himself.

For in one's heart one loves only one's child and one's work; and where there is great love of oneself, then is it the sign of pregnancy: thus have I discovered.

My children are still verdant in their first spring, standing near one another and shaken in common by the winds, the trees of my garden and of my best soil.

And truly! Where such trees stand beside one another, there *are* Happy Islands!

But one day I will uproot them and stand each by itself alone: that it may learn loneliness and defiance and foresight.

Gnarled and crooked and with flexible hardness it shall then stand by the sea, a living lighthouse of unconquerable life.

There where the storms rush down into the sea, and the snout of the mountain drinks water, each shall have its day and night watches, for *its* testing and recognition.

It shall be tested and recognized, to see whether it is my kind and race—whether it is master of a long will, silent even when it speaks, and giving such that it *takes* in giving:—

—that it may one day become my companion and a fellow-creator and a fellow-rejoicer with Zarathustra:—such a one as writes my will on my tablets: for the fuller perfection of all things.

And for its sake and for those like it, I must perfect *myself*: therefore I now avoid my happiness and present myself to every unhappiness—for *my* final testing and recognition.

And truly, it is time that I went away; and the wanderer's shadow and the longest sojourn and the stillest hour—have all said to me: "It is high time!"

The wind blew to me through the keyhole and said "Come!" The door sprang cunningly open and said "Go!"

But I lay chained to my love for my children: desire spread this snare for me, the desire for love, that I should become the plunder of my children and lose myself to them.

To desire—for me now that means to have lost myself. *I possess you, my children*! In this possessing all should be security and nothing desire.

But the sun of my love brooded upon me, Zarathustra stewed in his own juice—then shadows and doubts flew past me.

I longed for frost and winter: "Oh, that frost and winter would again make me crack and crunch!" I sighed:—then icy mist arose out of me.

My past burst from its tomb, many pains buried alive woke up—: they had only been sleeping, concealed in burial shrouds.

Thus everything called to me in signs: "It is time!" But I—heard not: until at last my abyss stirred and my thought bit me.

Ah, abysmal thought, which is *my* thought! When shall I find strength to hear you burrowing and no longer tremble?

My heart rises to my throat when I hear you burrowing! Even your silence wants to choke me, you abysmal silent one!

As yet I have never dared to summon you *up*: it has been enough that I—have carried you about with me! As yet have I not been strong enough for my final lion's arrogance and playfulness.

Your weight was always terrible enough for me: but one day I shall find the strength and the lion's voice to summon you up!

When I have overcome myself in that, then I will overcome myself in that which is greater; and a *victory* shall be the seal of my perfection!—

Meanwhile I still travel on uncertain seas; chance flatters me, the smooth-tongued; I gaze forward and backward—still I see no end.

As yet the hour of my final struggle has not come to me—or does it come to me perhaps just now? Truly, sea and life gaze around me gaze at me with insidious beauty:

O afternoon of my life! O happiness before evening! O haven on high seas! O peace in uncertainty! How I mistrust you all!

Truly, I am mistrustful of your insidious beauty! I am like the lover who mistrusts the all-too-velvety smile.

As he thrusts the most beloved before him, tender even in his hardness, the jealous one—, thus I thrust this blissful hour before me.

Away with you, you blissful hour! With you there came to me an involuntary bliss! I stand here ready for my deepest pain:—you came at the wrong time!

Away with you, you blissful hour! Rather seek shelter there—with my children! Hurry! and bless them before evening with *my* happiness!

There evening already approaches: the sun sinks. Away—my happiness!—

Thus spoke Zarathustra. And he waited for his misfortune the whole night: but he waited in vain. The night remained clear and calm and happiness itself came closer and closer to him. But towards morning Zarathustra laughed in his heart and said mockingly: "Happiness runs after me. That is because I do not run after women. But happiness is a woman."

Before Sunrise

O HEAVEN ABOVE ME, you pure one! Deep one! You abyss of light! Gazing on you I tremble with godlike desires.

To cast myself into your height—that is *my* depth! To hide myself in your purity—that is *my* innocence!

The god is veiled by his beauty: thus you hide your stars. You do not speak: *thus* you proclaim your wisdom to me.

Mute over the raging sea you have risen for me today; your love and your modesty make a revelation to my raging soul.

That you came to me beautiful, veiled in your beauty, that you spoke to me mutely, manifest in your wisdom:

Oh, how could I fail to divine all the modesty of your soul! *Before* the sun you came to me—the loneliest.

We have been friends from the beginning: we have grief and dread and ground in common; even the sun is common to us.

We do not speak to each other, because we know too much—: we are silent together, we smile our knowledge to each other.

Are you not the light of my fire? Do you not have the sister soul to my insight?

Together we learned everything; together we learned to ascend beyond ourselves to ourselves and to smile cloudlessly:—

—to smile down cloudlessly out of luminous eyes and out of miles of distance, when constraint and purpose and guilt steam beneath us like rain.

And I wandered alone: for *what* did my soul hunger by night and in labyrinthine paths? And I climbed mountains: *whom* did I ever seek upon mountains, if not you?

And all my wandering and mountain climbing: it was merely sheer necessity and a help in my helplessness—my whole will wants only to *fly*, to fly into *you!*

And what have I hated more than passing clouds and whatever defiles you? And I have even hated my own hatred because it defiled you!

I detest the passing clouds, those stealthy cats of prey: they take from you and me what we have in common—the uncanny boundless Yes- and Amen-saying.

We detest these mediators and mixers, the passing clouds: those half-and-half ones, that have learned neither to bless nor to curse from the heart.

I would rather sit in a tub under closed heavens, rather sit in the abyss without a heaven, than see you, luminous heaven, defiled with passing clouds!

And often I have longed to pin them fast with the jagged golden wires of lightning, that I might, like the thunder, drum upon their hollow bellies:—

—an angry drummer, because they rob me of your Yes and Amen!—You heaven above me, you purer! More luminous! You abyss of light!—because they rob you of *my* Yes! and Amen!

For I would rather have noise and thunder and storm curses, than this deliberate doubting cat's repose; and also among men I hate most of all the soft-treaders and half-and-half ones and the doubting, hesitating passing clouds.

And "he who cannot bless shall *learn* to curse!"—this clear teaching fell to me from the clear heaven; this star stands in my heaven even in dark nights.

I, however, am a blesser and a Yes-sayer, if only you are around me, you pure one! Light! You abyss of light!—then into all abysses I carry my beneficent Yes-saying.

I have become a blesser and a Yes-sayer: and therefore I fought long and was a fighter, that I might one day have my hands free for blessing.

This, however, is my blessing: to stand above everything as its own heaven, its round roof, its azure bell and eternal security: and blessed is he who blesses thus!

For all things are baptized at the well of eternity and beyond good and evil; but good and evil themselves are only fugitive shadows and damp afflictions and passing clouds.

Truly, it is a blessing and not a blasphemy when I teach: "Above all things stands the heaven of chance, the heaven of innocence, the heaven of accident, the heaven of mischievousness."[6]

"By Chance"[7]—that is the oldest nobility in the world, I gave that back to all things, I emancipated them from bondage under purpose.

I set this freedom and heavenly cheerfulness like an azure bell above all things, when I taught that over them and through them no "eternal will"—wills.

I set this mischievousness and folly in place of that will, when I taught: "In everything one thing is impossible—rationality!"

A *little* reason, to be sure, a seed of wisdom scattered from star to star—this leaven is mixed in all things: for the sake of folly, wisdom is mixed in all things!

A little wisdom is indeed possible; but I have found this blessed certainty in all things: that on the feet of chance they prefer—*to dance.*

O heaven above me, you pure one! High! This is now your purity to me, that there is no eternal reason-spider and -spiderweb:—

—that to me you are a dance floor for divine chances, that to me you are a god's table for divine dice and dice players!—

But you blush? Did I speak the unspeakable? Did I blaspheme, when I meant to bless you?

Or is it the shame of being two that makes you blush!—Are you telling me to go and be silent, because now—*day* comes?

The world is deep—: and deeper than day had ever been aware. Not everything may be uttered in the presence of day. But the day is coming: so let us part!

O heaven above me, you modest one! Glowing one! O you, my happiness before sunrise! The day is coming: so let us part!—

Thus spoke Zarathustra.

On the Virtue that Makes Small

1

When Zarathustra was on firm land again he did not go straightway to his mountains and his cave, but made many wanderings and questionings and found out this and that, so that he said jokingly of himself: "Behold a river that flows back to its source in many windings!" For he wanted to learn what had happened *to men* while he had been away: whether they had become greater or smaller. And once he saw a row of new houses, and he marveled and said:

What do these houses mean? Truly, no great soul put them up as its likeness!

Perhaps a silly child took them out of its toy box? If only another child would put them back into the box!

And these rooms and chambers—can *men* go out and in there? They seem to be made for silk dolls; or for dainty nibblers who perhaps let others nibble with them.

And Zarathustra stood still and reflected. At last he said sorrowfully: "*Everything* has become smaller!

"Everywhere I see lower doorways: those of *my* kind probably still go through, but—he must stoop!

Oh, when shall I arrive again at my home, where I shall no longer have to stoop—shall no longer have to stoop *before the small ones!*"— And Zarathustra sighed and gazed into the distance.—

But the very same day he gave his speech on the virtue that makes small.

2

I pass through this people and keep my eyes open: they do not forgive me for not envying their virtues.

They bite at me, because I say to them that for small people, small virtues are necessary—and because it is hard for me to understand that small people are *necessary*!

Here I am still like a cock in a strange farmyard, at which even the hens peck: but I am not unfriendly to these hens on that account.

I am courteous towards them, as towards all small annoyances; to be prickly towards what is small seems to me the wisdom of hedgehogs.

They all speak of me when they sit around their fire in the evening— they speak of me, but no one thinks—of me!

This is the new stillness I have learned: their noise about me spreads a cloak over my thoughts.

They shout to one another: "What is this dark cloud about to do to us? Let us see that it does not bring a plague upon us!"

And recently a woman pulled back her child that was approaching me: "Take the children away," she cried, "such eyes scorch children's souls."

They cough when I speak: they think that coughing is an objection to strong winds—they know nothing of the roaring of my happiness!

"We have no time yet for Zarathustra"—so they object; but what matters a time that "has no time" for Zarathustra?

And if they praise me, how could I go to sleep on *their* praise? To me their praise is a belt of thorns: it scratches me even when I take it off.

And I also learned this among them: the praiser acts as if he gave back, but in truth he wants to be given more!

Ask my foot if it likes their way of lauding and luring! Truly, to such a measure and tick-tock beat it likes neither to dance nor stand still.

They would like to lure and praise me to a small virtue; they would like to persuade my foot to the tick-tock of a small happiness.

I pass through this people and keep my eyes open: they have become *smaller* and are becoming smaller—*but that is due to their doctrine of happiness and virtue.*

For they are modest even in virtue—because they want comfort. But only a modest virtue is compatible with comfort.

To be sure, they also learn in their way to stride on and stride forward: I call that their *limping*—. Thus they become a hindrance to all who are in a hurry.

And many of them go forward and at the same time look backward with stiff necks: I like running into these.

Foot and eye should not lie nor give the lie to each other. But there is much lying among small people.

Some of them *will*, but most of them are only *willed*. Some of them are genuine, but most of them are bad actors.

There are unconscious actors among them and involuntary actors—the genuine are always rare, especially genuine actors.

There is little of man here: therefore their women make themselves manly. For only he who is man enough will—*redeem the woman* in woman.

And I found this hypocrisy the worst among them: that even those who command feign the virtues of those who serve.

"I serve, you serve, we serve"—so prays here even the hypocrisy of the rulers—and ah, if the first lord is *only* the first servant!

Ah, into their hypocrisies too my eyes' curiosity flew astray; and well did I divine all their fly-happiness and their buzzing around sunny windowpanes.

I see as much weakness as kindness. As much weakness as justice and pity.

They are frank, honest, and kind to one another, as grains of sand are frank, honest, and kind to grains of sand.

To embrace a small happiness modestly—they call that "resignation"! And at the same time they look out for a new little happiness.

In their hearts they want one thing most of all: that no one hurt them. Thus they anticipate every one's wishes and do well to every one.

That, however, is *cowardice*: though it be called "virtue."—

And when they happen to speak harshly, these little people, *I* hear in it only their hoarseness—in fact every draft makes them hoarse.

They are clever, their virtues have clever fingers. But they lack fists, their fingers do not know how to close into fists.

Virtue for them is what makes modest and tame: with it they have made the wolf a dog and man himself man's best domestic animal.

"We set our chair in the *middle*"—so says their smirking to me—"and as far from dying warriors as from contented swine."

That, however, is—*mediocrity*: though it be called moderation.—

3

I pass through this people and let fall many words: but they know neither how to take nor how to keep them.

They are surprised that I did not come to revile their lusts and vices; and truly, I have not come to warn against pickpockets either!

They wonder why I am not ready to improve and sharpen their cleverness: as if they had not yet enough smartasses, whose voices grate on my ear like slate pencils!

And when I cry: "Curse all the cowardly devils in you, that would like to whimper and fold the hands and pray"—then they cry: "Zarathustra is godless."

And especially their teachers of resignation cry this;—but precisely in their ears I love to shout: "Yes! I *am* Zarathustra the godless!"

Those teachers of resignation! Wherever there is anything small and sick and scabby, there they creep like lice; and only my disgust prevents me from squashing them.

Well! This is my sermon for *their* ears: I am Zarathustra the godless, who says: "Who is more godless than I, that I may delight in his instruction?"

I am Zarathustra the godless: where shall I find my equal? And all those are my equals who give themselves their own will and renounce all resignation.

I am Zarathustra the godless! I cook every chance in *my* pot. And only when it is cooked through do I welcome it as *my* food.

And truly, many a chance came imperiously to me: but my *will* spoke still more imperiously to it, then it went down imploringly on its knees—

—imploring that it might find home and heart with me, and saying flatteringly: "See, O Zarathustra, how friend comes only to friend!"—

But why do I speak when no one has *my* ears! And so I will shout it out to all the winds:

You become ever smaller, you small people! You crumble away, you comfortable ones! You will yet perish—

—by your many small virtues, by your many small omissions, and by your many small resignations!

Too tender, too yielding: so is your soil! But for a tree to become *great*, it seeks to twine hard roots around hard rocks!

Also what you omit weaves at the web of mankind's future; even your nothing is a spider's web and a spider that lives on the blood of the future.

And when you take, it is like stealing, you small virtuous ones; but even among rogues, *honor* says: "One should steal only when one cannot rob."

"It is given"—that is also a doctrine of resignation. But I say to you, you comfortable ones: *it is taken* and will ever take more and more from you!

Ah, that you would renounce all *half* willing, and would decide to be idle like you decide to act!

Ah, that you understood my word: "Always do what you will— but first be such as *can will*!

"For all that love your neighbor as yourselves—but first be such as *love themselves*—

"—such as love with a great love, such as love with a great contempt!" Thus speaks Zarathustra the godless.—

But why do I speak when no one has *my* ears! It is still an hour too early for me here.

I am my own forerunner among this people, my own cockcrow in dark lanes.

But *their* hour comes! And mine comes too! Hourly they become smaller, poorer, more barren—poor herbs! poor soil!

And *soon* they shall stand before me like dry grass and prairie, and truly, weary of themselves and panting even more than for water—for *fire*!

O blessed hour of the lightning! O mystery before noon!—One day I shall turn them into running fires and heralds with flaming tongues:—

—one day they shall proclaim with flaming tongues: It is coming, it is near, *the great noon*!

Thus spoke Zarathustra.

On the Mount of Olives[8]

WINTER, A BAD GUEST, sits with me at home; my hands are blue from his friendly handshake.

I honor him, this bad guest, but I like to let him sit alone. I like to run away from him; and if one runs *well*, then one escapes him!

With warm feet and warm thoughts I run where the wind is calm, to the sunny corner of my mount of olives.

There I laugh at my stern guest and am still fond of him, for he drives the flies from my house and stills many little noises.

For he will not permit even a mosquito to buzz, far less two of them; and he makes the lanes lonely, so that the moonlight is afraid there at night.

He is a hard guest, but I honor him, and I do not pray, like the pampered, to the potbellied fire-idol.

Better even a little chattering of teeth than idol-worship!—so wills my nature. And I especially have a grudge against all fire idols in heat, steaming and musky.

Whom I love I love better in winter than in summer; now I mock my enemies better and more heartily since winter sits in my house.

Heartily, truly, even when I *crawl* into bed—: even there my hidden happiness laughs and plays pranks; even my deceptive dream laughs.

I, a—crawler? Never in my life have I crawled before the powerful; and if I ever lied, I lied out of love. Therefore I am glad even in my winter bed.

A simple bed warms me more than a rich one, for I am jealous of my poverty. And in winter it is most faithful to me.

I begin each day with a wickedness, I mock winter with a cold bath: my stern roommate grumbles at that.

I also like to tickle him with a wax candle: so that he may finally let the sky emerge from an ashen gray twilight.

For I am especially wicked in the morning: at the early hour when the pail rattles at the well and horses neigh warmly in grey lanes:—

Then I wait impatiently for the bright sky to dawn for me at last, the snow-bearded winter sky, the old man with his white hair,—

—the winter sky, the silent one, that often even stifles its sun!

Did I perhaps learn from him the long bright silence? Or did he learn it from me? Or has each of us devised it himself?

The origin of all good things is a thousandfold—all good playful things spring for joy into existence: how should they do so— once only!

Long silence is also a good playful thing, and to gaze like the winter sky from a bright, round eyed face:—

—like it, to stifle one's sun and one's inflexible solar will: truly, I have learned *well* this art and this winter playfulness!

It is my favorite sarcasm and art that my silence has learned not to betray itself by silence.

Clattering with discourse and dice, I outwit the solemn attendants: my will and my purpose shall elude all those stern inspectors.

That no one might see down into my profundity and my ultimate will—for that I devised my long bright silence.

So many clever I have found: they veiled their faces and muddied their waters so that no one might see through and under them.

But precisely to them came the cleverer distrusters and nutcrackers: precisely their most hidden fish were fished out!

But the bright, the forthright, the transparent—these seem to me the cleverest silent ones: in them the depth is so *profound* that even the clearest water does not—betray it.—

You snowbearded silent winter sky, you round eyed white haired above me! Oh you heavenly likeness of my soul and its pranks!

And *must* I not hide myself, like one who has swallowed gold, so that they shall not slit open my soul?

Must I not walk on stilts that they *overlook* my long legs—all those enviers and injurers around me?

These smoky, lukewarm, bedraggled, moldy, fretful souls—how *could* their envy endure my happiness!

Thus I show them only the ice and winter of my peaks—and *not* that my mountain still winds all the sunny belts around it!

They hear only the whistling of my winter storms: and do *not* know that I also travel over warm seas, like longing, heavy, hot southern winds.

They even pity my accidents and chances:—but *my* word says: "Let chance come to me: it is innocent as a little child!"

How *could* they endure my happiness, if I did not put accidents and winter distress and polar bear caps and mantles of snow clouds around my happiness!

—if I myself did not pity their *pity*: the pity of those enviers and injurers!

—if I myself did not sigh before them and chatter with cold, and patiently *let* myself be wrapped in their pity!

This is the wise playfulness and benevolence of my soul, that it *does not conceal* its winters and glacial storms; it does not conceal its chilblains either.

To one person loneliness is the flight of the sick; to another it is the flight *from* the sick.

Let them *hear* me chattering and sighing with winter cold, all those poor squinting rascals around me! With such sighing and chattering I still escape their heated rooms.

Let them sympathize with me and sigh with me on account of my chilblains: "He will yet *freeze to death* on the ice of knowledge!"—so they complain.

Meanwhile I run with warm feet here and there on my mount of olives: I sing in the sunny corner of my mount of olives and mock all pity.—

Thus sang Zarathustra.

On Passing By

THUS SLOWLY WANDERING THROUGH many peoples and diverse cities, Zarathustra returned by roundabout roads to his mountain and his cave. And behold, on his way he came unawares to the gate of the *great city*: but here a frothing fool with outstretched hands sprang at him and blocked his way. It was the same fool whom the people called "Zarathustra's ape": for he had gathered something of phrasing and cadence and perhaps also liked to borrow from his store of wisdom. But the fool spoke thus to Zarathustra:

O Zarathustra, here is the great city: here you have nothing to seek and everything to lose.

Why would you wade through this mire? Have pity on your feet! Rather spit on the gate of the city, and—turn back!

Here is the hell for hermits' thoughts: here great thoughts are boiled alive and reduced.

Here all great sentiments decay: only the smallest rattleboned feelings rattle here!

Don't you already smell the slaughterhouses and cookshops of the spirit? Does not this city steam with the fumes of slaughtered spirit?

Don't you see the souls hanging like limp dirty rags?—And they also make newspapers out of these rags!

Don't you hear how spirit has here become a play on words? It vomits out loathsome verbal swill!—And they make newspapers out of this verbal swill too.

They hound one another and don't know where! They inflame one another and don't know why! They rattle with their tins, they jingle with their gold.

They are cold and seek warmth from distilled waters; they are inflamed and seek coolness from frozen spirits; they are all sick and diseased with public opinion.

All lusts and vices are at home here; but the virtuous are here too, there are there is much serviceable serving virtue:—

Much serviceable virtue with scribbling fingers and behinds hardened to sitting and waiting, blessed with little chest decorations and padded, rumpless daughters.

There is also much piety here and much devout lick-spittleing and fawning before the God of Hosts.

Down "from on high" trickles the star and the gracious spittle; every starless chest longs for what comes from above.

The moon has her court, and the court has its mooncalves: to everything, however, that comes from the court, the serviceable mob and all serviceable beggar virtues pray.

"I serve, you serve, we serve"—thus all serviceable virtue prays to the prince: that the deserved star may at last be pinned on the narrow chest!

But the moon still revolves around all that is earthly: so too the prince revolves around what is earthliest of all—that, however, is the gold of the shopkeeper.

The God of the Hosts of is not the god of gold bars; the prince proposes, but the shopkeeper—disposes!

By all that is luminous and strong and good in you, O Zarathustra! Spit on this city of shopkeepers and turn back!

Here all blood flows putrid and tepid and frothy through all veins: spit on the great city that is the great trash heap where all the scum froths together!

Spit on the city of compressed souls and narrow chests, of slit eyes and sticky fingers—

—on the city of the importunate, the shameless, the scribble- and scream-throats, the overheated ambitious ones:—

—where everything infirm, infamous, lustful, gloomy, insipid, ulcerous, and conspiratorial festers together:—

—spit on the great city and turn back!—

But here Zarathustra interrupted the foaming fool and put his hand over his mouth.—

Stop at last! shouted Zarathustra, your speech and your kind have long disgusted me!

Why did you live so long by the swamp that you yourself had to become a frog and a toad?

Does not a tainted, frothy swamp-blood now flow in your own veins, when you have thus learned to croak and revile?

Why did you not go into the forest? Or till the earth? Is the sea not full of green islands?

I despise your contempt; and since you warned me—why did you not warn yourself?

Out of love alone shall my contempt and my warning bird take wing: but not out of the swamp!—

They call you my ape, you foaming fool: but I call you my grunting pig—by your grunting you are spoiling even my praise of folly.

What was it that first made you grunt? Because no one sufficiently *flattered* you:—therefore you sat yourself beside this filth, so that you might have cause for much grunting,—

—that you might have cause for much *revenge*! For revenge, you vain fool, is all your foaming; I have divined you well!

But your fools' words injure *me*, even when you are right! And even if Zarathustra's words *were* a hundred times justified: *you* would always—*do* wrong with my words!

Thus spoke Zarathustra; and he looked on the great city, sighed and was long silent. At last he spoke thus:

I am disgusted by this great city, too, and not only this fool. Here as there, there is nothing to better, nothing to worsen.

Woe to this great city!—And I wish that I already saw the pillar of fire in which it will be consumed!

For such pillars of fire must precede the great noon. But this has its time and its own fate.—

This precept, however, I give to you in parting, you fool: Where one can no longer love, there should one—*pass by!*—

Thus spoke Zarathustra and passed by the fool and the great city.

On Apostates

1

Ah, everything that lately stood green and many-hued on this meadow already lies faded and grey! And how much honey of hope have I carried away into my beehives!

All those young hearts have already become old—and not even old! only weary, ordinary, comfortable:—they put it: "We have become pious again."

Lately I saw them run forth in early morning with brave steps: but the feet of their knowledge grew weary and now they slander even the courage they had in the morning!

Truly, many of them once lifted their legs like the dancer, the laughter of my wisdom beckoned to them:—then they thought better of it. Just now I saw them bent—to creep to the cross.

Once they fluttered around light and freedom like gnats and young poets. A little older, a little colder: and already are they mystifiers and mumblers and homebodies.

Perhaps their hearts despaired because solitude swallowed me like a whale? Perhaps their ears longingly listened *in vain* for me and for my trumpet and herald calls?

—Ah, there are ever only a few whose hearts have a long courage and playfulness; and in these the spirit also stays patient. But the rest are *cowards*.

The rest: these are always the great majority, the commonplace, the superfluous, the many-too-many—those are all cowards!—

He who is of my type will also meet the experiences of my type on the way: so that his first companions must be corpses and jesters.

His second companions, however—they will call themselves his *believers*: a living swarm, with much love, much folly, much adolescent veneration.

He among men who is of my type shall not bind his heart to those believers; he who knows the fickle, fainthearted nature of mankind will not believe in those springtimes and many colored meadows!

If they *could* do otherwise, then they would also *will* otherwise. The half-and-half spoil every whole. That leaves will wither—what is there to wail about!

Let them fly and fall, O Zarathustra, and do not wail! Rather blow among them with rustling winds—

—blow among those leaves, O Zarathustra: so that all that is *withered* may run from you even faster!—

2

"We have become pious again"—so these apostates confess; and some of them are even too cowardly to confess it.

I look into their eyes,—then I tell it to their face and to the blush on their cheeks: You are such as *pray* again!

But it is disgrace to pray! Not for everyone, but for you and me and for whoever has his conscience in his head. For *you* it is a disgrace to pray!

You know it well: the cowardly devil in you who would like to clasp his hands and to fold his arms and to take it easier:—it was this cowardly devil who persuaded you: "There *is* a God!"

Through that, however, you have become one of those who dread the light, whom light never lets rest: now you must daily thrust your head deeper into night and fog!

And truly, you have chosen well the hour: for just now the nocturnal birds are flying again. The hour has come for all people who dread the light, the evening hour of rest, when they do not—"find rest."

I hear it and smell it: their hour for hunt and procession has arrived, not indeed for a wild hunt, but for a tame, lame, snuffling, pussyfooting, prayer-muttering hunt,—

—for a hunt after soulful sneaks: all mousetraps for the heart have again been set! And whenever I lift a curtain a little night moth rushes out.

Did it perhaps squat there along with another little night moth? For everywhere I smell little concealed communities; and wherever there are closets there are new devotees in them and the atmosphere of devotees.

They sit for long evenings beside one another, and say: "Let us again become like little children and say, 'dear God!'"—their mouths and stomachs upset by the pious confectioners.

Or they look for long evenings at a crafty, lurking cross-marked spider, that preaches prudence to the spiders themselves and teaches: "There is good spinning under crosses!"

Or they sit all day at swamps with fishing rods and on that account think themselves *profound*; but whoever fishes where there are no fish, I would not even call superficial!

Or they learn to play the harp in pious pleasure with a composer of songs who would like to harp himself into the hearts of young women—for he has tired of old women and their praises.

Or they learn to shudder with a scholarly half-madman who waits in darkened rooms for spirits to come to him—and the spirit has entirely departed!

Or they listen to an old, roving, whistling tramp who has learned the sadness of sounds from sad winds; now he whistles like the wind and preaches sadness in sad sounds.

And some of them have even become night watchmen: now they know how to blow horns and go about at night and awaken old things that had long fallen asleep.

Five sayings about old things I heard last night at the garden wall: they came from such old, sorrowful, desiccated night watchmen.

"For a father he does not care enough for his children: human fathers do it better!"—

"He is too old! He no longer cares for his children at all,"—answered the other night watchman.

"*Has* he any children? No one can prove it unless he himself proves it! I have long wished he would for once prove it thoroughly."

"Prove? As if *he* had ever proved anything! Proving is difficult to him; he lays great stress on one's *believing* him."

"Yes! Yes! Belief makes him blessed, belief in him.[9] Old people are like that! It's the same with us too!"—

—Thus the two old night-watchmen and light-scarecrows spoke together and then tooted sorrowfully on their horns: so it happened last night at the garden wall.

But my heart writhed with laughter as if it would break and knew not, where? and sank into my midriff.

Truly, it will be the death of me yet, to choke with laughter when I see drunken asses and hear night watchmen thus doubt God.

Has the time not *long* since passed for all such doubts? Who may still awaken such old slumbering light-shunning things!

With the old gods it has long since come to an end:—and truly, they had a fine gay godlike end!

They did not die in "twilight"—as some lie![10] Instead: one day they—*laughed* themselves to death!

That happened when the ungodliest word came from a god himself—the word: "There is one God! You shall have no other gods before me!"—

—an old grimbeard of a god, a jealous one, thus forgot himself:—

And all the gods laughed then and rocked on their chairs and cried: "Is it not precisely this godlike, that there are gods, but no God?"

Who has ears, let him hear.—

Thus Zarathustra discoursed in the town which he loved and which is called "The Motley Cow." For from here he had only two days to go to reach his cave again and his animals; but his soul rejoiced continually at the nearness of his return home.

The Return Home

O solitude! You my *home* solitude! Too long have I lived wildly in wild strange lands not to return home to you in tears!

Now shake your finger at me as mothers do, now smile at me as mothers smile, now say only: "And who was that, who like a storm wind once stormed away from me?—

"—who departing cried: 'I have sat with solitude too long, I have unlearned how to be silent!' *That*—you have surely learned now?

"O Zarathustra, I know everything, and that you were *more forsaken* among the many, you solitary one, than you ever were with me!

"To be forsaken is one thing, to be lonely another: *that*—you have learned now! And that among men you will always be wild and strange:

"—Wild and strange even when they love you: for above all they want to be *indulged*!

"But here you are at your own hearth and home; here you can say everything and pour out all reasons, nothing here is ashamed of hidden, hardened feelings.

"Here all things come caressingly to your discourse and flatter you: for they want to ride upon your back. On every image you here ride to every truth.

"Here you may speak to all things fairly and frankly: and truly, it sounds like praise in their ears for one to speak to all things—directly!

"But to be forsaken is another matter. For, do you remember, O Zarathustra? When once your bird screamed overhead, when you stood in the forest, irresolute? unsure where to go, beside a corpse:—

"—when you spoke: 'let my animals lead me! I found it more dangerous among men than among animals:'—*That* was forsakenness!

"And do you remember, O Zarathustra? When you sat on your island, a well of wine among empty buckets, giving and distributing, bestowing and pouring out among the thirsty:

"—until at last you sat alone thirsty among the drunk and wailed each night: 'Is it not more blessed to receive than to give? And more blessed to steal than to receive?'—*That* was forsakenness!

"And do you remember, O Zarathustra? When your stillest hour came and drove you away from yourself, when it said in an evil whisper: 'Speak and break!'—

"—when it made you repent all your waiting and silence and discouraged your humble courage: *That* was forsakenness!"—

O solitude! You my home solitude! How blissfully and tenderly your voice speaks to me!

We do not question each other, we do not complain to each other, we go openly together through open doors.

For all is open with you and clear; and here even the hours run on lighter feet. For in the dark time weighs heavier on one than in the light.

Here the words and word-shrines of all being spring open to me: here all being wants to become words, here all becoming wants to learn to speak from me.

But down there—all speech is in vain! There, forgetting and passing-by are the best wisdom: *that* I have learned now!

He who would grasp all human things must handle everything. But for that my hands are too clean.

I even dislike to inhale their breath; ah! that I have lived so long among their noise and bad breath!

O blissful stillness around me! O pure odors around me! O how this stillness draws deep breaths of pure air! O how it listens, this blissful stillness!

But down there—there everything speaks, there everything is unheard. One may ring in one's wisdom with bells: the shopkeepers in the market place will outjingle it with pennies!

Everything among them talks, no one knows any longer how to understand. Everything falls into the water, nothing falls any longer into deep wells.

Everything among them talks, nothing succeeds any longer and comes to an end. Everything cackles, but who will still sit quietly on the nest and hatch eggs?

Everything among them talks, everything is talked out. And that which yesterday was still too hard for time itself and its teeth, today hangs gnawed and scraped from the mouths of today's men.

Everything among them talks, everything is betrayed. And what was once called the secret and secrecy of profound souls, belongs today to the street trumpeters and other butterflies.

O human being, you strange thing! You noise in dark streets! Now again you are behind me:—my greatest danger lies behind me!

My greatest danger always lay in indulgence and pity; and all human being wants to be indulged and pitied.

With concealed truths, with a fool's hand and a fond foolish heart and rich in pity's little lies—thus I always lived among men.

Disguised I sat among them, ready to misunderstand *myself* that I might endure *them*, and gladly saying to myself: "You fool, you do not know men!"

One forgets about men when one lives among them: there is too much foreground in all men—what can far-seeing, far-seeking eyes do *there*!

And when they misunderstood me, I, fool that I am, indulged them more than I did myself: for I was used to being hard on myself and often even taking revenge on myself for the indulgence.

Bitten all over by poisonous flies and hollowed like a stone by many drops of malice: thus I sat among them and still told myself: "Everything small is innocent of its smallness!"

Especially those who call themselves "the good" I found to be the most poisonous flies: they bite in all innocence, they lie in all innocence; how *could* they—be just towards me!

Pity teaches him who lives among the good to lie. Pity makes stifling air for all free souls. For the stupidity of the good is unfathomable.

To conceal myself and my riches—*that* I learned down there: for I found everybody still poor in spirit. It was the lie of my pity that I knew in every one,

—that I saw and sniffed out in every one what was *enough* spirit for him and what was *too much* spirit for him!

Their stiff sages: I called them sagacious, not stiff—thus I learned to slur words. Their gravediggers: I called them researchers and scholars—thus I learned to confound words.

Gravediggers dig diseases for themselves. Bad vapors lie under old rubbish. One should not stir up the bog. One should live on mountains.

With blessed nostrils I breathe again the freedom of mountains. At last my nose is freed from the smell of all human being!

Tickled by the sharp air as with sparkling wine, my soul *sneezes*—sneezes and jubilates to itself: "*Gesundheit!*"

Thus spoke Zarathustra.

ON THE THREE EVILS

1

In a dream, in my last morning dream, I stood today in the foothills—beyond the world, I held a pair of scales and *weighed* the world.

Oh that the dawn came too early to me: she glowed me awake, the jealous one! She is always jealous of the glow of my morning dreams.

Measurable by him who has time, weighable by a good weigher, attainable by strong wings, divinable by divine nutcrackers: thus did my dream find the world:—

My dream, a bold sailor, half-ship half-hurricane, silent as a butterfly, impatient as a falcon: how did it have the patience and time today to weigh the world!

Did my wisdom perhaps speak secretly to it, my laughing, wakeful day-wisdom, which mocks at all "infinite worlds"? For it says: "Wherever there is force, *number* becomes master: it has more force."

How confidently did my dream contemplate this finite world, not inquisitively, not acquisitively, not timidly, not entreatingly:—

—as if a full apple presented itself to my hand, a ripe golden apple, with a soft, cool, velvety skin:—thus the world presented itself to me:—

—as if a tree nodded to me, a wide-branching, strong-willed tree, bent for reclining and a footstool for weary travelers: thus the world stood on my foothills:—

—as if delicate hands carried a casket towards me—a casket open for the delectation of modest, adoring eyes: thus the world presented itself before me today:—

—not riddle enough to frighten away human love, not solution enough to put to sleep human wisdom:—a humanly good thing the world was to me today, of which so many evil things are said!

How I thank my morning dream that I thus weighed the world this morning! As a humanly good thing it came to me, this dream and comforter of the heart!

And that I may do the same as it by day and learn and copy its best, now I will put the three most evil things on the scales and weigh them humanly well.—

He who taught how to bless also taught how to curse: what are the three most cursed things in the world? I will put these on the scales.

Sex, the lust to rule, selfishness: these three things have so far been most cursed and held in worst and falsest repute—these three things I will weigh humanly well.

Well then! Here are my foothills and there is the sea—*it* rolls here to me, shaggy, fawning, the faithful old hundred-headed canine monster that I love!—

Well then! Here I will hold the scales over the weltering sea: and I also choose a witness to look on—you, hermit tree, you fragrant, broad arched tree that I love!—

On what bridge does the present pass to the future? What compulsion compels the high stoop to the low? And what bids even the highest—to grow still higher?—

Now the scales stand level and still: I have thrown in three weighty questions, three weighty answers balance the other scale.

2

Sex: a sting and stake to all hair-shirted despisers of the body and cursed as "the world" by all afterworldly: for it mocks and makes fools of all teachers of confusion and error.

Sex: to the rabble the slow fire on which it is burnt; to all wormy wood, to all stinking rags, the ever-ready rut and oven.

Sex: for free hearts, innocent and free, the garden happiness of the earth, an overflowing of thanks to the present from all the future.

Sex: a sweet poison only to the withered, but to the lion-willed the great cordial and the reverently reserved wine of wines.

Sex: the great symbolic happiness of a higher happiness and highest hope. For marriage is promised to many, and more than marriage,—

—to many that are stranger to one another than man and woman:—and who has fully understood *how strange* man and woman are to one another!

Sex:—but I will have hedges around my thoughts, and even around my words, lest swine and swooners should break into my gardens!—

The lust to rule: the fiery scourge of the hardest of the hard-hearted; the cruel torture reserved by the cruelest for themselves; the dark flame of living pyres.

The lust to rule: the wicked gadfly mounted on the vainest peoples; the mocker of all uncertain virtues; which rides on every horse and every pride.

The lust to rule: the earthquake which breaks and breaks open all that is rotten and hollow; the rolling, rumbling, punitive demolisher of whited sepulchers; the flashing question mark beside premature answers.

The lust to rule: before whose glance man creeps and crouches and drudges and becomes lower than the snake and the swine—until at last the great contempt cries out of him—,

The lust to rule: the terrible teacher of the great contempt, which preaches in the face of cities and empires "away with you!"—until at last they themselves cry out "away with *me!*"

The lust to rule: which, however, rises alluringly even to the pure and solitary and up to self-sufficient elevations, glowing like a love that paints purple delights enticingly on earthly heavens.

The lust to rule: but who would call it *lust*, when the height longs to stoop for power! Truly, there is nothing sick or diseased in such longing and descending!

That the lonesome height may not for ever remain lonesome and self-sufficient; that the mountains may come to the valleys and the winds of the heights to the plains:—

Oh who could find the right baptismal and virtuous name for such longing! "Gift-giving virtue"—thus did Zarathustra once name the unnamable.

And then it happened too,—and truly, it happened for the first time!—that his word blessed *selfishness*, the wholesome, healthy self-ishness, that springs from the powerful soul:—

—from the powerful soul, to which pertains the exalted body, the handsome, triumphant, refreshing body, around which everything becomes a mirror:

—the supple, persuasive body, the dancer, whose symbol and epitome is the self-rejoicing soul. The self-rejoicing of such bodies and souls calls itself: "Virtue."

Such self-rejoicing protects itself with its words of good and bad as with sacred groves; with the names of its happiness it banishes everything contemptible from itself.

Away from itself it banishes everything cowardly; it says: "Bad—*that is* cowardly!" He who is always fretting, sighing, complaining, and who gleans even the slightest advantage seems contemptible to it.

It also despises all grievous wisdom: for truly, there is also wisdom that blooms in the dark, a nightshade wisdom, which always sighs: "all is vain!"

Shy distrust seems base to it, and every one who wants oaths instead of looks and hands: and all-too-mistrustful wisdom, for such is the mode of cowardly souls.

It regards as baser still the obsequious, doglike one, who immediately lies on his back, the submissive; and there is also wisdom that is submissive and doglike and pious and obsequious.

Altogether hateful to it and nauseating is he who will never defend himself, he who swallows down poisonous spittle and evil glances, the all-too-patient one, the all-suffering, all-satisfied one: for that is servile.

Whether they be servile before gods and divine kicks, or before men and the stupid opinions of men: it spits at *all* kinds of slaves, this blessed selfishness!

Bad: thus it calls all that is stooped and sordidly servile, constrained blinking eyes, oppressed hearts, and that false yielding manner that kisses with broad cowardly lips.

And sham wisdom: so it calls all wit that slaves and old men and the weary affect; and especially the whole wicked, nitwitted, witless foolishness of priests!

But the sham-wise, all the priests, the world-weary, and those whose souls are womanish and servile—oh how their game has all along cheated selfishness!

And precisely *that* was virtue and was called virtue—to cheat selfishness! And "selfless"—so all those world-weary cowards and cross-marked spiders wanted themselves, with good reason!

But for all those the day is now at hand, the change, the sword of judgment, *the great noon*: there much shall be revealed!

And he who proclaims the "I" wholesome and holy, and selfishness blessed, truly, he speaks also what he knows, a prophet: *"Behold, it comes, it is near, the great noon!"*

Thus spoke Zarathustra.

ON THE SPIRIT OF GRAVITY

1

My tongue—is of the people: I speak too crudely and heartily for silky rabbits. And my words sound still stranger to all ink-fish and pen-foxes.

My hand—is a fool's hand: woe to all tablets and walls and whatever has room for fool's scribbling, fool's scrawling!

My foot—is a horse's-foot; with it I trample and trot over stick and stone, in the fields up and down, and I am as happy as the devil in racing so fast.

My stomach—is surely an eagle's stomach? For it likes lamb's flesh best of all. But it is certainly a bird's stomach.

Nourished by a few innocent things, ready and impatient to fly, to fly away—that is my nature now: how could there not be something of the bird's nature in that!

And especially that I am enemy to the spirit of gravity, that is bird-nature: and truly, mortal enemy, archenemy, born enemy! Oh, where has my enmity not flown and strayed already!

I could sing a song about that—and *will* sing it: though I am alone in an empty house and must sing it to my own ears.

There are other singers, to be sure, whose voices are made soft, whose hands are made eloquent, whose eyes are made expressive, whose hearts are awakened, only by a full house—I am not like them.—

2

He who will one day teach men to fly will have shifted all boundary stones; the boundary stones themselves will fly into the air to him, and he will rebaptize the earth—as "the light."

The ostrich runs faster than the fastest horse, but even he buries his head heavily into the heavy earth: thus it is with the man who cannot yet fly.

He calls earth and life heavy, and so the spirit of gravity *wants* it! But he who would become light and a bird must love himself—thus *I* teach.

Not, to be sure, with the love of the sick and infected: with them even self-love stinks!

One must learn to love oneself—thus I teach—with a wholesome and healthy love: that one may endure to be with oneself and not to roam.

Such roaming calls itself "love of the neighbor": these words there have been so far the best for lying and dissembling, and especially by those who have been burdensome to every one.

And truly, to *learn* to love oneself is no commandment for today and tomorrow. Rather it is of all arts the finest, subtlest, last and most patient.

For all his possessions are well concealed from the possessor; and of all treasures, it is our own we dig up last—the spirit of gravity commands that.

Close upon the cradle are we presented with heavy words and values: this dowry calls itself "good" and "evil". For the sake of it we are forgiven for living.

And we suffer little children to come unto us, to forbid them in good time from loving themselves: thus the spirit of gravity commands it.

And we—we bear loyally what we have been given on hard shoulders over rugged mountains! And when we sweat we are told: "Yes, life is hard to bear!"

But only man is hard to bear! That is because he carries too much that is foreign on his shoulders. Like the camel he kneels down and lets himself be well laden.

Especially the strong, reverent spirit who would bear much: he loads too many *foreign* weighty words and values upon himself— now life seems like a desert to him!

And truly! Many a thing too that is *our own* is hard to bear! And much that is inside man is like the oyster, that is, repulsive and slippery and hard to grasp—

—so that a noble shell with noble adornment must plead for it. But one must learn this art too: to *have* a shell and a fair appearance and a shrewd blindness!

Again, it is deceiving about much in man that many a shell is poor and pitiable and too much of a shell. Much concealed goodness and power is never dreamt of; the most exquisite delicacies find no tasters!

Women know that, the most exquisite of them: a little fatter, a little thinner—oh, how much fate is in so little!

Man is difficult to discover, and most of all to himself; the spirit often lies about the soul. Thus the spirit of gravity commands it.

But he has discovered himself who says: That is *my* good and evil: with that he has silenced the mole and the dwarf who say: "Good for all, evil for all."

Truly, I do not like those who call everything good and this world the best. Those I call the all-satisfied.

All-satisfiedness, which knows how to taste everything,—that is not the best taste! I honor the refractory, fastidious tongues and stomachs, which have learned to say "I" and "Yes" and "No."

To chew and digest everything, however—that is to have a really swinish nature! Always to bray Yea-Yuh—that only the ass has learned, and those like it!—

Deep yellow and hot red: thus *my* taste wants it—it mixes blood with all colors. But he who whitewashes his house betrays to me a whitewashed soul.

Some fall in love with mummies, others with phantoms: both alike are enemies to all flesh and blood—oh, how repugnant are both to my taste! For I love blood.

And I do not want to stay and dwell where every one spits and spews: that is not *my* taste,—I would rather live among thieves and perjurers. Nobody has gold in his mouth.

Still more repugnant to me, however, are all lickspittles; and the most repugnant beast of a man that I found, I baptized parasite: it would not love, and yet wanted to live by love.

Wretched I call all who have only one choice: either to become evil beasts or evil tamers of beasts: among such men I would build no homes.

I also call wretched those who always have to *wait*,—they are repugnant to my taste: all tax collectors and shopkeepers and kings and other keepers of lands and shops.

Truly, I too learned to wait and profoundly so,—but only to wait for *myself*. And above all I learned to stand and to walk and to run and to leap and to climb and to dance.

But this is my teaching: he who wishes one day to fly, must first learn to stand and to walk and to run and to climb and to dance—one does not fly into flying!

With rope-ladders I learned to reach many a window, with nimble legs I climbed high masts: to sit on high masts of knowledge seemed to me no small happiness;—

—to flicker like small flames on high masts: a small light, certainly, but yet a great comfort to castaway sailors and the shipwrecked!

By diverse ways and windings I arrived at my truth: not by a single ladder did I mount to the height where my eye roves into my remoteness.

And it was only reluctantly that I ever asked the way—that has always offended my taste! Rather I questioned and tried the ways themselves.

A trying and a questioning has been all my traveling—and truly, one must also *learn* how to answer such questioning! But that—is my taste:

—not good, not bad, but *my* taste, of which I am no longer ashamed and which I have no more wish to hide.

"This—is now *my* way—where is yours?" thus I answered those who asked me "the way." For *the* way—that does not exist!

Thus spoke Zarathustra.

On Old and New Tablets

1

Here I sit and wait, old broken tablets around me and also new half-written tablets. When will my hour come?

—the hour of my descent, of my going under: for I want to go among men once more.

For that I am waiting now: for first the signs must come to me that *my* hour has arrived—namely the laughing lion with the flock of doves.

Meanwhile I talk to myself as one who has time. No one tells me anything new: so I tell myself to myself.

2

When I came to men, I found them resting on an old conceit: all of them thought they had long known what was good and evil for man.

All talk of virtue seemed an old and wearisome business to them; and he who wished to sleep well spoke of "good" and "evil" before retiring to rest.

I disturbed this sleepiness when I taught that *no one yet knows* what is good and evil—unless it be he who creates!

—But it is he who creates man's goal and gives the earth its meaning and its future: that anything at all is good and evil, *that* is his *creation*.

And I bade them overturn their old academic chairs and wherever that old conceit had sat; I bade them laugh at their great moralists and saints and poets and world-redeemers.

I bade them laugh at their gloomy sages and at whoever had at any time sat forebodingly on the tree of life like a black scarecrow.

I sat down by their great road of tombs among cadavers and vultures—and I laughed at all their past and its rotting, decaying glory.

Truly, like preachers of repentance and fools, I raised a hue and cry of wrath on all their greatness and smallness—that their best is so very small! That their worst is so very small!—thus I laughed.

My wise longing, born in the mountains, cried and laughed in me; a wild wisdom, truly!—my great broad-winged longing.

And often it carried me off and up and away and in the midst of laughter: then I flew quivering like an arrow with sun-drunken rapture:

—out into distant futures, which no dream has yet seen, into warmer Souths than artists ever dreamed: there where gods in their dancing are ashamed of all clothes:—

—that I may speak in parables and halt and stammer like the poets: and truly I am ashamed that I still have to be a poet!

Where all becoming seemed to me the dancing of gods and the playfulness of gods, and the world unloosed and unbridled and fleeing back to itself:—

—like many gods eternally fleeing and seeking one another, like many gods blessedly contradicting, communing, and belonging together again:—

Where all time seemed to me a happy mockery of moments, where necessity was freedom itself, which played happily with the goad of freedom:—

Where I also found again my old devil and archenemy, the spirit of gravity, and all that he created: constraint, law, necessity and consequence and purpose and will and good and evil:—

For must there not be that which is danced *over*, danced beyond? Must there not, for the sake of the nimble, the nimblest,—be moles and clumsy dwarfs?—

3

There it was too that I picked up the word "Übermensch" by the way, and that man is something that must be overcome,

—that man is a bridge and not a goal: rejoicing over his noon-tides and evenings, as advances to new dawns:

—Zarathustra's declaration of the great noon, and whatever else I have hung up over men like a purple afterglow of evening.

Truly, I also let them see new stars along with new nights; and over cloud and day and night I spread out laughter like a colored canopy.

I taught them all *my* poetry and aspiration: to compose and collect into one what is fragment in man and riddle and dreadful chance—

—as poet, reader of riddles, and redeemer of chance, I taught them to create the future, and to redeem by creating—all that *has been.*

To redeem what is past in man and to transform every "It was" until the will says: "But so I willed it! So shall I will it—"

—this I called redemption, this alone I taught them to call redemption.—

Now I await *my* redemption—that I may go to them for the last time.

For I want to go to men once more: I want to go under *among* them, in dying I will give them my richest gift!

I learned this from the sun when it goes down, the overrich: it then pours gold into the sea from inexhaustible riches,—

—so that even the poorest fisherman still rows with *golden* oars! For I saw this once, and did not tire of weeping to see it.—

Like the sun, Zarathustra too wants to go under: now he sits here and waits, old broken tablets around him and also new tablets—half-written.

4

Behold, here is a new tablet: but where are my brothers who will carry it with me to the valley and into hearts of flesh?—

Thus my great love of the farthest demands it: *do not spare your neighbor!* Man is something that must be overcome.

There are many diverse paths and ways of overcoming: see to that *yourself*! But only a jester thinks: "man can also be *jumped over.*"

Overcome yourself even in your neighbor: and a right that you can rob you should not accept as a gift!

What you do, no one can do to you in turn. Behold, there is no retribution.

He who cannot command himself should obey. And many a one *can* command himself, but much is still lacking before he obeys!

5

This is the nature of noble souls: they do not want something *for nothing*, least of all, life.

He who is of the mob wants to live for nothing; but we others, to whom life has given itself—we are always considering *what* we can best give *in return*!

And truly, it is a noble speech that says: "What life has promised *us, we* shall keep that promise—to life!"

One should not wish to enjoy where one has not given joy. And—one should not *wish* to enjoy!

For enjoyment and innocence are the most bashful things: neither likes to be sought. One should *have* them—but one should rather *seek* for guilt and pain!—

6

O my brothers, the first-born is always sacrificed. But now we are first-born!

We all bleed on secret sacrificial altars, we all burn and roast in honor of ancient idols.

Our best is still young: this excites old palates. Our flesh is tender, our skin is only lambs' skin:—how could we not excite old idol-priests!

In us ourselves he lives on still, the old idol-priest, who roasts our best for his feast. Ah, my brothers, how should the first-born not be sacrifices!

But so our kind wants it; and I love those who do not wish to preserve themselves. I love with my whole love those who go under and perish: for they cross over.—

7

To be truthful—few *can* do it! And those who can, will not! But the good can do this least of all.

Oh, these good men! *Good men never speak the truth*; to be good in this way is a disease of the spirit.

They yield, those good ones, they submit themselves, their heart repeats, their ground obeys: but he who obeys *does not listen to himself*!

All that the good call evil must come together that one truth may be born: O my brothers, are you evil enough for *this* truth?

The daring venture, the prolonged distrust, the cruel No, the tedium, the cutting to the quick—how seldom do *these* come together! But from such seed is—truth produced!

All *knowledge* thus far has grown up *beside* the bad conscience! Break, break, you knowers, the old tablets!

8

When the water is spanned by planks, when bridges and railings reach over the river: truly, then he is not believed who says: "Everything is in flux."[11]

Even the simpletons contradict him. "What?" say the simpletons, "everything in flux? But there are planks and railings *over* the stream!

"*Over* the stream all is stable, all the values of things, the bridges and bearings, all 'good' and 'evil': these are all *stable!*"—

But when the hard winter comes, the river animal-tamer: then even the cleverest learn mistrust; and then truly not only the simpletons say: "Should not everything—*stand still*?"

"Fundamentally everything stands still"—that is a fit winter teaching, a good cheer for unfruitful seasons, a great comfort for hibernators and fireside-squatters.

"Fundamentally everything stands still"—: but the thawing wind preaches to the *contrary*!

The thawing wind, an ox that is no plough-ox—a raging ox, a destroyer who breaks the ice with angry horns! But ice—*breaks bridges!*

O my brothers, is everything not *now in flux*? Have not all railings and bridges fallen into the water? Who could still *cling* to "good" and "evil"?

"Woe to us! Hail to us! The thawing wind blows!"—Preach thus, O my brothers, through every street!

9

There is an old illusion, which is called good and evil. Up to now the orbit of this illusion has revolved around soothsayers and astrologers.

Once man *believed* in soothsayers and astrologers: and *therefore* man believed: "Everything is fate: you shall, for you must!"

Then again man mistrusted all soothsayers and astrologers: and *therefore* man believed: "Everything is freedom: you can, for you will!"

O my brothers, concerning the stars and the future there has so far been only illusion, and not knowledge: and *therefore* concerning good and evil there has so far been only illusion and not knowledge!

10

"Thou shalt not rob! Thou shalt not kill!"—such words were once called holy; before them one bowed the knee and the head and took off one's shoes.

But I ask you: Where have there ever been better robbers and killers in the world than such holy words?

Is there not in all life itself—robbing and killing? And when such words were called holy was not *truth* itself—slain?

—Or was it a sermon of death that called holy what contradicted and opposed all life?—O my brothers, break, break the old tablets!

11

This is my pity for all the past that I see: it is abandoned,—

—abandoned to the favor, the spirit, the madness of every generation that comes and transforms all that has been into its own bridge!

A great despot could come, a cunning devil, who according to his pleasure and displeasure, might strain and constrain all the past: until it became his bridge and harbinger and herald and cockcrow.

This however is the other danger and my other pity—he who is of the mob remembers back to his grandfather—but with his grandfather time stops.

Thus all the past is abandoned: for one day the herd might become master and drown all time in shallow waters.

Therefore, O my brothers, a *new nobility* is needed to be the adversary of all mob rule and despotism and to write again the word "noble" on new tablets.

For many noble are needed, and noble of many kinds, *that there may be nobility*! Or, as I once said in a parable: "Precisely this is god-like, that there are gods, but no God!"

12

O my brothers, I consecrate and direct you to a new nobility: you shall become procreators and cultivators and sowers of the future—

—truly, not to a nobility which you could buy like shopkeepers with shopkeepers' gold: for whatever has its price has little value.

Not from where you have come will you find your honor henceforth, but from where you are going! Your will and your foot, which seek to step out beyond you—let them be your new honor!

Truly, not that you have served a prince—what do princes matter now!—nor that you have become a bulwark to that which stands, that it may stand more firmly!

Not that your family have grown courtly at courts and you have learned, like a flamingo, to stand for long hours in a colorful costume in shallow pools:

—For being *able* to stand is a merit among courtiers; and all courtiers believe that blessedness after death must comprise—being *allowed* to sit!

Nor that a ghost which they call holy led your ancestors into promised lands, which I do not praise: for where the worst of all trees grew, the cross,—in that land there is nothing to praise!—

—and truly, wherever this "holy ghost" led its knights, always in such campaigns—goats and geese and the contrary and crude ran *foremost*!—

O my brothers, your nobility shall not gaze backward, but *outward*! You shall be exiles from all father- and forefather-lands!

You shall love your *children's land*: let this love be your new nobility,—the undiscovered country in the remotest seas![12] For it I bid your sails search and search!

You shall *make amends* to your children for being the children of your fathers: *thus* shall you redeem all that is past! This new tablet I place over you!

13

"Why live? All is vanity! To live—that is thrashing straw; to live—
that is to burn oneself and yet not get warm."—

Such ancient babbling still passes for "wisdom"; it is honored all
the more *because* it is old and smells musty. Even mould enno-
bles.—

Children might speak thus: they *shrink* from the fire because it
has burned them! There is much childishness in the old books of
wisdom.

And he who is always "thrashing straw," why should he be allowed to slander thrashing! Such fools should be muzzled!

Such people sit down to dinner and bring nothing with them,
not even a good appetite—and then they slander: "All is vain!"

But to eat and drink well, my brothers, is truly no vain art! Break,
break the tablets of the never gay!

14

"To the clean are all things clean"—so the people say. But I say to
you: To the swine all things become swinish!

Therefore the swooners and drooping heads, whose hearts also
droop limply, preach: "The world itself is a filthy monster."

For all these have an unclean spirit; but especially those who
have no peace or rest unless they see the world *from behind*—the
afterworldly!

I tell *these* to their faces, although it may not sound pretty: the
world is like man in having a behind—*that much* is true!

There is much filth in the world: *that much* is true! But the world
itself is not therefore a filthy monster!

There is wisdom in the fact that much in the world smells badly:
disgust itself creates wings and water-divining powers!

Even in the best there is still something that nauseates; and even
the best is something that must be overcome!—

O my brothers, there is much wisdom in this, that there is much
filth in the world!—

15

Such sayings I heard the pious afterworldly speak to their consciences, and truly without malice or falsehood—although there is nothing more false in the world, or more malicious.

"Let the world be as it is! Do not even raise a finger against it!"

"Let whoever will strangle and stab and fleece and flay the people: do not raise a finger against it! Thus they will learn to renounce the world."

"And your own reason—you shall yourself stifle and choke it; for it is a reason of this world,—thus you shall yourself learn to renounce the world."[13]—

—Break, break, O my brothers, those old tablets of the pious! Break the maxims of those who slander the world!—

16

"Whoever learns much unlearns all violent desire"—that is whispered today in all the dark lanes.

"Wisdom wearies, nothing is worthwhile; you shall not desire!"—I found this new tablet hanging even in the public markets.

Break, O my brothers, break this *new* tablet too! The weary of the world hung it up, and the preachers of death and the jailer: for behold, it is also a sermon for slavery!—

Because they learned badly and the best things not at all, and everything too early and everything too fast; because they *ate* badly, from that their stomach-aches resulted,—

—For their spirit is a stomach-ache: *it* advises death! For truly, my brothers, the spirit *is* a stomach!

Life is a well of delight: but all wells are poisoned to him in whom the stomach-ache, the father of misery, speaks.

To know: that is *delight* to the lion-willed! But he who has become weary is himself merely "willed," he is the sport of every wave.

And such is always the nature of weak men: they lose themselves on their way. And at last their weariness asks: "Why did we ever go on the way? It is all the same!"

To them it sounds pleasant to have preached in their ears: "Nothing is worthwhile! You shall not will!" But that is a sermon for slavery.

O my brothers, Zarathustra comes as a fresh blustering wind to all the way-weary; he will yet make many noses sneeze!

My free breath blows even through walls, and into prisons and imprisoned spirits!

Willing liberates: for willing is creating: thus I teach. And you should learn *solely* in order to create!

And you shall first *learn* from me how to learn, how to learn well!—Who has ears, let him hear!

17

There stands the bark—over there perhaps is the way into the great nothingness. But who would embark on this "perhaps"?

None of you want to embark on the boat of death! How then could you be *world-weary*!

World-weary! And you have not yet even parted from the earth! I have always found you still greedy for the earth, still in love with your own earth-weariness!

Your lip does not hang down in vain—a small earthly wish still sits on it! And in your eye—does not a little cloud of unforgotten earthly bliss float there?

On the earth there are many good inventions, some useful, some pleasing: the earth is to be loved for their sake.

And there is such a variety of well-invented things that the earth is like a woman's breasts: useful as well as pleasing.

But you world-weary ones! You earth-idlers! You should be lashed with switches! With lashes one should make your legs sprightly again.

For: if you are not invalids and decrepit wretches of whom the earth is weary, then you are sly sloths or dainty, sneaking pleasure-cats. And if you will not *run* gaily again, then you shall—pass away!

One should not want to be a physician to the incurable: thus teaches Zarathustra—so you shall pass away!

But it takes more *courage* to make an end than to make a new verse: all physicians and poets know that.—

18

O my brothers, there are tablets framed by weariness and tablets framed by sloth, the rotten: although they speak similarly they want to be heard differently.—

Look at this languishing one! He is but an inch from his goal, yet from weariness he has laid himself down obstinately in the dust: this brave one!

He yawns from weariness at the path and the earth and the goal and himself: he will not go a step further,—this brave one!

Now the sun glows on him and dogs lick his sweat: but he lies there in his obstinacy and prefers to languish:[14]—

—to languish an inch from his goal! Truly, you will have to drag him into his heaven by the hair of his head—this hero!

Better still that you let him lie where he has lain down, that sleep may come to him, the comforter, with cooling murmuring rain.

Let him lie until he wakes of his own accord—until of his own accord he renounces all weariness and what weariness has taught through him!

Only, my brothers, drive the dogs away from him, the idle skulkers, and all the swarming vermin—

—all the swarming vermin of the "cultured," who—feast on the sweat of every hero!—

19

I form circles around me and holy boundaries; ever fewer climb with me up ever-higher mountains: I build a mountain range out of ever-holier mountains.—

But wherever you would climb with me, O my brothers, see to it that a *parasite* does not climb with you!

Parasite: that is a worm, a creeping, cringing worm that tries to fatten itself on your sick sore places.

And this is its art, that it finds where climbing souls are weary: in your grief and dejection, in your tender modesty, it builds its disgusting nest.

Where the strong are weak, where the noble are all-too-gentle—there it builds its disgusting nest; the parasite lives where the great have small sores.

Which is the highest type of being and which the lowest? The parasite is the lowest type; but he who is of the highest type feeds the most parasites.

For the soul which has the longest ladder, and can go deepest down: how could there not be the most parasites upon it?—

—the most comprehensive soul, which can run and stray and roam furthest in itself; the most necessary soul, which out of joy flings itself into chance—

—the soul which, having being, plunges into becoming; the possessor, which *wants* to will and desire:—

—the soul fleeing from itself which overtakes itself in the widest circle; the wisest soul, which folly exhorts most sweetly:—

—the soul which loves itself most, in which all things have their current and countercurrent and ebb and flow:—oh how should *the loftiest soul* not have the worst parasites?

20

O my brothers, am I then cruel? But I say: That which is falling should also be pushed!

Everything of today—it is falling, it is decaying: who would check it! But I—I even want to push it!

Do you know the delight that rolls stones into precipitous depths?—These men of today: just see how they roll into my depths!

I am a prelude to better players, O my brothers! A precedent! *Follow* my precedent!

And he whom you do not teach to fly, teach—*to fall faster!*—

21

I love the brave: but it is not enough to be a swordsman,—one must also know *against* whom to be a swordsman!

And often is it greater bravery to refrain and pass by: *in order* to reserve oneself for a worthier enemy!

You should have only enemies whom you hate but not enemies you despise: you must be proud of your enemy: thus I taught once before.

For the worthier enemy, O my brothers, you shall reserve yourselves: therefore must you pass by much,—

—especially much rabble, who din in your ears about the people and peoples.

Keep your eye clear of their for and against! There is much right, much wrong in it: whoever looks on grows angry.

Sighting and smiting—here they are the same thing: therefore depart into the forests and lay your sword to sleep!

Go *your* ways! And let the people and peoples go theirs!—dark ways, truly, on which not one hope flashes any more!

Let the shopkeeper rule where all that still glitters is—shopkeepers' gold. The time of kings is past: what today calls itself the people deserves no kings.

Just see how these peoples themselves now behave like the shopkeepers: they pick up the smallest advantage out of all kinds of rubbish!

They lie around lurking and spy around smirking—they call that "being good neighbors." O blessed distant time when a people said to itself: "I want to be—*master* over peoples!"

For, my brothers: the best shall rule, the best also *want* to rule! And where the doctrine is different, there—the best is *lacking*.

22

If *they*—had bread for nothing, ah![15] What would *they* cry for! Their sustenance—that is their true entertainment; and it should be hard for them!

They are beasts of prey: even in their "working"—there is robbery, even in their "earning"—there is fraud! Therefore it should be hard for them!

Thus they shall become better beasts of prey, subtler, cleverer, *more man-like*: for man is the best beast of prey.

Man has already robbed all the animals of their virtues: that is why of all animals it has been hardest for man.

Only the birds are still beyond him. And if man should yet learn to fly, ah! *to what height*—would his rapaciousness fly!

23

Thus I want man and woman: the one fit for war, the other fit to give birth, but both fit for dancing with head and legs.

And we should consider every day lost on which we did not dance *once*. And we should call every truth false which does not give *one* laugh!

24

Your wedlock: see that it is not a bad *lock*! You lock too quickly: so there *follows* from it—wedlock-breaking![16]

And yet better marriage breaking than marriage bending, marriage lying!—A woman spoke to me so: "Indeed I broke the marriage, but first the marriage broke—me!"

I have always found the badly paired to be the most revengeful: they make every one suffer for it that they are no longer single.

Therefore I would have the honest say to one another: "We love each other: let us *see to it* that we stay in love! Or shall our promise be a mistake?"

—"Give us a probation and a little marriage, so that we may see if we are fit for the great marriage! It is a big thing to be always together."

Thus I counsel all the honest; and what would be my love of the Übermensch and of all that is to come if I should counsel and speak otherwise!

To propagate yourselves not only onwards but *upwards*—toward that, O my brothers, may the garden of marriage help you!

25

He who has grown wise concerning old origins, behold, he will at last seek springs of the future and new origins.—

O my brothers, it will not be long until *new peoples* shall arise and new springs rush down into new depths.

For the earthquake—it chokes up many wells and causes much thirst: but it also brings inner powers and secrets to light.

The earthquake reveals new springs. In the earthquake of old peoples new springs burst forth.

And whoever calls out: "Behold, here is a well for many thirsty, one heart for many longing, one will for many instruments":—around him assembles a *people*, that is to say: many triers.

Who can command, who must obey—*that is tried out there*! Ah, with what long seeking and solving and failing and learning and trying again!

Human society: it is a trial, so I teach—a long seeking: but it seeks the commander!—

—a trial, oh my brothers! And *no* "contract"! Break, break that word of the soft hearted and half-and-half!

26

O my brothers! With whom lies the greatest danger to the whole human future? Is it not with the good and just?—

—with those who say and feel in their hearts: "We already know what is good and just, we have it too; woe to those who are still searching for it!

And whatever harm the evil may do, the harm the good do is the most harmful harm!

And whatever harm the slanderers of the world may do, the harm the good do is the most harmful harm!

O my brothers, one man once saw into the hearts of the good and just and said: "They are the pharisees." But he was not understood.

The good and just themselves could not understand him: their spirit is imprisoned in their good conscience. The stupidity of the good is unfathomably shrewd.

But it is the truth: the good *must* be pharisees—they have no choice!

The good *must* crucify him who invents his own virtue![17] That *is* the truth!

But the second one who discovered their country, the country, heart and soil of the good and just: it was he who asked: "Whom do they hate most?"

The *creator* is the one they hate most: him who breaks the tablets and old values, the breaker,—him they call the lawbreaker.

For the good—they *cannot* create: they are always the beginning of the end:—

—they crucify him who writes new values on new tablets, they sacrifice the future *to themselves*—they crucify the whole human future!

The good—they have always been the beginning of the end.—

27

O my brothers, have you really understood this word? And what I once said of the "last man"?—

With whom lies the greatest danger to the whole human future? Is it not with the good and just?

Break, break the good and just!—O my brothers, have you really understood this word?

28

You flee from me? You are frightened? You tremble at this word?

O my brothers, when I bade you to break the good and the tablets of the good, only then did I launch mankind upon its high seas.

And only now does the great terror, the great prospect, the great sickness, the great nausea, the great seasickness come to it.

The good taught you false shores and false assurances; in the lies of the good you were born and bred. Everything has been made fraudulent and twisted through and through by the good.

But he who discovered the country of "man," discovered also the country of "man's future." Now you shall be seafarers, valiant, patient!

Stand up straight in good time, oh my brothers, learn to stand up straight! The sea storms: many want to right themselves again with your help.

The sea storms: everything is at sea. Well then! Come on! You old seaman-hearts!

What of fatherland! Our helm wants to fare *away*, out where our *children's land* is! Out that way, stormier than the sea, storms our great longing!—

29

"Why so hard!"—said the kitchen coal one day to the diamond; "are we not then close kin?"—

Why so soft? O my brothers thus *I* ask you: are you not then— my brothers?

Why so soft, so submissive and yielding? Why is there so much negation and abnegation in your hearts? So little fate in your glances?

And if you will not be fates and the inexorable: how can you—conquer with me?

And if your hardness will not flash and cut and cut to pieces, how can you one day—create with me?

For creators are hard. And it must seem bliss to you to press your hand upon millennia as upon wax,—

—bliss to write upon the will of millennia as upon brass,—harder than brass, nobler than brass. Only the noblest is entirely hard.

This new tablet, O my brothers, I put over you: *become hard!*—

30

O you my will! You end of all need, *my own* necessity! Keep me from all small victories!

You predestination of my soul, which I call destiny! You in-me! Over-me! Keep and save me for *one* great destiny!

And your last greatness, my will, save for your last—that you may be inexorable *in* your victory! Ah, who has not succumbed to his own victory!

Ah, whose eye has not dimmed in this drunken twilight! Ah, whose foot has not faltered and in victory forgotten—how to stand!—

—That I may one day be ready and ripe in the great noon: ready and ripe like glowing ore, like a cloud heavy with lightning and swollen milk-udders:—

—ready for myself and my most hidden will: a bow eager for its arrow, an arrow eager for its star:—

—a star, ready and ripe in its noon, glowing, pierced, blissful through by annihilating sun-arrows:—

—a sun itself and an inexorable sun-will, ready for annihilation in victory!

O will, you end of every need, *my* necessity! Save me for *one* great victory!—-

Thus spoke Zarathustra.

THE CONVALESCENT

1

One morning, not long after his return to his cave, Zarathustra sprang up from his bed like a madman, cried with a frightful voice, and acted as if some one still lay on the bed who did not wish to rise; and Zarathustra's voice resounded in such a way that his animals came to him in fright, and out of all the neighboring caves and hiding places all the creatures slipped away—flying, fluttering, creeping, jumping, according to the kind of foot or wing each had been given. But Zarathustra spoke these words:

Up, abysmal thought, out of my depths! I am your cock and dawn, sleepy worm: up! up! My voice shall soon crow you awake!

Loosen the fetters of your ears: listen! For I want to hear you! Up! Up! Here is thunder enough to make even the graves listen!

And wipe the sleep and all the dimness and blindness from your eyes! Hear me with your eyes, too: my voice is a balm even for those born blind.

And once you are awake you will always stay awake. It is not *my* way to awaken great-grandmothers out of their sleep in order to I bid them—sleep on!

You stir, stretch yourself, wheeze? Up! Up! Do not wheeze—you shall speak to me! Zarathustra the godless calls you!

I, Zarathustra, the advocate of life, the advocate of suffering, the advocate of the circle—I call you, my most abysmal thought!

Hail to me! You are coming—I hear you! My abyss *speaks*, I have turned my lowest depths into the light!

Hail to me! Come here! Give me your hand—ha! let go! Ha ha!——Disgust, disgust, disgust————woe is me!

2

No sooner had Zarathustra spoken these words than he fell down like a dead man, and long remained as one dead. But when however he came to himself again, then he was pale and trembling and remained lying down and for a long time would neither eat nor drink.

This condition continued for seven days; his animals, however, did not leave him day or night, except that the eagle flew off to fetch food. And whatever he fetched and collected he laid on Zarathustra's bed: so that at last Zarathustra lay among yellow and red berries, grapes, rosy apples, sweet-smelling herbs and pinecones. At his feet, however, two lambs were stretched, which the eagle had with difficulty robbed from their shepherds.

At last, after seven days, Zarathustra raised himself in his bed, took a rosy apple in his hand, smelt it and found its aroma pleasant. Then his animals thought the time had come to speak to him.

"O Zarathustra," they said, "now you have lain like that for seven days with heavy eyes: will you not now get on your feet again?

"Step out of your cave: the world waits for you as a garden. The wind plays with heavy fragrance which seeks for you; and all the brooks would like to run after you.

"All things long for you, since you have been alone for seven days—step forth out of your cave! All things want to be your physicians!

"Has a new knowledge perhaps come to you, a bitter, grievous knowledge? You have lain like leavened dough, your soul has risen and swelled over all its rims.—"

—O my animals, replied Zarathustra, chatter on like this and let me listen! It refreshes me to hear your talk: where there is talk, the world is like a garden to me.

How charming it is that there are words and sounds: are not words and sounds rainbows and illusive bridges between things eternally separated?

Every soul is a world of its own; to each soul every other soul is an afterworld.

Illusion deceives most beautifully precisely between what is most alike: for the smallest gap is the most difficult to bridge.

For me—how could there be an outside-of-me? There is no outside! But we forget that when we hear sounds; how delightful, that we forget!

Have not names and sounds been given to things that man may refresh himself with them? Speech is a beautiful folly: with it man dances over everything.

How lovely is all speech and all the lies of sounds! With sounds our love dances on many-colored rainbows.—

—"O Zarathustra," his animals said, "all things themselves dance for those who think as we do: they come and offer their hand and laugh and flee—and return.

"Everything goes, everything returns; the wheel of being rolls eternally. Everything dies, everything blossoms forth again; the year of being runs eternally.

"Everything breaks, everything is joined again; the house of being builds itself the same eternally. Everything parts, everything greets every other thing again; the ring of being is eternally true to itself.

"In every Now being begins; the ball There rolls around every Here. The center is everywhere. The path of eternity is crooked."—

—O you jokers and barrel-organs! answered Zarathustra and smiled again, how well you know what had to be fulfilled in seven days:—

—and how that monster crept into my throat and choked me! But I bit off its head and spat it away from me.

And you—have you already made a hurdy-gurdy song out of it? But now I lie here, still exhausted with that biting and spitting-away, still sick with my own redemption.

And you watched all this? O my animals, are you also cruel? Did you like to look at my great pain as men do? For man is the cruelest animal.

At tragedies, bullfights, and crucifixions he has so far felt best on earth; and when he invented hell for himself, behold, that was his heaven on earth.

When the great man cries—: immediately the little man comes running; his tongue hangs out of his mouth with lasciviousness. But he calls it his "pity."

The little man, especially the poet—how zealously he accuses life in words! Listen to it, but do not fail to hear the delight that is in all accusation!

Such accusers of life: life overcomes with a wink. "You love me?" she says impudently; "wait a little, as yet I have no time for you."

Towards himself man is the cruelest animal; and in all who call themselves "sinners" and "bearers of the cross" and "penitents," do not overlook the voluptuousness in their complaints and accusations!

And I myself—do I want to be man's accuser? Ah, my animals, this alone have I learned, that man needs what is most evil in him for what is best in him,—

—that whatever is most evil is his best *power*, and the hardest stone for the highest creator; and that man must grow better *and* more evil:—

Not to *this* torture-stake was I tied, that I know: man is evil—rather that I cried as no one has cried before:

"Ah, that his most evil is so very small! Ah, that his best is so very small!"

The great disgust with man—*it* choked me and had crept into my throat: and what the soothsayer truly said: "All is the same, nothing is worthwhile, knowledge chokes."

A long twilight limped on before me, a mortally weary, dead drunk sadness which spoke with a yawning mouth.

"He returns eternally, the man of whom you are weary, the small man"—so my sadness yawned and dragged its feet and could not go to sleep.

Man's earth became a cave to me, its breast sunken, everything living became to me human decay and bones and mouldering past.

My sighs sat on all human graves and could no longer rise; my sighs and questions croaked and gagged and gnawed and wailed day and night:

—"Ah, man recurs eternally! The small man recurs eternally!"[18]

Once I saw both of them naked, the greatest man and the smallest man: all-too-similar to one another—even the greatest, all-too-human!

The greatest all-too small!—that was my disgust at man! And the eternal recurrence even of the smallest!—that was my disgust at all existence!

Ah, Nausea! Nausea! Nausea![19]—Thus spoke Zarathustra, and sighed and shuddered; for he remembered his sickness. But his animals would not let him speak further.

"Say no more, you convalescent!"—so answered his animals, "but go out where the world waits for you like a garden.

"Go out to the roses and bees and flocks of doves! But especially to the songbirds: so that you may learn *singing* from them!

"Singing is precisely for the convalescent; let the healthy talk. And when the healthy too wants songs, he wants different songs than the convalescent."

—"O you jokers and barrel-organs, be silent!" replied Zarathustra, and smiled at his animals. "How well you know what consolation I invented for myself in seven days!

That I have to sing once more—*that* consolation I invented for myself and *this* convalescence: would you also make another hurdy-gurdy song out of that?"

—"Say no more," his animals replied again; "rather, you convalescent, first prepare a lyre for yourself, a new lyre!

"For behold, O Zarathustra! New lyres are needed for your new songs.

"Sing and bubble over, O Zarathustra, heal your soul with new songs: that you may bear your great destiny, which has not yet been any one's destiny!

"For your animals know it well, O Zarathustra, who you are and must become: behold, *you are the teacher of the eternal return,*—that is now *your* destiny!

"That you must be the first to teach this teaching—how could this great destiny not be your greatest danger and sickness!

"Behold, we know what you teach: that all things eternally return and we ourselves with them, and that we have already existed an infinite number of times, and all things with us.

"You teach that there is a great year of becoming, a monster of a great year: it must, like an hourglass, turn itself over again and again, so that it may run down and run out again:—

—"so that all these years are alike in what is greatest and also in what is smallest, so that we ourselves are alike in every great year, in what is greatest and also in what is smallest.

"And if you wanted to die now, O Zarathustra: behold, we know too what you would then say to yourself—but your animals ask you not to die yet!

"You would speak and without trembling, rather gasping with happiness: for a great weight and oppression would be taken from you, you most patient one!—

" 'Now I die and disappear,' you would say, 'and in a moment I am nothing. Souls are as mortal as bodies.

" 'But the knot of causes in which I am intertwined returns,—it will create me again! I myself am part of the causes of the eternal return.

" 'I come again with this sun, with this earth, with this eagle, with this snake—*not* to a new life or a better life or a similar life:

—" 'I come again eternally to this identical and selfsame life, in its greatest and its smallest, to teach again the eternal return of all things,—

—" 'to speak again the word of the great noon of earth and man, to proclaim the Übermensch to man again.

" 'I spoke my word, I break on my word: thus my eternal lot wants it—as a proclaimer I perish!

" 'Now the hour has come for him who goes under to bless himself. Thus—*ends* Zarathustra's going under.' "—

When the animals had spoken these words they were silent and waited for Zarathustra to say something to them: but Zarathustra did not hear that they were silent. On the contrary, he lay quietly with closed eyes like a sleeper, although he was not asleep: for he was conversing with his soul. The serpent, however, and the eagle, when they found him thus silent, respected the great stillness around him and discreetly withdrew.

ON THE GREAT LONGING

O MY SOUL, I taught you to say "today" as well as "once" and "formerly" and to dance your dance over every Here and There and Yonder.

O my soul, I delivered you from all nooks, I brushed dust, spiders and twilight from you.

O my soul, I washed the petty shame and the nook-virtue from you and persuaded you to stand naked before the eyes of the sun.

With the storm that is called "spirit" I blew across your surging sea; I blew all clouds away, I even strangled the strangler called "sin."

O my soul, I gave you the right to say No like the storm and to say Yes as the open sky says Yes: you are as still as light and now you walk through denying storms.

O my soul, I gave you back the freedom over the created and the uncreated: and who knows, as you know, the voluptuousness of future things?

O my soul, I taught you the contempt that does not come like the gnawing of a worm, the great, the loving contempt, which loves most where it despises most.

O my soul, I taught you to be so persuasive that you persuade even the elements themselves to come to you: like the sun, which persuades the sea to rise even to its height.

O my soul, I took all obeying and knee-bending and obsequiousness from you; I myself gave you the names, "cessation of need" and "destiny."

O my soul, I have given you new names and colorful toys, I have called you "destiny" and "circumference of circumferences" and "time's umbilical cord" and "azure bell."

O my soul, I gave your soil all wisdom to drink, all new wines, and also all immemorially old strong wines of wisdom.

O my soul, I poured every sun out on you and every night and every silence and every longing:—then you grew up for me as a vine.

O my soul, now you stand exuberant and heavy, a vine with swelling udders and full clusters of golden brown grapes:—

—crowded and weighed down by your happiness, waiting from superabundance and yet bashful in your expectancy.

O my soul, there is nowhere a soul more loving and comprehensive and spacious! Where could future and past be closer together than with you?

O my soul, I have given you everything and my hands have been made empty by you—and now! Now you say to me smiling and full of melancholy: "Which of us owes thanks?—

—"does the giver not owe thanks to the receiver for receiving? Is giving not a necessity? Is receiving not—mercy?"—

O my soul, I understand the smile of your melancholy: your overabundance itself now stretches out longing hands!

Your fullness looks forth over raging seas, and seeks and waits: the longing of overfullness looks forth from the smiling heaven of your eyes!

And truly, O my soul! Who could see your smiling and not melt into tears? The angels themselves melt into tears through the over-graciousness of your smiling.

It is your graciousness and overgraciousness that does not want to complain and weep: and yet, O my soul, your smile longs for tears, and your trembling mouth for sobs.

"Is not all weeping complaining? And all complaining, accusing?" Thus you speak to yourself, and therefore, O my soul, you will rather smile than pour forth your grief—

—pour forth in gushing tears all your grief at your fullness and at the craving of the vine for the vintner and his knife!

But if you will not weep, not weep out your purple melancholy, then you will have to *sing*, O my soul!—Behold, I myself smile, I who foretold this to you:

—sing with a roaring song until all seas grow still to listen to your longing,—

—until over still longing seas the bark glides, the golden marvel, around whose gold all good, bad, marvelous things leap:—

—also many great and small beasts, and everything that has light marvelous feet, that can run on paths as blue as violets,—

—towards the golden marvel, the voluntary bark and its master: he, however, is the vintner who is waiting with his diamond-studded knife,—

—your great deliverer, O my soul, the nameless one—for whom only future songs will find names! And truly, your breath is already fragrant with future songs,—

—already you glow and dream, already you drink thirstily at all deep echoing wells of comfort, already your melancholy reposes in the bliss of future songs!—

O my soul, now I have given you everything and even the last that I have, and all my hands have been made empty by you:—*that I bade you sing*, behold, that was the last I had to give!

That I bade you sing, speak now, speak: *which* of us now—owes thanks?—But better still: sing to me, sing, O my soul! And let me thank you!—

Thus spoke Zarathustra.

THE OTHER DANCE SONG

1

Into your eyes I gazed lately, O life: I saw gold glint in your night eyes,—my heart stood still with delight:[20]

—I saw a golden bark glinting on darkened waters, a sinking, drinking, winking, golden tossing bark!

At my feet, frantic to dance, you cast a look, a laughing questioning melting tossing look:

Twice only you stirred your rattle with your small hands—then my feet already swung with the fury of dance.—

My heels raised themselves, my toes listened to understand you: for the dancer has his ears—in his toes!

I sprang to your side: then you fled back from my leap; and the tongue of your fleeing, flying hair licked me in its swing!

I sprang away from you and your serpents: then you stood there, half-turned, with your eyes full of desire.

With crooked glances—you teach me crooked ways; on crooked ways my feet learn—guile!

I fear you near, I love you far; your flight allures me, your seeking cures me—I suffer, but for you what would I not bear gladly!

Whose coldness inflames, whose hatred seduces, whose flight binds, whose mockery—induces:

—who would not hate you, you great woman who binds, enwinds, seduces, seeks, finds! Who would not love you, you innocent, impatient, wind-swift, child-eyed sinner!

Where do you lure me now, you unruly paragon? And now you are fleeing from me again, you sweet wildcat and ingrate!

I dance after you, I follow even your faint traces. Where are you? Give me your hand! Or only a finger!

Here are caves and thickets: we shall go astray!—Stop! Stand still! Don't you see owls and bats flitting past?

You owl! You bat! You want to confuse me? Where are we? You have learned such barking and howling from a dog.

You gnaw on me sweetly with little white teeth, from under your curly little mane your evil eyes flash at me!

This is a dance over stock and stone: I am the hunter—will you yet be my dog or my catch?

Now beside me! And quickly, you malicious leaper! Now up! And over!—Ah! In leaping I fell!

Oh, see me lying there, you prankster, and begging for grace! I would gladly walk with you—in some lovelier place!

—in love's paths through silent mottled bushes! Or there along the lake: where goldfishes dance and swim!

Are you tired now? Over there are sheep and the red of evening: isn't it nice to sleep while the shepherd plays his flute?

You are so very tired? I will carry you there, just let your arm sink! And if you are thirsty—indeed I have something, but your mouth would not like to drink it!—

—Oh this accursed, nimble, supple snake and slippery witch! Where have you gone? But from your hand two spots and red blotches itch on my face!

I am truly weary of always being your sheepish shepherd. You witch, if I have so far sung to you, now *you* will—cry to me!

You will dance and cry to the rhythm of my whip! But did I forget my whip?—No!"—

2

Then life answered me thus and kept her gentle ears closed:

"O Zarathustra! Do not crack your whip so terribly! You surely know: noise murders thought—[21] and just now such tender thoughts are coming to me.

"We are both two real good-for-nothings and evil-for-nothings. Beyond good and evil we discovered our island and our green meadow—we two alone! Therefore we better like each other!

"And even if we do not love each other from the heart—must we then have a grudge against each other if we do not love each other from the heart?

"And that I like you, often too well, that you know: and the reason is that I am jealous of your wisdom. Ah, this mad old fool of wisdom!

"If your wisdom should one day run away from you, then would my love would quickly run away from you too."—

At that life looked thoughtfully behind and around herself and said softly: "O Zarathustra, you are not faithful enough to me!

"You do not love me nearly so much as you say; I know you are thinking of leaving me soon.

"There is an old heavy heavy booming bell: it booms out at night up to your cave:—

"—when you hear this bell beat the hour at midnight, then between one and twelve you think—

"—you think, O Zarathustra, I know it, of leaving me soon!"—

"Yes," I answered hesitatingly, "but you also know—" And I said something into her ear, in the midst of her tangled yellow foolish tresses.

"You *know* that, O Zarathustra? No one knows that.——"

And we gazed at each other and looked at the green meadow, over which the cool evening was just passing, and we wept together.—But then life was dearer to me than all my wisdom had ever been.—

Thus spoke Zarathustra.

3

One!

O man! Take care!

Two!

What does the deep midnight speak?

Three!

"I slept, I slept—,

Four!

"From the deepest dream I awoke:—

Five!

"The world is deep,

Six!

"And deeper than the day had thought.

Seven!

"Deep is its woe—,

Eight!

"Joy—deeper yet than heartache:

Nine!

"Woe says: Go!

Ten!

"But all joy wants eternity—,

Eleven!

"—wants deep, deep eternity!"

Twelve!

THE SEVEN SEALS
(OR: THE YES- AND AMEN-SONG)

1

If I am a soothsayer and full of that soothsaying spirit which wanders on high ridges, between two seas,—

wanders between the past and the future like a heavy cloud,—enemy to sultry plains and to all that is weary and can neither die nor live:

ready for lightning in its dark bosom and for the redeeming flash of light, pregnant with lightning bolts that say yes! that laugh yes! soothsaying lightning bolts:—

—but he is blessed who is thus pregnant! And truly, long must he hang like a heavy storm on the mountain, who shall one day kindle the light of the future!—

oh how should I not lust for eternity and for the wedding ring of rings—the ring of return?[22]

Never yet did I find the woman by whom I wanted children, unless it be this woman, whom I love: for I love you, O eternity!

For I love you, O eternity!

2

If ever my wrath burst tombs, moved boundary stones and rolled old broken tablets into steep depths:

If ever my mockery scattered moldy words to the winds, and if I came like a broom to cross-marked spiders and as a cleansing wind to old sepulchers:

If ever I sat rejoicing where old gods lay buried, world-blessing, world-loving, beside the monuments of old world-slanderers:—

—for I love even churches and the tombs of gods, if only heaven looks through their ruined roofs with pure eyes; I like to sit like grass and red poppies on ruined churches—

oh how should I not lust for eternity and for the wedding ring of rings—the ring of return?

Never yet did I find the woman by whom I wanted children, unless it be this woman, whom I love: for I love you, O eternity!

For I love you, O eternity!

3

If ever a breath of the creative breath has come to me, and of the heavenly necessity that compels even chances to dance star-dances:

If ever I have laughed with the laughter of the creative lightning, which the long thunder of the deed grumblingly, but obediently follows:

If ever I have played dice with the gods at the divine table of the earth, so that the earth quaked and ruptured and snorted forth streams of fire:—

—for the earth is a divine table, and trembling with creative new words and dice throws of the gods:

oh how should I not lust for eternity and for the wedding ring of rings—the ring of the return?

Never yet did I find the woman by whom I wanted children, unless it be this woman, whom I love: for I love you, O eternity!

For I love you, O eternity!

4

If ever I have drunk a full draft of the foaming spice- and blend-mug in which all things are well mixed:

If ever my hand has mingled the furthest with the nearest and fire with spirit and joy with sorrow and the harshest with the kindest:

If I myself am a grain of the redeeming salt which makes everything in the mixing bowl mix well:—

—for there is a salt that units good with evil; and even the most evil is worthy to be a spice and a last foaming over:—

Oh how should I not lust for eternity and for the wedding ring of rings—the ring of the return?

Never yet did I find the woman by whom I wanted children, unless it be this woman, whom I love: for I love you, O eternity!

For I love you, O eternity!

5

If I love the sea and all that is sealike, and love it most when it angrily contradicts me:

If the delight in seeking, which drives sails to the undiscovered, is in me if a seafarer's delight is in my delight:

If ever my rejoicing has cried: "The shore has vanished—now the last chain has fallen from me—

"—the boundless roars around me, far out glisten space and time, well then! come on! old heart!"—

Oh how should I not lust for eternity, and for the wedding ring of rings—the ring of the return?

Never yet did I find the woman by whom I wanted children, unless it be this woman, whom I love: for I love you, O eternity!

For I love you, O eternity!

6

If my virtue is a dancer's virtue, and if I often sprung with both feet into emerald golden rapture:

If my wickedness is a laughing wickedness, at home among rose banks and hedges of lilies:

—for in laughter all evil is present, but it is sanctified and absolved by its own bliss:—

And if it is my alpha and omega that everything heavy shall become light, every body a dancer, all spirit a bird: and truly, that is my alpha and omega!—

Oh how should I not lust for eternity and for the wedding ring of rings—the ring of the return?

Never yet did I find the woman by whom I wanted children, unless it be this woman, whom I love: for I love you, O eternity!

For I love you, O eternity!

7

If ever I spread out a still sky above me and flew into my own sky with my own wings:

If I swam playfully in the deep luminous distances, and the bird-wisdom of my freedom came:—

—but bird-wisdom speaks so:—"Behold, there is no above, no below! Throw yourself about, out, back, you light one! Sing! speak no more!

"—are not all words made for the heavy? Do not all words lie to the light? Sing! speak no more!"—

Oh how should I not lust for eternity and for the wedding ring of rings—the ring of the return?

Never yet did I find the woman by whom I wanted children, unless it be this woman, whom I love: for I love you, O eternity!

For I love you, O eternity!

FOURTH AND LAST PART

Ah, where in the world has there been greater folly than among the pitying? And what in the world has caused more suffering than the folly of the pitying?

Woe to all lovers who do not have a height that is above their pity!

Thus spoke the devil to me once: "God too has his hell: it is his love of man."

And most recently I heard him speak this word: "God is dead: God died of his pity for man."

—*Zarathustra, "On the Pitying"*

[*1892*]

The Honey Sacrifice

—And again months and years passed over Zarathustra's soul, and he did not heed them; but his hair became white. One day, as he sat on a stone in front of his cave and looked silently out,—but there one gazes out on the sea, and across winding abysses,—his animals went thoughtfully around him, and at last placed themselves in front of him.

"O Zarathustra," they said, "you gaze out perhaps for your happiness?"—"What matters happiness!" he answered, "I have long ceased to strive any more for happiness, I strive for my work."—"O Zarathustra," the animals said then, "you say that as one who has an excess of good things. Don't you lie in a sky-blue lake of happiness?"—"You jokers," answered Zarathustra and smiled, "how well you chose the image! But you know too that my happiness is heavy, and not like a fluid wave: it oppresses me and will not leave me, and is like molten pitch."—

Then his animals went thoughtfully around him and placed themselves once more in front of him. "O Zarathustra," they said, "is *that* why you yourself always become yellower and darker, although your hair looks white and flaxen? Behold, you are sitting in your pitch of hard luck!"—"What do you say, my animals?" said Zarathustra and laughed, "truly I slandered when I spoke of pitch. As it happens with me, so is it with all fruits that turn ripe. It is the *honey* in my veins that makes my blood thicker, and also my soul stiller."—"So it will be, O Zarathustra," answered his animals, and pressed up to him; "but will you not climb a high mountain today? The air is pure, and today one sees more of the world than ever."—"Yes, my animals," he answered, "your advice is admirable and according to my heart: I will climb a high mountain today! But see that honey is there ready to hand, yellow, white, good, ice-cool golden honey in the comb. For know that at the summit I will make the honey-sacrifice."—

But when Zarathustra had reached the summit, he sent home the animals that had accompanied him, and found that he was now alone—then he laughed heartily, looked around him, and spoke thus:

That I spoke of sacrifices and honey-sacrifices was merely a ruse and, truly, a useful folly! Up here I can now speak more freely than in front of hermits' caves and hermits' pets.

What sacrifice! I squander what is given to me, a squanderer with a thousand hands: how could I call that—sacrificing?

And when I desired honey I only desired bait and sweet mucus and mucilage, for which even growling bears and strange, sulky, evil birds put out their tongues:

—the best bait, such as huntsmen and fishermen need. For if the world is like a dark forest of animals and a pleasure-ground for all wild huntsmen, it seems to me rather, and preferably, a fathomless, rich sea;

—a sea full of colorful fishes and crabs, for which even the gods might long and might be tempted to become fishers in it and casters of nets: so rich is the world in wonderful things, great and small!

Especially the human world, the human sea—now towards *it* I cast my golden fishing rod and say: open up, you human abyss!

Open up and throw me your fish and shining crabs! With my best bait shall I bait today the strangest human fish!

—my happiness itself I cast out far and wide, between sunrise, noon, and sunset, to see if many human fish will not learn to kick and tug at my happiness.

Until, biting at my sharp hidden hooks, they have to come up to *my* height, the most mottled abysmal groundlings to the most wicked of all fishers of men.

For *that* is what I am through and through, reeling, reeling in, raising up, raising, a raiser, trainer, and taskmaster, who not in vain once advised himself: "Become who you are!"

Thus may men now come *up* to me: for as yet I await the signs that it is time for my descent; as yet do I not myself go under, as I must, among men.

Therefore I wait here, crafty and scornful upon high mountains, no impatient one, no patient one, rather one who has forgotten even patience—because he no longer "suffers in patience."

For my destiny gives me time: perhaps it has forgotten me? Or does it sit in the shade behind a big stone and catch flies?

And truly, I am well disposed to my eternal destiny, because it does not dog and hurry me, but leaves me time for jests and mischief: so that today I have climbed this high mountain to catch fish.

Did ever any one catch fish upon high mountains? And though what I seek and do here is folly, it is still better than if I became solemn down there from waiting, and green and yellow—

—to become a posturing wrath-snorter from waiting, a holy howling storm from the mountains, an impatient one that shouts down into the valleys: "Listen, or else I will lash you with the scourge of God!"

Not that I bear a grudge against such wrathful ones for that: they are good enough for a laugh! How impatient they must be, those big drums of alarm, which find a voice now or never!

But I and my destiny—we do not speak to today, neither do we speak to the never: for speaking we have patience and time and more than time. For one day it must come and may not pass by.

What must one day come and may not pass by? Our great Hazar, our great, remote empire of man, the Zarathustra empire of a thousand years—

How remote may such "remoteness" be? What does it concern me? But on that account to me it is nonetheless sure—I stand secure with both feet on this ground;

—on an eternal ground, on hard primordial rock, on this highest, hardest, primordial mountain ridge to which all winds come as to the breaking storm, asking where? and whence? and whither?

Here laugh, laugh, my bright healthy sarcasm! From high mountains cast down your glittering mocking laughter! With your glitter bait for me the finest human fish!

And whatever belongs to *me* in all seas, my in-and-for-me in all things—fish *that* out for me, bring *that* up to me: for that I wait, the wickedest of all fishermen.

Out! out! my fishing rod! In, down, bait of my happiness! Drip your sweetest dew, honey of my heart! Bite, my fishing rod, into the belly of all black misery!

Look out, look out, my eye! Oh, how many seas ring round about me, what dawning human futures! And above me—what rose-red stillness! What unclouded silence!

The Cry of Distress

The next day Zarathustra was again sitting on the stone in front of his cave, while his animals roved about in the world outside to bring home new food—new honey too: for Zarathustra had spent and squandered the old honey to the very last drop. But as he was sitting there with a stick in his hand, tracing the shadow of his figure in the ground, reflecting, and truly! not about himself and his shadow,—suddenly he startled and shrank back: for he saw another shadow beside his own. And when he hastily looked around and stood up, behold, there stood the soothsayer beside him, the same who had once eaten and drunk at his table, the proclaimer of the great weariness, who taught: "All is the same, nothing is worthwhile, the world is without meaning, knowledge chokes." But his face had changed since then; and when Zarathustra looked into his eyes, his heart was startled once more: so many evil prophecies and ashen lightning bolts ran over that face.

The soothsayer, who had perceived what went on in Zarathustra's soul, wiped his face with his hand as if he wanted to wipe it away; Zarathustra did the same. And when both of them had thus silently composed and strengthened themselves, they shook hands as a sign that they wanted to recognize each other.

"Welcome," said Zarathustra, "you soothsayer of the great weariness, not in vain shall you once have been guest at my table. Eat and drink with me again today, and forgive a cheerful old man for sitting at the table with you!"—"A cheerful old man?" replied the soothsayer, shaking his head, "but whoever you are, or would be, O Zarathustra, you shall not be up here much longer—in a little while your boat shall no longer be stuck on dry land!"—"Am I stuck on dry land?"—asked Zarathustra laughing.—"The waves around your mountain," answered the soothsayer, "rise and rise, the waves of great distress and misery: they will soon raise your boat too, and carry you away."—At that Zarathustra was silent and wondered.—"Do you still hear nothing?" continued the soothsayer: "does it not rush and roar out of the depth?"—Zarathustra was silent once more and listened: then heard he a long, long cry, which the abysses threw to one another and passed on; for none wished to keep it: so evil did it sound.

"You proclaimer of bad tidings," Zarathustra said at last, "that is a cry of distress and the cry of a man; it may well come out of a black sea. But what does human distress matter to me! My last sin, which has been reserved for me, do you know what it is called?"

—"*Pity!*" answered the soothsayer from an overflowing heart, and raised both his hands—"O Zarathustra, I have come to seduce you to your last sin!"[1]—

And hardly had those words been uttered when the cry sounded once more, and longer and more anxious than before, also much nearer. "Do you hear? Do you hear, O Zarathustra?" cried the sooth-sayer, "the cry is for you, it calls you: come, come, come, it is time, it is high time!"—

Zarathustra was silent at that, confused and shaken; at last he asked like one who is hesitant in his own mind: "And who is it that calls me?"

"But you know it, certainly," answered the soothsayer vehemently, "why do you conceal yourself? It is *the higher man* that cries for you!"

"The higher man?" cried Zarathustra, horror-stricken: "what does *he* want? What does *he* want? The higher man! What does he want here?"—and his skin was bathed in sweat.

The soothsayer, however, did not hear Zarathustra's alarm, but listened and listened toward the depth. But when it had been still there for a long while, he looked back and saw Zarathustra stand-ing there trembling.

"O Zarathustra," he began in a sorrowful voice, "you do not stand there like one whose happiness makes him giddy: you better dance or else you will fall!

"But even if you dance for me, leaping all your side-leaps, no one may say to me: 'Behold, here dances the last cheerful man!'

"In vain would anyone come to this height who sought *him* here: he would find caves, indeed, and caves behind caves, hiding places for the hidden, but not mines of happiness nor treasure chambers nor new gold veins of happiness.

"Happiness—how indeed could one find happiness among the buried and the hermits! Must I yet seek the last happiness on the happy islands and far away among forgotten seas?

"But all is the same, nothing is worthwhile, seeking is pointless, there are no happy islands any more!"

Thus sighed the soothsayer; with his last sigh, however, Zarathustra again became serene and assured, like one who has come out of a deep chasm into the light. "No! No! Three times no!" he exclaimed with a strong voice, and stroked his beard—"I know better than *that*! There are still happy islands! Silence *about that*, you sighing bag of sorrows!

"Stop splashing *on that*, you rain cloud of morning! Do I not stand here already wet with your misery and drenched like a dog?

"Now I shall shake myself and run away from you, so that I may become dry again: don't be surprised at that! Do I seem discourteous to you? But this is *my* court.

"But as regards the higher man: well! I shall seek him at once in those forests: his cry came *from there*. Perhaps he is being attacked by an evil beast.

"He is in *my* domain: here he shall not come to harm! And truly, there are many evil beasts about me."—

With those words Zarathustra turned to go. Then the soothsayer said: "O Zarathustra, you are a rogue!

"I know it well: you would like to be rid of me! You would rather run into the forest and lay snares for evil beasts!

"But what good will it do you? In the evening you will have me back again; I will sit in your own cave, patient and heavy as a block—and wait for you!"

"So be it!" shouted back Zarathustra as he went away: "and whatever is mine in my cave is yours too, my guest!

"But if you find honey in there, well! just lick it up, you growling bear, and sweeten your soul! For in the evening we must both be cheerful;

—"cheerful and gay, because this day has come to an end! And you yourself will dance to my songs, as my dancing bear.

"Don't you believe it? You shake your head? Well! Cheer up, old bear! But I too—am a soothsayer."

Thus spoke Zarathustra.

CONVERSATION WITH KINGS

1

Before Zarathustra had been an hour on his way in the mountains and forests he suddenly observed a strange procession. Right on the path which he was about to descend two kings came walking, adorned with crowns and purple belts and as colorful as flamingos: they drove before them a laden ass. "What do these kings want in my domain?" said Zarathustra in astonishment to his heart, and he quickly hid behind a bush. But when the kings drew near he said half aloud, like someone talking to himself: "Strange! Strange! How does this fit together? I see two kings—and only one ass!"

At that the two kings halted, smiled, looked towards the spot from which the voice came, and then looked at one another. "We might think such things too," said the king on the right, "but we do not say them."

The king on the left, however, shrugged his shoulders and answered: "Perhaps that is a goatherd. Or a hermit who has lived too long among rocks and trees. For no society at all also spoils good manners."

"Good manners?" the other king replied angrily and bitterly: "what is it we are trying to get away from? Is it not 'good manners'? Our 'good society'?

"Better, truly, to live among hermits and goatherds than with our gilded, false, painted mob—though it call itself 'good society.'

—"though it call itself 'nobility.' But everything there is false and foul, above all the blood, thanks to evil old diseases and worse quacks.

"The best and dearest to me today is a healthy peasant, coarse, shrewd, obstinate and enduring: that is the noblest type today.

"The peasant is the best today; and the peasant type should be master! But ours is the kingdom of the mob—I no longer let myself be deceived. Mob, however, means hodgepodge.

"Mob hodgepodge: in that everything is mixed with everything, saint and swindler and gentleman and Jew and every beast out of Noah's ark.

"Good manners! Everything is false and foul with us. No one knows any longer how to revere: it is precisely *that* we are running away from. They are insipid, obtrusive curs; they gild palm leaves.

"This disgust chokes me, that we kings ourselves have become false, draped and disguised with the old yellowed pomp of our grandfathers, showpieces for the stupidest and the craftiest and whoever traffics for power today!

"We *are not* the first—and yet must *represent* them: we have at last become weary and disgusted with this deception.

"We have gone away from the rabble, from all those ranters and scribbling bluebottles, from the stench of shopkeepers, the ambitious wriggling, the bad breath—: phew, to live among the rabble;

—phew, for representing the first men among the rabble! Ah, disgust! disgust! disgust! What do we kings matter now!"—

"Your old sickness is upon you," said the king on the left, "your disgust seizes you, my poor brother. But you know that someone is listening to us."

Just then Zarathustra, who had opened his ears and eyes wide at this talk, rose from his hiding place, advanced towards the kings and began:

"He who listens to you, he who likes to listen to you, O kings, is called Zarathustra.

"I am Zarathustra, who once said: 'What do kings matter now!' Forgive me, it delighted me when you said to each other: 'What do we kings matter now!'

"But here is *my* realm and my dominion: what might you be seeking in my domain? But perhaps on your way you have *found* what *I* seek: namely, the higher man."

When the kings heard this, they beat their breasts and said with one voice: "We have been recognized!

"With the sword of these words you sever the thickest darkness of our hearts. You have discovered our distress, for behold! we are on our way to find the higher man—

"—the man who is higher than we: although we are kings. To him we convey this ass. For the highest man shall also be the highest lord on earth.

"There is no worse misfortune in all human destiny than when the mighty of the earth are not also the first men. Then everything becomes false and distorted and monstrous.

"And when they are even the last men, and more beast than man, then the price of the mob rises and rises, and at last mob virtue even says: 'Behold, I alone am virtue!' "—

"What have I just heard?" replied Zarathustra; "what wisdom from kings! I am enchanted, and truly, I already feel the urge to make a rhyme about it:—

"—even if it should be a rhyme not fit for every one's ears. I unlearned long ago to have consideration for long ears. Well then! Come on!"

(But here it happened that the ass too found speech:[2] it said distinctly and maliciously, Yea-Yuh.)

> Once upon a time—I believe, in the year of our grace
> number one—
> the Sybil spoke, drunk without wine:
> "Woe, now all goes to pieces!
> "Decay! Decay! The world never sank so deep!
> "Rome sank to a whore and to a whorehouse,
> "Rome's Caesar sank to a beast, God himself—to Jew!"

2

These rhymes of Zarathustra delighted the kings; but the king on the right said: "O Zarathustra, how well we did to set out to see you!

"For your enemies showed us your image in their mirror: there you looked out with the sneering grimace of a devil: so that we were afraid of you.

"But what good did it do! You always stung us again in our hearts and ears with your sayings. Then we said at last: What does it matter how he looks!

"We must *hear* him, him who teaches: 'You shall love peace as a means to new wars, and the short peace more than the long!'

"No one ever spoke such warlike words: 'What is good? To be brave is good. It is the good war that hallows every cause.'

"O Zarathustra, our fathers' blood stirred in our veins at such words: it was like the voice of spring to old wine-casks.

"When the swords ran wild like red spotted snakes, then our fathers grew fond of life; the sun of every peace seemed to them languid and lukewarm, but the long peace made them ashamed.

"How they sighed, our fathers, when they saw brightly polished, dried-up swords on the wall! Like them they thirsted for war. For a sword thirsts to drink blood and sparkles with desire."——

—When the kings spoke thus and talked eagerly of the happiness of their fathers, Zarathustra was overcome with no small temptation to mock their eagerness: for obviously they were very peaceful kings whom he saw before him, kings with old and refined features. But he restrained himself. "Well!" he said, "there leads the way, there lies the cave of Zarathustra; and this day shall yet have a long evening! But at present a cry of distress calls me urgently away from you.

"It will honor my cave if kings want to sit and wait in it: but, to be sure, you will have to wait long!

"Well! What of that! Where today does one learn better to wait than at court? And all the virtue left to kings—is it not today called: *being able* to wait?"

Thus spoke Zarathustra.

THE LEECH

AND ZARATHUSTRA WENT THOUGHTFULLY on, further and deeper, through forests and past swampy valleys; but as happens with those who meditate on hard matters he accidentally stepped on a man. And behold, suddenly a cry of pain and two curses and twenty little invectives splashed into his face so that in his fright he raised his stick and also struck the man he had stepped on. Immediately afterwards, however, he regained his composure; and his heart laughed at the folly he had just committed.

"Forgive me," he said to the man he had stepped on, who had got up enraged and sat down again, "forgive me, and hear first of all a parable.

"As a wanderer who dreams of remote things on a lonesome highway runs unawares against a sleeping dog, a dog which lies in the sun:

"—as both of them then stare up and snap at each other, like deadly enemies, these two mortally frightened beings—so did it happen to us.

"And yet! And yet—how little was lacking for them to caress each other, that dog and that solitary! Are they not both—solitaries!"

—"Whoever you are," said the trodden one, still enraged, "you come too near me with your parable, and not only with your foot!

"Behold, am I then a dog?"—And at that the sitting one got up, and pulled his naked arm out of the swamp. For at first he had lain outstretched on the ground, hidden and indiscernible, like those who lie in wait for a swamp animal.

"But what are you doing!" cried Zarathustra in alarm, for he saw blood streaming over the naked arm,—"what has hurt you? Has an evil beast bit you, you unfortunate one?"

The bleeding one laughed, still angry, "What do you care!" he said, and was about to go on. "Here am I at home and in my province. Whoever will question me, let him: but I will not reply to a moron."

"You are mistaken," said Zarathustra sympathetically, and held him fast; "you are mistaken. Here you are not at home, but in my domain, and here no one shall receive any harm.

"But call me what you will—I am who I must be. I call myself Zarathustra.

"Well! Up there is the way to Zarathustra's cave: it is not far,— won't you tend to your wounds at my home?

"It has gone badly with you, you unfortunate one, in this life: first a beast bit you, and then—a man trod upon you!"——

But when the trodden one had heard the name of Zarathustra, he changed. "What has happened to me!" he exclaimed, "*who* concerns me so much in this life as this one man, Zarathustra, and that one animal that lives on blood, the leech?

"For the sake of the leech I have lain here by this swamp, like a fisher, and already my outstretched arm had been bitten ten times, when now a finer leech bites at my blood, Zarathustra himself!

"O happiness! O miracle! Praised be the day that enticed me into the swamp! Praised be the best, the liveliest cupper living today, praised be the great leech of conscience, Zarathustra!"—

Thus spoke the man Zarathustra had stepped on, and Zarathustra rejoiced at his words and their refined, respectful style. "Who are you?" he asked and gave him his hand, "there is much to clear up and elucidate between us: but already, it seems to me, the day dawns pure and bright."

"I am *the conscientious in spirit*," answered he who was asked, "and in matters of the spirit it is difficult for any one to take it more rigorously, more strictly, and more severely than I, except him from whom I learned it, Zarathustra himself.

"Better to know nothing than to half-know many things! Better to be a fool on one's own account, than a sage in other people's estimation! I—get to the bottom:

—"what does it matter if it is great or small? If it is called swamp or sky? A hand's breadth of ground is enough for me, if it really is ground and bottom!

—A hand's breadth of ground: one can stand on that. In the conscience of knowledge there is nothing great and nothing small."

"So perhaps you are an expert on leeches?" asked Zarathustra; "and you investigate the leech to its ultimate grounds, you conscientious one?"

"O Zarathustra," answered the trodden man, "that would be an immensity, how could I presume to do so!

"But what I am master of and expert on is the *brain* of the leech:—that is *my* world!

"And it is also a world! But forgive me that my pride speaks out here, for here I do not have my equal. Therefore I said: 'here I am at home.'

"How long have I investigated this one thing, the brain of the leech, so that here the slippery truth might no longer slip from me! Here is *my* domain!

"For the sake of this I cast everything else aside, for the sake of this everything else becomes indifferent to me; and close beside my knowledge lies my black ignorance.

"My spiritual conscience requires of me that it should be so, that I should know one thing and not know everything else: I am disgusted by all the half-spirited, all the hazy, hovering, and visionary.

"Where my honesty ends I am blind, and also want to be blind. But where I want to know I also want to be honest, namely, hard, rigorous, strict, cruel, inexorable.

"Because *you* once said, O Zarathustra: 'Spirit is life that itself cuts into life,' that led and seduced me to your teaching. And truly, with my own blood I have increased my own knowledge!"

—"As the evidence indicates," broke in Zarathustra; for the blood was still flowing down the naked arm of the conscientious one. For ten leeches had bitten into it.

"O you strange fellow, how much this evidence tells me, namely from you yourself! And perhaps I could not pour all of it into your strict ears!

"Well then! We part here! But I would like to meet you again. Up there is the way to my cave: tonight you will be my welcome guest!

"I would also like to make amends to your body for Zarathustra treading upon you with his feet: I shall think about that. Just now, however, a cry of distress calls me hastily away from you."

Thus spoke Zarathustra.

The Magician

1

But when Zarathustra had gone around a rock he saw on the same path, not far below him, a man who threw his limbs about like a maniac, and at last tumbled to the ground on his belly. "Stop!" Zarathustra said then to his heart, "he there must surely be the higher man, from him came that dreadful cry of distress,—I will see if I can help him." But when he ran to the spot where the man lay on the ground, he found a trembling old man who stared; and all of Zarathustra's efforts to lift him and set him again on his feet were in vain. The unfortunate one, too, did not seem to notice that someone was beside him; on the contrary, he continually looked around with pathetic gestures, like one forsaken by and isolated from all the world. At last, however, after much trembling, convulsion, and contortion, he began to wail thus:

> Who warms me, who loves me still?
>> Give hot hands!
>> Give charcoal-warmers of the heart!
> Stretched out, shuddering,
> Like the half dead, whose feet one warms—
> Shaken, ah! by unknown fevers,

Shivering with sharp icy frost-arrows,
Hunted by you, thought!
Unnamable! Veiled! Terrible!
You hunter behind clouds!
Struck down by your lightning bolt,
You mocking eye that stares at me from the dark:
                                        —thus I lie,

bent, twisted, convulsed
With all eternal torture,
Struck
By you, cruelest hunter,
You unknown—*god*!

Strike deeper!
Strike yet *once* more!
Stake through, break this heart!
Why this torture
With blunt-toothed arrows?
Why do you keep looking,
Not tired of human pain,
Pleased to see suffering with gods' lightning eyes?
You do not want to kill,
Only torture, torture?
Why—torture *me*,
You sadistic, unknown God?—
Ha ha! You are stealing near?
In such midnight
What do you want? Speak!
You crowd me, press me—
Ha! far too closely!
Away! Away!
You hear me breathing,
You overhear my heart,
You jealous—
Jealous of what?
Away! Away! Why the ladder?
Do you want *in*,
Into my heart,

Climb in, deep into my most secret
Thoughts to climb?
Shameless! Unknown—thief!
What do you want with your stealing?
What do you want with your listening?
What do you want with your torturing,
You torturer!
You—hangman-god!
Or shall I, like the dogs,
Roll for you?
Cringing, enraptured, beside myself,
Wag with love—for you?

In vain! Stick further,
Cruelest thorn! No,
No dog—I am only your game,
Cruelest hunter!
Your proudest captive,
You robber behind clouds!
Speak at last!
You lightning-veiled! Unknown! Speak,
What do you want, highway-ambusher, from—*me*?
What do you want, unknown—God?——
What? Ransom?
What do you want with ransom?
Demand much—my pride advises that!
And be brief—my other pride advises that!

Ha ha!
Me—you want? Me?
Me—entirely? . . .
Ha ha!
And torture me, fool that you are,
Racking my pride?
Give *love* to me—who still warms me?
Who still loves me?—give hot hands,
Give charcoal-warmers of the heart,
Give me, the loneliest,
Whom ice, ah! sevenfold ice

Has taught to long for enemies,
For enemies themselves,
Give, yes yield,
Cruelest enemy,
to me—*yourself!*——

Away!
He himself fled,
My single last companion,
My great enemy,
My unknown
My hangman-god!—

—No! Come back,
With all your tortures!
To the last of all the lonely
O come back!
All the streams of my tears run
Their course to you!
And my last heart's flame—
Flares up to *you*!
O come back,
My unknown God! My *pain*!
My last—happiness!

2

—But here Zarathustra could no longer restrain himself, took his stick and struck the wailer with all his might. "Stop it!" he shouted at him with furious laughter, "stop this, you actor! You counterfeiter! You liar from the ground up![3] I know you well!

"I will warm your legs for you, you evil magician, for such as you I know very well how—to make things hot!"

—"Leave off," the old man said and sprang up from the ground, "strike me no more, O Zarathustra! I did it only for fun!

"That kind of thing belongs to my art; it was you that I wanted to try out when I gave this performance. And truly, you have seen quite through me!

"But you too—have given me no small proof of yourself: you are *hard*, you wise Zarathustra! You strike hard with your 'truths,' your stick forces from me—*this* truth!"

—"Do not flatter me," answered Zarathustra, still excited and frowning, "you actor from the ground up! You are false: why do you speak—of truth!

"You peacock of peacocks, you sea of vanity; *what* did you represent before me, you evil magician; *whom* was I meant to believe in when you wailed in this way?"

"*The ascetic of the spirit*," said the old man, "it was him—I represented; you yourself once invented this expression—

"—The poet and magician who at last turns his spirit against himself, the transformed one who freezes through his evil science and conscience.

"And just admit it: it was a long while, O Zarathustra, before you discovered my trick and lie! You *believed* in my distress when you held my head with both your hands,—

"—I heard you lament 'he has been loved too little, loved too little!' That I so far deceived you made my malice rejoice in me."

"You may have deceived subtler ones than I," said Zarathustra sternly. "I am not on my guard against deceivers, I *must* be without caution: so my lot wants it.

"But you—*must* deceive: so far do I know you! You must ever be equivocal, tri- quadri-, quinquivocal! Even what you just confessed is not nearly true enough nor false enough for me!

"You bad counterfeiter, how could you do otherwise! You would even rouge your disease if you showed yourself naked to your physician.

"Thus you rouged your lie before me when you said: 'I did so *only* for fun!' There was also *seriousness* in it, you *are* something of an ascetic of the spirit!

"I divine you well: you have become the enchanter of all, but against yourself you have no lie or cunning left—you are disenchanted with yourself!

"You have reaped disgust as your one truth. No word in you is genuine any more, but your mouth is so: that is, the disgust that clings to your mouth."—

—"Well who are you!" the old magician cried then with defiant voice, "who dares to speak thus to *me*, the greatest man living today?"—and a green flash shot from his eye at Zarathustra. But immediately afterward he changed, and said sadly:

"O Zarathustra, I am weary of it, I am disgusted with my arts, I am not *great*, why do I dissemble! But you know it well—I sought greatness!

"I wanted to appear to be a great man and persuaded many: but this lie is beyond my strength. It is breaking me.

"O Zarathustra, everything about me is a lie; but that I am breaking—this my breaking is *genuine*!"—

"It honors you," said Zarathustra gloomily and looking aside, "it honors you that you sought greatness, but it betrays you too. You are not great.

"You bad old magician, *that* is the best and the most honest thing I honor in you, that you have become weary of yourself, and have expressed it: 'I am not great.'

"*In that* I honor you as an ascetic of the spirit, and although only for the twinkling of an eye, in that one moment you were—genuine.

"But tell me, what are you looking for here in *my* forests and rocks? And lying down in *my* way, how did you want to try me?—

—in what did you test *me*?"

Thus spoke Zarathustra, and his eyes sparkled. The old magician was silent for a while, then he said: "Did I seek to test you? I—only seek.

"O Zarathustra, I seek a genuine one, a right one, a simple one, an unequivocal one, a man of all honesty, a vessel of wisdom, a saint of knowledge, a great man!

"Don't you know it, O Zarathustra? *I seek Zarathustra*."

—And here there was a long silence between them; but Zarathustra became profoundly absorbed in thought, so that he shut his eyes. But afterwards coming back to his companion in the conversation, he grasped the hand of the magician and said, full of politeness and cunning:

"Well! The way leads up there, there is the cave of Zarathustra. In it you may seek him whom you would like to find.

"And ask counsel of my animals, my eagle and my serpent: they shall help you to seek. But my cave is large.

"I myself, to be sure—I have as yet seen no great man. For what is great, even the subtlest eye today is too coarse. It is the kingdom of the mob.

"I have found many who stretched and inflated themselves, and the people cried: 'Look there, a great man!' But what good are all bellows! In the end, wind comes out.

"At last the frog bursts which has inflated itself too long: then out comes wind. To prick a swollen one in the belly, I call that good fun. Hear that, you boys!

"Today belongs to the mob: who still *knows* what is great and what is small! Who could successfully seek greatness there! Only a fool: fools succeed.

"You seek for great men, you strange fool? Who *taught* you to? Is today the time for it? Oh, you evil seeker, why do you—seek to test me?"[4]—

Thus spoke Zarathustra, comforted in his heart, and went laughing on his way.

Retired from Service

BUT NOT LONG AFTER Zarathustra had freed himself from the magician, he again saw a person sitting beside the path which he followed, namely a tall, black man, with a haggard, pale face: *this man* grieved him exceedingly. "Ah," he said to his heart, "there sits disguised misery, that looks to me like the priestly sort: what does *it* want in my domain?

"What! Hardly have I escaped from that magician: must another necromancer cross my path,—

"—Some wizard with the laying-on of hands, some somber wonder worker by the grace of God, some anointed world-slanderer: may the devil take him!

"But the devil is never in his proper place: he always comes too late, that damned dwarf and clubfoot!"—

Thus cursed Zarathustra impatiently in his heart, and he considered how he might slip past the black man with his face turned: but behold, it came about otherwise. For at the same moment the sitting one had already seen him; and not unlike one whom an unexpected happiness overtakes, he sprang to his feet and went straight towards Zarathustra.

"Whoever you are, you traveler," he said, "help a strayed one, a seeker, an old man, who may easily come to grief here!

"The world here is strange to me and remote, I heard wild beasts howling, too; and he who could have given me protection, he is no more.

"I was seeking the last pious man, a saint and a hermit, who, alone in his forest, had not yet heard of what all the world knows today."

"*What* does all the world know today?" asked Zarathustra. "Perhaps this, that the old God, in whom all the world once believed, no longer lives?"

"You say it," answered the old man sorrowfully. "And I served that old God until his last hour.

"But now I am retired from service, without master, and yet not free; likewise I am no longer merry even for an hour, except in recollections.

"Therefore I climbed into these mountains, that I might finally have a festival for myself once more, as becomes an old pope and church-father: for I am the last pope!—a festival of pious recollections and divine services.

"But now he himself is dead, the most pious of men, the saint in the forest, who praised his God constantly with singing and mumbling.

"I no longer found him when I discovered his hut—but I found two wolves inside it, which howled on account of his death,—for all animals loved him. Then I hurried away.

"Did I thus come in vain into these forests and mountains? Then my heart determined that I should seek another, the most pious of all those who do not believe in God—, my heart determined that I should seek Zarathustra!"

Thus spoke the old man and gazed with keen eyes at him who stood before him. But Zarathustra seized the hand of the old pope and regarded it a long while with admiration.

"Behold, you venerable one," he said then, "what a fine and long hand! That is the hand of one who has always dispensed blessings. But now it holds fast him whom you seek, me, Zarathustra.

"It is I, Zarathustra the godless, who says: 'Who is ungodlier than I, that I may delight in his instruction?' "—

Thus spoke Zarathustra, and penetrated with his glances the thoughts and afterthoughts of the old pope. At last the latter began:

"He who most loved and possessed him has now also lost him most—:

"—Lo, I myself am surely the most godless of us at present? But who could rejoice at that!"—

—"You served him to the last?" asked Zarathustra thoughtfully, after a deep silence, "You know *how* he died? Is it true what they say, that pity choked him,

"—that he saw how *man* hung on the cross, and could not endure it;—that his love for man became his hell, and at last his death?"—

But the old pope did not answer, but looked aside timidly, with a painful and dark expression.

"Let him go," said Zarathustra, after prolonged meditation, still looking the old man straight in the eye.

"Let him go, he is gone. And though it honors you that you speak only in praise of this dead one, yet you know as well as I *who* he was, and that he went curious ways."

"To speak before three eyes," said the old pope cheerfully (he was blind in one eye), "I am more enlightened than Zarathustra himself in divine matters—and appropriately so.

"My love served him for long years, my will followed all his will. A good servant, however, knows everything, and many a thing which a master hides even from himself.

"He was a hidden god, full of secrecy. Truly, he did not come by his son otherwise than by secret ways. At the door of his faith stands adultery.

"Whoever extols him as a God of love, does not think highly enough of love itself. Did not that God want also to be judge? But the loving one loves irrespective of reward and punishment.

"When he was young, that God out of the orient, then he was harsh and vengeful, and built a hell for the delight of his favorites.

"But at last he became old and soft and mellow and pitiful, more like a grandfather than a father, but most like a tottering old grandmother.

"There he sat shriveled in his chimney-corner, fretting on account of his weak legs, world-weary, will-weary, and one day he suffocated of his all-too-great pity."——

"You old pope," said Zarathustra interposing, "have you seen *that* with your eyes? It could well have happened in that way: in that way, *and* also otherwise. When gods die they always die many kinds of death.

"Well! At all events, one way or other—he is gone! He offended the taste of my ears and eyes; worse than that I should not like to say against him.

"I love everything that looks bright and speaks honestly. But he—you know it, indeed, you old priest, there was something of your type in him, the priest-type—he was equivocal.

"He was also vague. How he raged at us, this wrath-snorter, because we understood him badly! But why did he not speak more clearly?

"And if the fault lay in our ears, why did he give us ears that heard him badly? If there was dirt in our ears, well! who put it in them?

"Too much miscarried with him, this potter who had not learned thoroughly! That he took revenge on his pots and creations, however, because they turned out badly—that was a sin against *good taste*.

"In piety there is also good taste: *this* said at last: 'Away with *such* a god! Better to have no god, better to set up destiny on one's own account, better to be a fool, better to be god oneself!' "

—"What do I hear!" the old pope said then, listening intently; "O Zarathustra, you are more pious than you believe, with such unbelief! Some god in you has converted you to your ungodliness.

"Is it not your piety itself which no longer lets you believe in a God? And your over-great honesty will yet lead you even beyond good and evil!

"Behold, what has been reserved for you? You have eyes and hands and mouth, which have been predestined for blessing from eternity. One does not bless with the hand alone.

"Near to you, though you profess to be the ungodliest one, I scent a stealthy odor of holiness and well-being that comes from long benedictions: I feel glad and grieved through it.

"Let me be your guest, O Zarathustra, for a single night! Nowhere on earth shall I now feel better than with you!"—

"Amen! So shall it be!" said Zarathustra, with great astonishment; "up there leads the way, there lies the cave of Zarathustra.

"Gladly, indeed, would I conduct you there myself, you venerable one, for I love all pious men. But now a cry of distress calls me hastily away from you.

"In my domain no one shall come to grief; my cave is a good haven. And best of all I would like to put every sorrowful one again on firm land and firm legs.

"Who, however, could take *your* melancholy off your shoulders? For that I am too weak. Truly, we should have to wait long until some one reawakened your god for you.

For that old god lives no more: he is quite dead."—

Thus spoke Zarathustra.

The Ugliest Man

—And again Zarathustra's feet ran through mountains and forests, and his eyes sought and sought, but they nowhere found whom they wanted to see, the great sufferer and crier of distress. But all the time he was on his way he rejoiced in his heart and was full of gratitude. "What good things," he said, "has this day given me, as amends for its bad beginning! What strange interlocutors have I found!

"At their words I will now chew a long while as at good corn; my teeth shall grind and crush them small, until they flow like milk into my soul!"—

But when the path again curved round a rock, suddenly the landscape changed, and Zarathustra entered into a realm of death. Here black and red cliffs bristled up, without any grass, tree, or bird's voice. For it was a valley which all animals avoided, even the beasts of prey, except that a species of ugly, thick, green snake came here to die when they became old. Therefore the shepherds called this valley: "Snake's Death."

But Zarathustra became absorbed in dark recollections, for it seemed to him that he had once before stood in this valley. And much heaviness settled on his mind, so that he walked slowly and always more slowly, and at last stood still. Then, however, when he opened his eyes, he saw something sitting by the wayside shaped like a man and yet hardly like a man, something unspeakable. And suddenly there came over Zarathustra a great shame, because he had gazed on such a thing: blushing to the very roots of his white hair, he turned aside his glance, and raised his foot that he might leave this evil place. But then the dead wilderness resounded: for from the ground a noise welled up, gurgling and rattling, as water gurgles and rattles at night through stopped-up water-pipes; and at last it turned into human voice and human speech:—it sounded thus:

"Zarathustra! Zarathustra! Read my riddle! Speak, speak! What is the *revenge on the witness?*

"I entice you back; here is slippery ice! See to it, see to it, that your pride does not break its legs here!

"You think yourself wise, you proud Zarathustra! Read then the riddle, you hard nutcracker,—the riddle that I am! Say then: who am *I!*"

—But when Zarathustra had heard these words—what do you think took place in his soul then? *Pity overcame him*; and he sank down suddenly, like an oak that has long withstood many lumber-jacks,—heavily, suddenly, to the terror even of those who meant to fell it. But immediately he got up again from the ground, and his face became stern.

"I know you well," he said, with a brazen voice, "*You are the murderer of God!* Let me go.

"You could not *endure* him who saw *you*,—who ever saw you through and through, you ugliest man. You took revenge on this witness!"

Thus spoke Zarathustra and was about to go; but the unspeakable grasped at a corner of his garment and began again to gurgle and seek for words. "Stay," he said at last—

—"stay! Do not pass by! I have divined what axe it was that struck you to the ground: hail to you, O Zarathustra, that you are again upon your feet!

"You have divined, I know it well, how he who killed him feels,—the murderer of God. Stay! Sit down here beside me; it is not to no purpose.

"To whom would I go but to you? Stay, sit down! Do not however look at me! Honor thus—my ugliness![5]

"They persecute me: now *you* are my last refuge. *Not* with their hatred, *not* with their henchmen—oh, I will mock such persecution, and be proud and cheerful!

"Has not all success so far been with the well-persecuted? And he who persecutes well learns readily to *follow*—when once he is—put behind! But it is their *pity*—

—"it is from their pity that I flee away and flee to you. O Zarathustra, protect me, you, my last refuge, you the only one who saw into me:

—"you have divined how the man feels who killed *him*. Stay! And if you will go, you impatient one, do not go the way that I came. *That* way is bad.

"Are you angry with me because I have already mangled language too long? Because I have already advised you? But know that it is I, the ugliest man,

—"who also has the largest, heaviest feet. Where *I* have gone, the way is bad. I tread all paths to death and destruction.

"But that you passed me by in silence; that you blushed, I saw it well: by that I knew you as Zarathustra.

"Every one else would have thrown his alms to me, his pity, in look and speech. But for that—I am not beggar enough: you understood that—

"for that I am too *rich*, rich in what is great, frightful, ugliest, most unspeakable! Your shame, O Zarathustra, *honored* me!

"With difficulty I removed myself from the importunate crowd of the pitiful—that I might find the only one who at present teaches that 'pity importunes'—you, O Zarathustra!

—"whether it is the pity of a god, or whether it is human pity: it is offensive to modesty. And unwillingness to help may be nobler than the virtue that rushes to do so.

"But *that*, pity, is called virtue itself today by all little people— they have no reverence for great misfortune, great ugliness, great failure.

"I look beyond all these, as a dog looks over the backs of thronging flocks of sheep. They are little good-wooled good-willed grey people.

"As the heron looks contemptuously at shallow pools, with its head bent back, so I look at the throng of grey little waves and wills and souls.

"Too long have we acknowledged them to be right, those little people: *thus* we have at last given them power as well—and now they teach: 'good is only what little people call good.'

"And 'truth' today is what the preacher spoke who himself sprang from them, that singular saint and advocate of the little people, who testified of himself 'I—am the truth.'

"That immodest one has long made the little people greatly puffed up—he who taught no small error when he taught 'I—am the truth.'

"Has an immodest one ever been answered more courteously?— You, however, O Zarathustra, passed him by, and spoke: 'No! No! Three times no!'

"You warned against his error, you were the first to warn against pity—not all, not none, but you and your kind.

"You are ashamed of the shame of the great sufferer; and truly when you say 'from pity there comes a grey cloud, take care, mankind!'

—"when you teach 'all creators are hard, all great love is beyond pity:' O Zarathustra, how well versed in weather signs you seem to me!

"But you yourself—warn yourself too against *your* pity! For many are on their way to you, many suffering, doubting, despairing, drowning, freezing ones—

"I warn you too against myself. You have read my best, my worst riddle, myself, and what I have done. I know the axe that fells you.

"But he—*had to* die: he looked with eyes which saw *every-thing*,—he saw men's depths and dregs, all his hidden ignominy and ugliness.

"His pity knew no shame: he crept into my dirtiest corners. This most prying, over-intrusive, over-pitiful one had to die.

"He always saw *me*: on such a witness I would have revenge—or not live myself.

"The god who saw everything, *even man*: that god had to die! Man cannot *bear it* that such a witness should live."

Thus spoke the ugliest man. But Zarathustra got up and pre-pared to go on: for he was chilled to the marrow.

"You unspeakable," he said, "you warned me against your way. As thanks for it I recommend mine to you. Behold, up there is the cave of Zarathustra.

"My cave is large and deep and has many corners; there the best hidden finds his hiding place. And close beside it, there are a hundred lurking places and byways for creeping, fluttering, and hopping creatures.

"You outcast who cast yourself out, you will not live among men and men's pity? Well then, do as I do! Thus you will learn from me too; only the doer learns.

"And speak first and foremost with my animals! The proudest animal and the wisest animal—they may well be the best counselors for us both!"—

Thus spoke Zarathustra and went his way, even more thoughtfully and slowly than before: for he asked himself many things, and hardly knew what to answer.

"How poor indeed is man," he thought in his heart, "how ugly, how wheezing, how full of hidden shame!

"They tell me that man loves himself. Ah, how great must that self-love be! How much contempt is opposed to it!

"Even this man has loved himself, as he has despised himself,— he seems to me a great lover and a great despiser.

"No one yet have I found who despised himself more deeply: even *that* is height. Ah, was *he* perhaps the higher man whose cry I heard?

"I love the great despisers. But man is something that must be overcome."——

THE VOLUNTARY BEGGAR

WHEN ZARATHUSTRA HAD LEFT the ugliest man he felt chilled and alone: for much coldness and loneliness came over his spirit, so that even his limbs became colder. But when he wandered on and on, uphill and down, at times past green meadows, though also sometimes over wild stony lows, where formerly perhaps an impatient brook had made its bed: then suddenly he grew warmer and cheerful again.

"What has happened to me?" he asked himself, "something warm and living refreshes me, it must be nearby.

"Already I am less alone; unknown companions and brothers circle around me, their warm breath touches my soul."

But when he peered about and sought for the comforters of his loneliness, behold, there were cows standing together on a knoll; it was their nearness and odor that had warmed his heart. But the cows seemed to listen eagerly to a speaker, and paid no heed to him who approached. When, however, Zarathustra was quite near to them, then he heard plainly that a human voice spoke in the midst of the cows; and apparently all of them had turned their heads towards the speaker.

Then Zarathustra eagerly sprang up and pulled the animals aside, for he feared that someone had had an accident, which the pity of the cows could hardly relieve. But in this he was deceived; for behold, there sat a man on the ground who seemed to be persuading the animals to have no fear of him, a peaceable man and preacher on the mount, out of whose eyes goodness itself preached.[6] "What do you seek here?" called out Zarathustra in astonishment.

"What do I seek here?" he answered: "just what you seek, you disturber of the peace; that is, happiness on earth.

"But to that end I would like to learn from these cows. For I tell you that I have already talked half a morning to them, and just now they were about to give me their answer. Why do you disturb them?

"Unless we are converted and become as cows, we shall not enter into the kingdom of heaven. For we ought to learn one thing from them: ruminating.

"And truly, though a man should gain the whole world, and yet not learn one thing, ruminating, what would it profit him! He would not be rid of his misery,

—"his great misery: that, however, is today called *disgust*. Who today does not have his heart, his mouth and his eyes full of disgust? You too! You too! But regard these cows!"—

Thus spoke the preacher on the mount and then turned then his gaze towards Zarathustra—for so far it had rested lovingly on the cows—: but then he changed. "Who is it that I am speaking with?" he exclaimed, frightened, and sprang up from the ground.

"This is the man without disgust, this is Zarathustra himself, the overcomer of the great disgust, this is the eye, this is the mouth, this is the heart of Zarathustra himself."

And while he thus spoke he kissed with overflowing eyes the hands of him with whom he spoke, and behaved altogether like one to whom a precious gift and jewel has unexpectedly fallen from heaven. But the cows looked at it all and were amazed.

"Do not speak of me, you strange one! Dear one!" said Zarathustra, restraining his affection, "speak to me first of yourself! Are you not the voluntary beggar who once cast away great riches,—

—"Who was ashamed of his riches and of the rich, and fled to the poorest to give them his abundance and his heart? But they received him not."

"But they received me not," said the voluntary beggar, "you know it, indeed. So I went at last to the animals and to these cows."

"Then you learned," interrupted Zarathustra, "how much harder it is to give properly than to take properly, and that gift-giving well is an *art*—the last, subtlest master-art of kindness."

"Especially nowadays," answered the voluntary beggar: "at present, that is to say, when everything low has become rebellious and exclusive and haughty in its manner: in the manner of the mob.

"For the hour has come, you know it well, for the great, evil, long, slow mob and slave rebellion: it grows and grows!

"Now all charity and any little giving away provokes the base; and the overrich may be on their guard!

"Whoever drips today, like bulging bottles out of all-too-narrow necks—today the necks of such bottles are broken gladly.

"Lustful greed, bilious envy, sour vengefulness, mob pride: all this threw itself in my face. It is no longer true that the poor are blessed. The kingdom of heaven, however, is with the cows."

"And why is it not with the rich?" asked Zarathustra temptingly, while he kept back the cows which sniffed familiarly at the peaceful one.

"Why do you tempt me?" answered the other. "You know it yourself even better than I. What was it that drove me to the poorest, O Zarathustra? Was it not my disgust at the richest?

—"at the convicts of riches, with cold eyes and lewd thoughts, who pick up profit out of all kinds of rubbish, at this rabble that stinks to heaven,

—"at this gilded, debased mob, whose fathers were pickpockets or carrion crows or ragmen with compliant, lustful, forgetful wives—for they are all of them not much different from whores—

"Mob above, mob below! What are 'poor' and 'rich' today! I unlearned that distinction—then I fled away further and ever further, until I came to these cows."

Thus spoke the peaceful one and himself snorted and perspired with his words: so that the cows were again amazed. But Zarathustra kept looking into his face with a smile, all the time the man talked so severely, and then shook his head silently.

"You do violence to yourself, you preacher on the mount, when you use such severe words. Neither your mouth nor your eyes were made for such severity.

"Nor your stomach either, I think: *it* opposes all such rage and hatred and foaming over. Your stomach wants gentler things: you are no butcher.

"You seem to me rather a plant- and root-man. Perhaps you grind corn. But you are certainly disinclined to fleshly pleasures and you love honey."

"You have divined me well," answered the voluntary beggar, with lightened heart. "I love honey, I also grind corn, for I have sought out what tastes sweet and makes pure breath:

—"also what takes a long time, a day's-work and a mouth's-work for gentle idlers and loafers.

"To be sure, nobody has achieved more than these cows: they have devised ruminating and lying in the sun. They also abstain from all heavy thoughts that inflate the heart."

—"Well!" said Zarathustra, "you should also see *my* animals, my eagle and my serpent,—there is not their like on earth today.

"Behold, there leads the way to my cave: be its guest tonight. And talk to my animals of the happiness of animals,—

—"until I myself come home. For now a cry of distress calls me hastily away from you. Also, should you find new honey with me, ice-cold, golden-comb-honey, eat it!

"But now take leave of your cows at once, you strange one! Dear one! though it is hard for you. For they are your warmest friends and teachers!"—

—"One excepted, whom I hold still dearer," answered the voluntary beggar. "You yourself are good, O Zarathustra, and even better than a cow!"

"Away, away with you! you naughty flatterer!" cried Zarathustra mischievously, "why do you spoil me with such praise and honey of flattery?

"Away, away from me!" he cried once more and swung his stick at the affectionate beggar: who however ran nimbly away.

THE SHADOW

BUT SCARCELY HAD THE voluntary beggar gone in haste, and
Zarathustra was again alone, when he heard behind him a new
voice that called out: "Stop! Zarathustra! Wait! It is I, O Zarathustra, I, your shadow!" But Zarathustra did not wait, for a sud-
den irritation came over him on account of the crowd and the
crowding in his mountains. "Where has my solitude gone?" he
said.

"Truly, it is getting to be too much for me; these mountains are
swarming, my kingdom is no longer of *this* world, I need new
mountains.

"My shadow calls me? What matters my shadow! Let it run after
me! I—run away from it."

Thus spoke Zarathustra to his heart and ran away. But the one
behind followed after him, so that immediately there were three
runners, one after the other, namely, foremost the voluntary beggar, then Zarathustra, and thirdly and hindmost his shadow. But
not long had they run thus when Zarathustra became conscious
of his folly and shook off with one jerk all his irritation and
disgust.

"What!" he said, "haven't the most ludicrous things always happened to us old hermits and saints?

"Truly, my folly has grown high in the mountains! Now I hear six
foolish old legs rattling behind one another!

"But is Zarathustra really afraid of his own shadow? And anyway
I think that it has longer legs than mine."

Thus spoke Zarathustra, and, laughing with his eyes and his
guts, he stood still and turned around quickly—and behold, in
doing so he almost threw his shadow and follower to the ground, so
closely had the latter followed at his heels and so weak was he. For
when Zarathustra scrutinized him with his glance, he was frightened as if he suddenly saw a ghost, so slight, dark, hollow and spent
this follower seemed.

"Who are you?" asked Zarathustra vehemently, "what are you
doing here? And why do you call yourself my shadow? I do not
like you."

"Forgive me," answered the shadow, "that it is I; and you do not like me, well then, O Zarathustra! I admire you and your good taste for that.

"I am a wanderer, who has already walked long at your heels; always on the way, but without a goal, also without a home: so that truly, I am not far from being the Eternal Jew, except that I am not eternal and not a Jew.

"What? Must I ever be on the way? Whirled by every wind, unsettled, driven about? O earth, you have become too round for me!

"On every surface I have already sat, like tired dust I have fallen asleep on mirrors and windowpanes: everything takes from me, nothing gives; I become thin—I am almost like a shadow.

"But I have fled to you and followed you longest, O Zarathustra, and although I hid myself from you, I was nevertheless your best shadow: wherever you have sat I sat there too.

"I wandered about with you in the remotest, coldest worlds, like a ghost that voluntarily haunts winter roofs and snows.

"With you I have striven into all the forbidden, all the worst and the furthest: and if there is anything of virtue in me, it is that I have had no fear of any prohibition.

"With you I have broken up whatever my heart revered, I have overthrown all border stones and statues, I pursued the most dangerous wishes—truly, I once went beyond every crime.

"With you I unlearned the belief in words and values and great names. When the devil sheds his skin doesn't his name also fall away? It is also skin. The devil himself is perhaps—skin.

" 'Nothing is true, everything is permitted': so I said to myself. Into the coldest water I plunged with head and heart. Ah, how often I stood there naked on that account, like a red crab!

"Ah, where have all my goodness and all my shame and all my belief in the good gone! Ah, where is the lying innocence which I once possessed, the innocence of the good and of their noble lies!

"Too often, truly, I followed close on the heels of truth: then it kicked me in the face. Sometimes I meant to lie, and behold! then only did I hit—the truth.

"Too much has become clear to me: now it does not concern me any more. Nothing that I love lives any longer—how should I still love myself?

" 'To live as I wish, or not to live at all': so I want it; so also the holiest want it. But ah! how do *I* still have—desire?

"Do *I*—still have a goal? A haven towards which *my* sail is set?

"A good wind? Ah, only he who knows *where* he sails, knows what wind is good, and a fair wind for him.

"What still remains to me? A heart weary and insolent; a restless will; fluttering wings; a broken backbone.

"This seeking for *my* home: O Zarathustra, you know that this seeking has been *my* home-sickening, it consumes me.

'Where is—*my* home?' I ask and seek and have sought for it, I have not found it. O eternal everywhere, O eternal nowhere, O eternal—in vain!"

Thus spoke the shadow and Zarathustra's face lengthened at his words. "You are my shadow!" he said at last sadly.

"Your danger is not small, you free spirit and wanderer! You have had a bad day: see that a still worse evening does not overtake you!

"To such unsettled ones as you at last even a prison seems bliss. Have you ever seen how captured criminals sleep? They sleep quietly, they enjoy their new security.

"Beware or else in the end a narrow faith will capture you, a hard, rigorous illusion! For now everything that is narrow and fixed seduces and tempts you.

"You have lost your goal. Ah, how will you get over and laugh away that loss? With that—you have also lost your way!

"You poor traveler, rambler, you tired butterfly! would you have a rest and a home this evening? Then go up to my cave!

"There leads the way to my cave. And now I will run quickly away from you again. Already it is as if a shadow lay upon me.

"I will run alone, so that it may again become bright around me. Therefore I must still be a long time merrily upon my legs. But in the evening we shall—dance!"——

Thus spoke Zarathustra.

At Noon

—And Zarathustra ran and ran but he found no one else, and he was alone and ever found himself again, he enjoyed and drank his solitude and thought of good things for hours on end. About the hour of noon, however, when the sun stood exactly over Zarathustra's head, he passed an old, bent and gnarled tree, which was encircled by the abundant love of a vine, and hidden from itself: from it there hung yellow grapes in profusion, confronting the wanderer. Then he felt inclined to quench a little thirst, and to break off for himself a cluster of grapes. But when he had already reached out his arm to do so, he felt still more inclined for something else: namely, to lie down beside the tree at the hour of perfect noon and sleep.

This Zarathustra did; and no sooner had he laid himself on the ground in the stillness and secrecy of the mottled grass, than he forgot his modest thirst and fell asleep. For as the proverb of Zarathustra says: "One thing is more necessary than another." Only his eyes remained open—for they never grew weary of viewing and admiring the tree and the love of the vine. In falling asleep, however, Zarathustra spoke thus to his heart:

Hush! Hush! Has not the world become perfect just now? What has happened to me?

As a delicate wind dances invisibly upon parqueted seas, light, feather light: thus—sleep dances on me.

It does not close my eyes, it leaves my soul awake. It is light, truly! Feather light.

It persuades me, I know not how, it touches me inwardly with a caressing hand, it compels me. Yes, it compels me, so that my soul stretches itself out:—

—how long and weary it becomes, my strange soul! Has a seventh day's evening come to it precisely at noon? Has it already wandered too long, blissfully, among good and ripe things?

It stretches itself out, long, long—longer! it lies still, my strange soul. It has tasted too many good things, this golden sadness oppresses it, it twists its mouth.

Like a ship that puts into the calmest cove—now it draws up to the land, weary of long voyages and uncertain seas. Is not the land more faithful?

As such a ship hugs the shore, nestles the shore—there it's enough for a spider to spin its thread from the ship to the land. No stronger ropes are needed.

As such a weary ship in the calmest cove: so do I also repose now, near to the earth, faithful, trusting, waiting, bound to it with the lightest threads.

O happiness! O happiness! you will perhaps sing, O my soul? You lie in the grass. But this is the secret, solemn hour, when no shepherd plays his pipe.

Take care! Hot noon sleeps on the fields. Do not sing! Hush! The world is perfect.

Do not sing, you prairie bird, my soul! Do not even whisper! Look—hush! The old noon sleeps, it moves its mouth: does it not just now drink a drop of happiness—

—An old brown drop of golden happiness, golden wine? Something whisks over it, its happiness laughs. Thus—does a god laugh. Hush!—

—'For happiness, how little is sufficient for happiness!' Thus I spoke once and thought myself wise. But it was a blasphemy: *that* I have now learned. Wise fools speak better.

The least thing precisely, the gentlest thing, the lightest thing, a lizard's rustling, a breath, a whisk, a glance of an eye—*little* makes up the *best* happiness. Hush!

—What has happened to me? Listen! Has time flown away? Don't I fall? Have I not fallen—hark! into the well of eternity?

—What happens to me? Hush! It stings me—ah—to the heart? To the heart! Oh, break up, break up, my heart, after such happiness, after such a sting!

—What? Has not the world become perfect just now? Round and ripe? Oh, for the golden round ring—where does it fly? Let me run after it! Quick!

Hush——" (and here Zarathustra stretched himself, and felt that he was asleep.)

"Up!" he said to himself, "You sleeper! You noon sleeper! Well then, up, you old legs! It is time and past time; many a good stretch of road is still awaiting you—

Now you have slept your fill; for how long a time? A half-eternity! Well then, up now, my old heart! For how long after such a sleep may you—remain awake?"

(But then he fell asleep again, and his soul contradicted him and defended itself, and lay down again)—"Leave me alone! Hush! Has not the world become perfect just now? Oh, for the golden round ball!—

"Get up," said Zarathustra, "you little thief, you slacker! What! Still stretching yourself, yawning, sighing, falling into deep wells?

"Who are you then, O my soul!" (and here he became frightened, for a sunbeam shot down from the sky upon his face.)

"O heaven above me," he said sighing, and sat upright, "you gaze at me? You listen to my strange soul?

"When will you drink this drop of dew that fell down upon all earthly things,—when will you drink this strange soul—

—"when, you well of eternity! You joyous, awful, noon abyss! when will you drink my soul back into you?"

Thus spoke Zarathustra, and rose from his bed beside the tree, as if awakening from a strange drunkenness: and behold! the sun stood there still exactly above his head. But one might rightly infer from this that Zarathustra had not slept long.

The Greeting

IT WAS LATE IN the afternoon when Zarathustra, after long useless searching and strolling about, again came home to his cave. But when he stood over against it, not more than twenty paces from it, the thing happened which he now least of all expected: he heard again the great *cry of distress*. And extraordinary! this time the cry came out of his own cave. It was a protracted, manifold, strange cry, and Zarathustra plainly distinguished that it was composed of many voices: although heard at a distance it might sound like the cry of a single mouth.

At that Zarathustra rushed forward to his cave, and behold! what a spectacle awaited him after that concert! For there sat together all whom he had passed during the day: the king on the right and the king on the left, the old magician, the pope, the voluntary beggar, the shadow, the conscientious man of the spirit, the sorrowful soothsayer, and the ass; but the ugliest man had set a crown on his head, and had wound two purple belts around himself, for he liked, like all the ugly, to disguise himself and pretend to be beautiful. But in the midst of that melancholy company stood Zarathustra's eagle, ruffled and disquieted, for he had been expected to answer too many questions for which his pride had no answer; the wise serpent, however, hung round his neck.

All this Zarathustra saw with great astonishment; but then he scrutinized each individual guest with gentle curiosity, read their souls and wondered again. In the meantime the assembled ones had risen from their seats, and waited respectfully for Zarathustra to speak. But Zarathustra spoke thus:

"You despairing ones! You strange! So it was *your* cry of distress that I heard? And now I know also where he is to be sought, whom I have sought for in vain today: *the higher man*—:

—"he sits in my own cave, the higher man! But why do I wonder! Haven't I myself lured him to me by honey sacrifices and cunning bird calls of my happiness?

"But it seems to me that you are badly suited for company: you make one another's hearts fretful, you that cry for help, when you sit here together. There is one that must come first,

—"one who will make you laugh once more, a good jovial jester, a dancer, a wind, a wild romp, some old fool:—what do you think?

"But forgive me, you despairing ones, for speaking such trivial words before you, unworthy, truly, of such guests! But you do not divine *what* makes my heart frolic:—

—"You yourselves do it, and the sight of you, forgive me! For every one who beholds a despairing one becomes courageous. To encourage a despairing one—every one thinks himself strong enough to do so.

"To myself you have given this power,—a good gift, my honorable guests! An excellent guest's gift! Well, do not reprimand when I also offer you something of my own.

"This is my empire and my dominion: but that which is mine shall this evening and tonight be yours. My animals shall serve you: let my cave be your resting-place!

"No one shall despair at home and hearth with me, in my preserve I protect every one from his wild beasts. And that is the first thing I offer you: security!

"But the second thing is: my little finger. And when you have *that*, then take the whole hand, very well! and the heart too! Welcome here, welcome, my guests!"

Thus spoke Zarathustra and laughed with love and mischief. After this greeting his guests bowed once more and were respectfully silent; the king on the right, however, answered him in their name.

"O Zarathustra, by the way in which you have given us your hand and your greeting, we recognize you as Zarathustra. You have humbled yourself before us; you have almost injured our respect—:

—"but who could have humbled himself as you have done, with such pride? *That* uplifts us ourselves, it is a refreshment to our eyes and hearts.

"To see only this we would happily climb higher mountains than this. For we have come as eager sightseers, we wanted to see what brightens dim eyes.

"And behold, now all our cries of distress are finished. Now our minds and hearts are open and enraptured. Our spirits lack little to become gay.

"There is nothing, O Zarathustra, that grows more pleasingly on earth than a lofty, strong will: it is the finest growth. An entire landscape refreshes itself at one such tree.

"To the pine I compare him, O Zarathustra, who grows up like you—tall, silent, hardy, solitary, of the best, supplest wood, stately,—

—"but in the end grasping out for *its* dominion with strong, green branches, asking weighty questions of the wind, the storm, and whatever is at home on high places;

—"answering more weightily, a commander, a victor! Oh! who should not climb high mountains to see such growths?

"At your tree, O Zarathustra, the gloomy and ill-constituted also refresh themselves; seeing you even the wavering become steady and heal their hearts.

"And truly, many eyes today turn towards your mountain and your tree; a great longing has arisen, and many have learned to ask: 'Who is Zarathustra?'

"And those into whose ears you have at any time dripped your song and your honey: all the hidden ones, the lonesome and the twosome, have simultaneously said to their hearts:

" 'Does Zarathustra still live? Life is no longer worthwhile, every-thing is the same, all is in vain: or—we must live with Zarathustra!'

" 'Why doesn't he come who has so long announced himself?' thus many people ask; 'has solitude swallowed him up? Or should we perhaps go to him?'

"Now it comes to pass that solitude itself becomes fragile and breaks open, like a grave that breaks open and can no longer hold its dead. Everywhere one sees the resurrected.

"Now the waves rise and rise around your mountain, O Zara-thustra. And however high your height may be, many of them must rise up to you: your boat shall not rest much longer on dry ground.

"And that we despairing ones have now come into your cave, and already no longer despair:—it is only a sign and omen that better ones are on the way to you,—

—"for they themselves are on the way to you, the last remnant of god among men: that is, all the men of great longing, of great loathing, of great satiety,

—"all who do not want to live unless they learn again to *hope*—unless they learn from you, O Zarathustra, the *great* hope!"

Thus spoke the king on the right, and seized the hand of Zarathustra in order to kiss it; but Zarathustra resisted his adoration and stepped back frightened, as if fleeing silently and suddenly into the far distance. But after a little while he was again at home with his guests, looked at them with clear scrutinizing eyes, and said:

"My guests, you higher men, I will speak in plain and clear German with you. It is not for *you* that I have waited here in these mountains."

(" 'Plain and clear German?' Good God!" said the king on the left to himself; "one sees he does not know our dear Germans, this wise man from the East!

"But he means 'coarse German'—very well! That is not the worst taste in these days!")

"You may, truly, all of you be higher men," continued Zarathustra; "but for me—you are neither high enough, nor strong enough.

"For me, that is to say, for the inexorable which is now silent in me, but will not always be silent. And if you are a part of me, still it is not as my right arm.

"For he who himself stands, like you, on sickly and tender legs, wishes above all to be *spared*, whether he is conscious of it or hides it from himself.

"My arms and my legs, however, I do not treat indulgently, nor I do spare *my warriors*: how then could you be fit for *my* warfare?

"With you I should still spoil all my victories. And many of you would tumble over if you heard only the loud beating of my drums.

"Moreover, you are not sufficiently beautiful and well-born for me. I require pure, smooth mirrors for my teachings; on your surface even my own likeness is distorted.

"On your shoulders many a burden presses, many a recollection; many an evil dwarf squats in your corners. There is hidden mob in you too.

"And though you are high and of a higher type, much in you is crooked and misshapen. There is no smith in the world that could hammer you right and straight for me.

"You are only bridges: may higher ones pass over on you! You are steps: so do not be angry with him who climbs over you into *his* height!

"Out of your seed there may one day arise for me a genuine son and perfect heir: but that time is distant. You yourselves are not those to whom my heritage and name belong.

"Not for you do I wait here in these mountains; not with you may I descend for the last time. You have come to me only as omens that higher ones are on the way to me,—

—"*not* the men of great longing, of great loathing, of great satiety, and that which you call the remnant of god;

—"No! No! Three times No! For *others* I wait here in these mountains, and will not lift my foot from there without them;

—"for higher ones, stronger ones, more triumphant ones, merrier ones, for such as are built squarely in body and soul: *laughing lions* must come!

"O my guests, you strange ones—have you yet heard nothing of my children? And that they are on the way to me?

"Speak to me of my gardens, of my happy islands, of my new beautiful race—why do you not speak to me of them?

"This guests' present I ask of your love, that you speak to me of my children. For them I am rich, for them I became poor: what have I not surrendered,

—"what would I not surrender that I might have one thing: *these* children, *this* living garden, *these* life trees of my will and of my highest hope!"

Thus spoke Zarathustra, and stopped suddenly in his speech: for his longing came over him, and he closed his eyes and his mouth because of the agitation of his heart. And all his guests were silent too and stood still and were confounded: except that the old soothsayer gestured with his hands and his features.

THE LAST SUPPER[7]

FOR AT THIS POINT the soothsayer interrupted the greeting of Zarathustra and his guests: he thrust himself forward like one who had no time to lose, seized Zarathustra's hand and exclaimed: "But Zarathustra!

"One thing is more necessary than another, so you say yourself: well, one thing is now more necessary *to me* than all others.

"A word at the right time: did not you invite me to *a meal*? And here are many who have made long journeys. You do not mean to feed us merely with speeches?

"Besides, all of you have thought too much about freezing, drowning, suffocating, and other bodily dangers: none of you, however, has thought of *my* danger, namely, dying of hunger—"

(Thus spoke the soothsayer. But when Zarathustra's animals heard these words, they ran away in terror. For they saw that all they had brought home during the day would not be enough to fill this one soothsayer.)

"And dying of thirst," continued the soothsayer. "And although I hear water splashing here like words of wisdom—that is to say, abundantly and tirelessly, I—want *wine*!

"Not every one is a born water drinker like Zarathustra. Neither does water suit weary and drooping men: *we* deserve wine—*it* alone gives immediate vigor and improvised health!"

"On this occasion, when the soothsayer was longing for wine, it happened that the king on the left, the silent one, also found speech for once. "*We* took care," he said, "about wine, I, along with my brother the king on the right: we have enough wine,—a whole ass's load of it. So nothing is lacking but bread."

"Bread," replied Zarathustra laughing, "it is precisely bread that hermits do not have. But man does not live by bread alone, but also by the flesh of good lambs, of which I have two:

—"*these* we shall slaughter quickly and cook spicily with sage: that is how I like them. And there is also no lack of roots and fruits, good enough even for gourmets and epicures; nor of nuts and other riddles that need cracking.

"Thus we will have a good meal in a little while. But whoever wants to eat with us must also give a hand to the work, even the kings. For with Zarathustra even a king may be a cook."

This proposal appealed to the hearts of all of them, save that the voluntary beggar objected to the flesh and wine and spices.

"Just hear this glutton Zarathustra!" he said jokingly: "does one go into caves and high mountains to make such meals?

"Now indeed I understand what he once taught us: 'A little poverty is blessed!' And why he wishes to do away with beggars."

"Be of good cheer," replied Zarathustra, "as I am. Abide by your customs, you excellent one: grind your corn, drink your water, praise your own cooking: if only it makes you happy!

"I am a law only for my own, I am not a law for all. But he who belongs to me must be strong-limbed and nimble-footed,—

—"cheerful in war and feasting, no sulker, no dreamer, ready for what is hardest as for the feast, healthy and whole.

"The best belongs to me and mine; and if we are not given it, then we take it: the best food, the purest sky, the strongest thoughts, the fairest women!"—

Thus spoke Zarathustra; but the king on the right answered and said: "Strange! Has one ever heard such clever things out of the mouth of a wise man?

"And truly, it is the strangest wise man who is clever and no ass."

Thus spoke the king on the right and wondered; but the ass maliciously replied Yeah-Yuh. This, however, was the beginning of that long meal which is called "The Last Supper" in the history books. At this there was nothing else discussed but *the higher man*.[8]

The Higher Man

1

WHEN I CAME TO men for the first time, I committed the folly of hermits, the great folly: I appeared in the marketplace.

And when I spoke to all, I spoke to none. In the evening, however, tightrope walkers were my companions, and corpses; and I myself was almost a corpse.

With the new morning, however, there came to me a new truth: then I learned to say: "What are the marketplace and the mob and the mob's noise and long mob ears to me!"

You higher men, learn *this* from me: in the marketplace no one believes in higher men. And if you want to speak there, very well! But the mob blinks: "We are all equal."

"You higher men,"—so the mob blink—"there are no higher men, we are all equal, man is but man, before God—we are all equal!"

Before God!—But now this god has died. Before the mob, however, we will not be equal. You higher men, go away from the marketplace!

2

Before God!—But now this god has died! You higher men, this god was your greatest danger.

Only since he lay in the grave have you again arisen. Only now comes the great noon, only now does the higher man become—master!

Have you understood this word, O my brothers? You are frightened: do your hearts turn giddy? Does the abyss here yawn for you? Does the dog of hell here yelp at you?

Well! Take heart! you higher men! Only now is the mountain of man's future at labor. God has died: now *we* want—the Übermensch to live.

3

The most careful ask today: "How is man to be preserved?" But Zarathustra asks as the first and only one: "How is man to be *overcome?*"

I have the Übermensch at heart, *he* is the first and only thing to me—and *not* man: not the nearest, not the poorest, not the most suffering, not the best.—

O my brothers, what I can love in man is that he is an over-going and a going under. And in you too there is much that makes me love and hope.

That you have despised, you higher men, that makes me hope. For the great despisers are the great reverers.

That you have despaired, there is much honor in that. For you have not learned to submit, you have not learned petty prudence.

For today the petty have become master: they all preach submission and humility and prudence and diligence and consideration and the long *et cetera* of petty virtues.

What is of womanish, what stems from the slavishness and especially the hodgepodge of the mob: *that* now wants to be master of all human destiny—O disgust! disgust! disgust!

That asks and asks and never tires: "How is man to preserve himself best, longest, most pleasantly?" With that—they are the masters of today.

Overcome these masters of today, O my brothers—these little people: *they* are the Übermensch's greatest danger!

Overcome, you higher men, the petty virtues, the petty prudences, the sand-grain discretion, the ant's pretensions, the wretched contentment, the "happiness of the greatest number"—!

And rather despair than submit. And truly, I love you, because you do not know today how to live, you higher men! For thus *you* live—the best!

4

Do you have courage, O my brothers? Are you brave? *Not* courage before witnesses but hermit and eagle courage, which not even a god observes any more?

I do not call brave the cold souls, the mulish, the blind and the drunken. He has heart who knows fear but *conquers* it; who sees the abyss, but with *pride*.

He who sees the abyss, but with eagle's eyes—he who *grasps* the abyss with eagle's talons: *he* has courage.——

5

"Man is evil"—all the wisest have told me that to comfort me. Ah, if only it were still true today! For evil is man's best strength.

"Man must become better and more evil"—thus *I* teach. The most evil is necessary for the Übermensch's best.

It may have been good for that preacher of the little people to suffer and be burdened by men's sin. But I rejoice in great sin as my great *consolation*.—

But such things are not said for long ears. Neither does every word suit every mouth. These are subtle remote things: sheep's hooves should not reach for them!

6

You higher men, do you think that I am here to put right what you have put wrong?

Or that I wished henceforth to make cozier beds for you sufferers? Or show you restless, erring, straying ones new and easier footpaths?

No! No! Three times No! Always more, always better ones of your kind must perish—for life must be harder and harder for you. Thus alone—

—Thus alone man grows to the height where the lightning strikes and shatters him: high enough for the lightning!

My soul and my seeking go forth towards the few, the long, the remote: what are your many little brief miseries to me!

You do not yet suffer enough for me! For you suffer from yourselves, you have not yet suffered *from man*. You would lie if you said otherwise! None of you suffers from what *I* have suffered.——

7

It is not enough for me that the lightning no longer does any harm. I do not want to conduct it away: it shall learn—to work for *me*.—

My wisdom has long accumulated like a cloud, it becomes stiller and darker. So does all wisdom which shall one day bear *lightnings*.—

To these men of today I will not be *light*, nor be called light. *Them*—I will blind: lightning of my wisdom! put out their eyes!

8

Will nothing beyond your power: there is a wicked falseness in those who will beyond their power.

Especially when they will great things! For they awaken distrust in great things, these subtle counterfeiters and actors:—

—until at last they are false to themselves, squint-eyed, white-washed worm-eaten decay, cloaked with strong words, pretended virtues and glittering false deeds.

Take good care there, you higher men! For nothing today is more precious to me and rarer than honesty.

Is this today not the mob's? But the mob does not know what is great, what is small, what is straight and honest: it is innocently crooked, it always lies.

9

Have a good mistrust today you higher men, you stouthearted! You openhearted! And keep your reasons secret! For this today is the mob's.

What the mob once learned to believe without reasons, who could—refute it with reasons?

And in the marketplace one convinces with gestures. But reasons make the mob mistrustful.

And if truth triumphed there for once, then ask yourselves with good mistrust: "What strong error fought for it?"

Be on your guard too against the learned! They hate you: for they are sterile! They have cold, desiccated eyes, before which all birds lie unplumed.

Such people brag that they do not lie: but the inability to lie is far from the love of truth. Beware!

Freedom from fever is far from being knowledge! I do not believe frozen spirits. He who cannot lie does not know what truth is.

10

If you want to rise high, use your own legs! Do not let yourselves be carried up, do not sit on the backs and heads of strangers!

But you mounted a horse? You are now riding briskly up to your goal? Well, my friend! But your lame foot is also with you on horseback!

When you reach your goal, when you jump from your horse: precisely on your *height*, you higher man—you will stumble!

11

You creators, you higher men! One is pregnant only with one's own child.

Do not let yourselves be imposed upon or beguiled! For who is *your* neighbor? Even if you do things "for your neighbor"—you still do not create for him!

Unlearn this "for," you creators: your very virtue wants you to have nothing to do with "for" and "for the sake of" and "because." You should stop your ears against these false little words.

"For one's neighbor," is the virtue only of petty people: there they say "like attracts like" and "one hand washes the other"—they have neither the right nor the strength for *your* selfishness!

In your selfishness, you creators, is the caution and providence of the pregnant! What no one's eye has yet seen, the fruit: that is sheltered and indulged and nourished by your whole love.

Where your whole love is, with your child, there too is your whole virtue! Your work, your will is *your* "neighbor": let no false values beguile you!

12

You creators, you higher men! Whoever must give birth is sick; but whoever has given birth is unclean.

Ask women: one does not give birth for pleasure. The pain makes hens and poets cackle.

You creators, there is much in you that is unclean. That is because you had to be mothers.

A new child: oh, how much new filth has also come into the world! Go aside! And whoever has given birth should wash his soul clean!

13

Do not be virtuous beyond your strength! And do not ask anything improbable from yourselves!

Follow in the footsteps of your fathers' virtue! How would you climb high if the will of your fathers did not climb with you?

But he who wants to be a firstborn should see that he does not also become a lastborn! And where the vices of your fathers are you should not pretend to be saints!

If your fathers were for women, strong wine and wild boars, what would it be if you demanded chastity of yourself?

It would be folly! Truly, I think it would be much if such a one were the husband of one or of two or of three women.

And if he founded monasteries and wrote above their doors: "The way to holiness," I should still say: What of it! it is a new folly!

He founded a reformatory and a refuge for himself: much good may it do! But I do not believe in it.

In solitude there grows what anyone brings into it, the inner beast too. Therefore solitude is inadvisable to many.

Has there ever been anything filthier on earth than the saints of the wilderness? Around *them* not only the devil was loose—but also the swine.

14

Shy, ashamed, awkward, like a tiger whose spring has failed: thus, you higher men, I have often seen you slink aside. A *throw* you made had failed.

But what does it matter, you dice players! You have not learned to play and mock as one ought to play and mock! Don't we always sit at a great table of mocking and playing?

And if you have failed at great things, does that mean you your-selves are—failures? And if you yourselves have been failures, has another failure therefore been—man? But if man has been a failure: well then! come on!

15

The higher its type the less often a thing succeeds. You higher men here, are you not all—failures?

Be of good cheer; what does it matter! How much is still possi-ble! Learn to laugh at yourselves as you ought to laugh!

No wonder that you have failed and only half succeeded, you half-broken ones! Does there not strive and struggle in you—man's *future*?

Man's greatest distance and depth and what in him is lofty as the stars, his prodigious strength: does not all that foam together in your pot?

No wonder many a pot is shattered! Learn to laugh at yourselves as you ought to laugh! You higher men, oh how much is still possible!

And truly, how much has already succeeded! How rich this earth is in small good perfect things, in what has turned out well!

Set small good perfect things around you, you higher men! Their golden ripeness heals the heart. What is perfect teaches hope.

16

What has so far been the greatest sin here on earth? Was it not the word of him who said: "Woe to them who laugh here!"

Did he himself find no reasons on earth for laughter? Then he sought badly. Even a child finds reasons here.

He—did not love enough: otherwise he would have also loved us who laugh! But he hated and jeered at us, he promised us wailing and gnashing of teeth.

Must one then curse right away when one does not love? That—seems bad taste to me. But thus he acted, being unconditional. He sprang from the mob.

And he himself simply did not love enough: otherwise he would have raged less that he was not loved. All great love does not *want* love—it wants more.

Avoid all such unconditional ones! They are a poor sickly type, a mob-type: they look sourly at this life, they have an evil eye for this earth.

Avoid all such unconditional ones! They have heavy feet and sultry hearts—they do not know how to dance. How could the earth be light to such as these!

17

All good things approach their goal crookedly. Like cats they arch their backs, they purr inwardly at their approaching happiness—all good things laugh.

His step betrays whether a man walks *his own* way: behold me walking! But whoever approaches his goal dances.

And truly, I have not become a statue, not yet do I stand there stiff, stupid, stony, like a pillar; I love to run swiftly.

And although there are swamps and dense afflictions on earth, he who has light feet runs even across mud and dances as on swept ice.

Lift up your hearts, my brothers, high, higher! And do not forget your legs! Lift up your legs too, you good dancers, and better still, stand on your heads!

18

This laugher's crown, this rose garlanded crown.[9] I myself have put on this crown, I myself have consecrated my laughter. I found none other today strong enough for that.

Zarathustra the dancer, Zarathustra the light, who beckons with his wings, ready for flight, beckoning to all birds, ready and prepared, blissfully light-spirited one:—

Zarathustra the soothsayer, Zarathustra the soothlaugher, no impatient one, no unconditional one, one who loves leaps and side-leaps; I myself have put on this crown!

19

Lift up your hearts, my brothers, high, higher! And do not forget your legs! Lift up your legs too, you good dancers: and better still, stand on your heads!

In happiness too there are heavy animals in a state of happiness, there are club-foots through and through. They exert themselves strangely, like an elephant trying to stand on its head.

But better to be foolish with happiness than foolish with misfortune, better to dance awkwardly than to walk lamely. So learn from me my wisdom: even the worst thing has two good sides,—

—even the worst thing has good dancing legs: so learn, you higher men, to stand on your own proper legs!

So unlearn nursing melancholy and all the mob sorrow! Oh, how sad the jesters of the mob seem to me today! But this today is the mob's.

20

Be like the wind when it rushes forth from its mountain caves: it dances to its own piping, the seas tremble and leap under its footsteps.

That which gives wings to asses[10] and milks lionesses, all praise to that good, unruly spirit which comes like a hurricane to all the present and to all the mob—

—which is enemy to all thistle-heads and casuists' heads and to all withered leaves and weeds: all praise to that wild, good, free spirit of the storm, which dances upon swamps and afflictions as upon meadows!

Which hates the consumptive dogs of the mob, and all the ill-constituted, sullen brood:—praised be this spirit of all free spirits, the laughing storm, which blows dust into the eyes of all the melanopic and melancholic!

You higher men, the worst thing in you is: none of you has learned to dance as you ought to dance—to dance beyond yourselves! What does it matter that you are failures!

How much is still possible! So *learn* to laugh beyond yourselves! Lift up your hearts, you good dancers, high! higher! And do not forget good laughter!

This crown of laughter, this rose garlanded crown: I cast this crown to you my brothers! I have consecrated laughter; you higher men, *learn*—to laugh!

The Song of Melancholy

1

WHEN ZARATHUSTRA SPOKE THESE sayings, he stood near the entrance of his cave; but with the last words he slipped away from his guests and fled for a little while into the open air.

"O pure scents around me," he cried, "O blessed stillness around me! But where are my animals? Come here, come here, my eagle and my serpent!

"Tell me, my animals: these higher men, all of them—do they perhaps *smell* bad? O pure smells around me! Only now do I know and feel how I love you, my animals."

—And Zarathustra said again: "I love you, my animals!" But the eagle and the serpent pressed close to him when he spoke these words, and looked up at him. In this attitude all three were silent together, and sniffed and sipped the good air with one another. For the air here outside was better than with the higher men.

2

But hardly had Zarathustra left the cave when the old magician got up, looked cunningly about him, and said: "He is gone!

"And already, you higher men—let me tickle you with this complimentary and flattering name, as he himself does—already my evil spirit of deceit and magic attacks me, my melancholy devil,

—"who is an adversary of this Zarathustra from the bottom: forgive him for this! Now he *insists* on working spells before you, now he has *his* hour; I struggle with this evil spirit in vain.

"Of all of you, whatever verbal honors you like to assume, whether you call yourselves 'the free spirits' or 'the truthful,' or 'the ascetics of the spirit,' or 'the unfettered,' or 'the great longers,'—

—"of all of you who like me suffer *from the great disgust*, for whom the old God has died and as yet no new god lies in cradles and swaddling clothes—of all of you my evil spirit and devil of sorcery is fond.

"I know you, higher men, I know him—I know also this fiend whom I love in spite of myself, this Zarathustra: he himself often seems to me like the beautiful mask of a saint,

—"like a new strange masquerade in which my evil spirit, the melancholy devil, delights—I love Zarathustra, so it often seems to me, for the sake of my evil spirit.—

"But already *he* attacks me and compels me, this spirit of melancholy, this evening-twilight devil: and truly, you higher men, he has a longing—

—"open your eyes!—he has a longing to come *naked*, whether as man or woman I do not yet know: but he comes, he compels me, ah! open your senses!

"The day is fading away, to all things the evening now comes, even to the best things; hear now and see, you higher men, what devil—man or woman—this spirit of evening-melancholy is!"

Thus spoke the old magician, looked cunningly about him and then seized his harp.

3

In clarifying air,
When already the dew's comfort
Wells down to the earth,
Unseen, also unheard—
For tender shoes wear
The comforting dew, like all that gently comforts—:
Do you remember then, do you remember, hot heart,
How once you thirsted
For heavenly tears and dew showers
Singed and exhausted by thirst,
While on yellow paths in the grass
Wicked evening sun glances
Ran about you through dark trees
Blinding, glowing glances of the sun, pleased
at your suffering?

"Seducer of *truth*? You?"—so they taunted
"No! Only a poet!
An animal, cunning, preying, prowling,

That must lie,
That must knowingly, willingly lie:
Lusting for prey,
Colorfully masked,
A mask for itself,
Prey for itself-
This—the seducer of truth?
No! Only fool! Only poet!
Only speaking colorfully,
Only shrieking colorfully from the masks of fools,
Climbing around on mendacious word bridges,
On colorful rainbows,
between false heavens
And false earths,
Roving, floating about—
Only fool! *Only* poet!

This—the seducer of truth?
Not still, stiff, smooth, cold,
Become a statue,
A pillar of god,
Not set up before temples,
A God's gatekeeper:
No! an enemy to all such statues of truth,
More at home in every desert than at temples,
With feline mischievousness,
Springing through every window
Quickly! into every chance,
Sniffing for every jungle,
Eagerly, longingly sniffing,
That you in jungles
Among the mottled fierce creatures,
Should run sinfully healthy and colorful and beautiful,
With lustful lips,
Happily mocking, happily hellish, happily bloodthirsty,
Robbing, skulking, lying:—

Or like the eagle, which long,
Long stares into abysses,

Into *its* abysses:—
Oh, how they circle down,
Under, in,
In *ever* deeper depths!—
Then,
Suddenly, with straight aim
Quivering flight,
They pounce on *lambs*,
Headlong down, ravenous,
Lusting for lambs,
Hating all lamb souls,
Grim in hatred at all that look
Sheepish, lamb eyed, or curly woolled,
Grey, with lambs' sheeps' kindness!

Thus,
Eaglelike, pantherlike,
Are the poet's desires,
Are *your* desires beneath a thousand masks,
You fool! You poet!

You who have seen man
As god as sheep—:
To rend the god in man,
Like the sheep in man,
And rending *to laugh*—

That, that is your bliss!
A panther's and eagle's bliss!
A poet's and fool's bliss!——

In clarifying air,
When already the moon's sickle,
Green between purpled reds
And envious creeps forth:
—the day's enemy,
With every step secretly
Into hanging rose gardens
Sickling down, until they sink,

Sink down palely beneath night:—
So I sank once
Out of my madness of truth,
Out of my longing of days,
Weary of day, sick from light,
—Sank downwards, eveningwards, shadowwards:
With one truth
Scorched and thirsty:
—Do you still remember, do you remember, hot heart,
How you then thirsted?—
That I am banished
From all truth,
Only fool!
Only poet!

ON SCIENCE

THUS SANG THE MAGICIAN; and all who were present went like
birds unawares into the net of his cunning and melancholy voluptuousness. Only the conscientious in spirit was not caught: he at
once snatched the harp from the magician and called out: "Air! Let
in good air! Let in Zarathustra! You make this cave sultry and poisonous, you bad old magician!

"You seduce, you false one, you subtle one, to unknown desires
and wildernesses. And ah, that such as you should talk and worry
about the *truth*!

"Woe to all free spirits who are not on their guard against *such*
magicians! It is all over with their freedom: you teach and lure back
into prisons,—

—"you old melancholy devil, a seductive bird call sounds out of
your lament, you resemble those who with their praise of chastity
secretly invite to voluptuousness!"

Thus spoke the conscientious in spirit; but the old magician
looked about him, enjoying his triumph, and for that reason tolerated the annoyance that the conscientious caused him. "Be quiet!"
he said in a modest voice, "good songs want to echo well; after good
songs one should long be silent.

"Thus do all the higher men. But you have perhaps understood only little of my song? There is little of the spirit of magic in you."

"You praise me," replied the conscientious one, "when you distinguish me from yourself. Very well! But you others, what do I see? You still sit there, all of you, with lusting eyes—:

"You free souls, where has your freedom gone! To me you almost look like those who have long been watching naughty naked dancing girls: your souls themselves dance!

"In you, you higher men, there must be more of that which the magician calls his evil spirit of magic and deceit—we must indeed be different.

"And truly, we spoke and thought long enough together before Zarathustra came home to his cave, for me to know: we *are* different.

"We *seek* different things even up here, you and I. For I seek more *security*, that is why I came to Zarathustra. For he is still the most steadfast tower and will—

—"today, when everything totters, when all the earth quakes. But you, when I see what eyes you make, it almost seems to me that you seek *more insecurity*,

—"more horror, more danger, more earthquaking. You long, so it almost seems to me, forgive my presumption, you higher men—

—"you long for the worst and most dangerous life, which frightens *me* most, for the life of wild beasts, for forests, caves, steep mountains and labyrinthine gorges.

"And it is not those who lead *out of* danger that please you best, but those who lead you away from all paths, the misleaders. But if you *actually* harbor such longings, they seem to me nevertheless to be *impossible*.

"For fear—that is man's original and fundamental feeling; through fear everything is explained, original sin and original virtue. Through fear *my* virtue also grew, that is to say: science.

"For fear of wild animals—that has been fostered in man the longest, including the animal he conceals and fears in himself—Zarathustra calls it 'the beast within.'

"Such prolonged ancient fear, at last become subtle, spiritual, intellectual—today, I think, it is called: *science*."—

Thus spoke the conscientious one; but Zarathustra, who had just come back into his cave and had heard and understood the last speech, threw a handful of roses to the conscientious man and laughed at his "truths." "What!" he exclaimed, "what did I hear just now? Truly, I think you are a fool, or I myself am one: and I will straightaway stand your "truth" on its head.

"For *fear*—is the exception with us. But courage and adventure and delight in the uncertain, in the unattempted—*courage* seems to me the whole prehistory of man.

"He has envied the wildest and most courageous animals and robbed them of all their virtues: only thus did he become—man.

"*This* courage, at last become subtle, spiritual, intellectual, this human courage, with eagle's wings and serpent's wisdom: *this*, it seems to me, is today called—"

"*Zarathustra!*" cried all of them there assembled as if with a single voice, and burst out at the same time into a great laughter; and it was as if a heavy cloud lifted from them. Even the magician laughed and said cleverly: "Well! It is gone, my evil spirit!

"And did I not myself warn you against it when I said that he was a deceiver, a lying and deceiving spirit?

"Especially when he shows himself naked. But what can *I* do about his tricks! Have *I* created him and the world?

"Well! Let us be good again, and of good cheer! And although Zarathustra looks angry—just see him! he bears a grudge against me—:

—"before night comes he will learn again to love and praise me, he cannot live long without committing such follies.

"*He*—loves his enemies: he knows this art better than any one I have seen. But he takes revenge for it—on his friends!"

Thus spoke the old magician, and the higher men applauded him: so that Zarathustra went round, and mischievously and lovingly shook hands with his friends—like one who has to make amends and apologize to every one for something. But when he came to the door of his cave, behold, then he longed again for the good air outside, and for his animals—and he wanted to slip out.

Among Daughters of the Wilderness

1

"Do not go away!" said the wanderer who called himself Zarathustra's shadow, "stay with us, otherwise the old dark misery might fall on us again.

"Now that old magician has done his worst for our benefit, and behold, the good, pious pope has tears in his eyes, and has embarked again upon the sea of melancholy.

"Those kings there may well put on a good air before us yet: for *they* have learned that better than any of us today! But if they had no one to see them, I bet that with them too the bad game would commence again,—

—"the bad game of drifting clouds, of damp melancholy, of curtained heavens, of stolen suns, of howling autumn winds,

—"the bad game of our howling and crying for help! Stay with us, O Zarathustra! Here there is much hidden misery that wishes to speak, much evening, much cloud, much damp air!

"You have nourished us with strong food for men, and powerful proverbs: do not let the weakly, womanish spirits attack us again at dessert!

"You alone make the air around you strong and clear! Did I ever find anywhere on earth such good air as with you in your cave?

"Many lands have I seen, my nose has learned to test and estimate many kinds of air: but with you my nostrils taste their greatest delight!

"Except,—except—, oh forgive an old recollection! Forgive me an old after-dinner song, which I once composed among daughters of the wilderness:—

"For with them there was the same good, clear, oriental air; there I was furthest from cloudy, damp, melancholy old Europe!

"Then I loved such oriental girls and other blue kingdoms of heaven, over which hung no clouds and no thoughts.

"You would not believe how charmingly they sat there, when they did not dance, profound, but without thoughts, like little secrets, like ribboned riddles, like after-dinner nuts—

"colorful and foreign, indeed! but without clouds: riddles which can be guessed: to please such girls I then composed an after-dinner song."

Thus spoke the wanderer who called himself Zarathustra's shadow; and before any one answered him, he had seized the harp of the old magician, crossed his legs, and looked calmly and sagely around him:—but with his nostrils he inhaled the air slowly and questioningly, like one who in new countries tastes new foreign air. Thereupon he began to sing with a kind of roaring.

2

Wilderness grows: woe to him who harbors wildernesses!

—Ha! Solemnly!
Indeed solemnly!
A worthy beginning!
African solemnity!
Worthy of a lion
Or of a moral howler monkey—
—but it's nothing to you,
You most charming friends,
At whose feet I
For the first time,
A European under palm trees,
Am permitted to sit. Selah.

Truly wonderful!
Here I sit now,
The wilderness near, and yet I am
Again so far from the wilderness,
And in no way devastated:
That is, swallowed down
By this smallest oasis—:
—It opened simply yawning,
Its sweetest mouth,
Most sweet smelling of all little mouths:
Then I fell in,

Down, right through—among you,
You best beloved friends! Selah.

Hail, hail that whale,
If for its guests it made things
So pleasant!—you understand
My learned allusion?
Hail to his belly,
If it was
Lovely as the belly of an oasis
As this is: which, however, I call into question,
—since I come from Europe,
Which is more skeptical than any
Little old wife.
May God improve it!
Amen!

Here I sit now,
In this smallest oasis,
Like a date,
Brown, sweet, oozing gold, lusting
For the round mouth of a girl,
But even more for girlish
Ice-cold snow white cutting
Incisors: for after such
Pants the heart of all hot dates. Selah.

As the aforementioned southern fruit
Similar, all-too-similar,
I lie here, by little
Flying insects
Sniffed around and played around,
And also by still smaller,
More foolish more sinful
Wishes and notions,—
Enveloped by you,
You silent, you foreboding
Cat girls,

Dudu and Suleika,
—*Ensphinxed*, to crowd many feelings
Into a *single* word:
(Forgive me God
This sin of speech!)
—I sit here sniffing the best air,
Truly the air of paradise,
Bright buoyant air, streaked with gold,
As good air as ever
Fell from the moon—
Whether by chance,
Or did it happen from playfulness?
As the old poets relate.
But I, a doubter, call it
Into doubt, but with this I come
Out of Europe,
Which is more skeptical than any
Little old wife.
May God improve it!
Amen!

Drinking this finest air,
With nostrils swollen as cups,
Without future, without memories,
So I sit here, you
Best beloved friends,
And look at the palm tree,
How she, like a dancer,
Bows and bends and sways at the hips,
—one does it too, if one watches long!
Like a dancer who, it seems,
Stood long, dangerously long,
Always, always only on *one* leg?
—so that she has forgotten, it seems,
The other leg?
In vain, at least,
I searched for the missing
Twin jewel
—namely, the other leg—

In the holy vicinity
Of her dearest, most delicate
Flap- and flutter- and flicker-skirt.
Yes, if you would, you beautiful friends,
Believe me entirely:
She has lost it!
It is gone!
Gone forever!
The other leg!
Oh what a shame about that lovely other leg!
Where—may it be waiting and mourning forsaken?
The lonely leg?
Perhaps afraid of one
Grim blonde locked
Lion monster? Or perhaps even
Gnawed off, nibbled away—
Misery, alas! alas! Nibbled away! Selah.

Oh do not cry to me,
Gentle hearts!
Do not cry to me, you
Date hearts! Milk breasts!
You heart purses
Of candy!
Cry no more,
Pale Dudu!
Be a man, Suleika! Courage! Courage!
—Or should perhaps
Something bracing, heart bracing,
Fit here?
An unctuous proverb?
A solemn exhortation?—

Ha! Up now, dignity!
Virtuous dignity! European dignity!
Blow, blow again,
Bellows of virtue!
Ha!
Roar once more,

Moral roaring!
As a moral lion
Roar before the daughters of the wilderness!
—For virtuous howling,
You dearest girls,
Is more than anything else
European fervor, European hot hunger!
And here I stand now,
As a European,
I cannot do otherwise, God help me![11]
Amen!

Wilderness grows: woe to him who harbors wildernesses!

THE AWAKENING[12]

1

After the song of the wanderer and shadow, the cave suddenly became full of noise and laughter: and since the assembled guests all
spoke simultaneously and even the ass, thus encouraged, would no
longer remain silent, Zarathustra was overcome by a little aversion
and scorn for his visitors: although he rejoiced at their gladness. For
it seemed to him a sign of convalescence. So he slipped out into the
open air and spoke to his animals.

"Where is their distress now?" he said, and already he felt re-
lieved of his petty disgust—"with me, it seems that they have unlearned their cries of distress!

—"though unfortunately not yet their crying." And Zarathustra
stopped his ears, for just then the Yeah-Yuh of the ass mixed
strangely with the noisy jubilation of those higher men.

"They are merry," he began again, "and who knows? perhaps at
their host's expense; and if they have learned to laugh from me, still
it is not *my* laughter they have learned.

"But what does that matter! They are old people: they recover in
their own way, they laugh in their own way; my ears have already
endured worse and have not become peevish.

"This day is a victory: he already yields, he flees, *the spirit of gravity*, my old arch-enemy! How well this day is about to end, which began so badly and gloomily!

"And it is *about to* end. Already the evening comes: it rides here over the sea, the good rider! How it bobs, the blessed one, the homecoming one, in its purple saddles!

"The sky gazes brightly on that, the world lies deep. Oh, all you strange ones who have come to me, it is already worthwhile to have lived with me!"

Thus spoke Zarathustra. And again came the cries and laughter of the higher men out of the cave: then he began again:

"They bite at it, they take my bait, their enemy, the spirit of gravity, departs from them too. Now they learn to laugh at themselves: is that what I hear?

"My strong food takes effect, my strong and savory sayings: and truly, I did not nourish them with gassy vegetables! But with warrior-food, with conqueror-food: I awakened new desires.

"New hopes are in their arms and legs, their hearts expand. They find new words, soon their spirits will breathe playfulness.

"Such food may not be proper for children, or for fond little women, old and young. Their stomachs are persuaded otherwise; I am not their physician and teacher.

"*Disgust* departs from these higher men; well! that is my victory. In my domain they become assured; all stupid shame flees away; they empty themselves.

"They empty their hearts, good times return to them, they relax and ruminate,—they become *thankful*.

"I take *that* as the best sign: they become thankful. It will not be long before they invent festivals and put up memorials to their old joys.

"They are *convalescents*!" Thus spoke Zarathustra joyfully to his heart and gazed out; but his animals pressed up to him, and honored his happiness and his silence.

2

But suddenly Zarathustra's ear was frightened: for the cave, which had so far been full of noise and laughter, became suddenly still as death; his nose, however, smelled a sweet scented vapor and odor of incense, as if from burning pinecones.

"What is happening? What are they up to?" he asked himself, and stole up to the entrance, so that he might see his guests unobserved. But wonder upon wonder! what was he then obliged to behold with his own eyes!

"They have all of them become *pious* again, they *pray*, they are insane!"—he said, and was astonished beyond measure. And indeed! all these higher men, the two kings, the pope retired from service, the evil magician, the voluntary beggar, the wanderer and shadow, the old soothsayer, the conscientious in spirit, and the ugliest man—they all lay on their knees like children and credulous old women, and worshipped the ass. And just then the ugliest man began to gurgle and snort, as if something unutterable in him tried to find expression; but when he actually found words, behold! it was a pious, strange litany in praise of the adored and incensed ass. And the litany sounded thus:

"Amen! And glory and honor and wisdom and thanks and praise and strength be to our god, from everlasting to everlasting!"

—But the ass brayed Yeah-Yuh.

"He carries our burdens, he has taken upon him the form of a servant, he is patient of heart and never says No; and he who loves his god chastises him."

—But the ass brayed Yeah-Yuh.

"He does not speak: except that he always says Yes to the world which he created: thus he extols his world. It is his subtlety that does not speak: thus is he rarely found wrong."

—But the ass brayed Yeah-Yuh.

"He goes modestly through the world. Grey is the body color in which he wraps his virtue. If he has spirit he conceals it; but every one believes in his long ears."

—But the ass brayed Yeah-Yuh.

"What hidden wisdom it is to wear long ears, and only to say Yes and never No! Has he not created the world in his own image, namely, as stupid as possible?"

—But the ass brayed Yeah-Yuh.

"You go straight and crooked ways; it concerns you little what seems straight or crooked to us men. Your domain is beyond good and evil. It is your innocence not to know what innocence is."

—But the ass brayed Yeah-Yuh.

"Behold, how you spurn no one, neither beggars nor kings. You suffer little children to come to you, and when bad boys tease you, then say you simply, Yeah-Yuh."

—But the ass brayed Yeah-Yuh.

"You love she-asses and fresh figs, you eat anything. A thistle tickles your heart when you happen to be hungry. There is the wisdom of a god in that."

—But the ass brayed Yeah-Yuh.

THE ASS FESTIVAL[13]

1

BUT AT THIS PLACE in the litany Zarathustra could no longer control himself; he himself cried out Yeah-Yuh, louder even than the ass, and sprang into the midst of his maddened guests. "Whatever are you about, you grown-up children?" he exclaimed, pulling up the praying ones from the ground. "Ah, if any one else, except Zarathustra, had seen you:

"Everyone would think you the worst blasphemers, or the very most foolish old women, with your new belief!

"And you yourself, you old pope, how can you bring yourself to adore an ass in such a manner as god?"—

"O Zarathustra," answered the pope, "forgive me, but in divine matters I am more enlightened even than you. And it is right that it should be so.

"Better to adore god thus, in this form, than in no form at all! Think over this saying, my exalted friend: you will readily see that in such a saying there is wisdom.

"He who said 'God is a Spirit' took the greatest step and leap so far made on earth towards unbelief: such a saying is not easily corrected!

"My old heart leaps and bounds because there is still something to adore on earth. Forgive an old, pious pope's heart that, O Zarathustra!—"

—"And you," said Zarathustra to the wanderer and shadow, "you call and think yourself a free spirit? And here you practice such priestly idolatries?

"Truly, you behave even worse here than with your naughty brown girls, you evil new believer!"

"It is bad enough," answered the wanderer and shadow, "you are right: but how can I help it! The old god lives again, O Zarathustra, you may say what you will.

"The ugliest man is to blame for it all: he has reawakened him. And if he replies that he once killed him, with gods *death* is always only a prejudice."

—"And you," said Zarathustra, "you evil old magician, what did you do! Who in this free age ought to believe in you any longer, when *you* believe in such divine asininities?

"What a stupid thing you have done; how could you, shrewd man, do such a stupid thing!"

"O Zarathustra," answered the shrewd magician, "you are right, it was a stupid thing, and it was hard enough to do it."

—"And even you," said Zarathustra to the conscientious in spirit, "consider, and put your finger to your nose! Does nothing go against your conscience here? Is your spirit not too clean for this praying and the exhalations of these devotees?"

"There is something to that," said the conscientious in spirit, and put his finger to his nose, "there is something in this spectacle which helps my conscience.

"Perhaps I dare not believe in god: but it is certain that god seems to me most worthy of belief in this form.

"God is said to be eternal, according to the testimony of the most pious: he who has so much time takes his time. As slow and as stupid as possible: *thereby* such a one can nevertheless go very far.

"And he who has too much spirit might well become infatuated with stupidity and folly. Think of yourself, O Zarathustra!

"You yourself—truly! even you could well become an ass through superabundance of wisdom.

"Does not the true sage willingly walk on the most crooked paths? The evidence teaches it, O Zarathustra,—*your own* evidence!"

—"And you yourself, finally," said Zarathustra, and turned towards the ugliest man, who still lay on the ground stretching up his arm to the ass (for he gave it wine to drink). "Speak, you unspeakable, what have you been about!

"You seem transformed, your eyes glow, the cloak of the sublime covers your ugliness: *what* did you do?

"Is it then true what they say, that you have again awakened him? And why? Was he not killed for good reasons and done away with?

"You yourself seem to me awakened: what did you do? why did *you* turn around? Why did *you* get converted? Speak, you unspeakable!"

"O Zarathustra," answered the ugliest man, "you are a rogue!

"Whether *he* lives still, or lives again, or is thoroughly dead—which of the two of us knows that best? I ask you.

"But one thing I do know—I once learned it from you yourself, O Zarathustra: he who wants to kill most thoroughly—*laughs*.

" 'One does not kill by anger but by laughter'—thus you spoke once, O Zarathustra, you hidden one, you destroyer without anger, you dangerous saint,—you are a rogue!"

2

But then it happened that Zarathustra, astonished at such public roguish answers, jumped back to the door of his cave and, turning towards all his guests, cried out with a strong voice:

"O you jokers, all of you, you jesters! Why do you dissemble and disguise yourselves before me!

"How the hearts of all of you convulsed with delight and malice, because you had at last become again like little children—namely, pious,—

—"Because you at last did again as children do—namely, prayed, folded your hands and said 'good God'!

"But now leave, I pray you, *this* nursery, my own cave, where today all childishness is carried on. Cool down, here outside, your hot childish playfulness and tumult of hearts."

"To be sure: unless you become like little children you shall not enter into *that* kingdom of heaven." (And Zarathustra pointed up with his hands.)

"But we certainly do not want to enter into the kingdom of heaven: we have become men,—*so we want the kingdom of Earth.*"

3

And once more Zarathustra began to speak. "O my new friends," he said,—"you strange ones, you higher men, how well you please me now,—

—"Since you have become gay again! Truly you have all blossomed forth: it seems to me that for such flowers as you, *new festivals* are required.

—"A little valiant nonsense, some divine service and ass festival, some old gay Zarathustra fool, some blusterer to blow your souls bright.

"Do not forget this night and this ass festival, you higher men! *That* you invented with me, that I take as a good omen,—such things only the convalescents invent!

"And should you celebrate it again, this ass festival, do it from love of yourselves, do it also from love of me! And in memory of me!"[14]

Thus spoke Zarathustra.

THE DRUNKEN SONG[15]

1

MEANWHILE ONE AFTER ANOTHER had gone out into the open air, and into the cool, thoughtful night; but Zarathustra himself led the ugliest man by the hand, so that he might show him his night world, and the great round moon, and the silvery waterfalls near his cave. There at last they stood still beside one another; all of them old people, but with comforted, brave hearts, and astonished in themselves that all was so well with them on earth; but the mystery of the night came closer and closer to their hearts. And once more Zarathustra thought to himself: "Oh, how well do they now please me, these higher men!"—but he did not say it aloud, for he respected their happiness and their silence.—

But then something happened which in this astonishing long day was most astonishing: the ugliest man began once more and for the last time to gurgle and snort, and when he had at length found expression, behold! a question sprang round and pure from his mouth, a good, deep, clear question, which moved the hearts of all who listened to him.

"My friends, all of you," said the ugliest man, "what do you think? For the sake of this day—*I* am for the first time content to have lived my entire life.

"And that I testify so much is still not enough for me. It is worth-while living on the earth: one day, one festival with Zarathustra, has taught me to love the earth.

"'Was *that*—life?' I will say to death. 'Well! Once more!'

"My friends, what do you think? Will you not, like me, say to death: 'Was *that*—life? For the sake of Zarathustra, well! Once more!'"—

Thus spoke the ugliest man; but it was not far from midnight. And what took place then, do you think? As soon as the higher men heard his question, they became suddenly conscious of their trans-formation and convalescence, and of him who was the cause of that: then they rushed up to Zarathustra, thanking, honoring, caressing him, and kissing his hands, each in his own peculiar way; so that some laughed and some wept. The old soothsayer, however, danced with delight; and even if he was then full of sweet wine, as some narrators suppose, he was certainly still fuller of sweet life, and had renounced all weariness. There are even those who say that then the ass danced: for not in vain had the ugliest man previously given it wine to drink. That may be the case, or it may be otherwise; and if in truth the ass did not dance that evening, there nevertheless hap-pened then greater and rarer wonders than the dancing of an ass would have been. In short, as the proverb of Zarathustra says: "What does it matter!"

2

But when this happened with the ugliest man, Zarathustra stood there like a drunk: his glance dulled, his tongue faltered and his feet staggered. And who could guess what thoughts then passed through Zarathustra's soul? But apparently his spirit retreated and fled in ad-vance and was in remote distances, and as it were "wandering on high mountain-ridges," as it is written, "between two seas, wandering like a heavy cloud between the past and the future." But gradually, while the higher men held him in their arms, he came back to himself a little, and resisted with his hands the crowd of the honoring and caring ones; but he did not speak. Suddenly, however, he turned his head quickly, for he seemed to hear something: then he laid his finger on his mouth and said: "*Come!*"

And immediately it became still and mysterious all around; but from the depth there came up slowly the sound of a bell. Zarathustra listened to it, like the higher men; then, however, he laid his finger on his mouth the second time, and said again: "*Come! Come! Midnight approaches!*"—and his voice had changed. But still he had not moved from the spot. Then it became yet stiller and more mysterious, and everything listened, even the ass, and Zarathustra's noble animals, the eagle and the serpent,—likewise the cave of Zarathustra and the big cool moon, and the night itself. Zarathustra, however, laid his hand upon his mouth for the third time, and said:

Come! Come! Come! Let us now wander! It is the hour: let us wander into the night!

3

You higher men, midnight approaches: then I will say something into your ears, as that old bell whispers it into my ear,—

—As mysteriously, as frightfully, and as cordially as that midnight bell whispers it to me, which has experienced more than any man:

—Which has already counted the throbbings of your fathers' hearts—ah! Ah! how it sighs! how it laughs in its dream! the old, deep, deep midnight!

Hush! Hush! Then many a thing is heard which may not be heard by day; but now in the cool air, when even all the tumult of your hearts has become still,—

—Now it speaks, now it is heard, now it steals into overwakeful, nocturnal souls: ah! Ah! how the midnight sighs! how it laughs in its dream!

—Do you not hear how it mysteriously, frightfully, and cordially speaks to *you*, the old deep, deep midnight?

O man, take care!

4

Woe to me! Where has time gone? Have I not sunk into deep wells? The world sleeps—

Ah! Ah! the dog howls, the moon shines. I will rather die, die, than say to you what my midnight heart thinks now.

Already I have died. It is all over. Spider, why do you spin around me? You want blood? Ah! Ah! the dew falls, the hour comes—

—the hour which chills and freezes, which asks and asks and asks: "Who has heart enough for it?

—who shall be master of the earth? Who will say: "*thus* you shall flow, you great and small streams!"

—the hour approaches: O man, you higher man, take care! this talk is for fine ears, for your ears—*what does the deep midnight declare?*

5

I am carried away, my soul dances. Day's-work! Day's-work! Who shall be master of the earth?

The moon is cool, the wind is still. Ah! Ah! have you already flown high enough? You have danced: but a leg is not a wing.

You good dancers, now all delight is over: wine has become dregs, every cup has become brittle, the graves mutter.

You have not flown high enough: now the graves mutter: "Free the dead! Why is night so long? Doesn't the moon make us drunk?"

You higher men, open the graves, awaken the corpses! Ah, why does the worm still burrow? It approaches, it approaches, the hour,—

—the bell booms, the heart still rattles, the woodworm, the heartworm, still burrows. Ah! Ah! *The world is deep!*

6

Sweet lyre! Sweet lyre! I love your sound, your drunken, croaking sound!—from how long ago, from how far has your sound come to me, from the distance, from the pools of love!

You old bell, you sweet lyre! Every pain has torn your heart, the pain of a father, fathers' pain, forefathers' pain; your speech has become ripe,—

—ripe like the golden autumn and the afternoon, like my hermit heart—now you say: The world itself has become ripe, the grape turns brown,

—now it wants to die, to die of happiness. You higher men, do you not feel it? An odor wells up mysteriously,

—a scent and odor of eternity, a rosy blessed, brown, golden wine odor of old happiness,

—of drunken midnight's dying happiness, which sings: the world is deep, *and deeper than day had been aware!*

7

Leave me! Leave me! I am too pure for you. Do not touch me! Has not my world become perfect just now?

My skin is too pure for your hands. Leave me, you dull, doltish, stupid day! Is midnight not brighter?

The purest shall be masters of the earth, the least known, the strongest, the midnight souls, who are brighter and deeper than any day.

O day, you grope for me? You feel for my happiness? For you I am rich, lonesome, a treasure pit, a gold chamber?

O world, you want *me*? Am I worldly to you? Am I spiritual to you? Am I divine to you? But day and world, you are too coarse,—

—have cleverer hands, grasp after deeper happiness, after deeper unhappiness, grasp after some god; do not grasp after me:

—my unhappiness, my happiness is deep, you strange day, but yet I am no god, no god's-hell: *deep is its woe.*

8

God's woe is deeper, you strange world! Grasp at god's woe, not at me! What am I! A drunken sweet lyre,—

—a midnight lyre, a bellfrog, which no one understands, but which *must* speak before deaf ones, you higher men! For you do not understand me!

Gone! Gone! O youth! O noon! O afternoon! Now evening and night and midnight have come,—the dog howls, the wind:

—is the wind not a dog? It whines, it barks, it howls. Ah! Ah! how she sighs! how she laughs, how she wheezes and pants, the midnight!

How she just now speaks soberly, this drunken poetess! has she perhaps overdrunk her drunkenness? has she become overawake? does she ruminate?

—she ruminates over her woe, in a dream, the old, deep midnight—and still more her joy. For joy, although woe is deep, *joy is deeper yet than agony.*

9

You grapevine! Why do you praise me? Have I not cut you! I am cruel, you bleed—: what does your praise of my drunken cruelty mean?

"Whatever has become perfect, everything ripe—wants to die!" so you say. Blessed, blessed is the vintner's knife! But everything immature wants to live: ah!

Woe says: "Away! Be gone, you woe!" But everything that suffers wants to live, so that it may become ripe and lively and longing,

—longing for the further, the higher, the brighter. "I want heirs," so says everything that suffers, "I want children, I do not want *myself*,"—

Joy, however, does not want heirs, it does not want children,—joy wants itself, it wants eternity, it wants recurrence, it wants everything eternally like itself.

Woe says: "Break, bleed, you heart! Wander, you leg! You wing, fly! Onward! upward! You pain!" Well! Cheer up! O my old heart: *Woe says: "Go!"*

10

You higher men, what do you think? Am I a soothsayer? Or a dreamer? Or a drunkard? Or a dreamreader? Or a midnight bell?

Or a drop of dew? Or a fume and fragrance of eternity? Do you not hear it? Do you not smell it? Just now my world has become perfect, midnight is also midday,—

Pain is also joy, a curse is also a blessing, night is also a sun,—go away! or you will learn: the wise is also a fool.

Did you ever say yes to one joy? O my friends, then you said yes to *all* woe too. All things are entangled, ensnared, enamored,—

—if ever you wanted one moment to come twice; if ever you said: "you please me, happiness! Instant! Moment!"[16] then you wanted *everything* to return!

—All new, all eternal, all entangled, ensnared, enamored, oh, then you *loved* the world,—

—you eternal ones, you love it eternally and for all time: and to woe too you say: go, but return! *For all joy wants—eternity!*

11

All joy wants the eternity of all things, it wants honey, wants dregs, wants drunken midnight, wants graves, wants the consolation of the tears of the grave, wants golden evening glow—

—*what* doesn't joy want? It is thirstier, warmer, hungrier, more frightful, more mysterious than all woe: it wants *itself*, it bites into *itself*, the ring's will strives in it,—

—it wants love, it wants hate, it is overrich, it gives, it throws away, it begs for someone to take from it, it thanks the taker, it would be hated,—

—so rich is joy that it thirsts for woe, for hell, for hate, for shame, for the cripple, for the *world*,—for this world, O, yes you know it!

You higher men, it longs for you, this joy, the irrepressible, blissful—for your woe, you failures! All eternal joy longs for failures.

For all joy wants itself, therefore it also wants agony! O happiness, O pain! Oh break, heart! You higher men, learn it well, that all joy wants eternity.

—Joy wants the eternity of *all* things, it *wants deep, deep eternity!*

12

Have you now learned my song? Have you divined what it means? Well! Come on! You higher men, sing me now my round!

Now sing yourselves the song whose name is "Once more," whose meaning is "To all eternity!"—sing, you higher men, Zarathustra's round!

> O man! Take care!
> What does deep midnight declare?
> "I sleep, I sleep—,
> "From the deepest dream I awoke:—
> "The world is deep,
> "And deeper than day had been aware.
> "Deep is its woe—,
> "Joy—deeper yet than agony:
> "Woe says: Go!
> "But all joy wants eternity—,
> "wants deep, deep eternity!"

The Sign

BUT IN THE MORNING after this night Zarathustra jumped up from his bed, girded his loins and came out of his cave, glowing and strong, like a morning sun coming out of dark mountains.[17]

"You great star," he spoke as he had spoken once before, "you deep eye of happiness, what would be all your happiness if you had not *those* for whom you shine!

"And if they remained in their chambers while you had awakened and come and given and distributed, how angry would your proud shame be!

"Well! they still sleep, these higher men, while *I* am awake: *they* are not my proper companions! Not for them do I wait here in my mountains.

"I want to go to my work, to my day: but they do not understand the signs of my morning, my step—is no awakening call for them.

"They still sleep in my cave, their dream still drinks at my drunken songs. The ear that listens for *me*—the *heedful* ear is missing from them."

—Zarathustra said this to his heart when the sun arose: then he looked inquiringly into the air, for he heard above him the sharp call of his eagle. "Well!" he shouted upward, "so do I like it, so do I deserve it. My animals are awake, for I am awake.

"My eagle is awake, and like me honors the sun. With eagle talons he grasps at the new light. You are my proper animals; I love you.

"But I still lack my proper men!"—

Thus spoke Zarathustra; but then he suddenly became aware that he was surrounded as if by innumerable swarming and fluttering birds: the whirring of so many wings and the crowding around his head, however, was so great that he shut his eyes. And truly, it was as though a cloud descended on him, like a cloud of arrows that pours upon a new enemy. But behold, here it was a cloud of love, and it showered upon a new friend.

"What is happening to me?" thought Zarathustra in his astonished heart, and slowly seated himself on the big stone that lay close to the exit from his cave. But while he grasped about with his hands, around him, above him and below him, and repelled the tender birds, behold, something still stranger happened to him: for he reached unawares into a mass of thick, warm, shaggy hair; but at the same time a roar sounded out,—a long, soft roar of a lion.

"*The sign comes*," said Zarathustra, and a change came over his heart. And in truth, when it turned clear before him, there lay a yellow, powerful animal at his feet, resting its head on his knee,— unwilling to leave him out of love, and behaving like a dog which again finds its old master. But the doves were no less eager with their love than the lion; and whenever a dove brushed its nose, the lion shook its head and wondered and laughed.[18]

While all this went on Zarathustra spoke only a sentence: "*My children are near, my children*"—, then he became quite silent. But his heart was loosed and from his eyes tears dropped down and fell upon his hands. And he took no further notice of anything, but sat there motionless, without repelling the animals further. Then the doves flew to and fro, and perched on his shoulder, and caressed his white hair, and did not tire of their tenderness and joyousness. But the strong lion always licked the tears that fell on Zarathustra's hands, and roared and growled shyly. Thus these animals acted.—

All this went on for a long time, or a short time: for properly speaking, there is *no* time on earth for such things—. But meanwhile the higher men had awakened in Zarathustra's cave, and marshaled themselves for a procession to go to meet Zarathustra, and give him their morning greeting: for they had found when they awakened that he no longer remained with them. But when they reached the door of the cave and the noise of their steps had preceded them, the lion started violently; it turned away suddenly from Zarathustra and, roaring wildly, sprang towards the cave. But the higher men, when they heard the lion roaring, all cried aloud as with one voice, fled back and vanished in an instant.

But Zarathustra himself, stunned and spellbound, rose from his seat, looked around him, stood there astonished, questioned his heart, recollected, and saw he was alone. "What did I hear?" he said at last, slowly, "what happened to me just now?"

And at once his memory returned and he took in at a glance all that had happened between yesterday and today. "Here indeed is the stone," he said, and stroked his beard, "I sat on *it* yesterday morning; and here the soothsayer came to me, and here I first heard the cry which I heard just now, the great cry of distress.

"O you higher men, it was *your* distress that the old soothsayer foretold to me yesterday morning,—

—"He wanted to seduce and tempt me to your distress: 'O Zarathustra,' he said to me, 'I come to seduce you to your last sin.'

"To my last sin?" cried Zarathustra, and laughed angrily at his own words: "*what* has been reserved for me as my last sin?"

—And once more Zarathustra became absorbed in himself, and sat down again on the big stone and meditated. Suddenly he sprang up, "*Pity! Pity for the higher men!*" he cried out, and his face changed to brass. "Well! *That*—has had its time!

"My suffering and my pity—what do they matter! Should I strive for my *happiness*? I strive for my *work*!

"Well! The lion has come, my children are near, Zarathustra has grown ripe, my hour has come:—

"This is *my* morning, *my* day begins: *arise now, arise, you great noon!*"——

Thus spoke Zarathustra and left his cave, glowing and strong, like a morning sun that comes out of dark mountains.

ENDNOTES

Prologue

1. (p. 7) *When Zarathustra was thirty years old, he left his home and the lake of his home and went into the mountains:* Zarathustra's emergence from the cave, as we suggest in the Introduction, parallels the emergence of the philosopher in the Myth of the Cave in *Republic* 7, by Plato (c.427–347 B.C.). A key difference is that while the cave in Plato's account is a realm of illusion, Zarathustra's cave is a realm of insight that can supplement the illumination provided by the sun's light. Zarathustra's retreat into solitude at the age of thirty, before his mission begins, is accurate with respect to the historical Zarathustra. It also alludes to the experience of Jesus, who was thirty when he went into the wilderness for forty days before beginning his mission.

2. (p. 7) go under: "Go under"—or, frequently, "going under"—is the literal translation of *untergehen*, a term also used for "perishing" or "dying," and for the sun setting; the latter meaning suggests both "perishing" and "regeneration." The conjunction of destruction and reappearance is also found in the German *Aufhebung* (literally, "picking up," but also with connotations of "keeping" and of "abolishing"), a significant term in the philosophy of Georg Wilhelm Friedrich Hegel (1770–1831). *Aufhebung* implies the end of one stage but also the "lifting up" of the contents from that stage to a new, more encompassing configuration. Hegel used this term in reference to different historical stages. Nietzsche suggests the desirability of such a process, but stresses the necessity of the destruction of the current situation if such a transformation is to occur.

3. (p. 8) *"Then you carried your ashes into the mountains; would you now carry your fire into the valleys?":* The phoenix is consumed by fire but rises again from its ashes.

4. (p. 9) *"Do not go to men, but stay in the forest! Go rather even to the animals! Why not be like me—a bear among bears, a bird among birds?":* The saint in the forest recalls a story applauded by Arthur Schopenhauer (1788–1860), in which a saintly hermit in the forest renounces his will to such an extent that he stops eating and subsequently dies. This story sums up what Nietzsche rejects in Schopenhauer's philosophy, its "anti-life" tendency. The characterization of the saint as one who loves animals but no longer loves men is also reminiscent of Schopenhauer, who perpetually found fault with other people but loved animals.

5. (p. 9) "God is dead!": Nietzsche also makes this statement in *Die fröhliche Wissenschaft* (1882; *The Gay Science*, sections 108 and 125), but the line is not original with him. It appears in a Lutheran hymn for Holy Saturday, "Ein trauriger Grabgesang" ("A Sorrowful Dirge"), by Johann Rist (1607–1667), which commemorates the period after Christ's crucifixion but before his resurrection. The cantata "Christ lag in Todesbanden" ("Christ Lay in Death's Bonds"), by Johann Sebastian Bach (1685–1750), focuses on the same period and uses similar imagery. The line also appears in Hegel's *Phänomenologie des Geistes* (1807; *Phenomenology of Spirit*) as a characterization of the stage of consciousness called "unhappy consciousness," which resembles the condition of modern nihilism that Nietzsche diagnoses. Nietzsche considers this condition to have ambivalent significance, however. He follows Ludwig Feuerbach (1804–1872), who claimed that human beings have always projected their own traits onto God, with the consequence that they do not recognize their own powers; the turn toward atheism in the modern West, while unsettling, has the potential to awaken Western humanity to its own powers. The expression "God is dead" represents for Nietzsche both the current spiritual crisis and what Nietzsche envisions as it optimal resolution.

6. (p. 9) I teach you the Übermensch: *Übermensch* means "superman"; it has sometimes been translated—literally, if inaccurately—as "overman." Because the term has become so widely recognized, we have chosen to leave it in the original German. It is perhaps best understood as a technical term that Zarathustra introduces and characterizes in his opening speech. The prefix *über* (which translates as "over" or "super") contributes to the ongoing play of "over" and "under" words that recurs throughout the book: undergoing, overcoming, going over, etc. The term is not original to Nietzsche. It occurs in certain eighteenth-century German religious texts, in German Romanticism, and in the work of Johann Wolfgang von Goethe (1749–1832). The word is also discussed in some detail in the Introduction.

7. (p. 9) overcome: This is the translation of *überwunden*. The central metaphorical theme of the book is developed through the contrast of elevation and descent. Thus Nietzsche constantly uses word combinations employing "over" and "under," "above" and "beneath," "high" and "low," etc.

8. (p. 9) man is more of an ape than any ape: The reference to apes and men alludes to the theory of evolution proposed by Charles Darwin (1809–1882). Nietzsche assumes that the theory of evolution is basically correct, but in some contexts he criticizes Darwin's contention that the fittest survive. Nietzsche thinks that in the human species, at least, the "higher" specimens are most vulnerable, and that survival is most assured for the mediocre. Nietzsche certainly does not think that the *Übermensch* will assuredly evolve, as he makes clear in Zarathustra's portrait of "the last man" (the man who has no evolutionary descendents) in Prologue 5 (p. 13).

9. (p. 13) *"We have invented happiness"—say the last men, and blink:* As we mention in the Introduction, Nietzsche challenges utilitarianism in this portrait. By defining the moral goal as "the greatest good for the greatest number" and defining the good as pleasure and the absence of pain, the utilitarians, according to Nietzsche, seek mere contentment. Although we seem to be the highest product of evolution thus far, as Nietzsche sees it, the utilitarian ideal renders this evolutionary achievement pathetic.

10. (p. 14) *"Prologue":* This is a translation of *Vorrede,* which translates literally as "before speech"; a *Rede* is a speech. Zarathustra is about to begin his speeches. The play on words does not translate into English.

11. (p. 16) *"Zarathustra has made a fine catch of fish today!":* Some of Jesus' most important disciples, including Saint Peter, were fishermen. He tells them, "Come, follow me, and I will make you fishers of men" (see the Bible, Matthew 4:18–19; Mark 1:16–17; compare Luke 5:9 [New International Version; henceforth, NIV]).

12. (p. 17) *"whoever knocks at my door must take what I offer him. Eat, and be off!":* This hermit's insistence that everyone, even the dead, eat the bread and wine he has to offer, is a lampoon of Jesus' words at the Last Supper: "Take and eat; this is my body. . . . Drink from it [the cup] . . . This is my blood" (see the Bible, Matthew 26:26–29 [NIV]; compare Mark 14:22–25; Luke 22:14–20, and 1 Corinthians 11:23–25). Nietzsche thinks that the Christian Church, by insisting that everyone must join it or be damned, is as indiscriminate and unreasonable as the hermit in this section.

13. (p. 18) *"Zarathustra shall not be the shepherd and dog of a herd!":* Zarathustra rejects the role that Jesus assumes when he claims, "I am the good shepherd" (see the Bible, John 10:11 [NIV]).

First Part

1. (p. 26) *he lived in the town that is called: The Motley Cow:* The name of the town suggests that its inhabitants are members of the human "herd," a term Nietzsche frequently uses to refer to the tendency of human beings to conform to the behavior of their fellows. The name is also a possible translation of Kalmasadalmya (Pali: Kammasuddamam), the name of a town the Buddha visited while wandering.

2. (p. 26) *On the Teachers of Virtue: Lehrstühlen,* literally "teach-chairs," has here been translated as simply "teachers." It might also be translated as "chairs" (as in an academic chair). Throughout the book Zarathustra pokes fun at academics, and this section initiates his attack. The suggestion in this section that one's virtues are like fair little women quarreling with each other makes reference to the fact that "virtue" (*Tugend*) is a feminine noun in German.

3. (p. 29) *On the Afterworldly: Hinterwelter,* translated here as "afterworldly," can also be translated as "afterworlder." It refers to those who believe in another world or a world after this one. In German it is easy to create words that refer to a class of persons, and Nietzsche does this throughout the book. For example, where we would say "afterworldly people," he simply says "afterworlders." This is a problem over and over again for the translator, as the reader will see.

4. (p. 29) *a poor fragment of a man and "I":* The German here is *Ich*, or simply "I." Previous translators have rendered the "Ich" here and elsewhere as "Ego" because it emphasizes the fact that Zarathustra is using "Ich" not to refer to himself but to the concept of the self, the "I." We prefer "I," because it is faithful to the text and does not carry the Freudian baggage of "Ego." We have placed the "I" in quotation marks to minimize confusion. There are no such quotation marks in the original text.

5. (p. 32) *"soul is only the name of something about the body":* This model of the human being contrasts straightforwardly with the account by René Descartes (1596–1650), in which the soul and the body are distinct substances, the soul being the more important. It also opposes Plato's model, in which the body and the soul are separate, and in which the body and its appetites and desires must be subordinate to reason, the highest part of the soul. In Zarathustra's model, the body is reason and the soul is a subordinate component.

6. (p. 42) *My brothers in war!:* Nietzsche uses many martial metaphors throughout the text. They should not be understood literally. The same advice applies to his many metaphorical uses of the concepts of "man" and "woman."

7. (p. 42) *I love you thoroughly:* The German expression *von Grund aus*—literally, "from the ground up"—is a favorite of Zarathustra's. Here translated as "thoroughly," it is also sometimes rendered as "from the very heart," "through and through," or "from bottom," depending on the context.

8. (p. 46) *where the marketplace begins . . . poisonous flies:* The "marketplace" recalls the location in which Socrates conducted his philosophical conversations, the marketplace (*agora*) of Athens. He described himself as a "gadfly" of the people he encountered. The reference to the marketplace also alludes to the warnings of Francis Bacon (1561–1626) against the "idols of the marketplace," which refers to the ways in which everyday lingusitic usage misleads and inhibits the progress of science. Zarathustra similarly objects to the messages of the popular "jesters" of the marketplace, who impede the progress of the creative individuals who might create new values.

9. (p. 48) *Whatever is thought about a great deal is at last thought suspicious:* There is a nice play on words here between *Denken* ("to think") and *bedenklich* ("suspicious"). This is just one example of many such plays upon words and puns that have been lost in translation.

10. (p. 54) *But I tell you: your love of the neighbor is your bad love of yourselves:* Jesus says in the Bible, Luke 10:25–28, that the whole law and the prophets

can be summed up in two commandments, " 'Love the Lord your God with all your heart and with all your soul and with all your strength and with all your mind'; and, 'Love your neighbor as yourself.' " See also Mark 12:29–31.

11. (p. 58) *On Little Old and Young Women:* The German here is *Weiblein* or "little women." So, literally translated, the title of this speech is "On Old and Young Little Women." We have followed Walter Kaufmann in translating it as "Little Old and Young Women" so as to catch the familiar English expression "Little Old Women." We discuss this strange, infamous, and highly metaphorical section in our Introduction. It is helpful when reading this section to remember that Nietzsche's next book after this one, *Jenseits von Gut und Böse* (1886; *Beyond Good and Evil*), which he saw as a kind of commentary on *Also sprach Zarathustra* (1883–1885; *Thus Spoke Zarathustra*), begins with a question: "Suppose truth is a woman: what then?" (The question plays on the fact that the German word for "truth" [*Wahrheit*] is a feminine noun.) If, as some scholars have done, one takes Nietzsche's question in *Beyond Good and Evil* seriously, and replaces every occurrence of the words "woman" and "women" in this speech with the word "truth," startling new meanings of the speech emerge (it is an experiment worth trying). Later in the book, Zarathustra insists that "happiness is a woman." The point, of course, is to resist the easy and silly *literal* reading of the speech.

12. (p. 58) *I met a little old woman who spoke thus to my soul:* Zarathustra's relationship to the little old woman, who teaches him about love, recalls Socrates' claim in Plato's *Symposium* that a woman, Diotima, taught him what he knows about love. In the *Symposium* Diotima interprets love in terms of a response to the timeless, immaterial form of Beauty; in this passage, the little old woman interprets it in terms of the power dynamics inherent in any sexual relationship. Although Zarathustra has imagined that a woman will just go along with his vision of her as "the most dangerous plaything," the old woman's comment reminds him that real women have minds of their own and that in approaching women he'd better be able to defend himself.

13. (p. 66) *All names of good and evil are parables: Gleichnisse,* or "parables," also means "likenesses," "similes," or "images." This is another of Zarathustra's favorite terms.

14. (p. 66) *spirit: Geist,* or "spirit," is a very complicated German word with a long religious and philosophical history. Nietzsche does not intend anything "otherworldly" when he uses it. By the "spirit" of a person he means something much more like what we mean when we speak of the "spirit of the times."

15. (p. 69) *therefore all belief comes to so little:* The German *Glaube,* or "belief," is also the word for "faith."

Second Part

1. (p. 75) *On the Happy Islands:* "The Happy Islands" (also translated as "The Blessed Islands") refers to the ancient Greek abode of heroes in the afterlife.

2. (p. 77) *"The knower walks among men* as *among animals":* Der Erkennende, or "the knower," could also be translated as "the wise one" or "the one who knows" or even "the enlightened man."

3. (p. 77) *I do not like them, the merciful who feel blessed in their pity: they are much too lacking in shame:* Mitleid, or "pity," may also be translated as "compassion." Literally, it means "suffering with." In rejecting pity or compassion, Zarathustra rejects Schopenhauer's ethics, which are based on compassion for all that live. Zarathustra's attacks on pity have made many readers suspicious of his ethical position. But one should note that the force of Zarathustra's attack is not directed against feeling pity or sympathy for others as such, but against feeling pity or sympathy for others for the wrong sorts of reasons (such as in order to feel better about oneself). The section concludes with Zarathustra's provocative reformulation of Christ's great ethical precept "Love thy neighbor as thyself."

4. (p. 83) *"I am just—revenged!":* As R. J. Hollingdale noted in his translation of *Thus Spoke Zarathustra*, in German gerecht ("just") is pronounced exactly like gerächt ("revenged").

5. (p. 85) *Life is a well of delight:* Lust, or "delight," may also be translated as "pleasure" or "joy"; in some contexts its translation is its obvious English cognate, "lust." In the still sexually restrained time of nineteenth-century Germany, *Thus Spoke Zarathustra* is intended as a paean to the human body and its pleasures (including sexual pleasure), and the many different uses of *Lust* is one expression of that. Nietzsche himself, it should perhaps be added, lived a relatively ascetic life.

6. (p. 87) *this is the tarantula's hole!:* We have taken a small poetic liberty in translating the German Höhle as its English cognate, "hole." Elsewhere we have generally translated it as "cave"; indeed, Zarathustra lives in a *"Höhle."*

7. (p. 89) *"Men are not equal":* Die Menschen is here translated as "men," when the word in fact means "mankind." For reasons of natural English usage, terms that are gender-neutral in German have often been rendered as "man" (or some other gendered formulation) in English, which simply does not have the ease with gender-neutral terms that many other languages enjoy. This unfortunately often creates the impression that Nietzsche is referring only to men, when he is referring to human beings generally, and at times it can make him sound misogynistic. The reader should be reassured that this is a fault of the translation and not a fault of Nietzsche's. In fact (and especially for his time), Nietzsche was unusually conscientious about avoiding gendered terms, often preferring to reserve their use for particular poetic, metaphorical, and philosophical purposes.

8. (p. 90) *On the Famous Wise Men:* Here is an example of the point made in the preceding endnote. We have rendered the German *Weisen* as "wise men" but could also have translated it as "wise ones." In the German it is simply *Weisen* ("the wise," as a noun rather than an adjective).

9. (p. 99) *That is your entire will, you wisest men, as a Will to Power:* Schopenhauer claims that the fundamental reality behind all phenomena (sentient beings and well as insentient forces of nature) is the "will to live," and he emphasizes the efforts every creature makes to keep existing. Zarathustra opposes this interpretation with the notion that life is, instead, the expansive and overabundant "will to power."

10. (p. 104) *The Land of Culture:* The German word *Bildung,* or "culture," is sometimes also translated as "education" or even as "edification" or "maturity," and is almost as complicated a word as the aforementioned *Geist* (see endnote 14 to the first part). A *Bildungsroman* is a "novel of education" or a "novel of up-building," in which the hero, usually a young man, travels about in order to experience life and usually goes through a process of disillusionment to come to a more mature appreciation of life. The *Bildungsroman* was a very popular form of literature in the nineteenth century, especially in Germany; Goethe wrote a particularly famous *Bildungsroman: Wilhelm Meisters Lehrjahre* (1795–1796; Wilhelm Meister's Apprenticeship). All of *Thus Spoke Zarathustra* may be read as a kind of *Bildungsroman,* in which the youth being educated about life is, of course, Zarathustra himself.

11. (p. 107) *"To be happy in gazing: with a dead will . . . but with intoxicated moon-eyes!":* Zarathustra opposes here the aesthetic theories of Kant and Schopenhauer, both of whom claim that aesthetic experience depends on a disinterested, dispassionate approach to what is observed. Zarathustra encourages an eroticized, interested appreciation of the world instead.

12. (p. 110) *On Poets:* This section incorporates a number of witty allusions to the poetic tradition.

13. (p. 110) *"Why did you say that the poets lie too much?":* Zarathustra made this comment previously in "On the Happy Islands." Zarathustra's claim that the poets lie too much repeats Socrates' contention in Plato's *Republic* that the poets deceive people, putting words into their heroes' mouths and stating untruths about the gods. According to Plato, Socrates would ban poetry on this account unless poetry could demonstrate that it actually did serve reason and good government. Zarathustra, by contrast, contends that fictionalizing is necessary, even though he has his own complaints against poets. "Belief does not make me blessed . . . least of all belief in myself." This alludes to Martin Luther's "Faith makes blessed," a statement defending his view that faith alone justified the soul in relation to God, and that good works do not ensure salvation. Zarathustra states, "And we desire even those things which old women tell one another in the evening. This we call the eternal-feminine in us." Goethe refers to the Eternal-Feminine in *Faust* (1808–1832), where it is the

idea that there is a pure form of the feminine that inspires men to perfect themselves. In *Faust* Helen of Troy is a personification of the Eternal-Feminine (See Johann Wolfgang von Goethe, *Faust: Part One and Sections from Part Two*, translated by Walter Kaufmann, Garden City and New York: Doubleday, 1961, p. 503.) Nietzsche is skeptical of this idea.

14. (p. 112) *"Ah, there are so many things between heaven and earth of which only the poets have dreamed!":* This is a reference to Hamlet's statement to his friend Horatio, "There are more things in heaven and earth, Horatio, / Than are dreamt of in your philosophy" (Shakespeare, *Hamlet*, act 1, scene 5). Relevant to this context is also the remark by Plato's Socrates: "Of that place beyond the heavens none of our earthly poets has yet sung, and none shall sing worthily" (Plato, *Phaedrus* 247c, in *The Collected Dialogues of Plato, Including the Letters*, edited by Edith Hamilton and Huntington Cairns, Bollingen Series LXXI, Princeton, NJ: Princeton University Press, 1961.)

15. (p. 112) *for all gods are poet's parables, poet's prevarications! Truly, it always lifts us upward—that is to the land of the clouds: on these we set our motley bastards and call them gods and Übermenschen":* The land of the clouds may allude to Cloud Cuckooland in Aristophanes' play *The Birds?*; it is the farcical realm of birds. Cloud Cuckooland is literally run by birdbrains, and one of its inhabitants is Socrates, whom Aristophanes lampoons. The idea that gods and *Übermenschen* are human beings' "motley bastards" is in keeping with Ludwig Feuerbach's notion that human beings project human traits onto all gods without realizing it. As our unacknowledged progeny, the gods are therefore bastards.

16. (p. 116) *"All is empty, all is alike, all has been!":* The soothsayer's message that "all has been" is a depressing version of the idea of eternal recurrence, for it suggests that the recurrence of time amounts to a script from the past from which one cannot deviate.

17. (p. 123) *his glances pierced their thoughts and afterthoughts: Hintergedanken* is here translated as "afterthoughts"; it also means "reservations." We have translated it as "afterthoughts," to catch the play on words with *Gedanken* ("thoughts").

Third Part

1. (p. 133) *with anger and longing Zarathustra wept bitterly:* When Zarathustra "wept bitterly," he did the same as Saint Peter after denying his association with Jesus. See the Bible, Matthew 26:75 and Luke 22:62.

2. (p. 134) *"O Zarathustra . . . you philosopher's stone"!":* The philosopher's stone is mercury, the catalyzing agent in alchemy that is supposed to transform lead into gold. The dwarf pouring lead into Zarathustra's ear is reminiscent of the murder of Hamlet's father, whose brother killed him by pouring lead into his ear.

3. (p. 134) *Then the dwarf was silent; and it lasted long:* As a friend of Indologist Peter Deussen, Nietzsche may have been aware that a dwarf, representing ignorance, appears beneath the feet of Shiva Nataraja, the dancing Shiva. This initial scene in the third part of *Zarathustra* reverses that picture, for the dwarf stands on Zarathustra.

4. (p. 136) *Lamefoot:* The most famous lamefoot in the Western tradition is Oedipus, who unwittingly kills his father at a crossroads and marries his mother. The ominous nature of Zarathustra's position in this section is evident in that he approaches a gateway at which roads converge, suggesting that he is facing his own crossroads. Perhaps the suggestion that Zarathustra is a lamefoot alludes to Achilles, too, suggesting that despite Zarathustra's heroism, he is clearly vulnerable to destruction. He is more at risk than Achilles, however, who is vulnerable only at the ankle.

5. (p. 137) *a young shepherd, writhing, choking . . . and a heavy black snake hung out of his mouth:* The serpent that bites its own tail, the uroboros (or ouroboros), originally a Greek symbol for the cosmic sea that surrounds the world, and also an alchemical symbol for the recurring cycle of time. In effect, the shepherd becomes the front of the serpentine circle of time by biting the head off the snake that assails him.

6. (p. 142) *"the heaven of chance . . . the heaven of mischievousness":* Himmel, or "heaven," also means simply "sky."

7. (p. 142) *"By Chance":* Nietzsche adds the German honorific *von* here to the name of "Chance," suggesting that chance is of noble origin. (The translation of *Ohngefähr* could also be "Accident.") We left *von* untranslated.

8. (p. 148) *On the Mount of Olives:* This recalls the garden of olives, Gesthemane, where Jesus confronted his fears in solitude on the night before his crucifixion. Zarathustra is similarly alone in this scene, but he seems to prefer solitude as well as the lack of human warmth he is experiencing.

9. (p. 156) *"Belief makes him blessed, belief in him":* Here again the word *Glaube* ("belief") might also have been rendered as "faith."

10. (p. 156) *They did not die in "twilight"—as some lie!:* This is a reference to the opera *Götterdämmerung* (*Twilight of the Gods*), by Richard Wagner (1813–1883). Nietzsche will use a similar title later for his masterpiece *Die Götzen-Dämmerung* (1889; *Twilight of the Idols*).

11. (p. 172) *"Everything is in flux":* The Greek philosopher Heraclitus (c.535–c.475 B.C.) famously claimed that one cannot step into the same river twice. Nietzsche admired him and considered his own emphasis on becoming and on transformation to be akin to Heraclitus' views.

12. (p. 174) *children's land . . . the undiscovered country in the remotest seas!* The reference to the "children's land" reverses the image of the Fatherland. With this reversal Zarathustra suggests that one's loyalty should not be to the past and tradition, but to the future that one is helping to create.

13. (p. 176) *"And your own reason—you shall yourself stifle and choke it; for it is a reason of this world,—thus you shall yourself learn to renounce the world":* Martin Luther objected to pride in human reason, and he urged Christians to discipline and reject the pretensions of reason.

14. (p. 178) *Now the sun glows on him and dogs lick his sweat; but he lies there in his obstinacy and prefers to languish:* The Bible's Psalm 22 compares menacing, evil men to dogs closing in, and also refers to the speaker's extreme thirst and his being left for dead. According to John 19:28, Jesus says "I am thirsty" (NIV) while on the cross. In John 19:23–24 the Evangelist explicitly quotes Psalm 22, saying that incidents surrounding Jesus' crucifixion fulfill the words of the Psalm.

15. (p. 180) *If they—had bread for nothing, ah!:* The suggestion of "free bread" is reminiscent of the Roman imperial policy of giving the people "bread and circuses" to keep them content.

16. (p. 181) *Your wedlock: see that it is not a bad lock! You lock too quickly: so there* follows *from it—wedlock-breaking!:* The play here on "wedlock," "lock," and "breaking" is much more natural in German. The breaking of wedlock in the German expression used by Nietzsche here is generally associated with adultery.

17. (p. 182) *the good* must *crucify him who invents his own virtue!:* This whole passage refers to Jesus. Despite Nietzsche's many attacks on the Christian Church, his comments on Jesus are usually favorable.

18. (p. 188) *"Man recurs eternally! . . . The small man recurs eternally!":* "Recurrence" and "return" are both used in the context of Nietzsche's idea of the "eternal recurrence" or the "eternal return." What Nietzsche means by "the eternal return," a notion that is discussed in various places in his corpus, is a matter of great scholarly controversy. (See the Introduction and endnote 16 to the second part.)

19. (p. 188) *Nausea!: Ekel* ("nausea") is a frequent alimentary complaint of Zarathustra. Like "going under" and many other repeated terms in the work, however, it does not seem to be used strictly in a literal sense. It can also be translated as "disgust."

20. (p. 193) *Into your eyes I gazed lately, O life: I saw gold glint in your night eyes,— my heart stood still with delight:* In the German the verses in part 1 rhyme. As elsewhere in the text, we have not tried to reproduce Nietzsche's rhymes, choosing rather to follow the meaning of the text as closely as possible.

21. (p. 194) *"noise murders thought":* This is a line from Schopenhauer's essay "On Noise," in which he complains, among other things, about the practice of merchants cracking whips to attract attention to their wares.

22. (p. 196) *should I not lust for eternity and for the wedding ring of rings:* This is a reference to Wagner's *Ring* cycle (a set of four operas), which features a ring that bestows power but destroys the person who wears it. Zarathustra's lust for the ring of rings—that is, time itself—similarly empowers by rendering mortal, as it does to whomever "weds" eternity, the entire ring of time. Zarathustra speaks of eternity as the only woman he would want to wed.

Fourth and Last Part

1. (p. 207) *"Zarathustra, I have come to seduce you to your last sin!":* Zarathustra's "last sin" contrasts with "original sin," the stain of sin with which every human being is born, according to Christian doctrine, as a consequence of the sin of the biblical forefather, Adam. The notion of Zarathustra's final sin suggests a return to innocence in the future, in contrast to the Christian doctrine, which restricts innocence to the distant past.

2. (p. 211) *the ass too found speech:* The ass's effort to speak here is reminiscent of the situation of the ass in *The Golden Ass*, a text by Apuleius (c.124–c.170) that despite its comic character traces the protagonist's spiritual development. In that work, a man who uses a stolen magic potion expects to be transformed into a bird but is actually transformed into an ass. The book recounts his adventures attempting to acquire the antidote: roses. At several times, in the possession of a series of owners, he attempts to speak but can only bray.

3. (p. 218) *You liar from the ground up!:* The accusation that the magician is only an actor suggests that he is modeled on Richard Wagner, whom Nietzsche criticized for being an actor more than a musician. Wagner suggested early in his career that he composed opera as a means of making drama more powerful than it would be without music. Nietzsche suggests that Wagner never revised his priorities—that is, he always saw music as subordinate to theater.

4. (p. 221) *"You seek for great men, you strange fool? . . . Oh, you evil seeker, why do you—seek to test me?":* There is a complicated word play here between *suchen* ("to seek" or "to search") and *versuchen* ("to experiment" but also "to test" or "to try" and "to tempt"). Plays between *versuchen* and *suchen* occur frequently in the text, and help emphasize Nietzsche's questioning, tentative, and experimental (rather than dogmatic or systematic) approach to knowledge.

5. (p. 226) *"Honor thus—my ugliness!":* Socrates was notoriously ugly, and Nietzsche considered his ugliness to be an underlying motivation for his attempt to seduce young men with words. Socrates was convicted on the grounds that he had corrupted the youth and denied the gods of the city.

6. (p. 230) *a peaceable man and preacher on the mount, out of whose eyes goodness itself preached:* This figure shares similarities with both the Buddha and Jesus. The Buddha renounced his position as a prince and urged compassion for all sentient beings, cows included. Jesus is the historical "preacher on the mount." (See the Bible, Matthew 5:1–12; Luke 6:17–23.)

7. (p. 243) *The Last Supper:* This is the final dinner Jesus had with his disciples, a Seder meal for the observance of Passover. He was crucified the following day. The dinner party of this section also resembles that of Plato's *Symposium*.

8. (p. 244) the higher man: After the dinner party in Plato's *Symposium*, each participant makes a speech about the nature of love. By contrast, after this party, Zarathustra alone makes a speech, and his topic is "the higher man."

9. (p. 252) *this rose garlanded crown:* When rose wreaths are carried by in a procession in honor of the goddess Isis, the ass in Apuleius' tale (see note 2 in this section) is finally able to get roses, the antidote he needs to turn himself back into a man.

10. (p. 253) *"which gives wings to asses":* In *The Golden Ass*, by Apuleius (see note 2 in this section), the ass is promised a statue in his honor (called "Escape on Ass-back") if he helps a kidnapped heroine escape. Later the ass is amused by a pathetic portrayal of Pegasus in a procession, in which wings have been attached to the back of an ass.

11. (p. 266) *And here I stand now, / As a European, / I cannot do otherwise, God help me!:* This is a reference to what is reported as Martin Luther's concluding statement at the Diet of Worms in April 1521: "Here I stand. I can do no other." He had been summoned to defend himself before the imperial Diet, having been formally excommunicated by the Pope. The Diet responded by issuing an edict that declared Luther to be an outlaw and by banning his writings.

12. (p. 266) *The Awakening:* This refers to a Lutheran movement in which both of Nietzsche's parents were involved. It emphasized public confession, and its adherents frequently used the image of "little children" in reference to themselves. (See the Bible: Matthew 19:13–15; Mark 10:13–16; and Luke 18:15–17.) The song sung here is very similar to "The Song of the Ass," which was sung in connection with the Ass Festival, a festival celebrated in a number of churches in medieval Europe in which the deacons, the lowest echelon of the clergy, behaved in carnivalesque fashion. Among other debaucheries, the festival sometimes included a procession of an ass up to or into the church, as well as participants who brayed at Mass.

13. (p. 269) *The Ass Festival:* This is the festival described in the preceding note. Zarathustra's return resembles Moses' return from Mount Sinai with the tablets of the Law only to discover that his followers were worshiping a golden calf.

14. (p. 272) *And in memory of me!:* "Do this in remembrance of me" is what Jesus says, according to the Bible, Luke 22:19 and 1 Corinthians 11:25 (NIV), after telling his disciples to eat the bread and drink the wine, which he offers to them as his body and his blood. The Mass, which includes this line, is celebrated in accordance with this command.

15. (p. 272) *The Drunken Song:* The title of the song suggests a relationship to Dionysus, the god of wine and revelry. The dancing recalls the behavior of Apuleius' ass (see note 2 in this section), whose dancing amuses his owners and leads to his ultimately being in a position to eat the antidote that will return him to human form.

16. (p. 278) *if ever you said: "you please me, happiness! Instant! Moment!":* In Goethe's *Faust*, Faust makes a bargain with the devil Mephistopheles. In return for giving Faust supernatural powers, Mephistopheles can take Faust's soul if he ever reaches a point of complete contentment in which he says "Moment, abide."

17. (p. 279) *Zarathustra jumped up from his bed . . . glowing and strong, like a morning sun coming out of dark mountains:* Like Socrates the morning after the Symposium, Zarathustra awakens early and rises while his dinner companions continue to sleep.

18. (p. 280) *the lion shook its head and wondered and laughed:* The laughing lion seems to represent a point between the lion stage and the child stage of the spirit, described in *On the Three Metamorphoses*, the section that begins the first part of the book. The suggestion is that the lion stage is giving way to that of the child.

German composer Richard Strauss, best known for his operas *Salomé* (1905), *Elektra* (1909), and *Der Rosenkavalier* (1911), began his musical career composing impressionistic tone poems. The best-known, *Also sprach Zarathustra* (*Thus Spoke Zarathustra*), was, according to Strauss, "freely based on Friedrich Nietzsche." When it premiered in Frankfurt in November 1896, *Thus Spoke Zarathustra* stunned audiences with its now-famous opening depicting the sunrise. Bold trumpets announce an open chord in C major, ascend to the fifth, and then climb to C an octave higher before resting in C minor. This simple musical gesture is followed by a foreboding series of tympani booms. Painting an epic panorama of the cosmos, the trumpet blasts ascend repeatedly and finally resolve to C major—two octaves above the opening note. Throughout the piece, Strauss makes use of C major to symbolize nature and the cosmos, while the neighboring and dissonant key of B stands for humanity. The clash between humans and the rest of the universe forms the music's core.

Strauss was in many ways the perfect man to represent Nietzsche's book in quintessentially modern program music (instrumental music inspired by or suggestive of a narrative or setting, a kind of precursor to the modern film score). Canadian piano prodigy Glenn Gould said of Strauss's work:

> It presents and substantiates an argument which transcends all the dogmatisms of art—all questions of style and taste and idiom—all the frivolous, effete preoccupations of the chronologist. It presents to us an example of the man who makes richer his own time by not being of it, who speaks for all generations by being of none. It is an ultimate argument of individuality—the argument that a man can

create his own synthesis of time without being bound by the conformities that time imposes.

Just as that other great individualist Nietzsche came to be misappropriated by Hitler and National Socialism, Strauss too was forced to work for the Nazis; he served for a short time as the president of their Reichsmusikkammer (state music office). In 1948 a "denazification" tribunal exonerated him of all collaboration with the National Socialists.

Director Stanley Kubrick made Strauss's *Thus Spoke Zarathustra* the fitting and memorable musical centerpiece of his 1968 cinematic masterpiece *2001: A Space Odyssey*. For the film's story, Kubrick (*Lolita, Dr. Strangelove*) collaborated with British author Arthur C. Clarke, from whom he commissioned a novel about man's place in the universe. In the 1960s Clarke was a member of a triumvirate of science-fiction writers that also included Isaac Asimov and Robert A. Heinlein. Clarke had already begun to expand to novel length his 1951 short story "The Sentinel," about man's first contact with intelligent life beyond Earth, when Kubrick offered him the commission.

Kubrick's film begins with a wide, Cinerama shot of the aligned moon, sun, and Earth, accompanied by Strauss's stirring opening bars. The music returns in the film's "Dawn of Man" segment when a tribe of apes—aided somehow by a perfect, black monolith of mysterious origin—discover they can use bones as weapons and thus defeat a rival tribe. Strauss, in his program note for *Thus Spoke Zarathustra*, could have been describing Kubrick and Clarke's vision:

> I did not intend to write philosophical music or to portray in music Nietzsche's great work. I wished to convey by means of music an idea of the development of the human race from its origin, through the various phases of its development, religious and scientific, up to Nietzsche's idea of the superman. The whole symphonic poem is intended as an homage to Nietzsche's genius, which found its greatest expression in his book *Thus Spoke Zarathustra*.

2001's final shot is legendary: A fetus floats star-like in the gorgeously textured, womb-like galaxy. Of all moments in Kubrick's innovative, high-concept film, this one is the most reminiscent of

Nietzsche's philosophy. In *Zarathustra*, the poet-philosopher describes the prophet, as he emerges enlightened from his mountain cave, as having become a child. And in Zarathustra's tale of the "metamorphoses of the spirit" (p. 25), the spirit changes into a camel, then a lion, and finally a child. "The child is innocence and forgetting, a new beginning, a game, a self-propelled wheel, a first movement, a sacred Yes-saying" (p. 26). Nietzsche also has Zarathustra utter maxims that ring with cosmic import, such as "one must still have chaos in oneself to give birth to a dancing star" (p. 13). Strauss's music swells one final time, and as it rises two octaves it underscores Nietzsche's and Kubrick's narrative arcs.

The Academy of Motion Picture Arts and Sciences nominated Kubrick for an Oscar for his direction and Clarke and Kubrick for their screenplay, which was nearly devoid of dialogue. The film was also nominated for art direction, and it won the award for special visual effects, which hold up beautifully even today. In 1996 the American Film Institute celebrated its hundred-year anniversary by selecting the top hundred films made since the inception of American cinema. *2001: A Space Odyssey* came in at twenty-two.

COMMENTS & QUESTIONS

In this section, we aim to provide the reader with an array of perspectives on the text, as well as questions that challenge those perspectives. The commentary has been culled from sources as diverse as reviews contemporaneous with the work, letters written by the author, literary criticism of later generations, and appreciations written throughout the work's history. Following the commentary, a series of questions seeks to filter Friedrich Nietzsche's Thus Spoke Zarathustra *through a variety of points of view and bring about a richer understanding of this enduring work.*

Comments

A. VON ENDE

The growth of Nietzsche corresponds with that of the new school; first he threw off the burden of the historical and traditional past; then he shattered with the hammer of his genius all the small, low, and weak ideals of the present; and finally, upon the ruins he preached to his apostles the gospel of the only one—the *Übermensch*. This over-human being, discarding all humanity with the great herd, and from the unscaled heights of his temple throwing thunderbolts which flash upon the whole world—this Over-man, with all his consciousness of superiority and his claim of being beyond good and evil, felt too human, all too human, to dispense with being in touch with his fellow-beings. Nietzsche himself was the least free of free men; but his soul, wavering from pole to pole, asking questions and not answering them, found a universal echo, and this echo is the keynote of the poetry of young Germany.

—from *The Critic* (February 1900)

THOMAS COMMON
Besides being a philosopher, Nietzsche is at the same time the most interesting of all writers for cultured men and women to read. In brilliancy of style and originality of thought he is perhaps unequalled. He is not only the most serious and profound of writers, he is also the gayest and most cheerful. There has never been such a master of aphorisms. As a prophetic writer also he stands alone.
—from *Nietzsche as Critic, Philosopher, Poet and Prophet* (1901)

GEORGE BERNARD SHAW
Nietzsche is worse than shocking, he is simply awful: his epigrams are written with phosphorus on brimstone. The only excuse for reading them is that before long you must be prepared either to talk about Nietzsche or else retire from society, especially from aristocratically minded society (not the same thing, by the way, as aristocratic society), since Nietzsche is the champion of privilege, of power, and of inequality. . . . His pungency; his power of putting the merest platitudes of his position in rousing, startling paradoxes; his way of getting underneath moral precepts which are so unquestionable to us that common decency seems to compel unhesitating assent to them, and upsetting them with a scornful laugh: all this is easy to a witty man who has once well learnt Schopenhauer's lesson, that the intellect by itself is a mere dead piece of brain machinery, and our ethical and moral systems merely the pierced cards you stick into it when you want it to play a certain tune. So far I am on common ground with Nietzsche. But not for a moment will I suffer any one to compare me to him as a critic. Never was there a deafer, blinder, socially and politically inepter academician. . . . To him modern Democracy, Pauline Christianity, Socialism, and so on are deliberate plots hatched by malignant philosophers to frustrate the evolution of the human race and mass the stupidity and brute force of the many weak against the beneficial tyranny of the few strong. This is not even a point of view: it is an absolutely fictitious hypothesis: it would not be worth reading were it not that there is almost as much evidence for it as if it were true, and that it leads Nietzsche to produce some new and very striking and suggestive combinations of ideas. In short, his sallies, petulant and impossible as some of them are, are the work of a rare spirit and are pregnant with its vitality.
—from *Dramatic Opinions and Essays*, Volume 1 (1906)

FRIEDRICH NIETZSCHE

Among my writings my *Zarathustra* stands to my mind by itself. With that I have given mankind the greatest present that has ever been made to it so far. This book, with a voice bridging centuries, is not only the highest book there is, the book that is truly characterized by the air of the heights—the whole fact of man lies *beneath* it at a tremendous distance—it is also the *deepest*, born out of the innermost wealth of truth, an inexhaustible well to which no pail descends without coming up again filled with gold and goodness. Here no "prophet" is speaking, none of those gruesome hybrids of sickness and will to power whom people call founders of religions. Above all, one must *hear* aright the tone that comes from this mouth, the halcyon tone, lest one should do wretched injustice to the meaning of its wisdom. . . .

It is no fanatic that speaks here; this is not "preaching"; no *faith* is demanded here: from an infinite abundance of light and depth of happiness falls drop upon drop, word upon word: the tempo of these speeches is a tender adagio. Such things reach only the most select. It is a privilege without equal to be a listener here.

—translated by Walter Kaufmann, from *Ecce Homo* (1908)

H. L. MENCKEN

Despite Nietzsche's conclusion that the known facts of existence do not bear it out, and the essential impossibility of discussing it to profit, the doctrine of eternal recurrence is by no means unthinkable. The celestial cycle put forward, as an hypothesis, by modern astronomy—the progression, that is, from gas to molten fluid, from fluid to solid, and from solid, by catastrophe, back to gas again—is easily conceivable, and it is easily conceivable, too, that the earth, which has passed through an uninhabitable state into a habitable state, may one day become uninhabitable again, and so keep see-sawing back and forth through all eternity.

But what will be the effect of eternal recurrence upon the superman? The tragedy of it, as we have seen, will merely serve to make him heroic. He will defy the universe and say "yes" to life. Putting aside all thought of conscious existence beyond the grave, he will seek to live as nearly as possible in exact accordance with those laws laid down for the evolution of sentient beings on earth when the cosmos was first set spinning. But how will he know when he has attained this end? How will he avoid going mad with doubts about his own knowledge? Nietzsche gave much thought, first and last, to this epistemological problem, and at different times he leaned toward different schools, but his writing, taken as a whole, indicates that the fruit of his meditations was a thorough-going empiricism. The superman, indeed, is an empiricist who differs from Bacon only in the infinitely greater range of his observation and experiment. He learns by bitter experience and he generalizes from this knowledge. An utter and unquestioning materialist, he knows nothing of mind except as a function of body. To him speculation seems vain and foolish: his concern is ever with imminent affairs. That is to say, he believes a thing to be true when his eyes, his ears, his nose and his hands tell him it is true. And in this he will be at one with all those men who are admittedly above the mass today. Reject empiricism and you reject at one stroke, the whole sum of human knowledge.

—from *The Philosophy of Friedrich Nietzsche* (1908)

MAX NORDAU

There are two kinds of men who have a natural propensity for exaggerated language: madmen and charlatans. The insane, who suffer from systematic delirium and maniacal excitement, receive very few impressions, but they are very strong. Their consciousness is filled with a very small number of ideas, often by a single one around which all their thoughts revolve in an impetuous whirl, as the waters of a rushing torrent boil around a rock that rises in the midst of their course. These sufferers have no connection with reality, and no comprehension of it. The violence of their subjective feelings renders them insensible to outside impressions. Their obsessions drive from their minds every other thought, and cover with their shadow the entire image of the world. They have lost the sense of proportions, and the faculty of comparing objective phenomena among them and with their reflection in their minds. The contents of their consciousness, feelings, or images, have for them the importance of the absolute, and when by language they express their impulses and their inward visions, no word, no expression seems strong enough to do justice to the peerless importance of their mental pictures. The writings of Nietzsche, especially those of the last period, the fourth and last portion of *Thus Spake Zarathustra*, the

Antichrist, and so forth, are good examples of these overstrained modes of speech, always rising to the most extreme tonality of madmen attacked by acute or chronic mania. Among charlatans, the case is incomparably more simple. Extreme exaggeration is not with them an internal necessity, but a very external one, not an organic impulse, but a deliberate intention with an object in view. They raise the voice powerfully to dominate the noise of the friars, to attract attention imperiously to themselves, to disturb, to deafen, to hypnotise the hearers and, by paralysing their faculty of judgment, subject them to their suggestion.

The natural superlativists, madmen and charlatans, serve as models for many imitators, who employ their grotesque and piercing shouts not by instinctive impulse, but in a coldly methodical fashion, because the method seems to them impressive, fine, efficacious, and above all, the very latest modern fad.

—from *The Bookman* (March 1912)

EDWARD GARNETT

Nietzsche's appearance in European thought marks a strong, savage reaction against the waves of democratic beliefs and valuations now submerging the old aristocratic standards, more or less throughout Europe. Other philosophers such as Herbert Spencer have made their protest against modern tendencies; other thinkers, as Ibsen, have put some of Nietzsche's questions in a tentative spirit; but Nietzsche is the first man to fall foul of democratic values altogether, and try to formulate his aristocratic standards of life into a definite creed—Master-Morality versus Slave-Morality.

There lies Nietzsche's value. It is because Nietzsche challenged Modernity, because he stood and faced the modern democratic rush which is backed by rank on rank of busy specialists today, because he opposes a creative aristocratic ideal to negate the popular will, instincts, and practice, that he is of such special significance. He showed the way the crowd is not going. Than this, nothing is more valuable in an age where the will of the majority is apt to become an imitation of its chance environment, a will to copy the majority; when the "standard of values" is chiefly given by the mass of minds that are anxious to think and do what they are told the majority is thinking and doing. And Nietzsche's antipathy to the crowd largely springs from his conviction that to give the reins of power over to the popular mind is to put a premium on the "wholesale," the "average," and "machine-made" ideal, for that suits it, that pleases it, that it is its instinct to follow. . . .

Nietzsche's special inspiration, the key that unlocked his most secret depths, was pain. Pain, cruel and prolonged, pursued, chased, and captured him, deepened the world for him, and forced into the light all the tendencies of his nature. It was pain attacking his aristocratic soul that brought out all his endurance, pain that emphasized so violently the will-to-power. For what is this philosophy, in his case, but the definition of the spirit in which he dared it, and scorned to bend. And this power to face suffering, the lack of which casts the weak, delicate, or ordinary mind outside itself, into the arms of "reliance on a God," exhibited in a satiric light to Nietzsche the sufferings of inferior natures, and made vulgar all sentimentalism, expression of suffering, the daily illusions of mankind, and the panaceas of the priests. And suffering also threw into Nietzsche's mind the deep light of understanding as to how life fabricates in man his petty concepts of what is good and what is evil, what he wishes to avoid and escape—i.e., what he is afraid of. Thus pain brought to Nietzsche the necessity for hardness, courage, sternness even cruelty, if mankind is to be shaped on fine, strong, and heroic lines. Pain also it was that gave him aspiration towards joy, gaiety, and the mocking spirit, because these are the antithesis to the weak despairing soul. But to give in to suffering! to give in to life! that is the part of the vulgar soul; to face reality, to triumph over it, was the fundamental instinct of Nietzsche's indomitable spirit. Pain therefore it was that made Nietzsche inhuman, intensified his caste bias, and transformed his natural distaste for the cheap idealism and shallow optimism of the mass of men (who cannot either suffer life nobly or enjoy nobly) into a virulent hatred of Modernity, that Modernity which advertises all its benefits aloud! and is afraid to even recognize its weaknesses. Suffering it was that made Nietzsche isolate himself from the outer world, and concentrate on himself on the immensely richer world of passions, tastes, hatred and distastes within him. Pain forces him to revise all his acquired opinions, to cast away his enthusiasms, his first idealistic interpretations of life, and it forces himself also into keen self-analysis, into a passion for analysing all "goodness" and discovering its motive.

—from *Friday Nights* (1922)

EDWIN MUIR

It was Nietzsche's fate to be always more true and interesting than his philosophy. However unsound his thesis might be, he uttered truths in supporting it which came clean out of reality, so that he seemed sometimes to hear life itself speaking. This union of something artificial and something true in his nature is what makes him so difficult and so interesting.

—from *Latitudes* (1924)

CARL JUNG

Zarathustra is in a way a document of our time, and it surely has much to do with our own psychological condition. I quite understand that it may have very bad effect, I myself often felt when I was plowing through the text that it had disagreeable effects upon me. There are passages which I intensely dislike and they really are irritating. But when you plow through your own psychology you also come across certain irritating places. So when I am irritated in those places in *Zarathustra* I say, well, here is a sore spot or an open wound. I take note of it, and then I know where the trouble is. I would advise you to take it in the same way, and then I think we can get safely through. You see, when we can stand *Zarathustra* we can stand a part of our modern world, particularly our European world: we feel it here very immediately.

—from *Nietzsche's* Zarathustra: *Notes of the Seminar Given in 1934–1939* (1988)

CRANE BRITON

Zarathustra . . . would be lost without his "saith" and "thou" and "yet," helpless without his exclamation points. In English translation he sounds very pseudo-biblical, like the King James version gone wrong. . . . Indeed, *Thus Spoke Zarathustra* has become, for a certain type of half-educated intellectual throughout the world, a kind of Enchiridion. . . . Yet the long white robes, prophetic beard, and phosphorescent glances of Zarathustra . . . have unquestionably

helped Nietzsche to his present prestige in . . . Germany. . . .
Zarathustra sounds as far-off as any Hebrew prophet, and much
more unreal. All the better for Nazi use. The vagueness, the
dithyrambic energy, the mantic arts, the tortured rhetoric of Nietzsche—Zarathustra seems able to move men in a way no concrete
proposals at the level of mere laws or arrangements ever can move
them.

—from *Nietzsche* (1941)

ALBERT CAMUS

Nietzsche's philosophy, undoubtedly, revolves around the problem
of rebellion. More precisely, it begins by being a rebellion. With
him, rebellion begins at "God is dead," which is assumed as an established fact; then rebellion hinges on everything that aims at
falsely replacing the vanished deity and reflects dishonour on a
world which undoubtedly has no direction but which remains the
only proving-ground of the gods.

—translated by Anthony Bower, from *The Rebel* (1951)

BRAND BLANSHARD

I must confess that often, when I have tried to read the most pop-
ularly effective of German philosophical writers, Nietzsche, I have
felt like throwing the book across the room. He is a boiling pot of
enthusiasms and animosities, which he pours out volubly, skillfully,
and eloquently. If he were content to label these outpourings
"Prejudices," as Mr. Mencken so truly and candidly labels his own,
one could accept them in the spirit in which they were offered. . . .
But he obviously takes them as philosophy instead of what they
largely are, pseudo-Isaian prophesyings, incoherent and unreasoned
Sibylline oracles.

—from *On Philosophical Style* (1954)

KARL JASPERS

Thus Spake Zarathustra (1883–85) is basically a series of addresses
by Zarathustra to crowds, companions, the "higher men," his animals, and himself, within a frame of situations and actions of this
fictitious figure. What Nietzsche regarded as his magnum opus resists all traditional means of classification: it is to be taken as poetry

as well as prophecy and philosophy, and still it cannot be viewed as precisely any one of these.

—translated by Charles F. Wallraff and Frederick J. Schmitz, from *Nietzsche: An Introduction to the Understanding of His Philosophical Activity* (1965)

MARTIN HEIDEGGER

We must learn how to learn from the teacher, even if it were only to raise questions that go beyond him. Only then shall we one day discover who Zarathustra is—or we will never discover it.

—translated by Bernd Magnus, from *Review of Metaphysics* (March 1967)

WALTER KAUFMANN

After all has been said, *Zarathustra* still cries out to be bluepenciled; and if it were more compact, it would be more lucid too. Even so, there are few works to match its wealth of ideas, the abundance of profound suggestions, the epigrams, the wit. What distinguishes *Zarathustra* is the profusion of "Sapphires in the mud." But what the book loses artistically and philosophically by never having been critically edited by its author, it gains as a uniquely personal record.

—from the editor's preface to *Thus Spoke Zarathustra* in *The Portable Nietzsche* (1968)

HAROLD ALDERMAN

Thus Spoke Zarathustra is a work of fiction; that is to say it contains no facts or empirical arguments and no metaphysical axioms from which Nietzsche purports to deduce eternal verities. Philosophers, however, have been bothered by the fictional character of *Thus Spoke Zarathustra* to the point of saying that it is not a work of philosophy; such philosophers apparently do not realize that all philosophy is fiction. For Nietzsche, however, this fact was one of the clearest things about the nature of philosophy; it was so clear that he decide to emphasize the fictive character of philosophy by constructing his major work as a conversation among a number of fictional characters.

—from *Nietzsche's Gift* (1977)

HANS-GEORG GADAMER
The style of this text is not for everyone's taste, at any rate not for my taste or the taste of my generation.

—translated by Zygmunt Adamczewski, from
The Great Year of Zarathustra (1881–1981),
edited by David Goicoechea (1983)

JACQUES DERRIDA
The future of the Nietzsche text is not closed. But if, within the still-open contours of an era, the only politics calling itself—proclaiming itself—Nietzschean will have been a Nazi one, then this is necessarily significant and must be questioned in all of its consequences.

—translated by Peggy Kamuf, from *The Ear of the Other:
Otobiography, Transference, Translation* (1985)

J. HILLIS MILLER
The basic idea of *Thus Spoke Zarathustra* is the thought of the eternal return, with its associated presupposition of the idea of the death of God. . . . Why is it appropriate for this thought to be expressed in the form of a fictional narrative in which Nietzsche projects himself into an imaginary protagonist, namely Zarathustra, and then doubles that protagonist with a narrator or witness who reports what Zarathustra said and did, as the gospel-makers reported the doings and sayings of Jesus?

—from *International Studies in Philosophy* XVII:2 (1985)

ALAN WHITE
The labyrinthine nature of Nietzsche's Zarathustra is apparent to all who have struggled with it; this book "for everyone and no one" contains a wealth of details, presented in an order that often seems simply chaotic.

—from *Within Nietzsche's Labyrinth* (1990)

DAVID ALLISON
If the very title of the work—*Thus Spoke Zarathustra: A Book for Everyone and No One*—suggests a profound enigma, the specific themes Nietzsche engages are at least recognizable from the start:

the dynamics of the human will, the death of God, the critique of traditional Christian morality, the will to power, the eternal return, and the overman (the higher form of humanity, envisaged by Nietzsche, which has not yet been attained). Nevertheless, despite the breadth and recognizability of these often-discussed topics, there remains a deeply personal, largely hidden stratum to *Zarathustra*, wherein Nietzsche reflectively engages his own most personal, philosophical, and emotional concerns. Foremost among these personally perplexing issues were the questions about his own capacity to effectively communicate his idea, the stress brought on by his continually failing personal health, and the disastrous state of his personal relations during this period.

—from *Reading the New Nietzsche* (2001)

THOMAS K. SEUNG

The epic of self-relation is Nietzsche's daunting invention. Nobody has ever attempted such an inventive task before or after his Zarathustra. Especially unique is the nature of Nietzsche's epic hero. He is so unique that he does not fit the traditional mold of an epic hero. Sometimes he even behaves like an anti-hero. But he does not really fit this model, either, because he has the power to wrestle with his cosmic self. Hence it is hard to classify the Nietzschean hero by using standard labels. . . . Nietzsche has constructed his epic of the soul by naturalizing the Christian God. Zarathustra's epic journey is sustained by the visible power of God, Mother Nature, and it is a secular offshoot of the long venerable tradition of Christian sacred epics. In this secular form . . . Nietzsche's psychological epic reads more like the Zen fable of ox-herding on enlightenment and redemption than the Christian psychological epics.

—from *Nietzsche's Epic of the Soul: Thus Spoke Zarathustra* (2005)

Questions

1. Is Zarathustra a blowhard who postures, struts, and puffs up his chest in an attempt to prove to his audience and himself that he is *not* a blowhard? Does Nietzsche side with Zarathustra or does he make fun of him?

2. H. L. Mencken describes Nietzsche's thought as "a thorough-going empiricism," the work of an "utter and unquestioning materialist." What does Mencken mean? Do you agree with him?

3. Suppose as an experiment in thought (not in action) you were to throw out the distinctions between good and evil—throw out the very concepts of good and evil—and renounce all that religion, philosophy, and tradition have to say about them. Would the result be a crippling anxiety or a sense of liberation? Would it follow from this experiment that you should contemplate acts that most people have almost always considered evil?

4. Does Nietzsche include material in *Thus Spoke Zarathustra* that undercuts Zarathustra as a speaker, that makes him ambiguous? Would you characterize Zarathustra's overall message as a doctrine or a life-affirming fiction?

FOR FURTHER READING

Other Works by Friedrich Nietzsche

Beyond Good and Evil. 1886. Translated by Walter Kaufmann. New York: Vintage Books, 1966.

The Birth of Tragedy and The Case of Wagner. 1872; 1888. Translated by Walter Kaufmann. New York: Vintage Books, 1967.

Daybreak: Thoughts on the Prejudices of Morality. 1881. Translated by R. J. Hollingdale. Cambridge: Cambridge University Press, 1982.

The Gay Science. 1882. Translated by Walter Kaufmann. New York: Vintage Books, 1974.

Human, All Too Human. 1878–1880. Translated by R. J. Hollingdale. Cambridge and New York: Cambridge University Press, 1986.

On the Genealogy of Morals and Ecce Homo. 1887, 1908. Translated, respectively, by Walter Kaufmann and R. J. Hollingdale, and by Walter Kaufmann. New York: Vintage Books, 1967.

The Portable Nietzsche. Edited by Walter Kaufmann. New York: Viking Press, 1954. Includes another translation of *Zarathustra.*

Selected Letters of Friedrich Nietzsche. Edited and translated by Christopher Middleton. Chicago: University of Chicago Press, 1969.

Twilight of the Idols, Or How to Philosophize with a Hammer. 1889. Together with *The Antichrist.* Translated by R. J. Hollingdale. Harmondsworth: Penguin, 1968.

Untimely Meditations. 1873–1876. Translated by R. J. Hollingdale. Cambridge and New York: Cambridge University Press, 1983.

The Will to Power. 1901. Translated by Walter Kaufmann and R. J. Hollingdale. New York: Random House, 1967.

Works About Thus Spoke Zarathustra

Gooding-Williams, Robert. *Zarathustra's Dionysian Modernism.* Stanford: Stanford University Press, 2001.

Higgins, Kathleen M. *Nietzsche's Zarathustra.* Philadelphia, PA: Temple University Press, 1987.

Jung, C. G. *Nietzsche's Zarathustra: Notes of the Seminar Given in 1934–1939.* Edited by James L. Jarrett. Princeton, NJ: Princeton University Press, 1988.

Lampert, Laurence. *Nietzsche's Teaching: An Interpretation of Thus Spoke Zarathustra.* New Haven: Yale University Press, 1986.

Rosen, Stanley. *The Mask of Enlightenment: Nietzsche's Zarathustra.* Cambridge and New York: Cambridge University Press, 1995.

Seung, Thomas K. *Nietzsche's Epic of the Soul:* Thus Spoke Zarathustra. Lanham, MD: Lexington Books, 2005.

Works About Nietzsche

Allison, David B., ed. *The New Nietzsche: Contemporary Styles of Interpretation.* New York: Dell, 1977.

———. *Reading the New Nietzsche.* Lanham, MD: Rowman and Littlefield, 2001.

Chamberlain, Lesley. *Nietzsche in Turin: An Intimate Biography.* New York: Picador USA, 1998.

Clark, Maudemarie. "Nietzsche's Misogyny." *International Studies in Philosophy* 26:3 (fall 1994), pp. 3–12.

———. *Nietzsche on Truth and Philosophy.* Cambridge, MA: Cambridge University Press, 1990.

Danto, Arthur C. *Nietzsche as Philosopher.* New York: Macmillan, 1965.

Diethe, Carol. *Nietzsche's Sister and the Will to Power: A Biography of Elisabeth Förster-Nietzsche.* Urbana: University of Illinois Press, 2003.

Gilman, Sander L., ed. *Conversations with Nietzsche: A Life in the Words of His Contemporaries.* Translated by David J. Parent. New York: Oxford University Press, 1987.

Hayman, Ronald. *Nietzsche: A Critical Life.* New York: Oxford University Press, 1980.